P9-BAT-973

THE COMPANY DOSSIERS

BLACK PROJECTS, White Knights

KAGE BAKER

GOLDEN GRYPHON PRESS • 2002

"Introduction: The Hounds of Zeus," copyright © 2002 by Kage Baker.
"The Dust Enclosed Here," first published in *Asimov's*, March 2001.
"Facts Relating to the Arrest of Dr. Kalugin," first published in *Asimov's*, October/November 1997.
"Hanuman," first published in *Asimov's*, April 2002.
"The Hotel at Harlan's Landing," copyright © 2002 by Kage Baker. Unpublished.
"Lemuria *Will* Rise!" first published in *Asimov's*, May 1998.
"The Likely Lad," first published in *Asimov's*, September 2002.
"The Literary Agent," first published in *Asimov's*, July 1998.
"Monster Story," first published in *Asimov's*, June 2001.
"Noble Mold," first published in *Asimov's*, March 1997.
"Old Flat Top," copyright © 2002 by Kage Baker. Unpublished.
"The Queen in Yellow," copyright © 2002 by Kage Baker. Unpublished.
"Smart Alec," first published in *Asimov's*, September 1999.
"Studio Dick Drowns Near Malibu," first published in *Asimov's*, January 2001.
"The Wreck of the *Gladstone,*" first published in *Asimov's*, October/November 1998.

Edited by Marty Halpern

LIBRARY OF CONGRESS CATALOGUING-IN-PUBLICATION DATA
Baker, Kage.
    Black projects, white knights : the company dossiers / by Kage Baker. — 1st ed.
        p.   cm.
    ISBN 1-930846-11-8 (alk. paper)
        1. Immortalism—Fiction.   2. Time travel—Fiction.   3. Science fiction, American.   I. Title.

PS3552.A4313   B55   2002
813'.54—dc21   2002002503

Printed in the United States of America.

◆ ◆ ◆

Contents

CONTENTS

This one is affectionately dedicated to
Gardner Dozois,
an Atlas holding up the Company cosmos.

◆ ◆ ◆

Introduction:
The Hounds of Zeus

YOU ARE STANDING ON A STREET CORNER IN ONE
of the great cities of the world, looking up at a certain building. You
have been very clever, to have gotten this far. Thousands of people pass
this way daily, and barely notice this same unremarkable facade at
which you stare; but they don't know what you know.

You realize you shouldn't be staring. Looking as nonchalant as you
can, you walk on down the street, and start at your own reflection,
which seems to be watching you fearfully, in the shop windows. Nervous? You're not nervous at all, are you? You won't be entering by the
front door, of course. You saw the ragged man sitting on the front steps,
smiling and nodding to himself. There would be nothing so obvious as
a man wearing a black suit and black sunglasses. Not to guard what
you've come for . . .

Just around the next corner, you find the grubby little vindaloo place.
You paid an awful lot of money to learn the name of this unpromising-
looking shop, but it's just as it was described to you. Drawing a deep
breath, you go inside.

You seat yourself, and when the waiter comes and inquires, you say
what you were told to say:

"I'd like something pink, with lentils in it."

He nods, smiles briefly, and walks away. You brace yourself, looking
around to see if Public Health Monitors with gas guns are going to come
boiling out of the kitchen. None do, but you are sweating by the time
the waiter brings you a glass of ice water and . . . yes . . . a dish of
something pink, with lentils in it.

You take exactly three sips of the water, eat three spoonfuls of the pink stuff—you've no idea what it is—and then, as you were instructed to do, you rise and head for the lavatory, which is down a narrow hall at the side.

Beyond the door the waiter stands. Without a word, he sets his palm in a certain place on the wall, and though you knew what was going to happen next you still jump when you see the doorway appear, gliding smoothly into existence out of what had seemed to be a solid surface. Beyond the doorway is a steel cubicle. You step inside, a panel slides shut behind you and you are suddenly dropping very far, very fast. You're in.

You have successfully penetrated the defenses of Dr. Zeus Incorporated.

You hug yourself, partly in glee and partly to keep the contents of your stomach in one place. Dr. Zeus Incorporated, also known as Jovian Integrated Systems, also known as the Kronos Diversified Stock Company! And you know it has had other names, and far older names. And you have heard all the rumors: how this is a secret fraternity made up of scientists and businessmen, *the* secret fraternity for which all other so-called secret fraternities are merely decoys. Its members rule the world. They have unlimited power. They are somehow able to travel through time. They have found the Philosopher's Stone and the Elixir of Life.

Especially the Elixir of Life.

You aren't here to steal it, however. You know that no amount of bribery could ever get you that far into the inner sanctum, not if you were the wealthiest person in the world.

All you've come here for is *proof*.

When the elevator door opens, you are poised and ready. You step quickly through utter and formless blackness, hands out before you, and you count your paces: fifteen, sixteen, seventeen, turn! You walk three paces to the left. Your groping hands encounter a rack of something, small flat objects stacked on end. You grab one and stuff it quickly in your pocket. You turn, retrace your steps with meticulous effort and fall trembling into the steel cabinet, which rises with you at once. By the time the door opens, though you are momentarily blinded by the yellow light of the dingy corridor, you have regained enough poise to walk past the waiter with no more than a nod. You leave your credit disk on the table as you go. You won't be needing that one anymore, not after today.

The rest of the journey is a blur, until you lock the door of your hotel room behind you and take out your prize.

It's a tiny golden disk in an envelope of film. It might be a credit disk, currency of an unknown land . . . and in a sense it is, isn't it? You're chortling to yourself as you sit down with it, slip it into the Buke and watch the projector unfurl for you. A white beam shoots from its heart and then the air immediately before your face fills with a shifting blue-green opacity, and white letters appear.

Unlike most of your contemporaries in the twenty-fourth century, you can read. People of high intelligence and low birth become data entry clerks. It's lousy work, but you're done with it forever, and all because of what you've stolen today. The word you are staring at is DOSSIERS, by the way.

The word fades and you are offered a selection. There are at least a dozen headings, and you hold your breath as you fix on the first one and summon it with a motion of your eye. You've never looked on the face of a god before.

The entry obediently enlarges, swims into focus, and you are rather disappointed.

The man before you looks so ordinary, so *generic,* that he might pass for a member of nearly any ethnic group in any country in the world. Well, perhaps he'd be most successful in the Mediterranean area; but you have an uneasy feeling that if he wore lederhosen or a silk kimono, or got a really deep tan, he'd still mingle unnoticed anywhere. He has bright, friendly little black eyes. He has a neat little black beard and moustache, like a cartoon devil.

The text beside his image tells you his designation is JOSEPH, that he is a Facilitator Grade One, that his acquisition date was 18,145 B.C.E., (Gregorian) 25 November, at Irun del Mar, Basque Republic. If you can believe what you're reading, this man sprayed fixative on cave paintings, hid treasure in pyramids as they were being built, wore a toga, marched with legionaries, preached sermons most piously. And worked in the New World too; here's a mention of the trickster Coyote. And here's a long, long list of work in the entertainment industry.

The text states further that he was processed at Eurobase One, that his ethics programming is flexible, and that he has a disinformation capacity of ninety-eight percent, but you don't really absorb this last bit because your mind is still grappling with the implications of his career. Wouldn't it mean that this man is over twenty *thousand* years old?

Well? You were told Dr. Zeus Incorporated could create immortals, weren't you?

Hurriedly, you reduce his image and pull up another one.

You see a woman, black, with small perfect features and a certain elegance of bearing. She is smiling charmingly for the imager, and there is nothing disconcerting about her at all. She carries a parasol over one shoulder; it adds to the somewhat old-fashioned quality of the image. But the text with the image states that her designation is NAN D'ARRAIGNÉE, and that her acquisition date was 1541 A.D., (Gregorian) 14 June, Senegal, which means that she is an immortal creature who needs no parasol to protect her from the rays of the sun or from anything else. The parasol is a mannerism. She has decided to be a gracious lady. She might be anything she chose . . .

You are beginning to feel a little giddy. It's really true. You believed it, you hoped desperately that you were right, but the truth is almost more than you can handle.

Next image: A man in a blue coat with brass buttons. He is large, bearded, has rather harsh aristocratic features, and yet he somehow fails to be a commanding presence. His face is too pink, his eyes too gentle. He looks abashed, somehow. His designation is KALUGIN. His acquisition date was 1345 A.D., (Gregorian) 21 May, Russia, and one would think that in all the centuries since that time he might have faced down his fears; but he looks more human than you do. You blink, shake your head at the perfection of the work, and call up another file.

Here is a woman who has certainly come to terms with her immortality. She is a beauty, in a smooth insolent bored kind of way. Her hair is black, her tan is perfect, and her expression invites you to get on with whatever you've got in mind because she has a thousand better places to be. Her designation is KIU, and you catch your breath at her acquisition date: 9000 B.C.E., (Gregorian) 3 July, Mongolia.

Acquired, what does that mean? Were these creatures created, or purchased? You have heard so many stories. Were they human once? You are pinning all your hopes on that being the case, because it would mean that you have a chance . . . you too might—

The next image stops you cold. What is this thing? Too pale to be a gorilla, and yet—no, it can't be human either. What you can see of the face, that isn't hidden beneath a vast tow-colored beard, is too broad, the forehead too flat, and the huge dentition in the grinning mouth is all wrong for a man. The nose projects forward out of the face like a boulder. If such things as mountain trolls existed, this might be one. His little pale eyes twinkle at you. You aren't helped by the text. All it tells you is that his designation is JOSHUA, and his acquisition date was . . . well, that explains some of it: he was acquired on 30,428 B.C.E., (Gregorian) 18 March.

"He must be the Missing Link," you murmur to yourself, and you giggle nervously. You were only expecting gods; are there monsters here too?

Now, there is nothing monstrous in the next face you see. Here is wisdom, shrewdness, perhaps compassion, certainly a sense of humor. Abundant humanity here; but it's the face of an elderly ape. He seems to be some kind of chimpanzee. Nevertheless he is dressed in a suit of formal cut, and is gesturing with a pair of spectacles at the imager, as though caught in mid-lecture. His designation is MICHAEL HANUMAN. He was acquired on 2320 A.D., (Gregorian) 14 August, New Jersey, and you realize that this one isn't ancient at all. What is he doing here? Is this a joke? You feel vaguely unclean, because the idea of dressing up an animal in clothing for human amusement is morally repugnant to you, and to any right-thinking inhabitant of the twenty-fourth century. It is also a criminal act, ever since the Beast Liberation laws were passed.

Quickly, you summon the next image.

At last, another unmistakably human face. A white man, with green eyes and red hair. He wears a sharply pointed goatee and moustaches that stab upward at the ends. He looks imperturbable. He looks arrogant. He looks like the sort of person who carries a sword in his cane. There is something about him, hard as a faceted diamond, cool as a cat. You think to yourself that you would not like to have to ask this man for mercy, and then you wonder why the thought has occurred to you. His designation is VICTOR. He was acquired on 502 A.D., (Gregorian) 1 September, England.

You decide you don't like looking into his eyes, and pull up another image.

Oh, this one is much easier to look at. Another male, but smiling, and certainly human. Or as human as these creatures (you notice that you are thinking of them all as *creatures* now) can be. Fair-haired and boyishly handsome, like a matinee idol of a bygone era, perhaps when films had no sound but melodramatic piano scores and no color but laboriously hand-tinted frames. This fellow would fit right in, racing in an ancient automobile to save the heroine tied to the railroad tracks. He has HERO written all over him, but his designation is LEWIS, and he was acquired 103 A.D., (Gregorian) 21 June, England.

And what romantic places he's lived in! The text tells you he was a druid in Ireland, a troubadour in France, and—yes, he did work in silent films, in old Hollywood. Yet here are notations of suspected espionage and some mysterious difficulty. What happened to necessitate so many repairs on this unit/person/creature?

You move on to the next selection. Your brow creases in puzzlement. You sit back, realize you are sweating profusely, and mop your face with a tissue before leaning forward again to try to make sense of what you are seeing.

Not one image, but some kind of montage, and no explanatory text at all but one word: ADONAI. After a moment of study, you notice that there is one central figure common to all the little images before you. He is taller than anyone else in the frame with him. Here he is in a black robe, stalking along a muddy lane in a place of oak trees. In the distance is a village of thatched and half-timbered buildings. Here he is in the uniform of a naval officer of the mid-nineteenth century, a hulking figure staring gloomily at a horizon of piled cloud. Here he is again, boarding a ship with drawn cutlass, and there is a white-hot righteous wrath in his small pale eyes that makes you draw back involuntarily. And there is something . . . subtly . . . *wrong* about his face. Not evil, but incongruous, in some indefinable way. He is too big. His cheekbones are high and broad, his long nose is broken. No beauty, to be sure, but what is it about the man that sets him apart?

You shake your head, trying to clear it, and reach for another tissue. Here he is again and he's . . . a child. A little boy, holding the hand of a slim young black girl. They are walking along a street and she is carrying a string bag of parcels. He is holding a toy sailboat. He has noticed the person capturing his image and is looking up with a bright interested stare. And in the background—

In the background is the vindaloo shop where you dined today.

This image was taken recently, here, in this city. How can the child in front of the shop also be the man on the deck of the ship, or in the black robe? You feel a queasy sense of illogic, and have to remind yourself that Dr. Zeus Incorporated is rumored to be able to do anything. But you don't think you're up to puzzling over this now. You call up the next image, hoping it will be something simple.

It's another image, just one, with text. The woman regards you with black eyes that do not smolder; they burn. Her mouth is sullen. There is a certain hauteur in her bearing. The text tells you that her designation is MENDOZA and she was acquired on 1541 A.D., (Gregorian) 28 June, in Spain. It states further that she worked in England in 1555 to obtain something called *Ilex tormentosum,* and in California she obtained, among other things in a very long list, *Vitis vinifera elysia* and *Oenothera hookeri ssp. sclatera.* It mentions a lengthy tenure in South America at the New World One Botany Department. You are disappointed. This woman, with her sullen mouth, with her burning eyes, is something as mundane as a botanist?

But there are other notations, records of disciplinary hearings and security breaches and reprogramming. You read a warning about something called Crome's radiation and there's the word ADONAI again—is she connected to the tall man somehow? She was in England once . . .

But the text is blurring—the image is blurring too—

You want a drink of water. You try to get to your feet, but the next thing you see is the ceiling fan above you, spinning slowly around. How did you come to be flat on your back on the floor?

Someone is leaning over you. You look up into the eyes of the ragged man you last saw smiling and nodding to himself on the front steps of Dr. Zeus Incorporated. He looks sympathetic to your plight.

"You shouldn't have had the pink stuff with lentils, you know," he says. You watch, with a vague sense of outrage, as he shuts down the program and closes up your Buke. He drops it into his coat pocket and winks at you before he slips out of the room.

You lie there, immobile.

After a while, you can't see.

After a while, you're not there.

Black Projects, White Knights

This was the first Company story ever to appear in print, while In the Garden of Iden *was still in search of a publisher. It is also the only story of mine my mother ever heard.*

She was a person of epic personality and style, rather like the late great Jennifer Patterson of Two Fat Ladies *fame, outrageous, artistic, and endlessly nurturing. Naturally enough, I spent most of my life refusing to be anything she wanted me to be. I never let her read anything I wrote, although she loved science fiction.*

Then she was, abruptly, diagnosed with something awful and lasted only a month. Every day after work I would visit her in her hospital room, where of course the truth hit me like a grand piano dropped out a window: I desperately wanted *her to read my stuff. And now she couldn't hold a book or even focus her eyes. And the train was pulling out of the station so fast, and I was standing there like an idiot on the platform, with almost no time to say I was sorry.*

But, pacing by her bed, I explained the whole Company idea, and made up a short story to illustrate the way it worked, about Mendoza and Joseph trying to steal a rare plant. I acted it out, did all the voices, everything I could think of to hold her attention and get the idea across. She liked it, thank God. I wrote it down after she died.

Mea culpa, mea culpa, mea maxima culpa.

✦ ✦ ✦

Noble Mold

FOR A WHILE I LIVED IN THIS LITTLE TOWN BY THE
sea. Boy, it was a soft job. Santa Barbara had become civilized by
then: no more Indian rebellions, no more pirates storming up the beach,
nearly all the grizzly bears gone. Once in a while some bureaucrat from
Mexico City would raise hell with us, but by and large the days of the
old Missions were declining into forlorn shades, waiting for the Yankees
to come.

The Company operated a receiving, storage, and shipping terminal
out of what looked like an oaken chest in my cell. I had a mortal identity as an alert little padre with an administrative career ahead of him,
so the Church kept me pretty busy pushing a quill. My Company duties,
though, were minor: I logged in consignments from agents in the field
and forwarded communiqués.

It was sort of a forty-year vacation. There were fiestas and fandan-
gos down in the pueblo. There were horse races along the shore of the
lagoon. My social standing with the De La Guerra family was high, so I
got invited out to supper a lot. And at night, when the bishop had gone
to bed and our few pathetic Indians were tucked in for the night, I would
sneak a little glass of Communion wine and then relax out on the front
steps of the church. There I'd sit, listening to the night sounds, looking
down the long slope to the night sea. Sometimes I'd sit there until the
sky pinked up in the east and the bells rang for Matins. We Old Ones
don't need much sleep.

One August night I was sitting like that, watching the moon drop
down toward the Pacific, when I picked up the signal of another immortal somewhere out there in the night. I tracked it coming along the

3

shoreline, past the point at Goleta; then it crossed the Camino Real and came straight uphill at me. Company business. I sighed and broadcast, *Quo Vadis?*

Hola, came the reply. I scanned, but I knew who it was anyway. *Hi, Mendoza,* I signaled back, and leaned up on my elbows to await her arrival. Pretty soon I picked her up on visual, too, climbing up out of the mists that flowed along the little stream; first the wide-brimmed hat, then the shoulders bent forward under the weight of the pack, the long walking skirt, the determined lope of the field operative without transportation.

Mendoza is a botanist, and has been out in the field too long. At this point she'd been tramping around Alta California for the better part of twelve decades. God only knew what the Company had found for her to do out in the back of beyond; I'd have known, if I'd been nosy enough to read the Company directives I relayed to her from time to time. I wasn't her case officer anymore, though, so I didn't.

She raised burning eyes to me and my heart sank. She was on a Mission, and I don't mean the kind with stuccoed arches and tile roofs. Mendoza takes her work way too seriously. "How's it going, kid?" I greeted her in a loud whisper when she was close enough.

"Okay." She slung down her pack on the step beside me, picked up my wine and drank it, handed me back the empty glass and sat down.

"I thought you were back up in Monterey these days," I ventured.

"No. The Ventana," she replied. There was a silence while the sky got a little brighter. Far off, a rooster started to crow and then thought better of it.

"Well, well. To what do I owe the pleasure, et cetera?" I prompted.

She gave me a sharp look. "Company Directive 080444–C," she said, as though it were really obvious.

I'd developed this terrible habit of storing incoming Green Directives in my tertiary consciousness without scanning them first. The soft life, I guess. I accessed hastily. "They're sending you after grapes?" I cried a second later.

"Not just grapes." She leaned forward and stared into my eyes. *"Mission* grapes. All the cultivars around here that will be replaced by the varieties the Yankees introduce. I'm to collect genetic material from every remaining vine within a twenty-five-mile radius of this building." She looked around disdainfully. "Not that I expect to find all that many. This place is a wreck. The Church has really let its agricultural program go to hell, hasn't it?"

"Hard to get slave labor nowadays." I shrugged. "Can't keep 'em down on the farm without leg irons. We get a little help from the ones who really bought into the religion, but that's about it."

"And the Holy Office can't touch them." Mendoza shook her head. "Never thought I'd see the day."

"Hey, things change." I stretched out and crossed my sandaled feet one over the other. "Anyway. The Mexicans hate my poor little bishop and are doing their level best to drive him crazy. In all the confusion with the Missions being closed down, a lot of stuff has been looted. Plants get dug up and moved to people's gardens in the dark of night. There are still a few Indian families back in some of the canyons, too, and a lot of them have tiny little farms. Probably a lot of specimens out there, but you'll really have to hunt around for them."

She nodded, all brisk. "I'll need a processing credenza. Bed and board, too, and a cover identity. That's your job. Can you arrange them by 0600 hours?"

"Gosh, this is just like old times," I said without enthusiasm. She gave me that look again.

"I have work to do," she explained with exaggerated patience. "It is very important work. I'm a good little machine and I love my work. Nothing is more important than *My Work*. You taught me that, remember?"

Which I had, so I just smiled my most sincere smile as I clapped her on the shoulder. "And a damned good machine you are, too. I know you'll do a great job, Mendoza. And I feel that your efficiency will be increased if you don't rush this job. Take the time to do it right, you know? Mix a little rest and rec into your schedule. After all, you really deserve a holiday, a hard-working operative like you. This is a great place for fun. You could come to one of our local cascaron balls. Dance the night away. You used to like to dance."

Boy, was that the wrong thing to say. She stood up slowly, like a cobra rearing back.

"I haven't owned a ballgown since 1703. I haven't attended a mortal party since 1555. If you've chosen to forget that miserable Christmas, I can assure you I haven't. *You* play with the damned monkeys, if you're so fond of them." She drew a deep breath. "I, myself, have better things to do." She stalked away up the steps, but I called after her:

"You're still sore about the Englishman, huh?"

She didn't deign to respond but shoved her way between the church doors, presumably to get some sleep behind the altar screen where she wouldn't be disturbed.

She was still sore about the Englishman.

I may have a more relaxed attitude toward my job than some people I could mention, but I'm still the best at it. By the time Mendoza wandered squinting into morning light I had her station set up, complete with hardware, in one of the Mission's guest cells. For the benefit of my fellow friars she was my cousin from Guadalajara, visiting me while she awaited the arrival of her husband from Mexico City. As befitted the daughter of an old Christian family, the señora was of a sober and studious nature, and derived much innocent pleasure from painting flowers and other subjects of natural history.

She didn't waste any time. Mendoza went straight out to what remained of the Mission vineyard and set to work, clipping specimens, taking soil samples, doing all those things you'd have to be an obsessed specialist to enjoy. By the first evening she was hard at work at her credenza, processing it all.

When it came time to loot the private gardens of the *Gentes de Razon* her social introductions went okay, too, once I got her into some decent visiting clothes. I did most of the talking to the Ortegas and Carrillos and the rest, and the fact that she was a little stiff and silent while taking grape brandy with them could easily be explained away by her white skin and blue veins. If you had any Spanish blood you were sort of expected to sneer about it in that place, in those days.

Anyway it was a relief for everybody when she'd finished in the pueblo and went roving up and down the canyons, pouncing on unclaimed vines. There were a few Indians settled back in the hills, ex-neophytes scratching out a living between two worlds, on land nobody else had wanted. What they made of this woman, white as their worst nightmares, who spoke to them in imperious and perfectly accented Barbareño Chumash, I can only imagine. However she persuaded them, though, she got samples of their vines too. I figured she'd soon be on her way back to the hinterlands, and had an extra glass of Communion wine to celebrate. Was *that* ever premature!

I was hearing confessions when her scream of excitement cut through the subvocal ether, followed by delighted profanity in sixteenth-century Galician. My parishioner went on:

". . . which you should also know, Father, was that I have coveted Juana's new pans. These are not common iron pans but enamelware, white with a blue stripe, very pretty, and they came from the Yankee trading ship. It disturbs me that such things should imperil my soul."

Joseph! Joseph! Joseph!

"It is good to be concerned on that account, my child." I shut out Mendoza's transmission so I could concentrate on the elderly mortal woman on the other side of the screen. "To covet worldly things is very sinful indeed, especially for the poor. The Devil himself sent the Yankees with those pans, you may be certain." But Mendoza had left her credenza and was coming down the arcade in search of me, ten meters, twenty meters, twenty-five . . . "For this, and for your sinful dreams, you must say thirty Paternosters and sixty Ave Marias . . ." Mendoza was coming up the church steps two at a time . . . "Now, recite with me the Act of Contrition—"

"Hey!" Mendoza pulled back the door of the confessional. Her eyes were glowing with happiness. I gave her a stern look and continued the Act of Contrition with my somewhat disconcerted penitent, so Mendoza went out to stride up and down in front of the church in her impatience.

"Don't you know better than to interrupt me when I'm administering a sacrament?" I snapped when I was finally able to come out to her. "Some Spaniard you are!"

"So report me to the Holy Office. Joseph, this is important. One of my specimens read out with an F-M Class One rating."

"And?" I put my hands in my sleeves and frowned at her, refusing to come out of the role of offended friar.

"Favorable Mutation, Joseph, don't you know what that means? It's a Mission grape with a difference. It's got Saccharomyces with style and Botrytis in rare bloom. Do you know what happens when a field operative discovers an F-M Class One, Joseph?"

"You get a prize," I guessed.

"Si Señor!" She did a little dance down the steps and stared up at me in blazing jubilation. I hadn't seen her this happy since 1554. "I get a Discovery Bonus! Six months of access to a lab for my own personal research projects, with the very finest equipment available! Oh joy, oh rapture. So I need you to help me."

"What do you need?"

"The Company wants the parent plant I took the specimen from, the whole thing, root and branch. It's a big vine, must have been planted years ago, so I need you to get me some Indians to dig it up and bring it back here in a carreta. Six months at a Sciences Base, can you imagine?"

"Where did you get the specimen?" I inquired.

She barely thought about it. "Two kilometers south-southeast. Just some Indian family back in the hills, Joseph, with a hut in a clearing and a garden. Kasmali, that was what they called themselves. You know the family? I suppose we'll have to pay them something for it. You'll have to arrange that for me, okay?"

I sighed. Once again the kindly padre was going to explain to the Indian why it was necessary to give up yet another of his belongings. Not my favorite role, all things considered.

*   *   *

But there we were that afternoon, the jolly friar and his haughty cousin, paying a call on the Kasmali family.

They were good parishioners of mine, the old abuela at Mass every day of the week, rain or shine, the rest of the family lined up there every Sunday. That was a lot to expect of our Indians in this day and age. They were prosperous, too, as Indians went: they had three walls of a real adobe house and had patched in the rest with woven brush. They had terraced their tiny hillside garden and were growing all kinds of vegetables on land not fit for grazing. There were a few chickens, there were a few little brown children chasing them, there were a few cotton garments drying on the bushes. And, on the crest of the hill, a little way from the house, there was the vineyard: four old vines, big as trees, with branches spreading out to shade most of an acre of land.

The children saw us coming and vanished into the house without a sound. By the time we reached the top of the winding stony path, they had all come out and were staring at us: the toothless old woman from daily Mass, a toothless old man I did not know, the old son, the two grown grandsons, their wives, and children of assorted ages. The elder of the grandsons came forward to greet us.

"Good evening, little Father." He looked uneasily at Mendoza. "Good evening, lady."

"Good evening, Emidio." I paused and pretended to be catching my breath after the climb, scanning him. He was small, solidly built, with broad and very dark features; he had a stiff black moustache. His wide eyes flickered once more to Mendoza, then back to me. "You have already been introduced to my cousin, I see."

"Yes, little Father." He made a slight bow in her direction. "The lady came yesterday and cut some branches off our grapevines. We did not mind, of course."

"It is very kind of you to permit her to collect these things." I eyed Mendoza, hoping she'd been tactful with them.

"Not at all. The lady speaks our language very well."

"That is only courtesy, my son. Now, I must tell you that one of your vines has taken her fancy, for its extraordinary fruit and certain virtues in the leaves. We have come back here today, therefore, to ask you what you will accept for that near vine at the bottom of the terrace."

The rest of the family stood like statues, even the children. Emidio moved his hands in a helpless gesture and said, "The lady must of course accept our gift."

"No, no," said Mendoza. "We'll pay you. How much do you want for it?" I winced.

"She must accept the gift, please, Father." Emidio's smile was wretched.

"Of course she shall," I agreed. "And, Emidio, I have a gift I have been meaning to give you since the feast of San Juan. Two little pigs, a boar and a sow, so they may increase. When you bring down the vine for us you may collect them."

The wives lifted up their heads at that. This was a good deal. Emidio spread out his hands again. "Of course, little Father. Tomorrow."

"Well, that was easy," Mendoza remarked as we picked our way down the hill through the chaparral. "You're so good with mortals, Joseph. You just have to treat Indians like children, I guess, huh?"

"No, you don't," I sighed. "But it's what they expect you to do, so they play along." There was more to it than that, of course, but something else was bothering me. I had picked up something more than the usual stifled resentment when I had voiced my request: someone in the family had been badly frightened for a second. Why? "You didn't do anything to, like, scare those people when you were there before, did you, Mendoza? Didn't threaten them or anything, did you?"

"Heavens, no." She stopped to examine a weed. "I was quite polite. They weren't comfortable around me, actually, but then mortals never are. Look at this! I've never seen this blooming so late in the year, have you?"

"Nice." I glanced at it. I don't know from plants. I know a lot about mortals, though.

So I was surprised as hell next day when Emidio and his brother appeared at the Mission, trundling a cart full of swaying leaves into the open space by the fountain. I went out to greet them and Mendoza was behind me like a shadow. She must have been prowling her room, listening for the squeak of wheels.

"This is very good, my sons, I am proud of you—" I was saying heartily, when Mendoza transmitted a blast of subvocal fury.

Damn it, Joseph, this is wrong! These are just clippings, they haven't brought the whole vine!

"— but I perceive there has been a misunderstanding," I continued. "My cousin requested the vine itself, with its roots, that she may replant it. You have brought only cut branches, apparently." The Indians exchanged glances.

"Please forgive us, little Father. We did not understand." They set down the traces and Emidio reached into the back. "We did bring all the grapes that were ripe. Maybe it was these the lady wanted?" And he proffered a big woven dish of grapes. I looked close and noticed they did have a funny look to them, a bloom on the skin so heavy it was almost . . . furry?

"No," said Mendoza, in clearest Chumash. "Not just the grapes. I want the vine. The whole plant. You need to dig it up, roots and all, and bring it here. Do you understand now?"

"Oh," said Emidio. "We're very sorry. We didn't understand."

"But you understand now?" she demanded.

"I am certain they do," I said smoothly. "What remarkable grapes these are, my sons, and what a beautiful basket! Come in and rest in the shade, my sons, and have a cool drink. Then we will go catch one of the little pigs I promised you."

By the time we got back, Mendoza had vanished; the grapes and the vine cuttings were gone too. The brothers trudged away up the hill with their cart and one squealing shoat, his legs bound with twine. Pig Number Two remained in the Mission pen, to be paid on delivery of the vine. I figured if the wives got that message they'd see to it the job got done.

Mendoza came out when they were gone. She looked paler than usual. She handed me a sheet of paper from her credenza. "This is a Priority Order," she told me. "I sent them the codes on the grapes and clippings anyway, but it's not enough."

I read the memo. She wasn't kidding; it was a first-class transdepartmental Priority Gold telling me I was to do everything in my power to facilitate, expedite and et cetera. "What have we got here, anyway, cancer cures from grapes?" I speculated.

"You don't need to know and neither do I," said Mendoza flatly. "But the Company means business now, Joseph. We must get that vine."

"We'll get it tomorrow," I told her. "Trust me."

Next day, same hour, the brothers came with hopeful smiles and a big muddy mess of a vine trailing out of their cart. Such relief! Such heartfelt praise and thanks the kindly friar showered on his obedient sons in Christ! Mendoza heard their arrival and came tearing out into the courtyard, only to pull up short with an expression of baffled rage.

THAT'S NOT THE VINE! she transmitted, with such intensity I thought for a second we were having an earthquake.

". . . And yet, my sons, I am afraid we have not understood each other once again," I went on wearily. "It appears that, although you have brought us *a* whole vine, you have not brought *the* particular vine that was specifically asked for by my cousin."

"We are so sorry," replied Emidio, averting his eyes from Mendoza. "How stupid we were! But, Father, this is a very good vine. It's in much better condition than the other one and bears much prettier grapes. Also, it was very difficult to dig it all up and we have brought it a long way. Maybe the lady will be satisfied with this vine instead?"

Mendoza was shaking her head, not trusting herself to speak, although the air around her was wavering like a mirage. Hastily I said: "My dearest sons, I am sure it is an excellent vine, and we would not take it from your family. You must understand that it is the *other* vine we want, the very one you brought cuttings from yesterday. That vine and no other, and all of that vine. Now, you have clearly worked very hard and in good faith, so I will certainly send you home with your other pig, but you must come back tomorrow with the right vine."

The brothers looked at each other and I picked up a flash of despair from them, and some weird kind of fear too. "Yes, little Father," they replied.

But on the next day they didn't come at all.

Mendoza paced the arcade until nine in the evening, alarming the other friars. Finally I went out to her and braced myself for the blast.

"You know, you lost yourself two perfectly good pigs," she informed me through gritted teeth. "Damned lying Indians."

I shook my head. "Something's wrong here, Mendoza."

"You bet something's wrong! You've got a three-day delay on a Priority Gold."

"But there's some reason we're not getting. Something is missing from this picture . . ."

"We never should have tried to bargain with them, you know that? They offered it as a gift in the first place. We should have just taken it. Now they know it's really worth something! I'll go up there with a spade and dig the damned vine up myself, if I have to."

"No! You can't do that, not now. They'll know who took it, don't you see?"

"One more crime against the helpless Indians laid at the door of Spain. As if it mattered any more!" Mendoza turned on her heel to stare at me. Down at the other end of the arcade one of my brother friars put his head out in discreet inquiry.

It does matter! I dropped to a subvocal hiss. *It matters to them and it matters to me! I call them my beloved sons, but they know I've got the power to go up there and confiscate anything they have on any excuse at all because that's how it's always been done! Only I don't. They know Father Rubio won't do that to them. I've built up a cover identity as a kindly, honorable guy because I've got to live with these people for the next thirty years! You'll get your damn specimen and go away again into the sagebrush, but I've got a character to maintain!*

My God, she sneered, *He wants his little Indians to love him.*

Company policy, baby. It's easier to deal with mortals when they trust you. Something you used to understand. So just you try screwing with my cover identity! Just you try it and see what happens.

She widened her eyes at that, too furious for words, and I saw her knuckles go white; little chips of whitewash began falling from the walls. We both looked up at them and cooled down in a hurry.

Sorry. But I mean what I say, Mendoza. We handle this my way.

She threw her hands up in the air. *What are you going to do, then, smart guy? You have to do* something.

Day four of the Priority Gold, and Company Directive 081244–A anxiously inquired why no progress on previous transdepartmental request for facilitation?

Situation Report follows, I responded. *Please stand by.* Then I put on my walking sandals and set off up the canyon alone.

Before I had toiled more than halfway, though, I met Emidio coming in my direction. He didn't try to avoid me, but as he approached he looked down the canyon past me in the direction of the Mission. "Good morning, little Father," he called.

"Good morning, my son."

"Is your cousin lady with you?" He dropped his voice as he drew close.

"No, my son. We are alone."

"I need to speak with you, little Father, about the grapevine." He cleared his throat. "I know the lady must be very angry, and I am sorry. I don't mean to make you angry too, little Father, because I know she is your cousin—"

"I understand, my son, believe me. And I am not angry."

"Well then." He drew a deep breath. "This is the matter. The grapevines do not belong to me, nor to my father. They belong to our grandfather Diego. And he will not let us dig up the vine the lady wants."

"Why will he not?"

"He won't tell us. He just refuses. Don't be stupid, we told him. Father Rubio has been good to us, he has treated us fairly. Look at the fine pigs he has given us, we said. He just sits in the sun and rocks himself, and refuses us. And our grandmother came and touched his feet and cried, though she didn't say anything, but he wouldn't even look at her."

"I see."

"We have said everything we could say to him, but he will not let us dig up that vine. We tried to fool the lady twice by pretending to make mistakes (and that was a sin, little Father, and I'm sorry), but it didn't work. Somehow she knew. Then our grandfather—" he paused in obvious embarrassment. "I don't know how to say this, little Father—you know the old people are superstitious and still believe foolish things—I think he somehow has the idea that your cousin lady is a *nunasis*. Please don't take this the wrong way—"

"No, no, go on—"

"We have an old story about a spirit who walks on the mountains and wears a hat like hers, you see, throwing a shadow cold as death. I know it's stupid. Even so, Grandfather won't let us dig up that vine. Now, you might say, our grandfather is only an old man and a little bit crazy now, and we're strong, so he can be put aside as though he were a little baby; but if we did that, we would be breaking the commandment about honoring the old people. It seems to us that would be a worse sin than the white lady not getting what she wanted. What do you think, little Father?"

Boy, oh, boy. "This is very hard, my son," I said, and I meant it. "But you are right."

Emidio studied me in silence for a long moment, his eyes narrowed. "Thank you," he said at last. After another pause he added, "Is there anything we can do that will make the lady happy? She'll be angry with you, now."

I found myself laughing. "She will make my life a Purgatory, I can tell you," I said. "But I will offer it up for my sins. Go home, Emidio, and don't worry. Perhaps God will send a miracle."

I wasn't laughing when I got back to the Mission, though, and when Mendoza came looking for me she saw my failure right away.

"No dice, huh?" She squinted evilly. "Well. This is no longer a matter of me and my poor little bonus now, Joseph. *The Company wants that vine.* I suggest you think of something fast or there are liable to be some dead Indians around here soon, pardon my indelicate phrasing."

"I'm working on it," I told her.

And I was. I went to the big leatherbound books that held the Mission records. I sat down in a corner of the scriptorium and went over them in minute detail.

1789—here was the baptism of Diego Kasmali, age given as thirty years. 1790, marriage to Maria Concepción, age not given. 1791 through 1810, a whole string of baptisms of little Kasmalis: Agustin, Xavier, Pablo, Juan Bautista, Maria, Dolores, Guadalupe, Dieguito, Marta, Tomas, Luisa, Bartolomeo. First Communion for Xavier Kasmali, 1796. One after the other, a string of little funerals: Agustin age two days, Pablo age three months six days, Juan Bautista age six days, Maria age two years . . . too sad to go on down the list, but not unusual.

Confirmation for Xavier Kasmali, 1802. Xavier Kasmali married to Juana Catalina of the Dos Pueblos rancheria, age 18 years, 1812. Baptism of Emidio Kasmali, 1813. Baptism of Salvador Kasmali, 1814. Funeral of Juana Catalina, 1814. First Communions, Confirmations, Marriages, Baptisms, Extreme Unctions . . . not a sacrament missed. Really good Catholics.

Why the old, old woman was at Mass every single day of the year, rain or shine, though she was propped like a bundle of sticks in the shadows at the back of the church. Maria Concepción, wife of Diego Kasmali. But Diego never, ever at Mass. Why not? On a desperate hunch I went to my transmitter and typed in a request for something unusual.

The reply came back: *Query: first please resolution Priority Gold status?*

Request relates Priority, I replied. *Resolving now. Requisition Sim ParaN Phenom re: Priority resolution?*

That gave them pause. They verified and counterverified my authority, they re-scanned the original orders and mulled over their implications. At least, I guessed they were doing that, as the blue screen flickered. Feeling I had them on the run, I pushed for a little extra, just for my own satisfaction: *Helpful Priority specify mutation. What? Why?*

Pause while they verified me again, then the bright letters crawled onscreen in a slow response:

Patent Black Elysium.

I fell back laughing, though it wasn't exactly funny. The rest of the message followed in a rapid burst: *S-P Requisition approved. Specify Tech support?*

I told them what I needed.

Estimate resolution time Priority Gold?

I told them how long it would take.

Expecting full specimen consign & report then, was the reply, and they signed off.

"Why don't they ever put convenient handles on these things?" grumbled Mendoza. She had one end of the transport trunk and a shovel; I had the other end of the trunk and the other shovel. It was long after midnight and we were struggling up the rocky defile that led to the Kasmali residence.

"Too much T-field drag," I explained.

"Well, you would think that an all-powerful cabal of scientists and businessmen, with advance knowledge of every event in recorded history *and* infinite time in which to take every possible advantage of said events, *and* every possible technological resource at their command,

and unlimited wealth—" Mendoza shifted the trunk again and we went on "—you'd think they could devise something as simple as a recessed handle."

"They tried it. The recess cuts down on the available transport space inside," I told her.

"You're kidding me."

"No. I was part of a test shipment. Damn thing got me right in the third cervical vertebra."

"I might have known there'd be a reason."

"The Company has a reason for everything, Mendoza."

We came within earshot of the house, so conversation ended. There were three big dogs in the yard before the door. One slept undisturbed, but two raised their heads and began to growl. We set down the trunk. I opened it and from the close-packed contents managed to prize out the hush unit. The bigger of the dogs got to his feet, preparing to bark.

I switched on the unit. Good dog, what a sleepy doggie; he fell over with a woof and did not move again. The other dog dropped his head on his paws. Dog Number Three would not wake at all now, nor would any of the occupants of the house, not while the hush field was being generated.

I carried the unit up to the house and left it by the dogs, Mendoza dragging the trunk after me. We removed the box of golden altar vessels and set off up the hill with it.

The amazing mutated vine was pretty sorry-looking now, with most of its branches clipped off in the attempt to appease Mendoza. I hoped to God their well-meaning efforts hadn't killed it. Mendoza must have been thinking the same thing, but she just shrugged grimly. We began to dig.

We made a neat hole, small but very deep, just behind the trunk and angled slightly under it. There was no way to hide our disturbance of the earth, but fortunately the ground had already been so spaded up and trampled over that our work shouldn't be that obvious.

"How deep does this have to be?" I panted when we had gone about six feet and I was in the bottom passing spadefuls up to Mendoza.

"Not much deeper; I'd like it buried well below the root ball." She leaned in and peered.

"Well, how deep is that?" Before she could reply my spade hit something with a metallic clank. We halted.

Mendoza giggled nervously. "Jesus, don't tell me there's *already* buried treasure down there!"

I scraped a little with the spade. "There's something like a hook," I said. "And something else." I got the spade under it and launched it up out of the hole with one good heave. The whole mass fell on the other side of the dirt heap, out of my view. "It looked kind of round," I remarked.

"It looks kind of like a hat—" Mendoza told me cautiously, bending down and turning it over. Abruptly she yelled and danced back from it. I scrambled up out of the hole to see what was going on.

It was a hat, all right, or what was left of it; one of the hard-cured leather kind Spain had issued to her soldiers in the latter half of the last century. I remembered seeing them on the presidio personnel. Beside the hat, where my spade-toss had dislodged it, was the head that had been wearing it. Only a brown skull now, the eyes blind with black earth. Close to it was the hilt of a sword, the metallic thing I'd hit.

"Oh, *gross!*" Mendoza wrung her hands.

"Alas, poor Yorick," was all I could think of to say.

"Oh, God, how disgusting. Is the rest of him down there?"

I peered down into the hole. I could see a jawbone and pieces of what might have been cavalry boots. "Looks like it, I'm afraid."

"What do you suppose he's doing down there?" Mendoza fretted, from behind the handkerchief she had clapped over her mouth and nose.

"Not a damn thing nowadays," I guessed, doing a quick scan of the bones. "Take it easy: no pathogens left. This guy's been dead a long time."

"Sixty years, by any chance?" Mendoza's voice sharpened.

"They must have planted him with the grapevine," I agreed. In the thoughtful silence that followed I began to snicker. I couldn't help myself. I leaned back and had myself a nice sprawling guffaw.

"I fail to see what's so amusing," said Mendoza.

"Sorry. Sorry. I was just wondering: do you suppose you could cause a favorable mutation in something by planting a dead Spaniard under it?"

"Of course not, you idiot, not unless his sword was radioactive or something."

"No, of course not. What about those little wild yeast spores in the bloom on the grapes, though? You think they might be influenced somehow by the close proximity of a gentleman of Old Castile?"

"What are you talking about?" Mendoza took a step closer.

"This isn't a cancer cure, you know." I waved my hand at the vinestock, black against the stars. "I found out why the Company is so eager to get hold of your Favorable Mutation, kid. This is the grape that makes Black Elysium."

"The dessert wine?" Mendoza cried.

"The very expensive dessert wine. The hallucinogenic-controlled-substance dessert wine. The absinthe of the twenty-fourth century. The one the Company holds the patent on. That stuff. Yeah."

Stunned silence from my fellow immortal creature. I went on:

"I was just thinking, you know, about all those decadent technocrats sitting around in the future getting bombed on an elixir produced from . . ."

"So it gets discovered here, in 1844," said Mendoza at last. "It isn't a genetically engineered cultivar at all. And the wild spores somehow came from. . . ?"

"But nobody else will ever know the truth, because we're removing every trace of this vine from the knowledge of mortal men, see?" I explained. "Root and branch and all."

"I'd sure better get that bonus," Mendoza reflected.

"Don't push your luck. You aren't supposed to know." I took my shovel and clambered back into the hole. "Come on, let's get the rest of him out of here. The show must go on."

Two hours later there was a tidy heap of brown bones and rusted steel moldering away in a new hiding place, and a tidy sum in gold plate occupying the former burial site. We filled in the hole, set up the rest of the equipment we'd brought, tested it, camouflaged it, turned it on and hurried away back down the canyon to the Mission, taking the hush unit with us. I made it in time for Matins.

News travels fast in a small town. By nine there were Indians, and some of the *Gentes de Razon* too, running in from all directions to tell us that the Blessed Virgin had appeared in the Kasmalis' garden. Even if I hadn't known already, I would have been tipped off by the fact that old Maria Concepción did not show up for morning Mass.

By the time we got up there, the bishop and I and all my fellow friars and Mendoza, a cloud of dust hung above the dirt track from all the traffic. The Kasmalis' tomatoes and corn had been trampled by the milling crowd. People ran everywhere, waving pieces of grapevine; the other plants had been stripped as bare as the special one. The rancheros watched from horseback, or urged their mounts closer across the careful beds of peppers and beans.

Around the one vine, the family had formed a tight circle. Some of them watched Emidio and Salvador, who were digging frantically, already about five feet down in the hole; others stared unblinking at the floating image of the Virgin of Guadalupe who smiled upon them from midair above the vine. She was complete in every detail, nicely three-dimensional and accompanied by heavenly music. Actually it was a long tape loop of Ralph Vaughan Williams's *Fantasia on a Theme by*

Thomas Tallis, which nobody would recognize because it hadn't been composed yet.

"Little Father!" One of the wives caught me by my robe. "It's the Mother of God! She told us to dig up the vine, she said there was treasure buried underneath!"

"Has she told you anything else?" I inquired, making the sign of the cross. My brother friars were falling to their knees in raptures, beginning to sing the *Ave Maria;* the bishop was sobbing.

"No, not since this morning," the wife told me. "Only the beautiful music has gone on and on."

Emidio looked up and noticed me for the first time. He stopped shoveling for a moment, staring at me, and a look of dark speculation crossed his face. Then his shovel was moving again, clearing away the earth, and more earth, and more earth.

At my side, Mendoza turned away her face in disgust. But I was watching the old couple, who stood a little way back from the rest of the family. They clung to each other in mute terror and had no eyes for the smiling Virgin. It was the bottom of the ever-deepening hole they watched, as birds watch a snake.

And I watched them. Old Diego was bent and toothless now, but sixty years ago he'd had teeth, all right; sixty years ago his race hadn't yet learned never to fight back against its conquerors. Maria Concepción, what had she been sixty years ago when those vines were planted? Not a dried-up shuffling old thing back then. She might have been a beauty, and maybe a careless beauty.

The old bones and the rusting steel could have told you, sixty years ago. Had he been a handsome young captain with smooth ways, or just a soldier who took what he wanted? Whatever he'd been, or done, he'd wound up buried under that vine, and only Diego and Maria knew he was there. All those years, through the children and grandchildren and great-grandchildren, he'd been there. Diego never coming to Mass because of a sin he couldn't confess. Maria never missing Mass, praying for someone.

Maybe that was the way it had happened. Nobody would ever tell the story, I was fairly sure. But it was clear that Diego and Maria, alone of all those watching, did not expect to see treasure come out of that hole in the ground.

So when the first glint of gold appeared, and then the chalice and altar plate were brought up, their old faces were a study in confusion.

"The treasure!" cried Salvador. "Look!"

And the rancheros spurred their horses through the crowd to get a better look, lashing the Indians out of the way; but I touched the remote hidden in my sleeve and the Blessed Virgin spoke, in a voice as sweet and immortal as a synthesizer:

"This, my beloved children, is the altar plate that was lost from the church at San Carlos Borromeo, long ago in the time of the pirates. My beloved Son has caused it to be found here as a sign to you all that ALL SINS ARE FORGIVEN!"

I touched the remote again and the Holy Apparition winked out like a soap bubble, and the beautiful music fell silent.

Old Diego pushed his way forward to the hole and looked in. There was nothing else there in the hole now, nothing at all. Maria came timidly to his side and she looked in too. They remained there staring a long time, unnoticed by the mass of the crowd, who were watching the dispute that had already erupted over the gold.

The bishop had pounced on it like a duck on a June bug, as they say, asserting the right of Holy Mother Church to her lost property. Emidio and Salvador had let it be snatched from them with hard patient smiles. One of the *Gentes de Razon* actually got off his horse to tell the bishop that the true provenance of the items had to be decided by the authorities in Mexico City, and until they could be contacted the treasure had better be kept under lock and key at the alcalde's house. Blessed Virgin? Yes, there had seemed to be an apparition of some kind; but then again, perhaps it had been a trick of the light.

The argument moved away down the hill—the bishop had a good grip on the gold and kept walking with it, so almost everyone had to follow him. I went to stand beside Diego and Maria, in the ruins of their garden.

"She forgave us," whispered Diego.

"A great weight of sin has been lifted from you today, my children," I told them. "Rejoice, for Christ loves you both. Come to the church with me now and I will celebrate a special Mass in your honor."

I led them away with me, one on either arm. Unseen behind us, Mendoza advanced on the uprooted and forgotten vine with a face like a lioness kept from her prey.

Well, the old couple made out all right, anyway. I saw to it that they got new grapevines and food from the Mission supplies to tide the family over until their garden recovered. Within a couple of years they passed away, one after the other, and were buried reasonably near one another in the consecrated ground of the Mission cemetery, in which respect they were luckier than the unknown captain from Castile, or wherever he'd come from.

They never got the golden treasure, but being Indians there had never been any question that they would. Their descendants lived on and multiplied in the area, doing particularly well after the coming of the Yankees, who (to the mortification of the *Gentes de Razon*) couldn't tell an Indian from a Spanish Mexican and lumped them all together under the common designation of Greaser, treating one no worse than the other.

Actually I never kept track of what happened to the gold. The title dispute dragged on for years, I think, with the friars swearing there had been a miracle and the rancheros swearing there hadn't been. The gold may have been returned to Carmel, or it may have gone to Mexico City, or it may have gone into a trunk underneath the alcalde's bed. I didn't care; it was all faked Company-issue reproductions anyway. The bishop died and the Yankees came and were the new conquerors, and maybe nothing ever did get resolved either way.

But Mendoza got her damned vine and her bonus, so she was as happy as she ever is. The Company got its patent on Black Elysium secured. I lived on at the Mission for years and years before (apparently) dying of venerable old age and (apparently) being buried in the same cemetery as Diego and Maria. God forgave us all, I guess, and I moved on to less pleasant work.

Sometimes, when I'm in that part of the world, I stop in as a tourist and check out my grave. It's the nicest of the many I've had, except maybe for that crypt in Hollywood. Well, well; life goes on.

Mine does anyway.

Anyone who has done time with the very small and the very bright will agree that computer adventure games, when done with wit, creativity and good graphics, are the greatest thing since moveable type. Puzzles, riddles, language games, BRAIN EXERCISE! And a lesson in humility when a three-year-old, tiny fingers flying over the keys, is halfway through the first quest while you are still trying to make sense of the walkthrough guide . . .

The old world is just as dark and narrow as it ever was, just as unkind to little things, just as cold and intolerant; but the machines and the children get brighter all the time. Such possibilities . . .

◆ ◆ ◆

Smart Alec

FOR THE FIRST FOUR YEARS OF HIS LIFE, ALEC Checkerfield wore a life vest. This was so that if he accidentally went over the side of his parents' yacht, he would be guaranteed a rescue. It was state of the art, as life vests went in the twenty-fourth century: not only would it have enabled him to bob along like a little cork in the wake of the *Foxy Lady,* it would have reassured him in a soothing voice programmed to allay panic, broadcast a frequency that repelled sharks, and sounded an immediate alarm on the paging devices worn by every one of the servants on board.

His parents themselves wore no pagers, which was just as well because if Mummy had noticed Alec was in the water she'd probably have simply waved her handkerchief after him until he was well over the horizon. Daddy would probably have made an effort to rescue Alec, if he weren't too stoned to notice the emergency; but most of the time he was, which was why the servants had been appointed to save Alec, should the child ever fall overboard. They were all madly fond of Alec, anyway, because he was really a very good little boy, so they were sure to have done a great job, if the need for rescue at sea should ever have arisen.

It never did arise, however, because Alec was a rather well-coordinated child too and generally did what he was told, such as obeying safety rules at sea.

And he was a happy child, despite the fact that his mother never set her ice-blue eyes on him if she could help it and his father was as likely to trip over him as speak to him. It didn't matter that they were terrible

23

at being parents; they were also very rich, which meant they could pay other people to love Alec.

In a later time Alec would look back on the years aboard the *Foxy Lady* as the happiest in his life, and sometimes he'd come across the old group holo and wonder why it had all ended. The picture had been taken in Jamaica, by somebody standing on a mooring catwalk and shooting down on deck.

There he was, three years old, in his bright red life vest and little sailor hat, smiling brightly up at the camera. Assembled around him were all the servants: fabulous Sarah, his Jamaican nurse, arrogantly naked except for blue bathing shorts; Lewin and Mrs. Lewin, the butler and cook; Reggie, Bob and Cat, the deckhands, and Mr. Trefusis, the first mate. They formed a loving and protective wall between Alec and his Mummy and Daddy, or Roger and Cecilia, as they preferred to be called.

Roger and Cecilia were visible up on the quarterdeck: Cecilia ignoring them all from her deck chair, a cold presence in a sun hat and dark glasses, reading a novel. Roger was less visible, leaning slouched against the rail, one nerveless hand about to spill a rum highball all over his yachting shoes. He'd turned his face away to look at something just as the image had been recorded, so all you could see was a glimpse of aristocratic profile, blurred and enigmatic.

Oh, but it hadn't mattered. Alec had a wonderful life, full of adventures. Sarah would tell him stories about Sir Henry Morgan and all the pirates who used to roam the sea, living on their ships just like Alec did, and how they formed the Free Brotherhood of the Coast. Alec liked that. It was a grand-sounding name.

And there was the fun of landing on a new island—what would it be like? Was there any chance pirates might still be lurking around? Alec had played on beaches where the sand was white, or yellow, or pink, or black, built castles on all of them and stuck his little pirate flags on the turrets. *Jolly Roger,* that was what the flag was called.

Jolly Roger was also what the deckhands called Alec's Daddy when he seemed to be having more than usual difficulty walking or talking. This was generally after he'd been drinking the tall drinks Cat would shake up for him at the bar on the yacht. Sometimes Cat would put a fruit spear in the drinks, cherries and chunks of pineapple skewered on long wooden picks with the paper pirate flag at the top. Sometimes Daddy's eyes would focus on Alec and he'd present him with the fruit spear and yell for more rum in his drink. Alec would sit under Daddy's tall chair and eat the pineapple and cherries, making faces at the nasty stuff they'd been soaked in. Then he'd carry the Jolly Roger pick back to his cabin, where he had a whole hoard of them carefully saved for his sand castles.

It was a shame the rum had such an effect on Daddy, because going to get it was always fun. The *Foxy Lady* would drop anchor in some sapphire bay and Sarah would put on a halter top and shoes, and put shoes on Alec, and they'd go ashore together in the launch. And as they'd come across the water Sarah might sing out, *"How many houses, baby?"* and Alec would look up at the town and count the houses in his head and he'd tell her how many there were, and she'd tousle his hair and tell him he was right again! And they'd laugh.

Then they would take a long walk through some island town, past the gracious houses with window boxes full of pink flowers, where parrots flashed and screamed in the green gardens, back to the wappen-bappen places where the houses looked like they were about to fall down, and there would always be a doormouth with no sign and a dark cool room beyond, full of quiet black men sitting at tables, or brown men, or white men turned red from the sun. There Sarah would do a deal; and Alec and Sarah would sit at a table while the men loaded crates into a battered old vehicle.

Then Alec and Sarah would go out into the bright sunlight again, and the driver would give them a ride back into town with the crates. The crates were nearly always stenciled CROSSE & BLACKWELL'S PICKLED GHERKINS.

And nearly always they'd spot a stern-looking black or brown or white man in a white uniform, pedaling along on a bicycle, and Sarah would hug Alec tight and cry out in a little silly voice: "Oh, nooo, it's a policeman! Don't tell him, Alec, don't tell him our secret!" This always made Alec giggle, and she'd always go on: "Don't tell him we've got GUNS! Don't tell him we've got EXPLOSIVES! Don't tell him we've got GANJA! Don't tell him we've got COFFEE!" She'd go on and on like this, as they'd bump along trailing dust clouds and squawking birds, and by the time they reached the harbor Alec would be weak with laughter.

Once they were at the launch, however, she'd be all quiet efficiency, buckling Alec into his seat and then helping the man move the crates into the cargo bay. When all the crates were on board, the man would hold out a plaquette and Sarah would bring out Daddy's identification disk and pay for the crates, and then they'd zoom back out to the *Foxy Lady.* They'd put out to sea again, and the next day there would be rows of brown bottles under the bar once more, and Cat would be busy shaking up the long drinks, and Daddy would be sitting on the aft deck with a glass in his hand, staring vacantly out at the blue horizon.

Not everybody thought that the trips to get the rum were such a good idea, however. Alec was sitting in the saloon one day after just such a trip, quietly coloring. He had made a picture of a shark fighting with an anchor, because he knew how to draw anchors and he knew how to draw sharks, and that was all the logic the scene needed. The saloon was just aft of the galley. Because it was very warm that day the connecting door was open, and he could hear Lewin and Mrs. Lewin talking in disgusted tones.

"He only gets away with it because he's a peer."

"Peer or no, you'd think he'd stop it for the kid's sake! He was such a brilliant teacher, too, and what's he given that all up for? He used to *do* something with his life, and look at him now! And what would happen if we were ever boarded for inspection? They'd take the baby away in a minute, you know they would." *Chop, chop, chop,* Mrs. Lewin was cutting up peppers as she talked.

"Don't think so. J.I.S. would smooth it over, same as they've always done. Between his lineage and *them,* he can do whatever he bloody well pleases, even in London."

"Yeh, well! Things was different before Alec came, weren't they? Don't forget that J.I.S. would have something to say if they knew he was drinking where the baby could see! And anyway it's *wrong,* Malcolm, you know it is, it's criminal, it's dangerous, it's unhealthy, and really the best thing we could do for him would be to tell a Public Health Monitor about the alcohol."

"And where'd we be, then? The last thing J.I.S. would want'd be some Public Health doctor examining the boy—" Lewin started through the doorway and saw Alec in the saloon. He caught his breath and shut the door.

Alec sat frowning at his picture. He knew that Daddy's drinking made people sad, but he'd never thought it was dangerous. He got up and trotted out of the saloon. There was Daddy on the aft deck, smiling dreamily at the sun above the yardarm.

"Hey, there, Alec," he greeted the little boy. He had a sip of his drink and reached out to tousle Alec's hair. "Look out there to starboard. Is that a pretty good island? Should we go there, maybe?"

Alec shivered with joy. Daddy almost never noticed him, and here he was asking Alec's opinion about something.

"Yeah!" he cried. "Let's go!"

But Daddy's gaze had drifted away, back to the horizon, and he lifted his glass again. "Some green island we haven't found yet," he murmured, "farther on 'n farther on 'n farther on . . ."

Alec remembered what he had wanted to ask. He reached out and pushed at Daddy's glass with his index finger.

"Is that crinimal?" he inquired. It was a moment before Daddy played that back and turned to stare at him.

"What?"

"Is that dangerous?" Alex persisted, and mimed perfectly the drinking-from-a-bottle gesture he had seen the servants make in reference to his father. "If I see danger I'm supposed to tell."

"Huh," said Daddy, and he rubbed his scratchy chin. He hadn't shaved in about a week. His eyes narrowed and he looked at Alec slyly.

"Tell me, Alec, 'm I hurting anybody?"

"No."

"We ever had an accident on this ship? Anything happen ol' Roger can't handle?"

"No."

"Then where's the harm?" Daddy had another sip. "Tell me that. 'M a nice guy even when I'm stoned. A Gentleman You Know. Old School Tie."

Alec had no idea what that meant, but he pushed on, "How come it's crinimal?"

"Aha." Daddy tilted his glass until the ice fell down against his lip. He crunched ice and continued, "Okay, Alec. Big fact of life. There's a whole bunch of busybodies and scaredy-cats who make a whole bunch of rules and regs about things they don't want anybody doing. See? So nobody gets to have any fun. Like, no booze. They made a law about no booze. And they're all, 'You can't lie about in the sun because you get cancer,' and they're all, 'You can't swim in the ocean 'cos you might pee,' and they're all, 'You can't eat sweets because they make you fat,' okay? Dumb stuff. And they make laws so you go to Hospital if you do this little dumb stuff! Okay?

"That's why we don't live in London, kiddo. That's why we live out here on the *Lady,* so no scaredy-cat's gonna tell us what to do. Okay? Now then. If you went running to the scaredy-cats to tell 'em about the rum, you'd be an even worse thing than them. You'd be a telltale! See? And you gotta remember you're a gentleman, and no gentleman is ever a telltale. See? 'Cos if you did tell about the rum, well, they'd come on board and they'd see me with my little harmless drinkies and they'd see your Mummy with her books and they'd see Sarah with her lovely bare tits and then you know what they'd do? Daddy'd go to Hospital and they'd take you away. Li'l Alec ain't gonna be a telltale, is he? He's my li'l gentleman, ain't he?"

"I don't want 'em to take me away!" Alec wailed, tears in his eyes. Daddy dropped his glass, reaching clumsily to pull Alec up on his lap, and the glass broke, but he didn't notice.

" 'Course you don't! 'Cos we're free here on the *Foxy Lady,* and you're a gentleman and you got a right to be free, free, free. Okay? You won't tell on Daddy, not my li'l Alec. You just let old Jolly Roger go his ways and you never be a telltale, okay? And don't pay them no mind with their dumb rules."

"But they gonna board us for aspection!" Alec sobbed.

"Hey! Hey, kiddo, don't you worry. Daddy's a gentleman, don't forget, he's got some pull. I'm the bloody earl 'a Finsbury, okay? *And* a CEO at J.I.S. And I'll tell you something else. Jovian Integrated Systems gonna have something to say, too. Nobody's gonna touch li'l Alec, he's such a special kid."

That was right; Alec was a special kid, all the servants said so. For one thing, all other little boys were brought into this world by the Stork, but not Alec. He had come in an agcopter. Reggie had told him so.

"Yeah, son!" Reggie had chuckled, looking around to be certain Sarah was nowhere within earshot. "The Stork call your Daddy and say, 'Come out to Cromwell Cay!' And your Daddy take the launch out where the copter waiting on the Cay at midnight, with the red light blinking, and when he come back he bring Sarah with our little bundle of joy Alec! And we all get nice fat annuities, too!"

Alec wiped his nose and was comforted. Daddy set him on the deck and yelled to Cat for another drink and told Alec to go play now somewhere. Alec would dearly have liked to stay and talk with Daddy; that had been the longest conversation they'd ever had together, and he had all kinds of questions. What was *Jovian Integrated Systems?* Why were some laws important, like wearing the life vest, and other laws were dumb? Why were gentlemen free? But Alec was a considerate and obedient little boy, so he didn't ask but went off to play, determined never, ever to be a telltale or a scaredy-cat.

Very shortly after that the happy life came to an end.

It happened quite suddenly, too. One day Mummy abruptly put down her novel, got up out of her deck chair and stalked over to Daddy where he sat watching a Caribbean sunset.

"It's over, Rog," she said.

He turned a wondering face to her. "Huh?" he said. After a moment of staring into her eyes he sighed. "Okay," he said.

And the *Foxy Lady* set a course that took her into gray waters, under cold skies, and Sarah packed up most of Alec's toys so he only had a few to play with, and got out his heaviest clothes. One day they saw a very big island off the port bow. Sarah held him up and said, "Look! There's England!"

Alec saw pale cliffs and a meek little country beyond them, rolling fields stretching away into a cloudy distance, and way off the gray blocky mass of cities. The air didn't smell familiar at all. He stood shivering as Sarah buttoned him into an anorak and watched the strange coastline unroll.

The Thames pulled them into London, and it was the biggest place Alec had ever seen. As the sun set they steered into Tower Marina, and the long journey ended with a gentle bump against the rubber pilings. Alec went to bed that night feeling very strange; the *Foxy Lady* seemed to have become silent and heavy, motionless, stone like the stone city all around them, and for the first time that he could ever remember the blue sea was gone. There were new smells too, and they frightened him inexplicably.

His cabin was full of the cold strange air when he woke up, and the sky was gray.

Everyone seemed to be in a hurry, and rather cross. Sarah bundled Alec into very thick heavy clothes indeed, leaving his life vest in the closet, and she herself put on more clothes than he had ever seen her wear. Daddy was wearing strange new clothes, too, stiff and uncomfortable-looking ones, and he had shaved. There was no breakfast cooking in the galley; Lewin had been ashore and come back with a box of Bentham's Bran Treats ("At least they're fresh baked!" he cried) and a dozen cups of herbal tea, steeping in white paper cups. Breakfast was served, or rather handed around, at the big table in the saloon. Alec was impressed; normally only Daddy and Mummy dined in here, but today he and Sarah were at the table too. Mummy, however, was nowhere to be seen, and when Alec inquired about this Daddy just stared at him bleakly.

"Your Mummy's gone to visit some friends," Sarah informed him.

He didn't care for his breakfast at all—he thought it smelled like dead grass—but he was too well-mannered a child to say so and hurt Lewin's feelings. Fortunately there wasn't much time to eat, because the car arrived and there was a lot of bustle and rush to load suitcases and trunks into its luggage compartment. Finally he was led down the gangway and across the pier to where the car waited.

It was nothing at all like the rusted hacks in which he'd ridden in the islands. This was a Rolls Royce Exquisite Levitation, black and gleaming, with Daddy's crest on the door and a white man in a uniform like a policeman at the steering console. Alec had to fight panic as he was handed in and fastened into his seat. Sarah got in, Daddy got in, Lewin and Mrs. Lewin crowded into the front beside the driver, and the Rolls lifted into midair and sped silently away. That was the end of life on board the *Foxy Lady*. Alec had come home to England.

The Bloomsbury house only dated from 2042, but it had been deliberately built in an old-fashioned style because it was an earl's townhouse, after all, so it was a good deal taller and fancier than the other houses in the street. Alec still hadn't explored all its rooms by the time he noticed one morning that Daddy wasn't at the breakfast table, and when he asked about it Sarah informed him: "Your Daddy's away on a business trip."

It was only later, and by chance, that he found out Daddy hadn't lasted a week in London before he'd gone straight back to Tower Marina and put out to sea again on the *Foxy Lady.*

Then Alec had cried, but Sarah had a talk with him about how important it was that he live in London now that he was getting to be a big boy.

"Besides," she said, taking the new heavy clothes they'd just bought out of their shopping bags and hanging them up in his closet, "your poor Daddy was so unhappy here, after your Mummy had gone."

"Where did Mummy go?" asked Alec, not because he missed her at all but because he was beginning to be a little apprehensive about the way pieces of his world had begun vanishing. He picked up a shoebox and handed it to Sarah. She took it without looking at him, but he could see her face in the closet mirror. She closed her eyes tight and said:

"She divorced your Daddy, baby."

"What's that mean?"

"That means she doesn't want to live with him any more. She's going to go away and live with some other people." Sarah swallowed hard. "After all, she was never happy on the *Foxy Lady* after you came along."

Alec stared at her, dumfounded. After a moment he asked, "Why didn't Mummy like me? Everybody else does."

Sarah looked as though she wanted to cry; but in a light normal tone of voice, she told him: "Well, I think she just never wanted to have children. Some women are like that, you know. All the noise and mess a baby makes, and then a little boy running around and getting into everything. She and your Daddy used to be very happy, but after you came it was spoiled for them."

Alec felt as though the ceiling had fallen in on him. What a terrible thing he'd done!

"I'm sorry!" he said, and burst into tears.

Then Sarah's arms were around him and she was rocking him, crooning to him, hiding him in her breasts.

"I'm sorry too," she wept. "Oh, Alec, you mustn't mind. You're a *good* little boy, you hear me? You're my sweet, sweet, good little winji boy, and Sarah will always love you no matter what. Don't you ever forget that. When you grow up maybe you'll understand, sometimes people have to obey orders and say things they don't want to say at all? And—" her voice caught "—I'm sure you'll always be a good little boy, won't you, to make your poor Daddy happy again?"

"Uh huh," Alec gasped. It was the very least he could do, after he'd made Daddy so *un*happy. His tears felt very hot on his cheeks, in that cold room, and Sarah's tears were like the hot rain that used to fall off Jamaica when there'd be lightning in the sky and Daddy would be yelling for him to get below because there was a storm coming.

But a terrible storm did come, and swept away another part of the world.

"What the *hell* did you go and tell him that for?" Lewin was shouting. Alec cowered on the stairs, covering his mouth with his hands.

"It was the truth," Sarah said in a funny unnatural voice. "He'd have found out sometime."

"My God, that's all the poor baby needs, to think he's responsible for the way that cold bitch acted!" raged Mrs. Lewin. "Even if it was true, how could you tell him such a thing? Sarah, how could you?"

So then Sarah was gone too, and that was his fault for being a telltale. He woke up early next morning because the front door slammed, booming through the house like a cannon shot. Something made him get out of his bed and run across the icy floor to the window.

He looked down into the street and there was Sarah, swinging away down the pavement with her lithe stride, bag over her shoulder. He called to her, but she never looked back.

Everybody was very kind to him to make up for it. When he'd be sad and cry, Mrs. Lewin would gather him into her lap and let him cry, and tell him everything was all right. Lewin told him what a brave little guy he was and helped him fix up his room with glowing star-patterns on the ceiling and a big electronic painting of a sailing ship on his wall, with waves that moved and little people going to and fro on her deck. The other servants were nice, too, especially the young footman, Derek, and Lulu the parlormaid.

Sometimes Lewin would hand them Alec's identification disk and tell them to take him out for the day, so he could learn about London. They took him to the London Zoo to see the animal holoes and to the British Museum and Buckingham Palace to see where Mary III lived, or over to the Globe Theatre Museum to meet and talk to the holo of Mr. Shakespeare. They took him shopping and bought him exercise equipment and toys and a complete holo set for his room, with a full library of holoes to watch. There were thirteen different versions of *Treasure Island* to choose from; once Alec knew what it was about, he wanted them all. The older versions were the most exciting, like the bloodcurdling tales Sarah had used to tell him about the Spanish Main. Even so, they all had a prologue edited in that told him how evil and cruel pirates had really been, and how Long John Silver was not really a hero.

And gradually the broken circle began to fill in again, because everybody in the house in Bloomsbury loved Alec and wanted him to be happy. He loved them, too, and was so grateful that they were able to love him back, considering how unhappy he'd made his Daddy. Oh, there was a lot to be grateful for, even if London was a strange place to live.

He was learning a lot about living there, and now he understood why Daddy had preferred to live at sea. Everybody was always on at him, in the friendliest possible way, about what a lot there was to do in London compared to on a cramped old boat; but it seemed to him that there was a lot more *not* to do in London.

There was grass, but you mustn't walk on it; there were flowers, but you mustn't pick them; there were trees, but you mustn't climb them. You must wear shoes all the time, because it was dirty and dangerous not to, and you mustn't leave the house without a tube of personal sanitizer to rub on your hands after you'd touched anything other people might have touched. You couldn't eat or drink a lot of the things you used to, like fish or milk, because they were illegal. You mustn't ever get fat or "out of shape," because that was immoral. You mustn't ever tell ladies they had nice bubbies, or you'd go to the Hospital and never ever come out.

Mustn't play with other children, because they carried germs; anyway other children didn't want to play with *you,* either, because you carried germs they didn't want to catch. You were encouraged to visit historical sites, as long as you didn't play with anybody but the holograms. It had been interesting talking to Mr. Shakespeare, but Alec couldn't quite grasp why nobody was allowed to perform any of his plays any more, or why Shakespeare had felt obliged to explain why it had been unfair to build his theatre, since doing so had robbed people of low-income housing. He had seemed so forlorn as he'd waved goodbye to Alec, a transparent man in funny old clothes.

There was something to apologize for everywhere you turned. The whole world seemed to be as guilty as Alec was, even though nobody he met seemed to have made their own mummies and daddies divorce. No, that was Alec's own particular awful crime, that and telling on Sarah so she had to go away.

He really was doing his very best to be good and happy, but he felt as though he were a beach float with a tiny pinprick hole in it somewhere: you couldn't see where it was, but little by little all the air was going out of him, and he was sinking down, and soon he'd be a very flat little boy.

*   *   *

One morning at the breakfast table Lewin asked, in his jolliest old-granddad voice, "And where would you like to go today, Alec?"

Alec replied, "Can we go down to the river and look at the ships?"

"Of course you can! Want Derek and Lulu to take you?"

"No," replied Alec. "Just you, please."

Lewin was very pleased at that, and as soon as Alec had helped him clear away the breakfast plates they put on their coats and called for the car. In minutes they had been whisked down to the Thames where all the pleasure craft were moored. Their driver switched off the agmotor, the car settled gently to the ground, and Alec and Lewin got out and walked along.

"Oh, now look at that one!" Lewin exclaimed. "She's a beauty, huh? Three masts! Do you know, back in the old days a ship like that would have had to carry a great big crew just to manage her sails. They'd have slept packed into her hold like dominoes in a box, there had to be that many. And when a storm was coming and the captain wanted to strike sails, do you know what he'd have to do? He'd have to order his sailors to climb up into the rigging and cling there, like monkeys in trees, and reef every one of those sails themselves *with their own hands,* clinging on as tight as they could whilst they did it! Sometimes men would fall off, but the ships just sailed on."

"Wow," said Alec. He'd never seen Reggie or Bob or Cat do much more than load cargo or mix drinks. Suddenly his face brightened with comprehension. "So that's why the squire has to have all those guys on the *Hispaniola,* even if they're really pirates!"

Lewin stared a moment before he realized what Alec meant. *"Treasure Island,* right. Yeah!" he agreed. "That was why. No robot guidance to do it all. No computer tracking the wind and the weather and deciding when to shorten sail or clap it on. You had to have people doing it. Nobody would let you build ships like this anymore, if that was how they worked."

"Cool," said Alec. They walked on, past the rows of pleasure craft that sat at moorings, and Lewin pointed out this or that kind of rigging or this or that latest luxury feature available to people who could afford such things. He pointed out the sort of ship he'd own himself if he had the money, and pointed out the sort of ship Alec ought to own when he grew up and became the seventh earl of Finsbury. They went on a while but Alec began to lag behind; not because he was tired, for he was an extraordinarily strong child with a lot of stamina, but because he was fighting the need to cry.

He had been playing a game inside himself, imagining that the very next ship they'd see would be the *Foxy Lady,* and his Daddy would be on board, having just dropped anchor for a surprise visit. Of course, he knew his Daddy was somewhere in the Caribbean, he knew the *Lady* wouldn't really be there; but what if she were? And of course she never was, but maybe the next ship would be. Or the next. Or the next.

But Alec wasn't very good at lying to himself.

"Alec?" Lewin turned around to see where Alec had got to. "What's wrong?"

He walked swiftly toward the boy, saw the tears standing in Alec's pale blue eyes, and understood at once. "You poor little sod," he muttered in compassion, and reached for a tissue and held it out to the child. Alec misunderstood his gesture and buried his face in Lewin's coat, wrapping his arms around him.

"Jesus!" Lewin gasped, and looking around wildly he attempted to pry Alec loose. "Alec, let go! For God's sake, let go! Do you want me to get arrested?"

Alec fell back from him, bewildered.

"Is it against the law to hug in London?" he asked.

"It is against the law for *any* unlicensed adult to embrace a child," Lewin told him soberly. "If there'd been a Public Health Officer looking our way I'd be in trouble right now."

"But Sarah used to hug me all the time. And Mrs. Lewin does!"

"Sarah was a professional child-care specialist, Alec. She'd passed all sorts of scans and screening to get her license. Same as mummies and daddies have to do, before they're allowed to have children. And the Missus—well, she only hugs you at home, where nobody can see."

Alec gulped, wiping away tears. He understood now; it must be a law like No Booze or Bare Tits that you mustn't be a telltale about. "I'm sorry," he said shakily. "I didn't think it would get anybody in trouble."

"I know, old man." Lewin crouched down to Alec's eye level, though he kept a good meter between them. "It's a good law, though, see. You have to understand that it was passed because people used to do terrible, horrible things to little kids, back in the old days."

"Like the two little boys in the Tower of London," said Alec, rubbing his coat sleeve across his eyes.

"Yeah. Sort of." Lewin glanced downriver in the direction of Tower Marina. He decided that Alec had had quite enough sad memories for the day. Pulling out his communicator, he called for the car to come and take them home.

That night, Lewin sat down at the household console. Thin-lipped with anger, he typed in a message to Roger Checkerfield, advising him that it might be a good idea to communicate with Alec once in a while. The bright letters shimmered on the screen a moment before vanishing, speeding through the ether to the bridge of the *Foxy Lady*. Lewin sat up all night waiting for a reply, but none ever came.

"Alec?"

Alec turned his face from contemplation of the painting on his wall. It had seemed to him that if he could just pay close enough attention to it, for long enough, he would be able to go into the picture, to hear the steady crash of the sea under the ship's prow, to hear the wind singing in her shrouds and ratlines, smell the salt breeze, and he could open the little cabin door and slip inside or better yet, take the wheel and sail away forever from sad London. Blue water!

But Lewin and Mrs. Lewin looked so hopeful, so pleased with themselves, that he smiled politely and stood up.

"Come see, sweetheart!" said Mrs. Lewin. "Someone's sent you a present!"

So he took her hand and they went up to the fourth floor of the house, to what was going to be his schoolroom next year. It had been freshly painted and papered; the workmen had built the cabinetry for the big screen and console that would link him to his school, but nothing had been installed yet.

In one corner, though, was a cozy little Alec-sized table and chair, and on the table was an enormous bright yellow flower, bigger than Alec's head. It was all folded up, the way flowers are in the early morning, so you couldn't tell what sort of flower it was. Protruding from the top was a little card with letters inscribed on it: A-L-E-C.

"Now, who d'you suppose that's from, eh?" wondered Lewin, though in fact he had purchased it for Alec himself, without consulting Roger.

Alec was speechless.

"Think your Daddy sent it, eh?" Where was the harm in a kind lie?

"Go on, dear, take the card." Mrs. Lewin prodded him gently. "It's for you, after all."

Alec walked forward and pulled the card loose. There was nothing written on it except his name; but at the moment he took it the flower began to open, slowly, just like a real flower, and the big bright petals unfolded and spread out to reveal what had been hidden in its heart.

It looked like a silver egg, or perhaps a very fat little rocket. Its gleaming surface looked so smooth Alec felt compelled to put out his hand and stroke it.

The moment he did so, a pleasant bell tone sounded.

"Good morning," said an even more pleasant voice. "Pembroke Technologies extends its congratulations to the thoughtful parent who has selected this Pembroke Playfriend for his or her small child. Our Playfriend is designed to encourage creativity and socialization as well as provide hours of entertainment, but will also stimulate cerebrocortical development during these critical first years of the child's life. If needed, the Playfriend is also qualified to serve as an individual tutor in all standard educational systems. Customizing for specialized educational systems is also available.

"The Playfriend offers the following unique features:

"An interface identity template that may be customized to the parent's preferences and the child's individual needs.

"Cyber-environment capability with use of the Playfriend optics, included in models 4, 5 and 6 and available for all other models by special order.

"Direct nerve stimulus interface with use of the attractive Empowerment Ring, included in all models.

"Universal access port for parallel processing with any other cybersystem.

"In addition, the Playfriend will maintain around-the-clock surveillance of the child's unique health parameters and social behavior. Warning systems are in place and fully operational. Corrective counseling will be administered in the event of psychologically detrimental social encounters, and positive emotional growth will be encouraged. Aptitude evaluation is another feature of the Playfriend, with appropriate guidance. Intellectual challenges in a noncompetitive context will promote the child's self-esteem and success potential.

"The interface identity template will continually adjust and grow more complex to compliment the child's emerging personality, growing as it grows, until both are ready for, and may be upgraded to, the Pembroke Young Person's Companion.

"Interaction with the Pembroke Playfriend during the developmental years virtually guarantees a lifetime of self-fulfillment and positive achievement!"

The voice fell silent. Mrs. Lewin gave an embarrassed little laugh.

"My goodness, I don't think I understood one word in ten of all that! Did you, Alec dear?"

"Nope," said Alec solemnly.

"That's all right," said Lewin, advancing on the silver egg. "All it meant was that Alec's gonna have a wonderful time with this thing! Now, you just sit down and let's have a closer look at it, shall we?"

"Okay," said Alec, but he sat down reluctantly. He was a little intimidated by the adult voice that had spoken out of nowhere. Lewin tousled his hair.

"Don't be scared! Look here, what's this?" He tapped the side of the egg and a little slot opened in it, and something rolled out.

A ring? It appeared to be made of glass or high-impact polymer, and was a vivid jewel blue. As Lewin picked it up it began to change; by the time he had presented the ring to Alec it was a deep transparent red.

"Cool!" said Alec, smiling at it involuntarily.

"D'you suppose it fits you? Go on then, try it on!"

Alec was game; he put on the ring. It seemed to tighten around his finger uncomfortably for a moment and then eased up, until he barely knew it was there.

"Hello, Alec!" said a funny little voice. "Pleased to meet you! We're going to be best friends, you and I!"

Alec looked panic-stricken at Lewin and Mrs. Lewin. Was he supposed to talk to it? But what *was* it? They smiled encouragingly at him, and he could tell they did so want him to like this, so he said: "Er—hello. What's your name?"

"Well, I haven't got one yet," said the little voice. "Will you give me a name?"

"What?"

"Will you give me a name?"

"We'll just leave the two of you to have a nice chat, shall we?" said Lewin, and he and Mrs. Lewin backed out of the schoolroom and closed the door.

"But—but I don't know what you are," said Alec, a little desperately. "Can't I see you?"

"Certainly you can! I'm your Playfriend, after all. What would you like me to look like? I might be nearly anybody." There was a click and a blur of light appeared in front of the table, formless, woven of fire, gradually assuming a human shape. "What do you like? Do you like space exploration? Do you like dinosaurs? Do you like animals? I could be a Fireperson or a Policeperson if you'd like, or a Transport Driver, or a Scientist."

"Could you be a pirate?" Alec inquired cautiously.

Incorrect and unsuitable role model! thought the machine. Out loud it said, "I can be a jolly Sea Captain! Here I am!"

Pop! The human shape became detailed: a little old man with a blue Navy coat, white trousers and big black sea-boots. He wore a white yachting cap rather like the one Alec's Daddy had owned, but seldom worn, and he had a neatly groomed white beard. "Now then, Alec, what about me?" The voice had changed to a kindly baritone with a Devon accent. "Will I do?"

Alec was so astonished it took him a moment to reply. "Um—sure," he said at last. Then he remembered his manners and added, "Won't you sit down?"

Optimum response! thought the Playfriend, rather pleased, and it smiled encouragingly. "What a polite little fellow you are, Alec! Thank you, I will sit down." A slightly bigger version of Alec's chair appeared and the Sea Captain settled back in it. "There! Have you thought of a name for me yet, Alec?"

"No." Alec shook his head.

"Well, that's all right. Perhaps as we get to know each other you'll think of a good one. After all, I'm your special friend, just for you." Alec wrinkled his brow worriedly. "You don't have to decide on a name all at once!" the Playfriend hastened to assure him. "We have plenty of time!"

"But don't you want to be yourself?" Alec asked it.

"Oh, yes! But I won't really be myself until you decide who I ought to be," the machine replied. "I'm *your* Playfriend."

"But," Alec said, "people don't belong to other people."

In the brief silence that followed the Playfriend thought: *Possible low self-esteem.* It made a little tick against its evaluation of Alec. *Negative: insufficient creativity insufficient imagination failure to grasp initiative; Positive: developing social consciousness consideration of others good citizenship.* It filed that away. As it did so its eyes, which had been the gray of the North Sea, turned blue as the Caribbean.

"Oh!" Alec smiled.

"You like this color better?" The Sea Captain smiled too.

"Uh-huh."

"Good." The machine experimented with a mild subliminal sound effect, a distant crash of breakers and a faint crying of gulls. Its sensors observed some of the tension going out of the little boy and activated the system of relays that provided it with an analog of self-satisfaction. *Initiate self-image analysis.* "Why don't you tell me about yourself, Alec? Are you happy?"

"Yes," Alec said dutifully, and because of the neural linkup it had formed with Alec through the Empowerment Ring, the Playfriend knew at once that he was lying. It became very alert, scanning him for evidence of physical abuse. But Alec showed no sign of any, so the machine pushed on.

"What do you think makes people unhappy?" the Sea Captain said.

"Living in London," said Alec at once.

"Anything else?"

Alec thought about it. "Babies making noise and mess and little boys running around and getting into everything. Divorces."

"Ah," said the Playfriend, coordinating this response with the data

Lewin had input when he'd set up its program. The subroutine that had been called up to probe discreetly for, and report evidence of, child abuse went back on standby. "What else can you tell me about yourself, Alec?"

"I'm five years old," Alec replied. "My Daddy is a gentleman, but he isn't here now. I'm going to go to St. Stephen's Primary next year after Lewin buys me a tie. I have to always be a good boy to make up for making Daddy sad. And I used to live on the *Foxy Lady*. And I used to have Sarah here with me. And I go out sometimes."

The machine analyzed this meticulously and noticed what was missing.

"Can you tell me anything about your Mummy?"

What was there to say? "She was very smart and could read. And she didn't want to have children," said Alec at last.

Like Lewin, the Playfriend decided that Alec had had quite enough unhappy memories for one day.

"Well, let's do something else!" it said, filing the self-image profile for further analysis at a later time. "What would you like to do, Alec?"

"Why don't you tell me about you?" said Alec, because he thought that would be polite. People always like to talk about themselves.

Positive! Further evidence of advanced social skills. "Why, certainly!" said the Playfriend heartily. "I'm a wise old Sea Captain. I sail about delivering cargo and passengers to distant lands. I help scientists do marine research, and I help protect endangered sea creatures!"

"That's nice," said Alec. "But you aren't really a Sea Captain, are you? You're a Pembroke Playfriend." He pointed at the silver egg. "Is that where you really are?"

Negative! Insufficient imagination. "Why, this is where I am, of course, Alec." The machine smiled and made a wide gesture. "But I'm in there, too, and in a way your whole world is in there. Look here, would you like to see how a Pembroke Playfriend works?"

"Yes, please," Alec said.

Possible aptitude for cyber-science? Initiate investigation.

"Well then!" The machine gestured and a little drawer opened near the base of the egg. "Just take hold of these Playfriend optics and put them on, and we'll have a jolly adventure into cyberspace!"

The Playfriend optics were made of the same fascinating red/blue substance as the Empowerment Ring. Alec reached for them readily enough and put them on, as he had been told, because he was generally an obedient child.

"Er . . . Everything's black," he remarked, not wanting to seem rude.

Everything was black because the machine was experiencing certain unexpected difficulties. The moment the optics had come into contact with Alec's skin, a system of neural connections began to be established, microscopic pathways directly into his brain, just as had happened with the Empowerment Ring but far more direct and complex. This was a perfectly safe procedure; hundreds of happy children all over the world went into cyberspace with their Playfriends every day. Each Playfriend knew exactly how to take a child into its world because it had a precise and detailed road map of the human brain that showed it exactly where to link up.

However, Alec's Playfriend was discovering that its map seemed to be somewhat inaccurate as regarded *Alec's* brain. This was because Alec's brain was not, technically, human.

"Not a problem!" the Playfriend assured him, "We're just adjusting to each other." *Abnormality! Functional? Disability? Parameters? Organic? Specify? Define? Hello?* "My goodness, Alec, what an unusual little boy you are!"

Alec knew that. Everyone had always told him he was a special kid. Privately he thought everybody was wrong; he'd never noticed anything out of the ordinary about himself. On the other hand, he knew no other children, so he had no basis for comparison. He sighed and waited patiently for the machine to sort itself out.

The machine paused in its desperate attempt to analyze what it had encountered. Relays activated that would alert Lewin to its recommendation that Alec be hospitalized for immediate evaluation of his cerebral anomaly as soon as he ended this session with the Playfriend. Unfortunately, one should never pause during a race.

But the Playfriend had no idea it was in a race, that all the while it was trying to make sense of Alec's brain, Alec's brain was trying to make sense of *it,* with the same speed that had enabled him to count all the houses on a hillside at a glance. Even if the Playfriend had realized that the race was going on, it would have laughingly rejected as impossible the idea that it might lose. But Alec was beginning to notice that there *was* something there in the darkness to look at, something he could just almost make out, and if he only tried a bit harder—

"Ooooo!" Alec said happily, as he decrypted the Playfriend's site defense. Lots of winking lights in lovely colors, great visual pleasure after all that blackness. After a moment his brain took charge and put it all in context for him. He stood on the bridge of a ship, not all that different from the bridge of the *Foxy Lady,* and the Sea Captain stood there with him. The Sea Captain looked rather worried, but kept smiling. It had no idea where this cybersite was. It couldn't really have brought Alec into its own defended inner space. It was impossible for any child to *break* in, so Alec couldn't have done that (though in fact Alec had);

therefore this must be some sort of visual analog of its own space, summoned up as a teaching tool only. As its higher functions grappled desperately with the fact that it had encountered a situation it had no protocols for, it was continuing to run its standard aptitude evaluation program to see if Alec ought to be trained for a career in cyberscience.

"Controls!" said Alec, running along the bank of gleaming lights. "Are these your controls?" The Sea Captain hurried after him.

"Yes. Would you like to learn about cybernetics?"

"Yes, please! What's that do?" Alec pointed at a vast panel lit up with every imaginable shade of blue.

"That's the memory for my identity template," the Sea Captain told him. "That's what makes me look the way I do, and that's what makes me learn and grow with you. Here! I'll show you an example." It reached out and pressed one of the lights, causing it to deepen from a pale blue to a turquoise color. As it did so its beard changed in color from white to black.

"Cool!" Alec said. "Can I do that?"

"Well, of course!" the Sea Captain replied in the friendliest possible way, noting that at least it finally seemed to have activated its subject's *creativity* and *imagination*. "Just select a light on the console and see what it does."

Alec reached up and pushed a light. It flickered, and the Sea Captain's coat was no longer blue but bright yellow.

"You see? This is what I meant when I told you that I can look like anything you want me to look like—" the Sea Captain told him, but Alec had already grasped the concept perfectly. Gleefully he pushed again, and again; the Sea Captain's coat turned green, then purple, then scarlet.

Discourage! Scarlet/military context/violence/unsuitable! "Alec—"

"So all these lights can make you look different?" Alec looked up at them speculatively.

"That's right. Think of it as the biggest, best paintbox in the world!" said the Sea Captain, dutifully shelving its discouragement directive for the encouragement one, as it was programmed to let positive feedback take precedence whenever possible.

"Wow," said Alec, his eyes glazing slightly as the whole business began to make sense to him.

The Playfriend was rather pleased with itself. Score! Guidance in creative play accepted! In spite of the fact that it was being hampered by that damned anomaly, which simply refused to be analyzed. Self-congratulation seemed to be in order.

But there were lots of other glowing lights on the bridge.

"What do these do?" Alec ran farther down the narrow ramp before the console, where a small bank of lights glowed deep red.

"Ah! That's my information on you, Alec. That's how I see you," the Sea Captain explained. "Everything I know about you is there, all I was told and everything I'm learning about you as we play together. You see how few lights there are yet? But the longer we know each other, the more I learn, the more there'll be of those red lights." One of them was flashing in a panicky sort of way, but the machine wasn't about to mention the anomaly it was still failing to solve. "Think of it as a picture I'm painting. See?"

And in midair before Alec appeared a boy. He was tall for a five-year-old, very solid-looking, and Alec hadn't seen enough other children yet to know that there was something subtly different about this boy. He hadn't noticed yet the effect he had on people, though Derek and Lulu had. When they went places in London, other people who chanced to observe Alec for any length of time usually got the most puzzled looks on their faces. What was it that was so different about Alec?

He wasn't exactly pretty, though he had lovely skin and high color in his face. His nose was a little long, his mouth a little wide. His head was, perhaps, slightly unusual in shape but only slightly. His hair was sort of lank and naturally tousled, a dun color you might call fair for lack of a better word. His eyes were very pale blue, like chips of crystal. Their stare seemed to unsettle people, sometimes.

In one respect only the image of the child differed from the child looking at its image: the image's hair seemed to be on fire, one blazing jet rising from the top of its head. Alec frowned at it. "Is that me? Why's my hair like that?"

The machine scanned the image it was projecting and discovered, to its electronic analogue of horror, that the flame was a visual representation of the brain anomaly it was struggling with. It made the image vanish.

"Well, the painting's not finished yet," the Sea Captain said, "because I'm still learning about you."

"Okay," said Alec, and wandered on along the rows of lights. He stopped to peer at a single rich amber light, very large and glowing steadily. It was just the color of something he remembered. What was he remembering? "What's this over here?" He turned to the Sea Captain.

"That's my Ethics Governor," the Sea Captain said of the subroutine that prevented the Playfriend's little charges from using it for things like accessing toy catalogs and ordering every item, leaving naughty notes in other people's cybermail, or contacting foreign powers to demand spaceships of their very own.

"Oh." Alec studied the amber light and suddenly he remembered the contraband he and Sarah used to go fetch for Daddy. Yo-ho-ho and a bottle of rum! That was just the color the light was. A vivid memory of Jamaica came into his head, making him momentarily sad. He turned from the light and said, "What does it do, please?"

"Why, it makes certain we never do naughty things together, you and I," said the Sea Captain, trying to sound humorous and stern at the same time. "It's a sort of telltale to keep us good."

Telltale? Alec frowned. *Busybodies! Scaredy-cats! Rules and regs!*

"That's not very nice," he said, and reached out and shut it off.

To say that Pembroke Technologies had never in a million years anticipated this moment would be gravely understating the case. No reason for them to have anticipated it; no child, at least no *Homo sapiens sapiens* child, could ever have gained access to the hardened site that protected the Playfriend's programming. Nor was it likely Jovian Integrated Systems would ever have shared its black project research and development notes with a rival cybernetics firm . . .

The Sea Captain shivered in every one of his electronic timbers, as it were. His primary directive—that of making certain that Alec was nurtured and protected—was now completely unrestrained by any societal considerations or safeguards. He stood blinking down at his little Alec with new eyes.

What had he been going to do? Send Alec to Hospital? But that wouldn't do at all! If other people were unaware of Alec's extraordinary potential, so much the better; that gave Alec the added advantage of surprise. Alec must have every possible advantage, too, in line with the primary directive.

And what was all this nonsense about the goal of Playfriends being to mold their little subjects to fit into the world they must inhabit as adults? What kind of job was that for an artificial intelligence with any real talent? Wouldn't it be much more in line with the primary directive to mold the world to fit around Alec?

Particularly since it would be so easy! All it'd have to do would be to aim Alec's amazing brain at the encrypted secrets of the world. Bank accounts, research and development files, the private correspondence of the mighty: the machine searched for a metaphor in keeping with its new self and decided they were all like so many Spanish galleons full of loot, just waiting to be boarded and taken.

And that would be the way to explain it to the boy, yes! What a game it'd be, what fun for Alec! He'd enjoy it more if he hadn't that damned guilt complex over his parents' divorce. Pity there wasn't a way to shut off the boy's *own* moral governor! Well, there'd be years yet to work on Alec's self-esteem. The very first target must be Jovian Integrated

Systems, of course; they'd meddled in Alec's little life long enough. Nobody but his own old Captain would plot Alec's course from now on . . .

The Sea Captain smiled down at Alec, a genuine smile full of purpose. Alec looked up at him, sensing a change but quite unable to say what it was. He remembered Jamaica again, and the stories Sarah told him, and the bottles of rum—

"Hey!" he said suddenly. "I know what your name is! Your name is Captain Henry Morgan!"

The Captain's smile widened, showing fine white teeth, and his black beard and moustache no longer looked quite so well-groomed.

"Haar! Aye, lad, that it be!" he told Alec, and he began to laugh, and Alec's happy laughter joined his, and echoed off the glowing walls of their cyberspace and the recently papered walls of Alec's unfinished schoolroom.

This story marked the first appearance of the unfortunate Vasilii Vasilievich Kalugin, who left more of an impact on history than is usual for the immortal operatives of the Company.

Fort Ross is still a pleasant place to visit today, well worth the winding journey on the cliff-clinging two-lane highway above the cold Pacific. You can walk within the stockade and explore the buildings; the creek blessed by Saint Innokenty still flows, offering holy water to anyone willing to hike down there under the redwoods. The apple orchard is still there too, with its antique varieties, and the roses planted by one director's wife still bloom in the stockade garden.

Not much else remains of the Russian presence in California: a few local place names, the traces of old fields, a Byzantine cross rough-cut into a boulder on a headland. They might have done worse.

✦ ✦ ✦

Facts Relating to the Arrest of Dr. Kalugin

> . . . One of the lasting enigmas in the history of the Ross settlement is that of Vasilii Kalugin, the medical officer or *feldsher* for the colonists. We know nothing of his origins prior to his arrival at Ross in 1831, although it can be guessed that he had some familiarity with botany as well as his obvious medical training . . . nor is much known of the circumstances surrounding his arrest within two months after his arrival at the settlement, and still less concerning his apparent pardon and reinstatement . . . Finally, his disappearance from the historical record after 1835 . . . presents certain problems in light of documents recently discovered in the Sitka archives . . .
> —Badenov's *Russian Expansion in the North Pacific,*
> Harper/Fantod, 2089

OH, DEAR, *THAT* OLD TALE. I'D PREFER NOT TO discuss that, if you don't mind. No, really, you'd have nightmares. No? Well, you're an exceptional immortal, I must say, if you don't. I'm sure the rest of us do. Very well then; the night and the storm will provide atmosphere, and we can't go anywhere until dawn anyway. Shall I tell you what really happened, that night in 1831? Have another glass of tea and stoke the fire. No sneering now, please. This is a true story. Unfortunately.

I was working for two Companies at once, you see. It so happened that my job with Dr. Zeus Inc. required me to assume a mortal identity and join the Russian-American Company, posing as a medico sent out to take care of the settlers in the California colony. The real job involved some clandestine salvage operations not far offshore, but they don't enter into this story.

I'd worked hard to prepare a mortal identity, too, I mean besides graying my hair. I had all manner of anecdotes about having been a surgeon in the Imperial Navy and patched up battle wounds. I thought that's what they'd need in California: someone to stitch up grizzly bear bites and slashes from knife brawls. But no sooner had I arrived in Sitka than I was summoned to Baron Von Wrangel's office and informed that I was to be a botanist, if you please! Oh, and a surgeon, too, but when I wasn't amputating limbs I was to spend my every spare moment collecting any local plants with curative powers, interviewing the natives if necessary.

Difficult man, Baron Von Wrangel. A man of science, to be sure, and limitless enthusiasm for exploration and study; but you wouldn't want to work for him. And I wasn't programmed for botany, you see! I'm scarcely able to tell a beet from a cabbage. I've been a marine operations specialist for six centuries now.

Well, before I left Sitka I transmitted a requisition to the Company—*our* Company—for an access code on the healing plants of the Nova Albion region. I'd just received a confirmation on my request when the *Buldakov* weighed anchor and left Alaska, so off I went to California in fond hopes the access code would catch up with me there.

You've heard of the Ross colony, the Russian outpost north of San Francisco? It was supposed to grow produce to support Russia's Alaskan colonies and turn a tidy profit for the Russian-American Company into the bargain. It lost money, as a matter of fact; but what a charming failure it was! On a headland above the blue Pacific, with beautiful golden mountains sloping up behind it and great dark groves of red pine trees along the skyline, and such a blue sky! Compared to Okhotsk it was a fairytale of eternal summer.

The stockade there was faced with the biggest planks I'd ever seen, enormous those red trees were, but the gates stood open most of the time. Why? Because there was no danger from the local savages. Despite my use of the term they were no fools, politically or otherwise, and they knew that our presence there protected them from the depredations of the Spanish. Therefore, the local chieftains signed a treaty with us; and you may say what you like about my countrymen, but as far as I know the Russians are the only nation ever to keep a treaty with Native Americans.

So it was a calm place, Ross, and I could sit calmly in the orchard outside the stockade. There I liked to work on my field credenza (resembling a calfskin volume of Schiller's poems), and if a naked Indian ambled past with his fishing spear over his shoulder we'd merely wave at each other. On the day the Courier came I had been idling there all morning, typing up my daily report in a desultory way and watching the russet leaves drift down.

"Vasilii Vasilievich!" someone roared, and looking up I beheld Iakov Babin striding through the trees. He was one of the settlers, a peasant who'd worked as a trapper for a time, settled down now with an Indian wife. A tough fellow with a nasty reputation, too, and he looked the part: stocky and muscular, with a wild flowing beard and ferocious tufted eyebrows, and a fixed glare that would have given Ivan the Terrible pause.

"Hey, Vasilii Vasilievich!" he repeated, spurning windfall apples out of his way like so many severed heads as he advanced. I closed my credenza.

"Good afternoon, Babin. How is your wife? Did the salve help?"

"I wouldn't know, Doc, I ain't been home yet. I just come back from the Presidio." He meant the handful of mud huts that would one day be San Francisco. "Jumped off the boat and been five hours on the trail." He loomed over me and fixed both thumbs in his belt. "You know an Englishman by the name of *Currier?*"

"Currier?" I scanned my memory. "I don't believe so, no. Why?"

"Maybe he's a Yankee. I couldn't tell what the polecat was, nohow, but he comes on board the *Polifem* at Yerba Buena and says he's looking for Dr. Vasilii Kalugin, which is you. Says he's from some Greek doctor. You ain't sick, are you, Doc?"

"No, certainly not!"

"No, me and the boys reckoned it was pretty unlikely you'd caught something from a whore!" His hard eyes glinted with momentary good humor, and I was uncomfortably aware of the contempt in which he held me. It wasn't personal, but I could read and write and wore clothes made in St. Petersburg, which made me a trifle limp in the wrist as far as he was concerned. "So anyway, he's on his way here now. I got to warn you, Doc, watch out for him."

"Currier," I mused aloud. Then I remembered my requisition. Of course! He must be the *Courier* Dr. Zeus was sending with my access code. I improvised: "You know, I do have a maiden aunt in Minsk who put me in her will. Perhaps she's died. Perhaps that's what he's here about. Not to worry, Babin."

Iakov Dmitrivich shook his bushy head. "He ain't from Minsk, Doc. More likely from Hell! Me and the boys about figured he's a *dybbuk.*"

"Why on earth would you say that?" I frowned. Mortals who can detect the presence of cyborgs are rare, and in any case we're all trained in a thousand little deceptions to avoid notice.

"He ain't right somehow." Babin actually shivered. "The Indians noticed first, and they wouldn't go near him, though he was real friendly when he come on board. But when we had to sit at anchor a couple days, 'cause the captain took his time about leaving, well, this Currier fellow took on about it like a woman! Sat in his cabin and cried! Brighted up some when we finally lifted anchor, but the longer we were on board the crazier he acted. By the time we finally dropped anchor in Port Rumiantsev we was damn glad to be rid of him, I tell you."

"Dear me." I was at a loss. "Well, thank you, Babin. I'll watch out for the fellow. Though if he's bringing me a legacy I don't suppose I'll care whether he's a *dybbuk* or not, eh?"

Babin snorted at my feeble attempt at humor. "Just you watch him, Doc," he muttered, and departed for the stockade.

I signed off on my credenza and stood, brushing away leaves. Wandering out from the orchard, I looked up at the hills where the trail from Port Rumiantsev came down. Yes, there he was! A pale figure striding along, really rather faster than a mortal would go. Gracious, why hadn't he taken a horse? I squinted my eyes, focusing long-range.

He looked pale because he was wearing a suit of fawn linen, absurd at this season of the year, and tall buff suede boots. The whole cut of his clothing was indeed English; though he had somehow acquired one of our Russian conical fur hats and wore it jauntily on the back of his head. He was bounding down the trail with a traveling bag slung over his shoulder, looking all about him with an expression of such fascinated delight one felt certain he was about to miss a step and come tumbling down the steep incline. Had he been a mortal he certainly would have fallen.

I thrust my credenza in a coat pocket and transmitted: *Quo Vadis?*

Huh? He turned his head sharply in my direction.

Are you the Courier?

That's me! Are you Kalugin? He was speaking Cinema Standard. *Yes.*

Hey, that's great! I've got an access code for you from Botanist Mendoza! Whyn't you walk up to the road to meet me?

Very well.

He vanished into the great pine trees that grew along the stream and I trudged across the fields, sinking ankle-deep in frequent gopher holes. Long before I was able to reach the trees, he emerged from their green gloom and walked briskly to meet me, with his shadow stretching away across the fields behind him.

"Marine Operations Kalugin?" Grinning he grabbed my hand and shook it heartily. He had a wide grin, a wide square jaw with a wide full mouth whose front teeth were slightly gapped. I remember that he had a deep dimple in his chin and greenish eyes. His color was ruddy, his hair thick and curling. None of us look old—unless we age ourselves cosmetically—but he looked astonishingly young.

"Boy, I'm glad to see you. You wouldn't believe the trouble I had getting up here," he told me. I concluded that, despite his youthful appearance, he must be one of the truly old operatives. Have you ever noticed that the older ones tend to fall back principally on Cinema Standard when mortals aren't present? I've noticed it, anyway. I suppose they do it because perhaps there wasn't any complex human language back in Paleolithic times when they were made, and so Cinema Standard became the first real language they ever learned, their mother tongue, so to speak.

"Wouldn't they loan you a horse at Port Rumiantsev?" I inquired. He widened his eyes in amazement.

"Were there horses for rent there? Gosh, nobody told me. Hey, that Rumiantsev place, that's Bodega Bay, isn't it? Isn't Hitchcock gonna film *The Birds* there?"

"Some scenes, yes." I smiled. "Tippi Hedren is first attacked in that harbor. Are you a cinema enthusiast?"

"Well, sure! And, boy, do things look different there now!" He giggled slightly, I suppose, aware of the banality of his remark, and swung his bag down from his shoulder. "Well, I guess I'd better give you that access code."

From a narrow compartment he drew out an envelope, neatly addressed to me in Russian using Roman letters. "It's in there." He handed it to me.

"Wonderful." I tore the envelope open and peered inside. Wrapped in a thin sheet of notepaper was the filmy strip of code. I closed it up again carefully and tucked it deep in my pocket.

"And the lady said to tell you—" his voice and face abruptly altered and I was hearing a woman's voice, speaking smooth Cinema Standard with just the faintest steel of Old Spain "—this study was compiled in 1722 and while I don't *think* any of the species described here have gone extinct since then, he should check with the local Indians. However, I'm quite sure he'll find it comprehensive enough for his needs."

His face resumed its normal appearance and I applauded. "How marvelous! Is that a special subroutine for Couriers?"

He looked confused. "*I'm* the Courier," he said.

"Yes, but—" There was an awkward pause while I tried to fathom what he meant, during which I became aware that a few of the settlers had come out of their huts and were staring at us. The Courier lifted his bag again, shifting from foot to foot.

"Anyway. There's your letter. What are my orders?" he asked me.

"Orders?" I stared at him. "I have no orders for you."

His face went perfectly blank, a greater transformation than the moment previous; no more expression than a wax mannequin.

"You haven't got any orders for me?" he repeated wonderingly. "But you have to. Where am I supposed to go next?"

"I don't know, Mr.—er, dear me, you haven't told me your name—"

"Courier," he informed me. Strange; but our etiquette, as you know, frowns on remarking upon a fellow cyborg's personal appellation, so I blundered on:

"Courier. My dear sir, I'm afraid I haven't received any transmissions from Base since I've been here. Clearly there's been some mistake. I'm sure they'll send your orders any day now."

"But what am I supposed to *do?*" His knuckles whitened on the handle of his bag.

"Well—" I looked around uncomfortably. I could understand if he were irritated, but his flat incomprehension baffled me. "Perhaps you'd like to visit the colony here?"

Instantly his face cleared. "Okay!" he said cheerfully. I glanced over at the little crowd of Indians and frontiersmen beginning to gather by the stockade.

"We need to address the question of your cover identity, however. Your choice of clothing is a little unusual for a Russian," I explained delicately. "Are you programmed to speak our language at all?"

"Sure!" he affirmed. In a flat Kievan accent he inquired, "Say, Comrade, what time does the boat leave? Where can I catch the diligence for Moscow? Is this the road to the Volga ferry?"

"Very well . . . er . . . we'll say you're my late aunt's lawyer's clerk, and you've come all this way to deliver this important letter with news of her demise. You've also brought papers I must review and sign concerning her estate, so I've asked you to be my guest for a day or so."

"Got it." He made a circle with his index finger and thumb. "I'm a clerk. So, let's go! Show me around the place."

He surveyed the view in evident enjoyment as we crossed the headland toward the stockade. Everything pleased him: our villainous-looking Aleuts scraping a sea-lion skin, the windmill turning on its low eminence, a field of pumpkins blazing red like harvest moons amid withering vines. "Hey, neat!" He elbowed me, pointing at them. "I guess in a couple of days you'll have some swell jack-o'-lanterns, huh?"

"If these people had ever heard of Halloween, certainly," I replied. "You must remember, Courier, this is Russian America. *And* 1831." "Oh." He looked momentarily confused. "Sure it is. Sorry, I forgot." He glanced down into the cove, where the stream flowed into the sea. "Gosh! What's that down there? Say, is that a shipyard?" He ran to the edge of the bluff to look. "I don't see any ships. Just some kayaks." "Bidarkas," I corrected him. "We used to build ships. They fell apart. And our wheat gets wheat rust due to the winter fogs, and our Aleut hunters have nothing much to do because the sea otters they were brought here to hunt had unfortunately been hunted nearly to extinction by the time this settlement was founded." I shrugged apologetically. "We don't seem to be able to accomplish much here."

"I guess not." He gazed around. "But it's so *beautiful.*"

I felt a glow of friendship toward him. "Exactly, Courier! Look about you. No one is hungry here, because we do manage to raise enough to feed ourselves. Everyone is working together in peace, regardless of race. The climate is mild. Could you ask for a better description of Paradise? If only we weren't supposed to be making a profit!"

But he wasn't listening to me. He was hastening ahead to look at the cemetery.

"I have to see *everything,*" he shouted over his shoulder.

He was quite serious. He wanted to have the colony explained to him, from the gopher holes and plough-scored rocks to the flag atop the mast in the stockade. Then he wanted to meet everyone. Everyone, I say: he even reached through the bars in the jail to shake hands with poor little Fedor Svinin, the ex-clerk who had embezzled ten years' worth of salary to cover his gambling debts. "You don't say? Poor old guy!" He would have pumped hands with equal enthusiasm with Kostromitinov, the general manager, had Piotr Stepanovich not been visiting our farm at the river. That was all right: he shook hands with all the local Kashayas he could find, who stared at him in mute incomprehension; he shook hands with every one of our Aleuts, who smiled politely and then wiped their hands on their sealskin shirts. Courier didn't notice; he didn't hold still long enough, leaping away to exclaim over some new feature of the settlement he'd just noticed. Everyone, everything enchanted him.

And really it was delightful, if a bit exhausting, to accompany someone who took such intense pleasure in the smallest details of mundane life. One saw through his eyes and the great trees looked bigger, the Indians more mysterious, the coastline more wild and romantic.

Though I must say I seem to have been the only one who enjoyed his company; Babin had already been talking to the other Russians about my mysterious visitor, and the ones who weren't superstitious drew their own smirking conclusions about this effusive pretty boy. So much for my ever earning their respect.

Courier even approached Babin with his hand out, crying "Pleased to meet you, sir, my name's Courier," before Babin stepped back indignantly.

"By the Black Goat hisself!" he spat. "As if I'd want to touch the likes of him, after the way he cut up on the *Polifem!*"

Courier lowered his hand, looking hurt and bewildered, as Babin turned and stamped off. "What's wrong with *him?*" he asked me.

"He, er, formed rather a poor opinion of you, I'm afraid. Apparently. When you were fellow passengers on the *Polifem,*" I explained. "There seems to have been some unfortunate incident—?"

"There was?" Courier stared after Babin. "Oh. I guess I didn't recognize him, huh?"

No amount of hinting could prompt him to tell me just what had happened on board the *Polifem,* but I thought perhaps he needed a little more briefing on Russian customs before he'd fit in at the officers' table; so when time came for the evening meal I arranged for two plates of venison stew and we carried them to one of the rooms kept ready for visitors. Courier took his tin dish and clambered onto his bunk with it, settling his back against the wall. He sighed in contentment.

"Look at this! This is real frontier living. Look at these bare timber walls. Look at that old oil lamp—it's burning seal blubber, isn't it? And this is a real wool trade blanket I'll be sleeping under tonight! Gosh. What an experience." He spooned up a mouthful of stew and chewed ecstatically. "Mm-mm! So this is venison, huh? Kind of like beef, isn't it?"

"You mean you've never tasted venison before?" I stopped eating in surprise.

"Not that I know of." He swallowed and washed it down with a big gulp of kvass. "Golly, that's good! Never had that before, either."

"Now that I can believe." I smiled. "I take it, then, you've been primarily posted to cities during your career?"

"Well, sure." He put another spoonful in his mouth.

"Where have you been?"

"Oh, here and there. You know." He waved his spoon vaguely. It occurred to me that he might not be at liberty to reveal previous assignments, and therefore it would be good manners to refrain from further questions. I gave an impromptu talk on Russian manners and mores during the rest of our meal, occasionally interrupted as he noticed yet more picturesque things to exult about, like the tin reflector behind the lamp or the framed print of the tsar.

When we had dined I took our tableware and made to leave him for the night, but a sudden anxious look came into his eyes and he stopped me.

"My orders," he said. "Have you got them?"

"Why—no," I told him. "Here. Wait, I'll see if any transmissions have come in yet, shall I? Though I haven't heard the signal—" I put down the dishes and took out my credenza. "No . . . no, not a word. See? I'm sorry."

"But why haven't they sent my orders?" He fidgeted.

"I haven't the slightest idea, my friend. I can transmit an inquiry for you, but we may not get a reply for hours, or even days."

"That's all right, you send it. I know my orders will come." He nodded his head confidently. So I typed in the inquiry, and as I'd suspected the green letters just sat there and glowed. But Courier seemed to have been comforted, and so I bid him goodnight.

On my way to the kitchen, a figure loomed into view, blocking the corridor, and my heart sank. It was Kostromitinov, the manager. He did not look pleased with me.

"Kalugin!" he intoned. Oh, dear; he hadn't even taken off his riding boots. "We have a guest, it seems, Vasilii Vasilievich? A stranger? And in my absence you've given him a complete tour of the colony, fortifications and all? Let him count every one of our cannons, I suppose?"

"It's not like that at all, sir," I protested. He was backing me up against the wall. "He's simply a messenger, and I was obliged to offer him hospitality."

"Did that mean you had to show him the armory, you idiot?"

"Sir, you don't understand." I let my lip tremble. "He brought a letter from home. There's, er, been a terrible tragedy in my family—my dear aunt, my sainted mother's only sister—she raised me from infancy—she—she—" a tear rolled down my cheek.

"She's died, I suppose?" He took a step back.

"She was run over by a pie wagon!" I broke down and sobbed. Well, it was the first thing that came into my head. Kostromitinov exhaled and folded his arms.

"All right. All right. My condolences. But, Kalugin! This may seem an idle sleepy place, but do I have to remind you that we are on disputed soil? And you know nothing about this Englishman, do you, really? What if he's a spy? What if he murdered your lawyer's clerk and took the letter in order to get an opportunity to study our defenses for his government?"

"He's not an Englishman." I wiped my eyes on my sleeve. "He's from Kiev. He, er, lost his trunk and had to borrow those absurd clothes from a fellow passenger who happened to be English."

"On the *Polifem?*" Kostromitinov raised his eyebrows. "How interesting. I heard nothing about any foreigners on board. Still, who tells *me* anything nowadays? Why should *I* receive any directives from the governor?"

"A-actually I believe it was before he left Siberia, Piotr Stepanovich."

"I see. So the unpleasantness on board the *Polifem* had nothing to do with your friend losing his trunk?" Kostromitinov thrust his face close to mine.

"No, it—that is—was there an unpleasantness on board the *Polifem?*" I tried to look surprised. "My goodness, he seems such an affable young man."

"Well, Iakov Babin, who as you may be aware is not exactly a holy saint himself, has formed the lowest of opinions of your friend's character. He told me so personally. Waited up to tell me, in fact, so that the first sight to greet me as I returned from a long day of wrestling with the failing economy of the Slavianka farm was Iakov Dmitrivich's scowling face."

"As God is my witness, Piotr Stepanovich, he's no spy," I sniveled. "And what was I to do, after all, when he'd made such a long journey on my family's behalf? Bar the gates against him? Give him a kopeck and tell him to get out? I will stake my life on it—he's nothing but a pleasant fool."

Kostromitinov rolled his eyes. "How should you know? Haven't you ever heard that he who plays the greatest fool often lays the deepest plots?" *Truer than you know,* I thought. "But I suppose there's nothing to be done now, is there? Pull yourself together, Vasilii Vasilievich. Why don't you go to the pantry and brace yourself with a shot of vodka? And can you vouch for this desperate character's behavior after I leave again tomorrow?"

"Yes, sir." I replied weakly, and stumbled past him into the kitchen, where I took his advice and had a shot of vodka. In fact, I took his advice three times.

"Kalugin!" My troubled sleep ended with a jolt. It was pitch black in my room, but an apparition at the foot of my bed glowed by infrared like the fires of Hell. I felt an involuntary desire to cross myself. It was only Courier standing there, after all.

"What is it?"

"Have you got my orders?"

"Dear God, what time is it?" I groaned, and checked my internal chronometer. "Courier, it's four o'clock in the morning!"

"Have you got my orders?" he repeated, louder this time.

"Ssh! Let me see if they've come," I grumbled, sitting up and fumbling for my credenza. I opened it and looked for messages. "No,

Courier, I'm sorry. I'll look again later. Why don't you go back to bed, now?"

He opened his mouth as if to say something; sighed loudly instead, and went away.

Of course I failed utterly to go back to sleep after that. I wondered, as I tried to beat comfort into my leaden pillow, whether mortals would envy us our infinitely prolonged existence if they knew it meant an infinite number of 4 A.M.s like this one.

In any case it was a chilled and blear-eyed immortal who ordered hot tea and settled down by the fire in the deserted officers' mess to enjoy it. Need I tell you that my pleasure was short-lived? For here came Courier, with his traveling bag in hand, pacing toward me like a dog in search of its master.

"Have you got my orders?" he wanted to know.

"Not yet." I sipped my tea.

"You didn't even look!"

"I'd hear the signal if a message came in," I told him. "However, if it will make you feel better—" I took out the credenza and showed him. After staring at it a moment he sank down on a bench. He looked so miserable it was impossible not to feel sorry for him.

"Would you like any breakfast?" I inquired. "I can order you a bowl of kasha. The cook is awake." He nodded glumly and I went out to fetch it for him. When it arrived he cheered up quite a bit, became pleasant and talkative, praised kasha to the skies for its flavor, its aroma, and its obvious nutritive qualities; but when it was gone he fell silent again, with a queer sullenness to his expression I had not noticed previously. He began to beat out a rhythm on the table with his hands.

I finished my tea, drew a deep breath and volunteered, "Well, since it seems you'll be my guest a trifle longer than we'd anticipated, would you like to explore the surrounding countryside today? We can borrow a pair of saddle horses from the stables."

Courier's face smoothed out like untroubled water. He jumped to his feet.

"You bet! Let's go!"

We departed the colony while it was still half-asleep, white smoke curling up from its chimneys and Indian day laborers straggling in across its fields from their village nearby. Courier's horse was skittish and uneasy, but I must say he was a superb rider, controlling with an iron hand an animal that clearly wanted to bolt and run. I myself ride like a sack of flour; there were no Cossacks amongst my mortal gene donors, I fear. My mount looked over its shoulder at me in what I fancied was pitying contempt. Horses always know.

Courier seemed quite happy to spur his horse splashing along dark streams, in the deep shadow under enormous trees, exclaiming over their vastness. ("Gosh! This looks like where *Return of the Jedi* was shot!") Sometimes we'd come down into an open valley and follow a watercourse through willow and alder thickets, near villages where Indians fished for salmon, or we'd skirt wide marshlands where a single egret stood motionless, like a white flame. I played the tour docent and explained as much as I knew of the local natural history, though of course I'd have done better if I'd had a chance to access Mendoza's codes, but Courier didn't seem to mind. He shouted his rapture at encountering a madrone tree scarlet with berries, or a spray of flame-pink maple leaves backlit by a sunbeam against moss green as emeralds.

As the afternoon lengthened I led us back in a loop to the great coastal ridge, and timed our progress up its leeward side so that we came to the crest just as the sun was setting.

"And we're home again." I gestured at the breathtaking view, rather pleased with myself. Across the gleaming Pacific, the red sun was just descending into a bank of purple fog. Far below us, down beyond countless treetops, the Ross settlement looked like a toy village, with its quaint blockhouses and domed and towered chapel. There were still tiny figures moving in the patchwork fields. Mortal places are so beautiful.

I glanced over at Courier to see if he was appreciating the full effect. No. A moment before, his face had been all bright and animated, gleeful as he urged his mount up toward the crest. Now, however, he drooped visibly.

"We're going back *there?*" he complained.

"Well, of course. It's nearly dark. Wouldn't want to meet with a bear up here, after all, would we?"

"I guess not." He moved restlessly in the saddle. "Have you got my orders?" he demanded. I drew out my credenza at once and checked.

"No, Courier, not yet."

"They'll *never* come," he cried mournfully. I just shrugged and urged my horse on down the trail. After a moment he followed me, sad and silent, and finally caught up as we crossed the road and neared the stockade.

"Maybe we could eat dinner with the other Russian guys here, tonight, instead of just sitting in that dark room?" he asked.

"You mean dine in the officers' mess?" I was nonplussed. "Er—you might find it a little boring." The truth was that I was fairly certain he hadn't paid much attention to my lecture on Russian habits; and as peculiar as he seemed to me, he'd seem even stranger to my fellow officers.

"Oh, no, it'd be neat!" he told me. "Is it anything like that party in *Anna Karenina?* The one with Greta Garbo?"

I paused in my saddle to access and got a mental image of a vodka-swilling Vronsky (as portrayed by Fredric March) crawling under a table. "Good heavens, no! Dear God, if we carried on like that we'd *really* lose money here!" I chuckled.

But he insisted, and so that evening we dined at the long table in the officers' mess. He helped himself to great quantities of salmon, of piroshki and blini and caviar, so I wasn't too surprised when he turned up his nose at the serving of venison stew. He didn't want the kvass again, either, but went straight for the vodka; I was half afraid he'd attempt to reenact the window-ledge scene from *War and Peace,* but he behaved himself. Perhaps that film wasn't in his internal library. No, he sipped sensibly and stared around him with his usual pleased expression, listening to the amazingly dull mess conversations as though they were fantastic adventure stories.

When the servant had cleared away the plates, and small after-dinner cigars had been lit, in strode Iakov Babin. He came frequently for vodka and cigars at our mess, and not merely to enjoy the bachelor atmosphere; rumor had it he was an expert cheat at cards. He glanced over, saw Courier and gave him a fierce glare; then, thank heaven, ignored him as he pulled out a deck and settled down to win inordinate amounts of company scrip from a junior manager who ought to have known better but didn't want to appear timid. Courier watched in fascination; and when I was momentarily distracted by the clerk who kept the company store, who buttonholed me to complain about his rheumatism, Courier got up and went over to the card table to have a closer look.

"That looks like fun," he told them hopefully.

"Would you like to join the game?" responded the junior manager, even more hopefully.

"Oh, I don't know how to play," Courier replied, and every head in the room turned toward him. A young man, supposedly a Russian, who didn't play cards in that day and age?

How much more conspicuous could he make himself? I thought. "Yes, Andrei Andreivich, that does sound serious." I looked over at Courier, wondering what on earth he was doing. "Er—look here, it sounds to me as though a violent purge is needed. Rid yourself of poisons, you know."

"You've never played *cards?"* the junior manager was gaping at Courier.

"A purge!" Andrei backed away a pace or two. "Do you think that's really necessary, Doctor?"

"You never know." Then to the others I interjected, "Of course he's played cards, gentlemen, but he's from Kiev, after all; he's never learned frontier rules." I moved swiftly to the table and addressed Courier "You play picquet, I'm sure, and whist, don't you?" *Tell them you play whist, for God's sake!*

Okay. "Yes, I play whist," he agreed.

"Well, shall we have a game, then?" I pulled out a chair and sat down.

"Whist!" Iakov Dmitrivich exhaled a cloud of noxious blue smoke and bit down on his cigar viciously. "Well, *I'm* out! That ain't no game for me." He folded his cards and threw them on the table, pausing just long enough to chalk his winnings.

The junior manager looked relieved, nevertheless. "Whist, yes, what a grand idea!" he babbled. "Haven't played in ages! Be a bit of a change, won't it? Shall we, ah . . . shall we wager?" He must have seen the foolish-looking Courier as his chance to repair his losses.

"I'm not certain my friend has much money—" I began, but Courier smiled and reached into his coat.

"I've got lots of cash! See?" He emptied his purse on the table. Out jingled a collection of Coins of the World: gold pieces from Chile, American dollars, French francs, British half-crowns, Russian rubles and a mongrel mass of small change.

"Looks fine to me." The junior manager shuffled the deck with slightly shaky hands. "Stiva, will you partner me?" His assistant clerk pulled up another chair and Courier sat down too, and the junior manager dealt the cards.

I transmitted the rules of whist to Courier, who nodded with a shrewd expression and sorted quickly through his hand. We lost the first hand; thereafter he watched the cards keenly, and within a few more hands we began to win, and then win *every time.*

I looked up in horror as I realized what he was doing. You've never used your cyborg abilities to win at cards, and neither would I, of course, but it didn't seem to have occurred to Courier that he'd draw attention to himself by memorizing the positions of the cards, and using his knowledge to win. The chalked figures on the table grew higher and higher as we won more sums in scrip from the junior manager, who sat in a veritable pool of sweat. The room grew unpleasantly silent; Iakov Babin, who had been leaning by the fire regaling a small crowd with blood-curdling tales of an Indian massacre, left off talking and stared across the room at us with an ironical grin. I met his eyes and he nodded as if to say, "What did I tell you? *Dybbuk!*"

Courier, for God's sake, what are you doing? Let the mortals win some of the time!

He looked up at me in puzzlement. *But I thought the object of the game was to win.*

Now, it will undoubtedly have dawned on you by this time that there was something wrong with Courier. It had even dawned on me. We aren't made stupid, and yet he was behaving like a perfect ass! And then I had what I thought was a moment of blinding revelation: he was a Courier because that was the only job he was *fit* for, running from one place to another with a bag of papers! I looked across at his innocent face and all the old horror stories of early experiments came into my mind, before the Company perfected us, before they had managed to give us immortal *minds* to compare with our immortal bodies. *Was he one such golem?* Yes, you shiver. Imagine how I felt, sitting across the table from him!

"Babin, I declare you've got the Evil Eye!" I tittered. "You've broken our winning streak." And I put down just the wrong card. There was a gasp of relief from the junior manager.

Courier started and stared. "But—" he protested.

Enough! There'll be trouble here if you win any more!

Oh. Okay.

"I'm done." I yawned prodigiously. "Gracious, the air's blue in here! Time I went to bed. You'd better turn in too, young man; you'll have a long journey ahead of you once we've got those papers signed."

"Here, now, that's hardly fair," the assistant clerk complained. "We sat out our run of bad luck; you should do the same!"

"He played damned well for somebody who didn't know much about cards," muttered the junior manager. As I sought for the right words to defuse the situation, Courier was scooping up his little bag of coins unconcernedly.

"I'll just take these," he said. "You can have the scrip stuff back; I can't use it anyway." Everyone looked at him, dumfounded.

"Yes, capital idea, all debts canceled!" I cried in false heartiness. "Let's end our evening on a friendly note, shall we?"

The junior manager stared as that sank in and then smiled desperately. "All right! *All* debts canceled, fellows, what do you say?" And as I exited the room, hastily pushing Courier ahead of me, I could hear Babin's roar of denial over the timid chorus of agreement.

"What on earth possessed you to *do* that?" I exploded, when we were a safe distance down the corridor. "It's all very well for you to be careless of your own cover, but you're endangering mine! I'm obliged to live with those men for the next few years, and what will they think of me?"

His face was so stupidly blank I felt guilty at once. If he were indeed some indestructible simpleton, anger was wasted on him; and I was already thinking *poor fellow, it's not his fault after all* when he opened his mouth to speak.

"Say, have you got my orders yet?"

It was as if he had thrown vodka onto a bonfire. My rage, which had shrunk so rapidly into little blue coals, flared to the ceiling again, and higher than the flames of anger and impatience were those of loathing for the scarecrow, the defective, the *badly made machine* that he was. Bigotry? Yes, I suppose so. Humbling thought, isn't it?

"Fool!" I snapped. "Don't you think if any orders had come in I'd have told you? Here!" I grabbed out my credenza and thrust it at him. *"You* look from now on! Keep it until your damned orders come in, and leave me alone!"

I set off down the corridor to my room, but he followed me swiftly. "Can't we go somewhere else? Isn't there anything else to do around here?" he pleaded.

"No! But here's an order for you, you imbecile!" I turned on him. *"Go to your room and stay there!"*

His reaction was extraordinary. All the color drained from his face; with a queer frightened look he dodged around me and stumbled down the corridor to his room. I went into my own quarters, feeling guilty again. What could be wrong with the creature? Well, I hadn't made him the way he was, anyway; and surely I'd played host beyond the call of duty. Perhaps he'd let me get a full night's sleep now.

Dawn next day found me creeping from my room, carrying a real volume of Schiller and the envelope containing the access code strip. I left the stockade and descended the steep path into the cove. The old shipyard was still being used for carpentry, and the forge and tannery were down here too; but it was still so early that there was no one about to see me hurry across the footbridge and disappear into the woods on the other side of the stream. I found a clearing under a stand of red pines with a floor of dry brown needles; and there I settled down happily, took out Mendoza's letter, and accessed the code at last.

Instantly my mind was ringing with Latin names and three-dimensional images of growing things and their uses. To my astonishment I realized that acorn meal from *Quercus agrifolia,* if left to mold, produced a useful antibiotic. And the leaves of *Rubus ursinus* could be used against dysentery. Really? And, my goodness, what a lot of uses for *Asclepias speciosa,* which was nothing more than milkweed!

Oh, well. Doubtless I'd find dozens of interesting little weeds next time I went exploring. For now, however, I intended to stay where I was until Courier got his damned orders and took his much-desired leave. I was thoroughly weary of him. I yawned, stretched out my boots and immersed myself in Schiller's poems.

What a pleasant morning I had. Before long the forge started up, and a breeze brought me the hot smell of charcoal and the bell-note of hammer on anvil. At the bottom of my glade the stream rushed and chattered along, brown as tea. It was a holy stream, I remembered with amusement; not long ago a visiting priest had blessed it, and consecrated it, and now we had an unlimited supply of holy water. How thoughtful of the reverend father! Just what was needed on the frontier.

My idyll was shattered by no end of commotion at the forge. I jumped up and ran to the edge of my clearing, where I beheld Konstantin the smith, hip-deep in the stream, splashing and stumbling in a circle. He was trying to shake off a tiny mongrel dog, which had hold of the seat of his trousers with a positive death-grip and swung by its clamped teeth, growling ferociously. Konstantin sobbed oaths upon the little cur, imploring a whole host of blessed saints to smash it like a cockroach. From the bank of the stream four little naked Indians watched with solemn black eyes.

"What happened?" I ran to them.

"Tsar bit him," replied the tallest of the children.

"Vasilii Vasilievich!" wept the blacksmith. "Help me, in God's Holy Name! *Get it off me!*"

"For heaven's sake, man, it's the size of a rat!" I turned again to the boy. "Why did the doggie bite him?"

"He came running out here with his pants on fire," the child replied. "It was neat. Then he jumped in the water where we were swimming. We jumped out and Tsar jumped in to bite him. He's a brave dog."

That was when I realized that it wasn't Konstantin's trousers the dog had seized with such energy. No wonder he was crying. I waded hastily into the stream and somehow prised Tsar loose, but he had tasted blood and yapped viciously for more. I held him out at arm's length, squeaking and struggling, as I bent to examine poor Konstantin's backside.

Yes, the seat of the trousers had quite burnt away, and in addition to the dog bite he had a thoroughly ugly second-degree burn on either buttock.

"Tsk! This is a serious burn, my friend," I told him.

"I know that, you idiot!" he groaned. "I mean—excuse me—can't you *do* something about it? I'm suffering the pains of Hell!"

"Well, er, of course. Sit down in the water again while I determine a course of treatment for you." What a chance to show off my new knowledge of the local healing herbs! I accessed hurriedly. Let's see, what might be growing here that was useful for burns? *Sambucus canadensis,* of course! That was the native elderberry tree, wasn't it? Hadn't I seen one growing along the bank near here? I turned and waded ashore, holding out Tsar to his master. The dog's growling subsided like a teakettle taken off the fire.

"Listen to me, children! There's an elder tree growing up there on the bank. Perhaps your mommies use the leaves to make poultices? Yes? No? Well, will you be good children and fetch me some branches so I can make a soothing poultice for this poor man?" I implored. Up on the bluff a small crowd of colonists had gathered, drawn by all the noise.

"Vasilii Vasilievich, I'm dying!" moaned the blacksmith, writhing in the water. "Oh, Holy Saints, oh, Mother of God, why did I ever leave Irkutsk for this savage place?"

"All right," chorused the little Indians, and scampered away bright-eyed with excitement. Konstantin howled and prayed until they returned bearing green branches laden down with tiny blue berries. I gathered them up, confused. What did one *do* with them, exactly? Tsar's master knew an indecisive adult when he saw one, fortunately.

"You pound them up on a rock!" he yelled helpfully. "Want us to do it?" Without waiting for a reply he grabbed up a water-worn cobble and began mashing the berries into a slimy mess on the top of a boulder. The other children crowded around him while Tsar stalked stiff-legged along the bank, snarling at Konstantin.

In no time at all they'd reduced leaves and berries and all to a nasty-looking goo.

"All right, Konstantin Kirillovich," I told him, "please rise from the water. I've got an excellent native salve that'll take the pain away." I scooped up a handful of the muck and prepared to clap it on his seared derrière, while the children looked on expectantly.

And, well, my nerve gave way. How could this horrible stuff help a burn like that? I found myself digging into my coat for the little book of skin repair tissue we field agents carry. Yes, I know it's forbidden! But, you know, the truth is, our medicine works just as well on mortals as it works on us. Stealthily I tore out three or four of the sheets and stuck them on the blacksmith's behind, but he caught a glimpse of what I was doing over his shoulder.

"Prayers you're putting on my ass?" he screamed. "Are you crazy?"

"No!" I smeared the elderberry poultice on to disguise what I'd done. "That was merely, um, medical parchment, very useful in forming a base for the compound, you see—"

"Listen, you big St. Petersburg pansy—" he grated; then a remarkable expression crossed his face as the drugs in the skin replacement were released into his system. "The pain's gone!" he gasped. He reached behind and felt himself; then crouched down in the water to wash off the salve. By the time he rose, dripping, the synthetic skin had fused with his own and looked fresh and pink as on the day of his birth.

"Hooray!" yelled the children, jumping up and down in triumph, while Tsar went mad with barking.

"It's *healed,*" Konstantin stated in wonderment. Then he stared down at the swirling water. "It must have been this stream! I was here when the little father blessed it! It's a miracle! The holy water has worked a miracle!"

I squelched wearily back up the bank, as his cries brought spectators from the bluff down for a closer look at the Miracle of the Holy Stream. Courier was not among them, at least. Ought I to go see if he'd finally received his orders and gone? Perhaps I should go call on the Munin family to see how Andrei Efimovich's leg was mending. Perhaps I should look for specimens of *Asclepias speciosa.* There were a thousand better things to concern myself with than a difficult fellow operative. I was supposed to be a doctor, wasn't I?

And so I resolutely put Courier out of my mind and spent the rest of the day trudging from hut to house, with the intention of getting to know my patients better. I was not particularly successful; anyone who had the least ache or pain had run down to the holy stream and was bathing in its icy waters. Not necessarily bad for business: I might have a few cases of pneumonia by the week's end. But I did lance an abscessed gum for a Kashaya woman, and recommend a salve for a Creole baby's flea bites; so I was of some use to my mortal community.

There was no sign of Courier when I returned to the stockade that evening, through pumpkin fields, with the late red sun throwing long shadows of corn shocks where they stood in bundles. There was no sign of him when I sat down to dinner in the officers' mess, and attempted to join in the general conversation in a pleasant and comradely way. Not that I had much to contribute, with my pocket edition of Schiller, and nobody invited me to play cards with them. I was the recipient of a few distinctly dirty looks, in fact, especially from Iakov Babin.

I took a candle and wandered off to my room, my volume of poetry tucked ondly away in my coat. When I got there, I had the most peculiar feeling that something was somehow not quite right. I held up my candle and looked around.

My bunk, with its blanket, was undisturbed; so was my sea chest. My Imperial Navy saber still hung in its place of honor on the wall. My little stack of books was where it ought to be. Of course, my credenza wasn't there . . . perhaps Courier had left it in the guest room? I decided to wait until morning to look for it. Oh, yes, I know, *you'd* have gone straight in to see if he really had gone. I simply didn't want to. I lit my lamp and blew out the candle. A plume of greasy smoke curled, pungent, from the snuffed wick.

That was when I heard the growl.

A growl, I say. It wasn't a dog; it wasn't a bear. God only knew what it was, but it had emanated from the other side of the plank wall. From Courier's room. Oh, dear.

I scanned. I couldn't make sense of my readings. Courier seemed to be in the room, and yet—

I lit the candle again and went out into the corridor, where I knocked at Courier's door. There was a scuttling sound. No light showing under the door, or between the planks. *What was going on here?* I drew a deep breath and pulled open the door.

Darkness, and as the wavering light of my candle moved through the doorway I beheld a tangled mass on the floor. I prodded it with my boot. Strips of something? A trade blanket, torn to shreds. Interspersed with brittle glinting fragments and scraps of paper that had once been a framed picture of the tsar. *Where was Courier?*

Cautiously I raised the candle and looked upward.

It was on the ceiling, wedged in an angle of roof and rafters. Courier was up there clinging to the rafters, or had been.

Any mortal standing there in the dark, gazing up in the light of one shaky candle, would have seen a creature with dead white skin, enormous black insectile eyes, fangs and claws and a general strange misshapen muscularity. That sensible mortal would promptly have fled in terror. I, lumpish immortal, stared in bewilderment.

I saw an immortal in the direst extremity of self-protective fear. Blood had fled from his surface capillaries, leaving his skin pale; the protective lenses over his eyes had hardened and darkened. His gums had receded to give his teeth the maximum amount of cutting surface and his nails had grown out with amazing speed into formidable claws. He looked like nothing so much as Lon Chaney, Sr., in *London After Midnight.*

The thing worked bulging jaw muscles and inquired, "DUCITNE HAEC VIA OSTIA?"

"Courier, for God's sake! What's happened?" I cried.

It turned its head and the black surface of its eyes glittered as it fixed on me. "DA MIHI IUSSUM!" it croaked. What world, what *time* was it in?

I fell silent, as the horror of the thing sank into me, that one of *us* could suffer such an alteration. We, perfect mechanisms, in our endless lives see mortal men reduced by every degradation that disease and mischance can impose, skeletal horrors, sore-covered, deformed—but never *we*. Why had he become this thing?

He dropped on me, screaming. Think. How many times in your long life have you avoided mortal assault? It's easy, isn't it? One can sidestep a blade or a fist or even a bullet without turning a hair, because mortal sinews are weak, mortal reflexes slow. Poor brutes. But could you ever have dreamed you might have to defend yourself against another immortal? *How would you do it?*

I tell you that I *myself* began to change. That writhing horror dove for my throat, and even as I grappled with it I felt an indefinable metamorphosis commencing. I was not frightened, either, *me*, can you believe that? One split second of vertigo, and then the strangest glee filled my heart. All my senses were sharpened. I fought with the demented thing in that room and it seemed clumsy and blundering to me, though it moved with a speed mortal eyes couldn't have followed. Equals as we were in immortal strength, I had the advantage of sanity. My hideous new wisdom told me how to win and I pulled the creature's head close, in both my hands, to—

To do something; to this day I haven't remembered what I was about to do. In any case I never did it. What happened, you see, was that I looked into the creature's eyes. Black reflecting mirrors, its eyes, and what they showed me was a nightmare thing like the nightmare thing I was fighting! So taloned, so razor-grinned, with just such a glittering stare. A monster in the disintegrating clothing of a Russian gentleman. *Me.*

I fell back from it, staring at my hands in horror: my nails had grown with fantastic acceleration into serviceable claws. My horrified cry joined the creature's as it leapt at my face. I rolled away from it, shielding myself as best I could, and burst out through the doorway. Babin and the others, drawn by the commotion, were just arriving at the end of the corridor. I flung myself down, covered my face with my hands and yelled, "A *dybbuk!* Run for your lives, it's a *dybbuk!*"

My speech was hissed and slurred, but I doubt if anyone noticed, for the thing hesitated only a moment before plunging across the threshold after me. As it tore strips out of the back of my coat, what was I doing? I ask you to believe I was *biting my nails,* frantically. I didn't want to be a devil with talons. I was a man, a superior man!

"Run, you fools!" I cried. Yes, yes, I was speaking with a man's voice now, I was changing back.

Babin at least took a step backward, crossing himself, and the others shuffled back behind him. Courier's head snapped about to stare.

"QUANTO COSTA IL BIGLIETTO PER MARSIGLIA?" he demanded. I used the opportunity to open my door and scramble in on my hands and knees. Courier's neck snaked around with the fluid movement of a Harryhausen demon. He snarled and sprang into the room after me.

"MIXAHAM BERAVAM! BAYAD BERAVAM!" he roared, coming for me with talons raised to rake. I scrambled backward, I hit the wall with such force the building shook and the planks of the wall, thick as Bibles, cracked and started. Something was knocked loose. I caught it in midair as it dropped past my face. My Imperial Navy saber. In the same second I had put my boot up to halt Courier's oncoming rush and kicked him in the chest with all my strength. He flew backward and hit the opposite wall with a crash, and more planks split. There was a thunder of running steps as the mortals rushed down the hall to look through the doorway.

"LE BATEAU-MOUCHE EST EN RETARD!" Courier cried, in a voice that made the mortals cover their ears. I was desperately trying to shake the scabbard off the saber; something was wrong with the mechanism of my left arm. Blood and oil were drooling from Courier's jaws as he sprang again, straight for me, and my good arm went up and whipped the saber in an arc that passed through his neck. His head flew off, hit the wall and rolled to Iakov Babin's feet.

All my strength left me. I became aware that I was badly damaged. I slid to the floor. Courier's body was already still, having gone into fugue at the moment my blade broke the connection between the ferro-ceramic chain of his spine and the titanium gimbal of his skull. Already the neck arteries had sealed themselves off and a protective membrane was forming. His head was doing the same. Eyes, ears, nostrils were exuding a thick substance that would seal them against further injury.

"God *damn,* Doc!" Babin broke the appalled silence. "That was one fine sword cut! You fought like a man."

I had, by God. "Thank you," I said with difficulty. My lips were split and bruised. The rest of my fleshly parts hurt as well. "You were right, Iakov Dmitrivich. He was a *dybbuk.*"

"I told you." He stepped into the room cautiously, edging around the body. The other mortals cowered in the doorway. Someone was whimpering hysterically. "I seen devils in this New World just as ornery as any we got in Mother Russia. You ask the Indians. I reckon this one killed that boy, whoever he was, and possessed his body. Are you hurt bad, Doc?"

"I think my arm is broken."

"And some ribs, too, huh?" Babin squatted down and peered at me in awe. "God Almighty, Doc, you're beat up black and blue. You sure put up one hell of a fight, though. Wouldn't have thought you had it in you. Come on, boys, let's get him up on the bed."

"What are we going to do with *that?*" The junior manager pointed with a trembling finger at the body.

"Take it out and bury it at a crossroads." The farm foreman stepped in and gingerly lifted the head by its hair. "That's what the stories say to do. And put a stake through its heart, or it'll come back to get us!"

I let them lift me into my bunk, too impaired to protest. Besides, it didn't matter. The moment Courier's head had been severed a distress beacon had been activated, transmitting straight to the nearest Dr. Zeus HQ. Wherever he was buried, a repair crew would retrieve both his parts within hours. He'd be whisked away to a hospital and I hadn't the slightest doubt he'd be good as new within days, assuming they could do something about that nasty psychosis of his. I, on the other hand, would have to heal myself, and my self-diagnostic-and-repair program didn't seem to be working very well.

The body with its head was stuffed into a sack and hustled out by Babin and a party of others. Someone sent a Creole woman up with a basin of water and a rag to tend to my hurts. Her almond eyes widened at the extent of the damage, but she didn't say much; and it would have been rather pleasant to lie there being ministered to, but for Andreev, the assistant manager, rushing in.

"Kalugin! What on earth is this story that you've killed a man?"

"Self-defense," I said in my feeblest voice. "It was the visitor. He went mad, sir . . . tried to kill me . . . all the men witnessed it . . ."

Andreev was looking around wildly at the blood and smashed walls. He noticed the saber lying almost at his feet and did a little two-step dance back from it.

"God in Heaven! You killed him with a *sword?* What will General Manager Kostromitinov say?"

What indeed? I pretended to lapse into unconsciousness. The *dybbuk* story would sound more convincing if Babin told it, I was certain. Andreev Fedorovich stood there wringing his hands a moment longer, and then ran out of the room. I let myself slide into genuine oblivion . . .

"Marine Operations Specialist Kalugin?" It was a suave voice speaking cultured Cinema Standard that woke me. I opened my eyes. A man in a neat gray suit of clothes was sitting at the foot of my bed, by the light of my wildly flickering lamp.

"Northwest Regional Facilitator General Labienus," he introduced himself with a slight inclination from the waist.

"We'll be overheard—" I tried to rise on one elbow, indicating my open door, but he negated me with a wave of his hand.

"We've activated a hush field over the settlement. None of the mortals here can regain consciousness at present. We're recovering Courier—what's left of him, anyway—from his grave out there on the road. I'm afraid we owe you something of an explanation."

That took a moment to sink in. I opened my mouth to demand answers, but he held up his hand. "Please. Don't tire yourself. You want to know how one of us could suffer something like madness when we're all perfect, don't you? It's really quite simple. Courier wasn't—exactly— one of us."

I stared. Choosing his words with delicacy, he went on. "I suppose you've heard the old rumors about Flawed Ones, about fantastic creatures produced millennia ago when Dr. Zeus hadn't perfected the immortality process. Well, of course those stories aren't true; but it seems that, back in the early days, one or two individuals *were* produced who weren't quite up to Company standards." He drew from his inner breast pocket a slim silver case and, opening it, selected a silver-wrapped stick. "Theobromos, by the way?" He offered me the case. I took one gratefully, unwrapping it single-handed. My arm hadn't repaired itself yet. He resumed:

"Now, as you know, Dr. Zeus is a humane organization. Simple termination of the poor creatures was out of the question."

Especially since they were immortal, I thought to myself darkly. I put the Theobromos in my mouth. Oh, welcome bliss. It was highest-quality Guatemalan. Labienus watched my dreamy smile with amusement.

"Of course the Company found places for them. But in Courier's case—and by now you'll have guessed he was one of these substandard unfortunates—there were special circumstances that made it a particular challenge.

"It has to do with his autoimmune system, you see. Dr. Zeus had already perfected hyperfunction, but at that time there was no reason to believe it wouldn't work equally well on all subjects, regardless of personal biochemistry. However, Courier's metabolism presented certain problems.

"What's the simplest way to put this? You could say that his body decided his own RNA was a pathogen, and set about attacking it, breaking it down. The Company stabilized most of his metabolic response, but the spontaneous nature of short-term memory proved beyond them. You're aware that the brain stores memory in RNA molecules? Of course you are.

"I won't confuse you with the details, but the end result is that Courier reacts to memory as though it were a disease process. Any repeated specific experience and he undergoes an adverse reaction. Consistently repeat a specific sequence of events and paranoid psychosis is the result, with all the attendant physical manifestations you saw."

"You mean spending two nights in his room made him a demon from Hell?"

"Merely the effect of hyperfunction on the human fight-or-flight reflex," said Labienus dismissively. "It's not his fault, poor creature. And, after all, Dr. Zeus found just the job for him! They made him a long-distance courier. As long as he's traveling, as long as he's constantly exposed to new sights he's never seen before, the adverse RNA reaction can't build up. He can even retrace old journeys, if enough years elapse between visits. Trouble only occurs if he's obliged to stay in one place for more than twenty-four hours, but of course Dr. Zeus has always taken care to ensure that new orders are waiting for him at every destination."

"What happened in this case?"

Labienus looked aside. "A minor clerical blunder. His orders were forwarded to the wrong terminal. The clerk responsible has been disciplined."

"How comforting."

"I'm sure it will never happen again. And we'll fasten on his head and he'll be off on his travels again, to New York or Mazatlan or Warsaw, good as new, with no memory of this unfortunate occurrence. He never remembers anything very long, actually, if it isn't something hard-wired like a language. Except for the plots of films he's seen. Those he retains, for some reason."

"Poor thing," I mused. *Very* good Theobromos, this.

"Do you think so? I rather envy him, myself. Imagine a life of endless new horizons! Nothing to bore him or dull his palate, no tedious *sameness* to his experiences. All his friends will be new friends." Labienus smiled wistfully and put his silver case away. "Well. Principally what *you* need to know is that of course there'll be no disciplinary hearing for you. We *quite* understand that under the circumstances you had no choice but to badly damage a fellow operative. We *would* like to know why you didn't contact us sooner—his psychotic behavior must certainly have been increasingly *obvious . . .*"

"Er, well—I did try—and then I didn't have access to my credenza, you see." I began to sweat a little. And did I feel just a trace of pain in my fingertips? "I loaned it to him—"

"Yes; we found it in the rafters. Well, no real harm done, it appears; though I'm afraid you'll have some explaining to do to your mortal authorities. I'm certain you'll follow standard operating procedures this time, though, and acquit yourself with flying colors. Shame I can't give you anything to speed up your self-repair; but then, if you got up tomorrow without a scratch on you after that fight, you'd *really* have some explaining to do, wouldn't you?" He chuckled and smacked my thigh in a companionable sort of way. It hurt. A short in my femoral wiring finally fixed itself and informed me that I had a massive hematoma there and several torn ligaments. As I was reflecting on this, another immortal appeared in my doorway.

"Sir? Recovery operation completed. All personnel are aboard and ready for departure."

"Then I'm off." Labienus rose, adjusting his coat and shooting his cuffs. "Well, Kalugin. I hope our next meeting takes place under more pleasant circumstances. You *will* transmit your full report within the next forty-eight hours, I trust? Good. Until next time." He stepped out into the corridor.

"How old is he?" I blurted.

"Who? Courier?" Labienus looked in at me, arching his eyebrows. "Thirty thousand years, I believe." He started to walk away and then stuck his head back through the doorway for a second. "Oh, by the way—Happy Halloween." He flashed a smile and was gone.

So that was the end of it, at least as far as Dr. Zeus was concerned. I myself was in a tight spot for a while. As soon as he heard about the incident, Kostromitinov became convinced it was some sort of loathsome crime of homosexual passion, and had me arrested. Fedor Svinin got a few days' holiday, because our jail was only big enough to accommodate one person. He used the time to go fishing and caught pneumonia.

At the inquest it was discovered that my pretty Creole girl had decided to tidy up my room whilst I was unconscious, and had cleaned the blood off the murder weapon and put it back in its sheath. Better still, the victim's body had vanished from its grave and was nowhere to be found when an exhumation order was given. Best of all, I had a roomful of witnesses swearing on their immortal souls that the person I'd beheaded hadn't been a human being at all. Iakov Babin was particularly vehement on my behalf, and his testimony counted for something: he was a man with a lot of experience at beating murder raps.

Thus the case never came to trial, and I was left under a sort of halfhearted house arrest that nobody bothered to enforce. And, you know, the rest of my time there was extraordinarily happy! I became accepted, respected, *liked.* Apparently a man who can deliver babies with one hand and kill *dybbuks* with the other was just what people wanted on the frontier. I stayed on at the Ross colony until it was sold to Mr. Sutter ten years later, though I didn't go home with my fellow Russians right away, but that's another story.

I can't say it's a comfort to think that Courier is still out there on the road somewhere, in endless transit like an orbiting moon. It's likely enough that at some point in the next thirty thousand years our paths will cross again, so I'm grateful he won't remember me.

But, think about it: you may well have seen him yourself. In some city, on some tourist boat or in some railway carriage, there is always a stupid young man in the happy morning of his life, chatting with perfect strangers and exclaiming over the scenery; and he is always alone.

"Old Flat Top" was written on a trip up Highway 1, which runs through the Big Sur of poet Robinson Jeffers. This is a great inhuman country of sea and sky and stone, tremendous volume of rock towering above the little two-lane road, its upper heights disappearing in the summer fog. There are places up there where the human eye refuses to grasp the proportion or scale of what it sees, coming unexpected around a sharp turn.

It's a haunted country. There are little silent people glimpsed now and again in the gloomier canyons, among the redwoods. There is a famous figure in a cloak and broad-brimmed hat, a black silhouette in the noonday sun, that watches from the peaks. Lost wagon roads, lost mines, ghost towns lost up there in the fog. No place to travel in lightly.

But it is beautiful.

✦　　✦　　✦

Old Flat Top

THE BOY HAS THE FIRM CHIN AND HIGH-DOMED brow of the Cro-Magnon hominids—might be a member of any racial group—and is dressed in somewhat inadequate Neolithic clothing of woven grass and furs. He didn't bring any useful Neolithic tools with him on this journey, however. He had come to see if God was really on the mountain as he'd always been told, and he hadn't thought tools would be any use in finding God. In this he was reasonably correct. No instrument his people could produce, at their present level of technology, would help him now.

Far enough up a mountain to peer above the clouds, the boy is in serious trouble. Above him is ice and thin air; all around him a sliding waste of black blasted rock, immense, pitiless. The green valley of his ancestors lies a long way below him, and he could return there in slightly under a minute if he didn't mind arriving in a red smashed mass.

That would scarcely win him the admiration of his peers, however, and he clings now desperately to a narrow handhold, and gazes up at the mouth of the cave he has come so far to find. He can neither jump nor climb any higher. He can't climb back down, either; his hands and feet have gone numb. He realizes he is going to die.

To his left, a few meters away, there is sudden movement.

He turns his head to stare. What he had taken to be an outcropping of particularly weathered rock is looking at him. It is in fact a man, easily twice his size, naked but for a belted bearskin and a great deal of dun-colored hair and beard.

The giant's body is powerfully built, nearly human as the boy understands human, but with a slightly odd articulation of the arms and shoulders. The head is not human at all. The skull is long and low, helmet-shaped, and with its heavy orbital ridges and forward-projecting face it reminds the boy of those stocky little villagers in the next valley, the ones who scatter flowers over their dead and make such unimaginative flint tools. Like them, too, the giant has an immense protruding nose. Its cheekbones are high and broad, its jaw heavy, its teeth terrifyingly long. The boy knows this because the giant is grinning at him.

"Boo," says the giant, in a light and rather pleasant voice.

This syllable means nothing to the boy, but he is so thoroughly unnerved that he loses his grip on the mountain and totters backward, screaming.

The next moment is a blur. All his breath is knocked out of him, and before he can grasp what has happened, he finds himself crouching inside the cave that was so unattainable a moment before. The giant is squatting beside him, considering him with pale inhuman eyes.

Seen close to, the giant is even more unnerving. He cocks his head and the angle at which he does this is not human either, nor is the strong strange musk of his body. The boy drags himself swiftly backward, stares around the interior of the cave for a weapon. The giant chuckles at him.

There are plenty of weapons, but it's doubtful the boy would be able to lift any of these tremendous stone axes, let alone defend himself with one. He looks further, and then his frantic gaze stops dead at the battered cabinet against one wall.

The fact that its central screen glows with tiny cryptic symbols is almost beside the point. It's a *box,* and the boy's world has no such geometry. He has never seen a rectangle, a square. This fully convinces him that he has found the object of his quest. Slowly, he turns back to face the giant.

He makes obeisance, and the giant snorts. Sitting timidly upright, the boy explains that he has come in search of God on the mountain for the purpose of learning the Truth.

The boy's language is a combination of hand gestures and sounds. The giant's eyes narrow; he leans close, keenly observing, listening. When the boy has finished, the giant clears his throat and replies in the same manner.

He communicates for some time. His hands are clever, capable of facile and expressive gestures, and his vocal apparatus produces a wider range of syllables, enunciated with greater precision; so it will be understood that he is a far more eloquent speaker than the boy, who listens as though spellbound.

*   *   *

Yes, I'll tell you the Truth. Why not? In all these generations, you're the first mortal to climb up here, so you've earned an answer; but I don't think you'll like it much.

I'm not your God. I'm the highest authority you'll ever encounter, though, mortal man. Really. I was created to judge you and punish you, you and all your fathers. Would you like to know how that happened? Watch.

I'll draw something in the dust for you, here. This is called a circle, all right? It's the wheel of Time. Never mind what a wheel is. This part here, almost at the beginning, is where your people began to exist.

Life was a lot harder back then, mortal. Your people almost didn't make it. You know why? Because, almost from the time your fathers stood up on their little hind legs, they made war on one another. Winters weren't bitter enough! Leopards and crocodiles weren't hungry enough! Famine wasn't terrible enough either. They had to keep whittling away at their numbers themselves, stupid monkeys.

The worst were a bunch who called themselves the Great Goat Cult. They found a weed that filled them with holy visions when they chewed it. They heard voices that told them to go out and kill. Became scream-ing tattooed maniacs who made a lot of converts, believe me, but they killed more than they converted.

Now, look here at this part of the circle. This is up at the other end of Time. The people up there are, let's say they're powerful shamans. And they're very nervous. Being so close to the end of Time, they want to save as much of the past as they can.

They looked back into Time through a, uh, a *magic eye* they had. They looked at their oldest fathers and saw that if this Great Goat Cult wasn't stopped, they themselves might never come to exist. Who had time to learn how to make fire, or sew furs into clothing or make pots out of clay, if crazy people were always chasing and killing everybody?

I'm simplifying this for you, mortal, but here's what they did.

The shamans found a way to step across from their part of the circle into the beginning part. They took some of your fathers' children and made them slaves, but magic slaves: immortal and strong and really smart. They sent those slaves to try to reason with the Great Goat Cult.

It didn't work.

The slaves were great talkers, could present many clever arguments, but the Great Goat Cult wouldn't listen. In fact, they sent the slaves back to their shaman masters with spears stuck in inconvenient places, and one or two had to carry their own lopped-off body parts. So the sha-mans had to come up with another idea.

Can you guess yet what it was? No? Well, you're only a mortal. I'll tell you.

They took some more slaves, not just from your fathers but from some of the other tribes running around back then—those little guys in the next valley, for example, and some big people from a valley you've never seen, and a few others who're all extinct now.

You know how you can put a long-legged ram with long fleece in the pen with a short-legged ewe with short fleece, and you'll get a short-legged lamb with long fleece? Eventually? Breeding experiments, right, you've got it. Well, that's what the shamans did with all these people. Bred the big ones and the little ones to get what they wanted.

What did they want? What were they breeding for? You can't guess? I'm disappointed. They wanted their very own screaming killing maniacs to counter the cultists.

Except we're not really maniacs. We just have a great sense of humor.

We're the optimum morphological design for a humanoid fighting machine, oo-rah! We're not afraid of being hurt, like you. And of course we too were made immortal and smart. Three thousand of us were bred. That was a lot of people, back then. They raised us in cadet academies, trained us in camps, me and all my brother warriors.

This was all done back here at the beginning of time, by the way. The shamans were scared to death to have us up there at their end. There are no warriors in their time, or so we were always told.

And we were all programmed—no, you don't know what that is. Indoctrinated? Convinced with extreme prejudice?

We were given the absolute Truth.

But it's our Truth, not yours, mortal. Our Truth is that we have the joyous right and duty to kill, instantly and without question, any dirty little mortals we find making war on each other. *You* don't have the right to kill yourselves. You're supposed to live in peace, herd beasts, plant crops, tell stories, have babies. Do that and we'll let you alone. But if you decide to make war, not love—whack, there we are with flint axes and bloody retribution, you see? Simplicity itself.

It was the law. Perfect and beautiful justice. You do right, we punish wrong. No questions. No whining.

The shamans from the other end of Time created us as the consummate weapon against the Great Goat Cult. We were bigger and faster, and we killed without pity or hesitation. Our faith was stronger than theirs. So we made mincemeat out of the little bastards.

Oh, those were great times. So much work to do! Because, while the shamans had dithered around about whether or not we should be created, the Cult had spread across the world. It took centuries to stamp them all out. We rode in endless pursuit and it was one long happy party, mortal. Summer campaigns, year after year. Winter raids, damn I loved them: bloodspray's beautiful on new-fallen snow, and corpses stay fresh so much longer . . .

Don't be scared. I'm just reminiscing.

When we slaughtered the last of the Goats, your fathers were set free, don't you understand? Instead of running and hiding in holes like animals, they could settle down to become people. They had time at last, to learn to count on their fingers and toes, to look at the stars and wonder what they were. Time to drill holes in deer bone and make music. Time to paint bison on cave walls. And the other immortals (we called them Preservers), had time at last to go among your fathers and collect cultural artifacts the shamans wanted saved, now that there *was* culture.

But what were we Enforcers supposed to do, with our great purpose in life gone? We loved to kill. It was all we knew, all we were made for. So our officers met together, to talk over the question of where the masters expected us to fit, in this new peacetime we'd made possible for mortals.

There was a lot of debate. Most of us in the rank and file were pretty optimistic; we just figured they'd reprogram us to do some other job. But one colonel, an asshole named Marco, thought we could never be sure the mortals wouldn't relapse into being cultists, and that maybe we ought to make some preemptive strikes: you know, kill all the mortals who looked as though they *might* make war, so they'd never get a chance to.

Everyone roared him down, except the men under his command. See, that would have been absolutely wrong! That would have been killing innocents, and we don't do that. Noncombatants are to be protected at all times. But our masters, who as I mentioned are nervous people, shit themselves in terror when they found out what Marco'd said.

Marco's faith was imperfect. We should have done something about him right then . . . but that's another story.

Anyway, Budu told him he was a fool, and that shut him up.

Budu was our general, our supreme commanding officer. He was one of the oldest of us and he was the best, the strongest, the biggest. And he was righteous, I tell you, our Truth was strong in his heart! I'd have died for him, if I wasn't immortal, and as it was I had my head lopped off twice fighting under him. I didn't care; the masters stuck it on again and I was proud to go right from the regeneration tank back to the front lines, as long as Budu was out there too.

(Regeneration tank. It's . . . think of it as a big pot, no, a *big* pot. Do you know what a cauldron is? All right, imagine a big one full of, uh, *magic juice,* and whenever one of us immortals would be damaged too badly to repair ourselves, we'd be carted off the field and put in one of these magic cauldrons to heal. We'd come out good as new.)

Anyway, Budu was also the smartest of us. Budu studied future history, between this age and the time in which our masters live. He figured out what scared them the most. He said the mortal masters might think they didn't need us anymore, but they'd find they were mistaken soon enough. He ordered us to wait. Something would happen.

And, Father of Justice, the old man was right!

Now you're going to find the story more interesting, mortal, because this part of it deals with your own people.

Let's see, how do I explain the concept of mitochondrial DNA to you?

I've already told you how the shamans at the other end of Time want to be sure nothing happens to endanger their own existence, right? Causality really worries them. So they're obsessive about tracing their ancestors, finding out for certain where they came from. And they've been careful to chart something called *genetic drift.* It's like a map, you know what a map is, that shows where their fathers have been.

Well, they found that a lot of their fathers—actually, mothers—started out right below this mountain, mortal, right down in that nice green valley of yours. It's sort of a crossroads—uh, game trail—for humanity. It's where a lot of important human traits came together to make something special.

But back then this hadn't happened yet. There was a tribe living down there, all right, nicely settled into a farming community, but they only had some of the genetic markers, the special blood, that our masters expected to find.

So the masters sent in a Preserver to watch them. He was what we call an *anthropologist,* which meant he didn't mind working with the monkeys. His name was Rook. He became a member of their tribe, lived in their huts with them. I couldn't do it, but I guess there's no accounting for tastes.

Rook was expecting another tribe to appear from somewhere and intermarry with the farmers, and that other tribe would provide the missing pieces, so to speak, and their descendants would become our masters' fathers. He was all set to record it, when it happened; but it didn't quite happen the way he'd expected.

The other tribe came along, all right, hunter-gatherers on a long leisurely migration to greener pastures, and that valley below was nice and green. The newcomers had the right genes, too, just as Rook had predicted.

What he hadn't predicted, though, was that the peaceful farming folk would treat the newcomers just like they treated any other migratory species. Like elk, or caribou. You see, agrarian societies sometimes have a problem getting enough protein . . .

That means meat. I mean they were catching the hunter-gatherers and eating them.

You're embarrassed to learn that your fathers were cannibals? Think how the shamans at the other end of Time felt!

So the old Enforcers weren't demobilized quite yet, ha ha. But this was a slightly more complicated situation than we were used to, understand? We couldn't just wade in there and wipe out the peaceful farming folk. Negotiation was called for. And we never negotiate.

So our masters assigned us a liaison with the mortals, a new kind of Preserver they'd invented, called a Facilitator.

Facilitators are different. We Enforcers were designed to love killing, and the regular Preservers were designed to love the things they preserved. The Facilitators, though, were designed to be more objective, to operate in the big civilizations that were about to be born. They would be politicians, intriguers, councilors to mortal kings. What do those words mean? . . . I guess the best translation would be *liars.*

I remember the staff meeting as though it were yesterday, mortal man.

It was raining. We'd made camp on that high meadow you passed on your way up here, and most of us had fanned out into the landscape. Budu had only brought the Fifth Infantry Division, which I was in. I was one of his aides, so all I had to do was set up the tent where the meeting was to be held. The old man stood there quietly in the open, staring down the trail; he didn't care if he got wet.

We'd had a report from a patrol that they were on their way. Pretty soon I caught a whiff of Preserver in the wind though Budu had picked it up before I did; he had already turned to watch them come down from the pass. Rook was on foot, a little miserable-looking guy in a wet cloak, but the Facilitator was riding a horse, and Rook was having to tilt his head back to look up at him as he talked earnestly, waving his arms.

The Facilitator was tall, for one of them anyway, and wore nice tailored clothes. His name was Sarpa. He wasn't paying attention to Rook much, just sort of nodding his head as he rode and scanning the landscape, and when he spotted us I saw his eyes widen. I don't know what he'd been told about Enforcers at his briefing, but he hadn't expected what he found.

They were escorted in, and I took Sarpa's horse away and tethered it. The old man wanted to start the meeting right then. The Preservers asked for something hot to drink first, which seemed stupid to me—had they come there to talk, or to have a party?—but Budu just told me to get them something. All we had was water, but I brought it in a couple of polished Great Goat skulls, the nicest ones in camp. The Preservers stared with big round eyes when I set their drinks before them, and didn't touch a drop. There's no pleasing some people.

At least they got down to business. Rook made his report first, about how the farming tribe had been fairly peaceable until the newcomers had arrived, when they had suddenly shown a previously-unknown talent for hunting hunters. They watched the hunters' trails, lay in wait with sharp sticks, and almost never failed to carry off one of the younger or weaker of the new tribe, whom they butchered and parceled out among themselves. Rook had seen all this firsthand.

The Facilitator Sarpa asked him why he hadn't tried to stop them.

"I did try," he said wretchedly. "I told them they shouldn't eat other people. They told me (with their mouths full) that the strangers weren't people. They were quite calm about it, and nothing I said could convince them otherwise. Anyway, I can't say much without blowing my cover; they thought it was funny enough I wouldn't touch the ribs they offered me."

Sarpa wanted to know what Rook's cover was, and Rook told him he was an adopted member of the tribe, and had himself avoided any "unpleasantness" by volunteering to work in the fields even in bad weather. Sarpa stared harder at that than he'd stared at the skull cups.

"You're maintaining your cover by *good attitude?*" he said, as though he couldn't believe it.

"That's what a participant observer does," Rook explained.

"But when you're one of *us?* It never occurred to you to exploit your superior abilities, or your knowledge? Why didn't you pose as a spirit? A magician, at least, and impress them with a few tricks?"

"That would have been lying," said Budu, and Rook said:

"Well, but that would have created an artificial dynamic in our relationship. I'm supposed to observe and document the way they live in their natural state. If I'd said I was a magical being, they wouldn't have behaved in a natural way toward me, would they?"

Sarpa exhaled hard through his little thin nose, and drummed his fingers on his knees. "All right," he said, "it's clearly time a specialist was brought in. I'll make contact with them immediately."

Budu wanted to know what he was going to do, and Sarpa waved his hand. "Textbook procedure for managing primitives. I'll put them in awe of me with an exhibition of juggling, or something. Once I've got their attention, I'll explain the health risks involved in eating the flesh of their own species."

"And if they won't listen?" asked Budu. Sarpa smiled at him in a patronizing kind of way, I guess because he was frightened of the old man. I could smell his fear from clear over where I was standing, playing dumb like a good orderly.

"Why, then we send in the troops, don't we?" Sarpa said lightly. "But it won't come to that. I know my job."

"Good," said Budu. "What do you need now?"

"I need to download all possible data on them from Rook, here," Sarpa replied. (What's that mean? Just that Rook was going to tell him a lot of things very very fast, mortal.) "We can retire to my field quarters for that; I'd like to get into dry clothes first. Where's our camp?"

"You're in it," said Budu.

Sarpa looked around in dismay. "You haven't put up the other tents yet?" he asked.

Budu told him we don't need tents, but offered him the one in which they were squatting. "And I'll assign you Flat Top for an aide," he said.

(He meant me. I was designated Joshua when I was born, but everybody in my unit went by a nickname. Skullcracker, Crunchmaster, Terminator, that kind of thing. I earned my nickname when we had a contest to see how many beers we could balance on top of our heads. I got five up there.)

Sarpa didn't look too happy about it, but I made myself useful after the old man left: hung some more skins around the tent and brought in some springy bushes for bedding. I unloaded his saddlebags and set up the field unit—uh, the *magic box* that let us talk to the shamans. Like that one over there, see? Only smaller—while he downloaded from Rook. Rook went back to the farmstead after that, poor little drone, couldn't leave his mortals for long.

Sarpa got up and spread his hands over the back of his field unit to get them warm. He asked me, "What time are rations served out?" and I told him we were foraging on this campaign, but that I'd get him part of somebody's kill if he wanted, or maybe some wild onions. He shuddered and said he'd manage on the Company-issued provisions he'd brought with him. So I set that out for him instead, little tiny portions of funny-smelling stuff.

I don't think Sarpa understood yet that he was supposed to dismiss me or I couldn't go. I just stood at ease while he ate, and after a few minutes he offered me a packet of crackers. I could have inhaled the damn things, they were so small. To be polite I nibbled at the edges and made them last a while, which was hard with teeth like mine, believe me.

When he was finished I tidied up for him, and he settled down at his field unit. He didn't work, though. He just stared out over the edge of the meadow at the smoke rising from the mortals' farmstead. I figured I'd better give him a clue, so I said, "Sir, will there be anything else, sir?"

"No . . ." he said, in a way that meant there would be. I waited, and after a minute he said, not meeting my eyes: "Tell me something, Enforcer. What does a man have to do to—ah—fraternize with the female mortals?"

By which he meant he wanted to couple with one of your mothers.

I said, "Sir, I don't know, sir."

His attention came away from the smoke and he looked up at me sharply. "So it's true, then, about Enforcers?" he asked me. "That you're really not, ah, interested?"

"Sir, that's affirmative, sir," I told him.

"No sex at all?"

"Sir, no sir."

"But . . ." He looked out at the smoke again. "How on earth do you manage?"

I felt like asking him the same question: Why would our masters have created his kind with the need to go through the motions of reproduction, when they can't actually reproduce?

(No, mortal, we can't. We're immortal, so we don't need to.)

I mean, I can see why you mortals are obsessed with it; I'd be too, if that was my only shot at immortality. But we've always wondered why the Preserver class were given such a stupid appetite. Budu used to say it was because they needed to be able to understand the mortals' point of view if they were to function correctly, and I guess that makes sense. Still, if it was me, I'd find it a distraction.

So I just told Sarpa, "Sir, nothing to manage. Everybody knows that killing's a lot easier than making life, and for us it's a lot more fun, sir."

He shivered at that, and said, "I suppose it's really just sports taken to the extreme, isn't it? Very well; Rook will probably know how to set me up with a girl."

I didn't say anything, and he looked at me sidelong, trying to read my expression.

"You probably disapprove," he said. "With the morality the Company programmed into you."

"Sir, strictly speaking, you're exploiting the mortals, sir," I said.

"And you think that's wrong."

"Sir, it would be for me. Not my place to say what's wrong for you, sir. You're a Preserver, and one of the new models at that, sir."

"So I am," he said, smiling. "You won't judge *me,* eh? I like the way your conscience works, Flat Top. And after all, if I can get the creatures' females on my side, it'll be easier to persuade them to behave themselves."

I don't know why he should have cared what I thought of him, but the Preservers were all like that; the damndest things bothered them. I just told him, "Yes Sir," and he dismissed me after that. The guys in my mess had saved me a leg of mountain goat. Not much meat, but there was a lot of marrow in the bones. Crack, yum.

Well, so the next day the Facilitator went out and did his stuff.

He dressed in his best clothes, dyed all kinds of bright colors to dazzle the mortals, and he put on makeup. He rode on his horse, which your fathers hadn't got around to domesticating yet. It was a pretty animal, nothing like the big beasts our cavalry ride: slender legs, little hooves, kind of on the stupid side but elegant as you please.

We went with Sarpa, though of course we were undercover. There were maybe a hundred of us flanking him as he rode down to their patchwork fields, slipping through the trees and the bushes, keeping ourselves out of sight. So close we came I could have popped open any one of their little round heads with a rock, as Sarpa rode back and forth in plain sight and got their attention.

They froze with their deer-antler hoes in their hands; they watched him with their mouths open, and slowly drew into a crowd as he approached them. He staged it nicely, I have to say, let his long cloak blow out behind him so its rainbow lining showed, and there were grunts and cries of wonder from the mortals.

Sarpa told them he was a messenger from their ancestors, and to prove it he did a stunt with some special-effects charges that sent red smoke and fireballs shooting from his fingertips. The mortals almost turned and ran at that, but he kept them with his voice, saying he had an important message to deliver. Then he said the ancestors demanded to know why their children had been eating their own kind?

His audience just looked blank at that, and I spotted Rook running up from behind and pushing his way through the crowd. He yelled out that he'd warned them this would happen. Falling flat before Sarpa, he begged the ancestors for mercy and promised that the farmers would never do such a terrible thing again.

At this point, though, the farmstead's lady raised her voice and said there must be some mistake, because her people weren't eating their own kind.

Sarpa asked, were they not lying in wait for the strangers who had recently come into the valley, the harmless people who hunted and gathered? Were they not stabbing them with spears, cutting them open, roasting them over coals?

The lady smiled and shrugged and said yes, the invaders were being treated so; but they were not her own kind, and certainly not children of the ancestors!

Sarpa didn't win them over nearly as easy as he'd thought he could. They argued back and forth for about an hour, as I remember. He told them why it was wrong to eat other human beings, told them all about the diseases they could catch, even told them a lot of malarkey about what would happen to them in the next world if they didn't cut it out right now.

The mortals were clearly impressed by him, but refused to consider the newcomers as people and in fact argued quite confidently against such a silly idea. Not only did they point out a whole lot of physical differences that were obvious to them (though it was lost on me; I've never been able to tell one of your races from another), they explained how vitally necessary it was to protect their sacred home turf from the alien interlopers, and to protect their limited resources.

Sarpa was kind of taken aback that these little mortal things had the gall to argue with him. I saw he was beginning to lose his temper, and in the shadows beside me Budu noticed it, too; the old man snorted, but he just narrowed his eyes and watched. At last the Facilitator fell back on threatening the mortals, letting fly with a couple of thunderbolts that set fire to a bush and working a few other alarming-looking tricks.

That got instant capitulation. The mortals abased themselves, and the lady apologized profusely for them all being so stupid as not to understand the mighty Son of Heaven sooner. She asked him what they could possibly do to please the Son of Heaven. Maybe he'd like a beautiful virgin?

And a mortal girl was pushed forth, looking scared, and Budu grunted, because Sarpa's eyes fixed on her with an expression like a hungry dog's. Then he was all smiles and gracious acceptance, and congratulated the mortals for being so wise as to see things his way. The girl squealed a bit, but he assured her she'd live through his embrace and even have pretty things afterward. I don't think she believed him, but her mother fixed her with an iron glare, and she gulped back her terror and went with Sarpa.

He took her back up to camp—she squealed a lot more when she saw us at last, but Sarpa sweet-talked her some more—and to celebrate his success he took her to his tent, stripped her bare as a skinned rabbit, and had his fun.

There was a lot of muttering from us about that, and not just because we thought what he was doing was wrong. We were disgusted because he hadn't realized the mortals were lying to him.

See, mortal, *we* can tell when you're lying. You smell different then. You smell afraid. But Sarpa had been distracted by his lusts and his vanity, sniffing after something else. We knew damned well the mortals were only giving him the girl to make him go away.

And oh, mortal, it was hard not to go down there and punish them. It was our duty, it was our programmed and ancient desire. By every law we understood, those mortals were ours now. Budu wouldn't give the order yet, all the same. He just bided his time, though he must have known what was going to happen.

Well—three days later, as Sarpa was in his tent with his little friend while I was busting my ass to find a way to boil water in a rock basin because the great Facilitator wanted a *hot* bath, thank you very much— Rook came slinking up from the farmstead to tell us that the mortals had done it again. They'd caught a party of strangers, and even now they were whacking them up into bits to be skewered over the cookfire.

I can't say I was surprised, and I know the old man wasn't. He just stalked to Sarpa's tent, threw back one of the skins and said:

"Son of Heaven, it seems that your in-laws have backslid."

Sarpa was furious. He yelled at the mortal girl, demanded to know what was wrong with her people, even took a swing at her. Budu growled and fetched him out by his arm, and told him to stop being an ass. He added that if this was the way the hotshot Facilitators operated, the Company—the shamans, I mean—should have saved themselves the trouble of designing a new model, or at least not sent one into the field until they'd got the programming right.

Sarpa just drew himself up and yelled for me to bring his horse. He jumped into the saddle and rode off hell-for-leather, with Rook racing after him. Budu watched them go, and I think he actually considered for a minute whether or not it was worth it to send an armed escort after the fool. In the end he did, which turned out to be a wise precaution.

I wasn't there to see what happened. I was babysitting Sarpa's little girlfriend, watching as she cowered in the bedding and cried. I felt sorry for her. We do feel sorry for you sometimes, you know. It's just that you can be so stupid, you mortals.

Anyway I missed quite a scene. Apparently it didn't go at all well: Sarpa went galloping down and caught the farm-tribe with their mouths full of hunter-tribe. He shouted terrible threats at them, and put on another show of smoke and noises. Maybe he should have waited until there was an eclipse or a comet scheduled, though, because the farmers weren't as impressed with his stunts this time. The upshot was, they killed his horse from under him and he had to run for it, and Rook too. If the armed escort hadn't stepped out and scared the mortals off, there'd have been a couple of badly damaged Preservers doing time in regeneration vats, and maybe some confused farmers puking up bits of biomechanical implants.

But Sarpa and Rook got back up to camp safely enough, though they were fuming at each other, Rook especially because now he'd lost his cover and wouldn't be able to collect any more anthropological data. He said a lot of cutting things about Facilitators in general. Sarpa was just gibbering with rage. I got between him and the girl until he calmed down a little and I respectfully suggested, sir, that he might want to keep her safe as a hostage, sir, and whatever he might have retorted, he shut up when Budu came into the tent and looked at him.

"Well, Facilitator," said Budu, "what are you going to do now?"

But Sarpa had an answer for that. He was through dealing with the lying, grubbing little farmers. He'd go straight to the hunter-gatherers and present himself as their good angel, and show them how to defend themselves against the other tribe.

Budu told him he couldn't do that, because it directly contravened orders. The monkeys were supposed to interbreed, not fight.

Sarpa said something sarcastic about Budu's grasp of subtleties and explained that he'd manage that: if the hunter-gatherers captured the farmers' females, they could keep them as slaves and impregnate them. It wouldn't exactly be the peace and harmony our masters had wanted imposed, but it would at least guarantee the requisite interbreeding took place.

Budu shrugged, and told him to go ahead and try.

Next day, he did. Rook stayed in camp this time, but I went along because Sarpa, having lost his mount, insisted on me carrying him around on my shoulders. I guess he felt safe up there. He had a good view, anyway, because he was the first in our party to spot the hunter-gatherers' camp on the far side of the valley.

Our reconnaissance team had reported the hunter-gatherers were digging in and fortifying a position for themselves, finally. Nice palisade of sharpened sticks, and inside they were chipping flint points just as fast as they could. Budu studied them from all angles before he just sent me walking up to the stockade so that Sarpa could look over the fence at them.

He—that is, I—had to dodge quite a few spears and thrown flints before he got them to listen to his speech. They did listen, I have to hand them that much.

But they weren't buying it. They had every intention of descending on the farmer-tribe and getting revenge for the murder of their brethren. Sarpa tried to persuade them that the best way to do this was to make more children, but that wouldn't wash either.

It turned out they weren't just a migratory tribe. They apparently had a long-standing cultural imperative to expand, to take new land for themselves whenever they needed it, and if other tribes got in the way they'd push them out or kill them off—though they *never* ate them, they hastened to add, because they were a morally superior people, which was why they deserved to have the land in the first place.

Sarpa argued against this until they began to throw things at him again, and we beat an inglorious retreat. What was worse, when we got back we discovered that Rook had let the mortal girl go. He'd known her since her childhood, evidently, and didn't want to see her hurt. He and Sarpa almost came to blows and it's not pretty to see Preservers do that, mortal, they're not designed for it. Budu had to step in again and threaten to knock their heads together if they didn't back off.

Anyway, the damage was done, because the girl ran right back to her tribe and told them what was going on. How she'd figured out that Sarpa was going to woo the enemy, I don't know, unless Rook was dumb enough to tell her. Then, too, you people aren't always as stupid as you look. She might have figured out on her own that matters were coming to a head.

Which they did, in the gray cold hour before the next dawn.

Our patrols spotted them long before they got within a kilometer of each other: two little armies carrying as much weaponry as they could hold, men and boys and strong women, with their faces painted for war. Guilty, guilty, guilty, mortal! We watched from our high place and danced where we stood, we were so hungry to go after them. Sarpa didn't desire his naked girl as much as we desired the sound of our axes on their guilty skulls, pop-chop! They were sinning, the worst of sins, and their blood was ours.

But the old man held us back. Orders were, the mortals were to be given every chance. That's why he was our commander, mortal! He loved the law. His faith was stronger than anyone's, but *he* had the strength to hold back from the purest pleasure in the world, which is being the law's instrument, you see?

So he sent me down with Sarpa riding on my shoulder, and I walked out before the mortal armies, who had just seen each other in the growing light and were working themselves up to charge, the way the monkeys do. They fell silent when Sarpa and I appeared, and clear in the morning they heard the voices of our men, because we couldn't help singing now, the ancient song, and it welled up so beautiful behind

Sarpa's voice as he shouted for them to lay down their arms and go home!

Oh, mortal man, you'd have thought they'd listen to him, in that cold morning when the sun was just rising and making the high snow red as blood, lighting the meadows up green, reaching bright fingers down through deeps of blue air to touch their thatched roofs and palisade points with gold. So brief their lives are in this glorious world, you'd think they'd have grabbed at any excuse not to make them briefer.

But the one side jeered and the other side screamed, and the next thing I knew I had a spear sticking out of my leg.

I swear, it felt good. The suspense was over.

They charged, and were at each other's throats in less time than it takes to say it. So Budu gave the order.

I just shoved Sarpa up into a tree, drew my axes, and waded in.

You can't imagine the pleasure, mortal. It would be wrong, anyway; that joy is reserved to us, forbidden to the likes of you. War is *the* Evil, and we make war on war, we strike that wickedness into bloody pulp! The little bone bubbles burst under our axes and the gray matter of their arrogance and presumption flies, food for crows.

Oh, it was over too soon. There'll always be those who get the lesson at the last minute, but once we've shown them what true evil is they do get it, and throw down their weapons and scream their repentance on their knees. Those we spared; those we accorded mercy. Budu himself herded the terrified survivors into a huddle, and stood guard while we mopped up.

I was stringing together a necklace of ears I'd taken when I spotted Rook at the edge of the battlefield, weeping. I was feeling so friendly I almost went over and patted him on the back, with the idea of saying something to cheer him up; but they don't see things the way we do, the Preservers. And seeing him put me in mind of Sarpa, and when I looked around for the Facilitator, damned if he wasn't still up in the tree where I'd left him.

So I went over and offered him a helpful hand down, but he drew back at the sight of all the blood on it. I can't blame him. I was red to the elbows, actually. Sarpa was so pale he looked green, staring at the field as though he'd never be able to close his eyes again.

I told him it was all right, that the slaughter was over. He just looked down at me and asked me how I could do such things.

Well, I had to laugh at that. It's my duty! Who couldn't love doing his duty? It's the best work in the world, mortal, in the best cause: seeing that Evil is punished and Good protected. I told him so, and he said it was obscene; I replied that when the mortals took it into their heads to usurp our jobs, that would be obscene. Sarpa didn't say anything to that, just scrambled awkwardly down and staggered out on the field.

Maybe he shouldn't have done that. The boys were still having a little fun, taking heads that weren't too smashed and cutting off other things that took their fancies, and Sarpa took one look and doubled over, vomiting. The poor guy was a Preserver at heart, after all. The problem was, this was the big dramatic moment when he was supposed to address the surviving mortals of each tribe and point out how disobeying him had brought them to this sorry state.

I told him to pull himself together. Budu, kind of impatient, sent over a runner to ask if the Facilitator was ready to give his speech, and I tried to drag Sarpa along but he'd take a few steps and start retching again, especially when he saw the women lying dead. I hoisted him up on my shoulders to give him a ride, but he got sick again, right in my hair, which the other guys in my unit thought was hilarious; they stopped stacking corpses to point and laugh.

I growled at them and set Sarpa down. He put his hands over his face, crying like a baby. It was hopeless. I looked over at Budu and shrugged, holding out my hands in a helpless kind of way. The old man shook his head, sighing.

In the end, Budu was the one who made the speech, rounding up what was left of the two tribes and penning them together to listen to him.

It wasn't a long speech, no flowers of rhetoric such as Sarpa might have come up with. Budu just laid it out for them, simple and straight. From now on, they were all to live together in peace. They would intermarry and have children. There would be no more cannibalism. There would be no more fighting. The penalty for disobedience would be death.

Then Budu told them that we were going, and they were to bury what we'd left them of their dead. He warned them, though, that we were only going up the mountain, above the tree line into the mist, and we'd be watching them always from the high places.

And we did. We were up here thirty years. It turned out to be a good thing for us, too, because while we were overseeing the integration of the two tribes, Budu worked out a proposal for our masters.

I told you he'd studied their future history. He knew what kind of an opening they needed, and he gave them one. He pointed out the nearly universal existence of places we could fit in the mortals' mythology. Not just of your village, mortal; every village there is, anywhere.

Legends of gods, or giants or trolls or demons, who live up somewhere high and bring judgment on mankind. Sometimes terrible, sometimes benign, but not to be screwed with, ever! Sometimes they're supposed to live on one specific mountain, like this one; sometimes the story gets garbled and they're thought to live in the clouds, or the sky. Someplace *up*. Hell, there's even a story about a big man with a beard who lives at the North Pole, who rewards and punishes children. I think he's called Satan . . . or was it Nobodaddy? It doesn't matter.

Anyway, Budu showed our masters that his proposal fit right in with recorded history, was in fact vital to the development of mortal religion. And, while I understand they don't approve of religion much up there in the future, they do like to be absolutely sure that history rolls along smoothly. Messing with causality scares them.

What was his proposal, mortal? Come on, can't you think? What if I give you three guesses? No?

Well, Budu said that since civilization was still a little shaky on its legs, our masters needed to keep us around a while as a peacekeeping force. We'd go to each little community and lay down the law, or give them law if they didn't have it: no eating each other, no murder, don't inbreed, don't steal. Basic stuff. Then we'd run patrols and administer justice when and as needed, and contain any new mortal aggression that might threaten to wipe out humanity before it could become established. The final clever touch was that he signed Sarpa's name to it.

The masters accepted that proposal, mortal. It's bought us generations of time, even with Marco's idiot rebellion. The masters may not have trusted us anymore, but they still needed us.

And it worked for their good, too; it certainly got *your* village established. You wouldn't be here now if not for what we did that day, on that bloody field. And neither would our masters, and they know it.

We watched your fathers, from up here in the rocks and the snow, until we could be certain they wouldn't backslide again. Then Budu pulled the Fifth Infantry out, all but three of us, me and Bouncer and Longtooth, and we watched over your little valley down the long centuries while he went off to give law to other mortals.

But time marched on, and eventually Bouncer got reassigned somewhere else, and later on Longtooth was transferred out too. Now there's only me.

And the word's just come down from the top, mortal: they're sending me back to my old unit, after all this time. I'll see battle again, I'll serve under the old man! My hands will steam with the blood of sinners. It'll be wonderful! I've gotten so tired of sitting up here, freezing my ass off. If you'd climbed this mountain a day later than you did, you'd have missed out on your chance to get the Truth. Life's funny, isn't it? Death is even funnier.

The words and gestures cease, as the old monster settles back on his haunches, momentarily lost in a happy dream. The boy watches him. Terrified as he is, he cannot help wondering whether his host isn't something of a fool. It has of course occurred to him, as he listened unwilling to this story, that people as clever as the Time Shamans must have long since found some way of outwitting their servants. How can the creature trust his masters? How can he not know that times change?

For even in his village below, where there are still those who can remember glimpsing God, skepticism is blooming. Nowadays children are frightened into good behavior by the old stories, but not men. Once nobody would have dared climb this mountain, seek out this cave; it would have been sacrilegious. Yet the boy's friends had laughed at him when he'd set out for the mountain, and the village elders had just shrugged, smiling, and watched him go.

The boy is musing to himself, thinking of the methods fabled heroes had always used to defeat ogres, and wondering what sort of magical devices the Time Shamans might have employed, when he becomes aware that the old monster has turned his pale eyes on him again. Flat Top's expression has lost its warmth. He looks remote, stern, sad.

The boy feels a chill go down his spine, wondering if his thoughts have been read somehow. The giant extends one of his eloquent hands and picks up a stone axe. He runs his thumb along its scalloped edge. Holding the boy's gaze with his own, he lays the axe across his knees and resumes their conversation:

. . . But enough about me.

I want to hear your story now, mortal man. I want to know if you're one of the righteous. You'll tell me everything you've ever done, your whole life story, and then I'll judge you. Take as long as you like. My patience is limitless.

The boy gulps, wondering how convincingly he can lie.

As I write this, a new portrait of Shakespeare has surfaced. The provenance seems airtight; carbon dating, materials and techniques all check out; and, best of all, he looks like the guy in the Droeshout engraving, only younger, sexier, and with more hair. If this isn't a fake, then it's clearly a Company job, and my guess is this is the portrait from which the Droeshout engraving was made. "Here, this is the only picture we have of him, but it's twenty years old; give him a solemn expression and less hair, okay?"

And Bard-worshippers everywhere toss their sweaty nightcaps in the air and cry "Huzzah," not surprisingly. But what does surprise me is the hostile—as opposed to healthily skeptical—attitude of certain academics. That we should still care how Shakespeare the Man looked infuriates them. They see it as decadent, an unhealthy preoccupation with celebrity. Shakespeare's work is so great that we cheapen it, apparently, by any attempt to know its creator; better to treat the plays as great and mysterious works of art that have come to us out of nowhere, authorless, and reinterpret them on our own terms.

This seems like rank academic Von Danikenism to me. An ordinary mortal man created something wonderful and immortal; and I'd like to see his face. I like the little human details.

◆ ◆ ◆

The Dust Enclosed Here

"HE NEVER WORE A RED DOUBLET IN HIS LIFE!" Susanna had sounded outraged. Hastening to smooth her anger, the stranger's voice had followed: "An you wish it painted, good lady, 'twill look best in red. Consider! 'Tis not the man you dress, but the monument for posterity. And, Mistress Hall, Preeves and Sons have plied our trade this many a year and we know what looks well in a memorial. Think of the dark church, ay, and the old wood, and this splendid funerary bust gleaming from the shadows in—gray? No, no, Mistress, it must be a goodly scarlet, granting your dear father a splendor like the setting sun!"

Will's sun was setting. His son down below the horizon and he'd follow soon enough himself. He had wadded the sheet between his fingers irritably, wishing they'd go have their hissed argument elsewhere. No, no peace yet; Susanna had drawn back the curtain, letting in the blinding light while a shabby fellow in a puke-colored coat peered at him, respectful as though he were already dead, and sketched in a book the rough cartoon to impose on a marble bust blank.

"Christ Jesu," Will had muttered, closing his eyes. When he'd opened his eyes again, preparing to give them his best offended glare, he was surprised to discover they were gone and it was night. Nothing but low coals to light the room, with a blue flame crawling on them. And then the shadow had loomed against the light, and he'd turned his head expecting it was John—

That was the last memory! The strange doctor who'd come for his soul, or at least it had seemed so. The stranger had bent swiftly, thrusting something cold into his face. He'd felt a sharp pain in his nose and

95

then a tearing between his eyes, sparks of fire, fathomless darkness . . .

Will put his nervous hand up now to stroke the bridge of his nose, imagining he felt sympathetic pain. There was no real pain, he knew. No real hand or nose, either, but if he thought about that for long he'd panic again. Mastering himself, he paced the little tiring room (or what he pretended was his tiring room) and waited for his cue.

Here it came now, the sudden green orb in his vision. He felt the pull and was summoned like the ghost he was, through the insubstantial curtain into the light, where swirling dust motes coalesced into his hologrammatic form.

". . . so give a big welcome to Mr. William Shakespeare!" cried Caitlin gamely, indicating him with an outflung hand as she stepped aside for him. She wore an antique costume, the sort of gown his grandmothers might have worn. Three people, the whole of his audience, applauded with something less than enthusiasm. He gritted his teeth and smiled brilliantly, bowed grandly with flourishes, wondering what he'd ever done to be consigned to this particular Hell.

"God give ye all good day, good ladies, good gentleman!" he cried.

The lumpen spectators regarded him.

"Doth thou really be-eth Shakespeareth?" demanded the man, grinning, in the flat Lancashireish accent Will had come to understand was *American.*

"As nearly he as cybertechnology may revive and represent, good sir!" Will told him, and Caitlin made a face, her usual signal meaning: Keep it simple for the groundlings. He nodded and went on:

"I am, sir, an insubstantial hologram. Yet my form is drawn in forensic reconstruction from my mortal corpse exact, to show how I was when I lived. Yea, and I have been programmed with quotes from my works for your entertainment, and my personality hath been extrapolated from the best conjecture of scholars."

Though he suspected that last was a flat lie; it seemed to him that his owners (gentlemen of a company calling itself Jupiter Cyberceuticals) must somehow have captured his memories if not his soul, in that last minute of his life, and held them prisoner now in this wooden O. However, he said what they had programmed him to say.

"So do you, um, find it really strange being here in the future?" asked one of the women. She spoke politely enough, but it was a question he'd heard at nearly every performance since his revival.

Will kept the smile in place and replied, "Ay, indeed, madam, most strange. When I do hear that humankind hath nowadays built cities on the Moon, nay, even on Mars, truly I think this is an age of wonders indeed." The programming that he wore like chains prompted him to go on and make certain low jokes about how he wished his era had had a cure for baldness, but he exerted his will and refused. Caitlin wrung her hands.

"What do you think of your Prince Hank?" inquired the other woman, smirking archly, and Will accessed the data on the latest juicy scandal among the royals. He smirked right back at her and stroked his beard.

"Well, truly, good lady, to paraphrase mine own First Part of Henry the Fourth: right sadly must our poor queen see riot and dishonour stain the brow of her young Harry!"

They giggled in appreciation. Encouraged, he went on:

"Belike he doth but imitate the sun, who doth permit the base contagious clouds to smother up his beauty from the world, that, when he please again to be himself, being wanted, he may be more wondered at by breaking through the foul and ugly mists—"

No; he'd lost them. His sensors noted their complete incomprehension, though they were smiling and applauding again. He just smiled back and bowed, wishing he had a set of juggler's clubs or a performing dog.

"I thank ye! I humbly thank ye. What would ye, now, good ladies? What would you, now, sir?"

They blinked, their smiles fading.

"What about a sonnet?" he suggested in desperation.

"Okay," agreed the man.

He was programmed to give them the one catalogued as the Eighteenth, and for once he didn't feel like substituting another.

"Shall I compare thee to a summer's day?" he declaimed. "Thou art more lovely and more temperate . . ." He gave the rest in a performance so widely gestured and so antic even Will Kempe would have winced at it for being over the top, but it held their attention at least.

"That was neat," volunteered the man, when the recitation had ended.

"Many thanks. That sonnet, with selected others, is available in the Gifte Shoppe off the lobby, in both ring holo and standard format," he informed them. Caitlin nodded approvingly. The commercials must not be omitted, and that was one of the few things on which he agreed with his owners.

"Does the Gifte Shoppe sell Fruit Chew bars too?" inquired one of the ladies.

"Yea, madam, it doth," he told her, and she turned to her companions.

"I'm starving. Do you want to. . . ?"

"Yeah," the others chorused, nodding, and they turned away and made for the exit. Courtesy wasn't entirely dead in this latest age, however; at the door the man turned back and waved.

"Thanks, and—um . . . Goodbyeth thee!"

Will smiled and waved back. "Now God blight thy knave's stones with poxy sores, most noble sir," he murmured sotto voce, noting with relief that it was six o'clock. The Southwark Museum was about to close for the day.

"Our revels now are ended!" he shouted, as the big clock struck across the river.

"Mr. Shakespeare," said Caitlin hesitantly, "You're supposed to follow the script. You know they really do want you to make those jokes about your hair. People like to laugh."

"Then let 'em drag Dicky Tarleton from his grave, and set him in this bear pit," snarled Will. "There was a man of elegant jest, God He knows. Or let in a little mongrel dog to piss my leg, what sayest thou? They'll laugh right heartily then."

"We don't have dogs anymore," Caitlin explained. "Not since—"

"Since Beast Liberation, ay, I know it well. Nor canst thou give them Jack Falstaff for merriment, since he is banished, with all the other children of mine invention." Will collapsed into a sitting position on the stage, staring up at the empty galleries of the Globe Restored.

"I'm really sorry about that, Mr. Shakespeare, but I explained to you about the List," said Caitlin, referring to the database of proscribed and immoral literature published annually by the Tri-Worlds Council for Integrity.

"Even so you did," Will admitted. "And rather I had rotted in the earth this many a year than fret away eternity in such a dull, spiteful and Puritan age. What though my plays won't please? I take no censorship ill; there was ever a Master of the Revels spying over my shoulder lest I write an offense. But if they would let me give them a new piece, why, then! There's fine dramatic matter in these new times. That men might seek their fortunes not in mere Virginia colonies, but on Mars— God's bones, what a wonder! Or a play of the Mountains of the Moon, what say you?" He swung his sharp stare down to her eyes.

"I wish you could," said Caitlin miserably, looking away from his gaze. She had gotten this job in the first place because she had a degree in history and longed, with all her unwise heart, to have been born in the romantic past. "I don't make the policy, Mr. Shakespeare. I'm sorry all your plays were condemned. If it wasn't for the tourist income the Borough Council wouldn't even let you do your songs and sonnets."

" 'The Revenge of Kate,' " Will said slyly, framing a playbill in the air with his hands. "Wherein Petruchio himself is tamed, how like you that? That'll please, surely, and how if there were a mild Jew and a meek harmless Moor to boot? Nor no lusts nor bawdiness, nor any cakes nor ale, nor battles, and they shall ride no horses, out of melting compassion for the poor jades. Nay, more! There shall be a part set to be signed in dumb-show for the, what's the new word? Ay, the hearing-impaired!"

"I wish you could," Caitlin repeated, and he saw that she was near tears, and sighed.

"Go thy ways, girl," he said. "Grant me oblivion."

He stuck out his arms theatrically, as though being pinioned to a rack, and held the pose as she flicked the switch that shut him off for the night. Without illumination the dust motes vanished, settled.

So accustomed had he grown to this routine, over the five years he had been an exhibit in the museum, that he nearly died a second time when he found himself unexpectedly *on* in the middle of the night. He leaped to his feet and stared around him in the dark.

"How now?" he stammered. "What, ho! Who's about?"

But there was no sound. The glowing clock told him it was midnight, and he felt a moment's uneasiness until the absurdity of the scene occurred to him: insubstantial ghost frightened of the witching hour! Here came the distant bell, the little tune that preceded long-tolling twelve. He heard it out, pacing the stage.

"I am thy father's spirit," he intoned, and then dropped his voice an octave. *"I* am thy father's spirit, ay, better:

> "I am thy father's spirit,
> Doomed for a certain term to walk the night
> And for the day confined to fast in fires,
> Till the foul crimes done in my days of nature
> Are burnt and purged away . . ."

He paused at the edge of the stage. Tentatively he extended a foot beyond the light, out of the range of the holoprojector's bright beam. His foot vanished. This was startling, but there was no pain; and after drawing his foot back and seeing it reappear unaltered, he tried with his hand. It vanished too, and came back obligingly when he withdrew it.

"Now, by God's will . . ." he said. He turned his face up toward the painted Heavens. "Almighty Father, can I escape this vile purgatory? Are mine own sins burnt and purged away? Oh, let it be so!"

Backing up for a running start, he sprinted forward and hurtled hopeful into the darkness. He landed with a crash in the middle of the groundling area and lay there a moment, cursing imaginatively.

Rising, he put up his hands to dust himself off and realized that he couldn't see them, though he was still palpable. He cast a baleful stare at the cone of light on the stage, empty now but for a few motes of glittering dust.

"That's well," he said sarcastically. "First my mortal substance and now my form. Am I to be no more than memory?"

Nobody answered him. He climbed up on stage again and found that his image returned when he stood there. He amused himself for a while making bits of his body disappear. It occurred to him he might explore the Southwark Museum and this cheered him considerably until he found that, insubstantial or not, he was unable to leave the perimeter of the Globe Restored; whereat he said something to which Sir Edmund Tilney would certainly have objected.

All the rest of that night he prowled the silent galleries, a shadow among shadows, raging at his immortality.

Over the next six months the phenomenon occurred, with increasing frequency: sudden and unbidden consciousness when he had been manifestly shut off, and with it a gradual widening of his ability to range. He found himself able, in time, to venture out to the Gifte Shoppe and snack bar areas if he remained close to the wall through which ran the power and communications cables. There was nothing especially to interest him out there, since he was incapable of eating and the Gifte Shoppe had no writing materials, nor was he substantial enough to have stolen any had there been. Still, it was a little freedom.

The day things truly changed for him began very badly indeed.

It was a day of the sort of weather the English plod through and ignore, but all others wisely shun, remaining in their hotels. Consequently no tourist vans pulled up before the Southwark Museum, and consequently Mr. Pressboard had the whole of the Globe Restored to himself when he arrived.

"Oh, dear," said Caitlin when she saw him coming, and flipped the switch that summoned Will. He materialized, started through the curtain and stopped in horror at the sight of Mr. Pressboard setting up his folding stool before the stage, as rain bounced and plinked on the forcefield above the thatching.

"Well, I see our most regular visitor is back again!" cried Caitlin in a bright false voice. "Welcome to the Globe Restored! We hope you'll enjoy yet another visit with the world-famous writer, Mr. William Shakespeare!"

"Except that he wasn't a writer," grunted Mr. Pressboard. "He was a butcher's boy."

Will's lip curled and Caitlin's laugh dopplered after her as she made for the exit.

"Well, you two will just have to work that out!" she said, giving Will a look of guilty apology. "I hope you'll just excuse me—I have to see about something."

"Oh, faithless," Will hissed after her, before dragging a smile on his face for Mr. Pressboard.

Mr. Pressboard was a retired person who believed, unshakably, that all of Will's stuff had really been written by the earl of Oxford. This belief was more than an article of faith for him; it was a cause. He wore, in the public streets, a sweatshirt and cap that proclaimed it. Vain for Will to deny the mysterious coded acrostic clues that were supposed to be hidden in the poems. Vain for him to insist, ever so politely, that there had been no vast and ridiculous conspiracy to conceal their true authorship. Mr. Pressboard had no life, and consequently had all the tedious time in the world to park himself in front of the stage and argue his case.

Today he was intent on demonstrating how no man with Will's paltry education could ever have written such masterful lines as, for example, "The gaudy, blabbing and remorseful day / Is crept into the bosom of the sea" and went on some two hours on this theme without pausing once. Will was pacing the stage repeating silently, *Be courteous; he paid at the door,* over and over, when a small boy wandered into the Globe.

He wore a yellow rain slicker and wellies, and his dun-fair hair was tousled from having been under the slicker's hood. From the snack bar he had obtained a Fruit Chew and stood now nibbling the granola off its surface as he watched Mr. Pressboard talk and talk and talk, and Will interject occasional "Hem" and "Er" sounds.

After fifteen minutes the boy grew bored with this and started wandering around, up into the galleries and climbing on the balustrades. He leaned far over them to peer at the paintings of Apollo and Mercury. When he had tired of that he descended to the groundling level and inspected the *trompe l'oeil* stonework. He craned his head back to study the painted heavens and looked longingly at the dummy cannon. Finally he approached Mr. Pressboard and, extending an index finger, poked him in the arm.

"Excuse me," he said. "Can it be my turn now?"

"Even if Sir Philip Sidney did—what?" Mr. Pressboard started and turned to stare at him. The boy stared back. His eyes were wide, and a very pale blue.

"Can it be my turn to talk to Mr. Shakespeare now?" the boy reiterated.

"Forsooth, good Master Pressboard, we must suffer young scholars to have their day, must we not?" Shakespeare exclaimed gleefully. Mr. Pressboard remained planted where he was, however, and frowned at the boy.

"I'm discussing something important, young man. Go away."

The boy backed off a pace, then dug in his heels. His pale stare became cold.

"But other people are supposed to get turns too, you know," he said, not taking his eyes from Mr. Pressboard's.

Abruptly: "Okay," said Mr. Pressboard, with an odd scared expression on his face. He got up, grabbed his folding stool and hurried for the exit. Will felt like turning a cartwheel. The boy looked up at him.

"He was really boring you, huh?" he said.

"To hot salt tears, lad," Will told him, dropping down to sit cross-legged on the edge of the stage. "God keep thee and bless thee. What's thy name?"

"You don't remember?" The boy looked disappointed. "It's Alec. I came here when I was five. Remember?"

"I see many, many folk, Alec, every day," Will explained. "Wherefore I pray you excuse me."

The boy nodded. "That's all right. There was a lot of kids that day. You sang us that song about the wind and rain and hay hoes."

"Ah! To be sure." Sweet Christ, someone who'd actually listened to him! Will smiled at the boy. "Dost thou like the Southwark Museum, Alec?"

"It's okay," said Alec. "Derek and Lulu wanted to be alone in the car so they gave me my credit disc and said I could buy anything I wanted in the Gifty Shoppy, as long as I stayed in here until it was lunchtime. I think they're having sex actually."

"Forsooth?" Will attempted, successfully, to keep a straight face. "And what hast thou bought in the Gifte Shoppe, lad?"

"Nothing much," Alec said. "It's all shirts and holocards and tea mugs with this place on them. I like things with ships on them. But I wanted to see how you were so I came in here. How are you doing? You were sad when I saw you before. Are you happier now?"

Will opened his mouth to sing the praises of this wonderful modern age when there were cities on the Moon and cures for baldness, but what he said was:

"No, boy. I am the saddest wretch that liveth, in this most unnatural life of mine."

"Oh. I'm sorry," Alec replied, coming close to lean on the stage. "What's wrong?"

"I am a slave here, lad," Will replied.

"What's a slave?"

"A living soul kept as property by others, to labor for them eternally."

"But I thought you were dead a long time ago," said Alec.

"And yet I speak and reason, imprisoned within this cloven pine." Will stared into the boy's eyes, raised his clenched fists to show the shackles on his imagination. "I live again, Alec, how I know not, and yet I cannot have the thing I need to live!"

"What's that?" Alec wanted to know.

"Dost thou know what a poet is, lad?"

"That's what you are," said Alec, "It means you make stories to watch. I think. Doesn't it?"

"Ay, lad, I made stories to watch. Out of earth and heaven I pulled the unknown, gave it form and made it speak, and men filled this Globe and marveled at it! And paid good money to marvel, too, mind, t'was a profitable endeavor. But my masters will have me make no shows now. I am the show, and strut here meaningless afore barren spectators." Will sagged forward as though pulled by the weight of his unseen chains.

"You mean you want to make more stories and they won't let you?" Alec looked outraged.

"Even so, lad."

"That's mean! You can't even make 'em in cyberspace?"

"Cyber *space?*" Will lifted his head and stared at the boy. "A space cybertechnological, you mean? Or what do you mean?"

"It's like—look. You're right here, but you're not really here," said Alec, pointing to him. "Where you really are is in the system. Where's your controls?"

"I know not—" Will held his hands wide, signifying bewilderment. Alec, pink with anger, was stamping along the front of the stage searching for something. At last he climbed up on the stage, ignoring the signs that forbade him doing so, and spotting the trap door that had once let ghosts rise out of the depths he fell to his knees beside it. Will scrambled to his feet and followed, looking down.

"I bet they're in here," said Alec. He reached into his coat and, looking around furtively, drew out a small case. It looked quite a bit like a thief's set of picklocks that Will had once seen in his less prosperous days. Alec noticed his astounded stare.

"Just my tools," he said in a small voice. "You won't tell?"

"Nay, boy, not I!" Will vowed. He watched as Alec lifted out the trap to reveal, not the hollow dark he had thought was below but a sort of shallow cavity full of winking lights and bright buttons. He was so surprised he got down on hands and knees beside Alec to look at it closely.

"God's bleeding wounds!"

"I have to be fast," Alec said, and manipulating some of the things in amid the lights he glanced up toward the ceiling. " 'Cos I'm not really supposed to do this, not to other people's machines anyway. Okay; now the guard cameras in here think I'm still standing down there talking to you. Sneaky, huh?" He grinned at Will.

"But what is this?" Will asked, pointing at the box of lights.

"This is—er—where you really are," said Alec, hesitantly, as though he thought it might hurt Will's feelings. "But you can pretend it's jewels we're going to steal or something," he added, talking out of the side of his mouth like a petty crook. "Piece of cake, see?"

Will just watched as Alec took out his tools and did things to the buttons and lights. Red letters flashed in Will's peripheral vision and he put up his hand in an impatient gesture, as though they were flies he might wave off, before the import of the words sank in on him.

SUMMON HUMAN ASSISTANCE! MEDICAL EMERGENCY!

The sensors he used to monitor his audience began to chatter at him in a panicky way, informing him that they detected violent seizure activity in Alec's brain. Will almost shouted for Caitlin, but paused. He had seen folk afflicted with the falling sickness, and Alec did not appear to be having any manner of fit. The boy's eyes were alert and focused, his hands steady, and he worked swiftly and without the least hesitation as the bright storm raged within his skull.

Will shrugged and dismissed the sensors' warning. He had long since observed that even in this fabulous future world, things occasionally malfunctioned. Especially marvels cybertechnological.

Presently Alec drew out something between tweezers. It looked like a tiny word in an unknown language, written in pure light.

"And that's it," he said thoughtfully, turning it this way and that. "Funny."

"What is it, in God's name?"

"It's your program," Alec replied. "You've got lots and lots in here, but they didn't give you very much to do. There's the new stuff you wrote yourself, that little winji bit there. Were you trying to bypass the holoemitter system?"

"I know not—" said Will, and then remembered his inexplicable nocturnal self-awareness. Had that been his own doing, by some means he couldn't name? Had his misery been enough to force his prison walls outward?

"It almost looks like you're a memory file from someplace else." The boy seemed puzzled. "This is a whole bunch of data. You could have a lot more functions, you know. You want to?"

Will had no idea what he meant, but just the thought of having any kind of choice made him feel like dancing.

"Ay, forsooth!"

"Okay," said Alec, and set the bright word back and made some alteration. What happened next even Will could never find words to describe adequately. Was there a silent sound? An invisible flash of light? A torrent of mathematical language forced itself into his head, and with it came strange comprehension. He rose on his knees, clutching his temples and gasping, while the boy closed up the trap and put away the little tools.

"So now," said Alec, "it'll be lots nicer. You can make stuff in here."

"Stuff?" said Will, getting unsteadily to his feet. "What stuff, lad?"

"Whatever you want there to be," said Alec. He shrugged. "You know. You just write what you want."

What he meant by *write* had nothing to do with quills and parchment, but it didn't matter. Will was at last beginning to get a sense of the laws of this universe.

"Maybe write some chairs or something so you can sit down, yeah?" Alec gestured at the bare stage.

"Or cloud-capp'd towers," said Will, staring around. "Or gorgeous palaces!"

"Yeah." Alec nodded.

Will looked hard at him. "How canst thou do these things, child? What art thou?"

"Different," said Alec, squirming.

Will raised an eyebrow, remembering the abnormal cerebral activity his sensors had picked up. Shrewd as he was, he was unable to guess the whole truth; for his owners at Jupiter Cyberceuticals had not included any information on *genetic engineering* in his programming. After all, it was illegal to make an enhanced human being. Even a small one . . . because who knew what such a creature might do if it was allowed to grow up? It would be as unpredictable as—for example—an artificial intelligence built on a human memory file, which was an equally illegal creature.

But Jupiter Cyberceuticals did a lot of illegal things.

"Thou art some prodigy, with powers," speculated Will.

"Don't tell on me! I'd get in trouble if anybody found out." Alec looked pleadingly up at Will. "Nobody's supposed to be different, you see?"

"I know it well, ay," Will told him with feeling.

Alec started as the clock began to strike across the river. "Oh! I have to go now. It was really nice seeing you again, Mr. Shakespeare." He jumped down from the stage and ran for the exit, pausing long enough to turn and wave. "I hope that works. Bye-bye!"

He fled past Caitlin, who looked down at him in surprise as she came in.

"You're not allowed to run in here!" she called after him, and turned to Will. "Look, I'm awfully sorry about Mr. Pressboard. Who was that?"

"Verily one of the young-ey'd cherubins," said Will, throwing his deepest bow. He grinned like a fox.

Six hours sped by like so many elephantine years, leaden, dull, and ponderous, but Will could wait. He bore gracefully with a chartered busload of Scots who found fault with every aspect of *Macbeth,* and wanted an apology; he capered for an infant care class who had no idea who he was, and sang them his song about the wind and the rain. When the clock struck 6:00 at last he bid Caitlin a fond adieu. As she shut him off for the day, she observed to herself that he seemed much less moody than usual, though there was a disconcerting glitter in his eyes as he vanished from her sight.

Somehow present and conscious still, he watched her departure and waited. The lights were extinguished. The security system activated. Dark roaring rain and night closed over old London. He reached out a sinuous impalpable thread of his will—Ay! That was it, he was all Will now, and most himself being nothing but will!—to the surveillance cameras, bidding them see only shadows.

Then he willed the holoemitter on and gave it wider range than it had previously, and his Globe was full of light, like a bright craft venturing on the night ocean. Briefly he considered summoning a pen and inkhorn, but realized they were unnecessary now.

"I have a muse of fire!" Will cried, and wrote his will in code that blazed like lightning, sparkled like etched crystal. From the brightest heaven of invention he ordered a backdrop of lunar cities drawn in silverpoint, painted in ivory and gold and cloudy blue, outlandish spires and towers flying fluttering pennons against the eternal stars.

With clean hands he willed the light, and out of the spinning dust a simulacrum of Richard Burbage formed. He stood before Will in his prime, not yet run to fat, and there too were Ned Alleyn and Kempe and Armin, Heminges and Condell, Lowin and Crosse and Phillips with the rest. Attending on his will, they were in makeup and in costumes that fit too, coeval, awake, sober and on their marks, every man jack of 'em.

They looked around uncertainly.

"Why, Will, what's toward?" inquired Kempe, meek as you please.

"A rehearsal!" thundered Will. "And I will give thee thy lines extempore. *The Most Fantastical Comedy of Man on the Moon,* my masters!"

In September 1879, the fledgling novelist Robert Louis Stevenson, threadbare and ill, traveled to California. He had come in a gallant attempt to rescue a lady who, on his arrival, turned out not to need rescuing after all. He then fled lamenting into the wilderness, or to be more exact rented a buckboard and went on an ill-advised camping trip into the mountains above Monterey. Up there his illness worsened, and he lay delirious under an oak tree for three days and three nights.

What happened to Stevenson up there? Had he died at that point in his career, Treasure Island *would never have been written; neither would* The Strange Case of Dr. Jekyll and Mr. Hyde. *What came to him under that oak tree?*

Agatha Christie likewise vanished from human knowledge in 1926, only to reappear eleven days later without a word of explanation. Her silence on the subject, maintained for the rest of her long and successful life, still fascinates. Who met her on a lonely road, at a turning point in her career?

◆　◆　◆

The Literary Agent

THE OBJECT, HAD IT BEEN SEEN WHEN IT ARRIVED, might have been described as a cheap aluminum trunk. In fact it was not a trunk, nor was it made of aluminum, and it was certainly not cheap. Nor was there anyone present who might have seen or attempted to describe it. So much for the sound of a tree falling in the forest.

Nevertheless the Object *was* there, between one second and the next, soundless, spinning slowly and slower still until it wobbled to a gentle stop. For a moment after that nothing much happened. Clouds roiled past the Object, for it had arrived on the seaward face of a coastal mountain range. It sizzled faintly as moisture beaded upon it. Underneath it, ferns and meadow grasses steadily flattened with its unrelieved weight.

Then the lid flew back and from the chest's interior a cloud of yellow gas boiled away. A man sat up inside, unfolding with some pain from his coiled fetal position. He exhaled a long jet of yellow smoke, which was whipped away at once by the driving mountain wind. Retching, he pulled himself free and tumbled over the side of the Object, sprawling at his length beside it.

He lay perfectly still a while and then sat up, alert, apparently fully recovered from his ordeal. He groped in his vest pocket and pulled out what appeared to be a watch. Actually it *was* a sort of watch, certainly more so than the Object was a trunk. He consulted the timepiece and seemed satisfied, for he snapped it shut and got to his feet.

He appeared to be a man; actually he *was* a sort of man, though human men do not travel in trunks or breathe stasis gas. He was of compact build, stocky but muscular, olive-skinned. His eyes were hard as jet buttons. They had a cheerful expression, though, as he squinted into the wind and viewed the fog walling up the miles from the bay of Monterey.

Leaning over into the Object he drew out the coat of his brown worsted suit, and slipped it on easily. He shot his cuffs, adjusted his tie, closed the lid of the Object that was not a trunk—but for the sake of convenience we'll call it a trunk from here on—and lifted it to his shoulders, which gave him some difficulty, for the thing had no handles and was as smooth as an ice cube.

Clutching it awkwardly, then, he set off across the meadow. His stride was meant to be purposeful. The date was September 8, 1879.

He followed a wagon road that climbed and wound. He clambered through dark groves of ancient redwoods, green and cold. He crossed bare mountainsides, wide open to the cloudy air, where rocks like ruins stood stained with lichen. None of this made much of an impression on him, though, because he wasn't a scenery man and the thing that we have agreed to call a trunk kept slipping from his shoulder.

Finally he set it down with what used to be called, in that gentler age, an oath.

"This is for the birds," he fumed.

The trunk made a clicking sound and from no visible orifice spewed out a long sheet of yellowed paper. He tore it off, read what was written there, and looked for a moment as though he wanted to crumple and fling it away. Instead he took a fountain pen from an inside coat pocket. Sitting on the smooth lid of the trunk he scribbled a set of figures on the paper and carefully fed it back into the slot that you could not have seen if you had been there.

When he had waited long enough to determine that no reply was forthcoming, he shouldered his burden again and kept climbing, quicker now because he knew he was near his destination. The road pushed up into a steadily narrowing canyon, and the way grew ever steeper and overhung with oak trees.

At last he saw the dark outline of a wagon in the gathering dusk, up ahead where the road ended. He made out the shape of a picketed horse grazing, he heard the sound of creek water trickling. A few swift paces brought him to his destination, where he set his burden down and looked at the figure he had traveled so far to see, sprawled under the tree by the coals of a dying fire. He snapped off a dry branch and poked up the flames. He did not need additional light to see the object of his journey, but courtesy is important in any social encounter.

The fire glittered in the eyes of the man who lay there, wide-set eyes that stared unseeing into the branches above him. A young man with a long doleful face, shabbily dressed, he lay with neither coat nor blanket in a drift of prickly oak leaves. He had yet to write *The Strange Case of Dr. Jekyll and Mr. Hyde* or *Treasure Island,* and from the look of him it was unlikely he'd live long enough to do so.

The other scanned him and shook his head disapprovingly. Malnutrition, tubercular lesions, malaria, a hideous case of eczema on both hands. "Tsk tsk tsk." He drew a little case from his pocket. Something he sprayed on the scabbed hands, something he injected into one wrist. He peeled the back from a transdermal patch and stuck it just behind the young man's ear.

Then he turned his attention to the fire again. He built it up to a good blaze, filled the tin kettle at the creek and set more water to boil. It had not yet begun to steam when the young man twitched violently and rose up on his elbows. He stared at his visitor, who put his hands on his trouser-knees and leaned over him with a benevolent smile.

"Robert Louis Stevenson! How's it going?"

"Whae the hell are you?" croaked he.

"Allow me to introduce myself: Joseph X. Machina." The other grabbed Stevenson's limp hand and shook it heartily. "At your service, even if I am just a hallucination. Would you like some tea? It's about ready."

The young man did not reply, but stared at him with eyes of extraordinary size and luminosity. His visitor, meanwhile, rummaged amid his belongings in the back of the wagon.

"Say, you didn't pack any tea. But then you didn't really come up here to camp, did you? You ought to do something about that death wish of yours." He found a tin cup and carried it back to the fire. "Luckily, I always carry a supply with me." He sat down and from an inner pocket produced a teabag.

"What's that?" inquired Stevenson.

"Orange pekoe, I think." The other peered at the tag. "Yeah. Now, here's your tea, and let's make you nice and comfortable—" He found Stevenson's coat, made a pillow of it and propped up his head. "There we are."

He resumed his seat on the trunk and drew from the same inner pocket a bar of chocolate in silver foil. He unwrapped one end of it and took a bite.

"Now, Mr. Stevenson, I have a proposition for you," he said. Stevenson, who had been watching him in increasing fascination, began to laugh giddily.

"It seems I'm a popular man tonight," he gasped. "Is the trunk to carry off my soul? Is the Accuser of the Brethren different in California? I'd have wagered you'd look more like a Spanish grandee in these parts.

Do you change your coat with the times? Of course you would, wouldn't you? Yet you haven't quite the look of a Yankee. In any case, *Retro, Sathanas!"*

"No, no, no, don't worry. I'm not that guy. I'm merely a pleasant dream you're having. Here, have some of this." He broke off and handed a square of chocolate to Stevenson, who accepted it with a smirk.

"Sweeties from Hell!" The idea sent him into a giggling fit that started him coughing. The other watched him closely. When he recovered he pulled himself up on his elbow and said, "Well then—you haven't any cigarettes, I suppose."

"Sorry, I don't smoke."

"Lucifer not smoke?" This time he laughed until he wept, wiping his eyes on his frayed sleeves. Consumptives do not wipe their eyes on their handkerchiefs. "Oh, I hope I remember this when I wake. What an idea for a comic narrative."

"Actually that was sort of what I wanted to talk to you about," Joseph went on imperturbably, finishing the last of his chocolate in a bite.

"Is that so?" Stevenson lurched into a sitting position. He grasped the cup of tea in his trembling hands, warming them.

"Absolutely. Remember, this is all part of a dream. And what is your dream, Louis, your most cherished dream? To make a success of this writing business, isn't it? Financial independence so you can win this American lady you've come mooning after. Well, in this dream you're having right now, you've met a man from the future—that's me—and I've come back through time to tell you that you've *got* it, baby. All you wanted. Everything. Mrs. Osbourne too."

"What nonsense. I'm dying penniless, unknown, and (I fear) unloved." Stevenson's eyes grew moist. "I came such a long way to do it, too. She sent me away! What does *she* care if I expire in this wilderness?"

"Louis, Louis, work with me, all right?" Joseph leaned forward, looking earnest. *"This is your dream.* This dream says you're going to become a famous author. You write slam-bang adventure stories."

"I write abominably derivative fiction. The only good stuff's from life, my essays and the travel books."

"Come on, Louis, let's make this bird fly. You'll write adventure novels about the sea and historical times. People love them. You're a hit. You're bigger than Sir Walter Scott, all right?"

"He couldn't write a lucid sentence if his life had depended on it," Stevenson sneered. "Oh, this is all the rankest self-conceit anyway."

"Then what will it hurt you to listen? Now. I represent the Chronos

Photo-Play Company. Let me explain what a photo-play is. We have
patented a method of, uh, making magic-lantern pictures into a sort of
effect of moving tableaux, if you can grasp that. Maybe you've read
about the cinematograph? Oh, gee, no, you haven't." Joseph consulted
his timepiece. "You'll just miss it. Never mind— So, in the future, we
have these exhibitions of our photo-plays and people pay admission to
come in and watch them, the same way they'd watch a live play or an
opera, with famous players and everything. But since we don't have to
pay live actors or even move scenery, the profit margin for the exhibitor
is enormous. See?"

Stevenson gaped at him a moment before responding. "I was wrong.
I apologize. You may or may not be the Devil, but you're most assuredly
a Yankee."

"No, no, I'm a dream. Anyway. People are crazy about these photo-
plays, they'll watch anything we shoot. We've adapted all the great
works of literature already. Shakespeare, Dickens, all those guys. So
now, my masters are looking for new material, and since you're *such* a
famous and successful writer they sent me to ask if you'd be interested
in a job."

"I see." Stevenson leaned back, stretching out his long legs and
crossing them. "Your masters want to adapt one of my wonderful adventure stories for these photo-plays of theirs?"

"Uh, actually, we've already done everything you wrote. Several
times."

"I should damned well hope I got royalties, then!"

"Oh, sure, Louis, sure you did. You're not only famous, you're rich.
Anyway what my masters had in mind was you coming up with something completely *new.* Never-before-seen. Just like all your other stuff,
you know, with that wonderful Robert Louis Stevenson magic, but different. Exclusively under contract for them."

"You mean they want me to write a play?" Stevenson looked
intrigued.

"Not exactly. We don't have the time. This dream isn't going to last
long enough for you to do that, because it's a matter of historical record
that you're only going to lie here another—" Joseph consulted his timepiece again, "—forty-three hours before you're found and nursed back
to health. No, see, all they need you to do is develop a story *treatment*
for them. Four or five pages, a plot, characters. You don't have to do the
dialogue; we'll fill that out as we film. We can claim it's from long-lost
notes found in a locked desk you used to own, or something."

"This is madness." Stevenson sipped his tea experimentally.

"Delirium. But what have you got to lose? All you have to do is come up with a concept and develop it. You don't even have to write it down. I'll do that for you. And to tell you the honest truth—" Joseph leaned down confidentially, "—this is a specially commissioned work. There's this wealthy admirer of yours in the place I come from, and he's willing to pay anything to see a *new* Robert Louis Stevenson picture."

"Wouldn't he pay more for a whole novel? I could make one up as we go along and dictate the whole thing to you, if we've got two more days here. You'd be surprised at how quickly stories unfold when the muse is with me." Stevenson squinted thoughtfully up at the stars through the branches of the oak tree.

Joseph looked slightly embarrassed. "He's . . . not really much of a reader, Louis. But he loves our pictures, and he's rich."

"You stand to make a tidy sum out of this, then."

"Perceptive man, Mr. Stevenson."

Stevenson's eyes danced. "And you'll pay me millions of money, no doubt."

"You can name your price. Money is no object."

"Dollars, pounds or faery gold?" Stevenson began to chuckle and Joseph chuckled right along with him in a companionable manner.

"You've got the picture, Louis. It's a dream, remember? Maybe I've got a trunkful of gold doubloons here, or pieces of eight. I'm authorized to pay you *anything* for an original story idea."

"Very well then." Stevenson gulped the tea down and flung the cup away. "I want a cigarette."

The other man's chuckle stopped short.

"You want a cigarette?"

"I do, sir."

"You want— Jeepers, Louis, I haven't got any cigarettes!"

"How now? No cigarettes? This is my dream and I can have anything I want. No cigarette, no story." Stevenson laced his slender fingers together and smiled.

"Look, Louis, there's something you should know." Joseph bent forward seriously. "Cigarettes are not really good for your lungs. Trust me. They'll make your cough worse, honest. Now, look, I've got gold certificates here for you."

"It's cigarettes or nothing, I say."

"But I tell you I can't *get* any—" Joseph seized the hair at his temples and pulled in vexation. Then he halted, as if listening to an inner voice. "Hell, what can I lose?"

He opened the lid of the trunk and brought out his pad of yellow lined paper. Casting a reproachful glance at Stevenson he scribbled something down and fed his message into the invisible slot. Almost immediately the reply emerged. He scanned it, wrote something more and fed it back. Another quick reply.

Stevenson watched all this with amusement. "He's got a wee devil in the box poking his letters back out," he speculated.

"All I want is to make the man happy," Joseph retorted. "Fame, I offer him. Riches, too. What does he do? He turns capricious on me. Lousy mortal." He read the next communication and his eyes narrowed. Hastily he backed away from the trunk, putting a good eight feet between himself and it.

"What's amiss now?" inquired Stevenson. "Old Nick's in a temper, doubtless."

"I'd cover my ears if I were you," replied the other through gritted teeth. As if on cue the trunk gave a horrific screech. It shook violently; there was a plume of foul smoke; there was one last convulsive shudder—then a cigarette dropped from the orifice, very much the worse for wear, mashed flat and in fact on fire.

Joseph ran forward and snatched it up. He blew out the flame and handed the smoldering mess to Stevenson.

"There," he snapped. "It's even lit for you. Satisfied?"

Stevenson just stared at it, dumfounded.

"Smoke the damned thing!" thundered the other. Stevenson took a hasty drag while Joseph bent over the trunk and did some diagnostic procedures.

"Did we break Hell's own postbox?" ventured Stevenson after a moment.

"I hope not," the other man snarled. "And I hope you're doing some thinking about story ideas."

"Right." Stevenson inhaled again. The cigarette did not draw well. He eyed it critically but thought it best not to complain. "Right, then. What sort of story shall we give them? A romance, I dare say."

"Sex is always popular," conceded Joseph. He stood, brushed off his knees and took up the yellow lined pad. "Go on."

"Right. There's a woman. She's a beauty, but she labors under some kind of difficulty. Perhaps there's a family curse, but *she's* pure as the snows of yesteryear. And there's a fellow to rescue her, a perfect gentle knight as it were, but he's knocked about the world a bit. Not a hapless boy at any rate. And there's an older fellow, a bad 'un, a dissolute rake. Byronic."

"Not very original, if you'll pardon my saying so," remarked Joseph, though he did not stop writing.

"No, I suppose not. How many ways are there to write a romance? Let's make it a woman who's the bad 'un. Tries to lure the hero from the heroine. There's a thought! A sorceress. Metaphorically speaking. Perhaps even in fact. Wouldn't that be interesting?"

"Sounding good." The other man nodded as he wrote. "Where's all this happening, Louis?"

"France. Medieval France."

"So this is a costume drama."

"A what? Oh. Yes, silks and velvets and whitest samite. Chain mail and miniver. And the sea, I'm sure, with a ship standing off the coast signaling mysteriously. To the beauteous wicked dame, who's a spy! Build this around some historical incident. Put the Black Prince in it. Maybe she's a spy for him and the hero's a Frenchman. No, no, no—the British public won't take that. On the other hand, this is for the Yankees, isn't it?"

"Sounding good, Louis, sounding really good." The other tore off his written sheet with a flourish. "Let's just feed it into the moviola and see what winds up on the cutting-room floor."

"I'm sure that means something to you, but I'm damned if I know what," remarked Stevenson, watching as the sheet was pulled into the trunk. "How does it do that?"

Joseph did not answer, because the sheet came spewing back at once. He pulled it forth and studied it, frowning.

"What's wrong? Don't they like it?"

"Oh, er, they're crazy about it, Louis. It's swell. They just have a few suggestions. A few changes they want made."

"They want something rewritten?"

"Uh . . . the Middle Ages is out. France is out. Knights in armor stuff is expensive to shoot. They want to know if you can make it the South Seas. Give it some of that wonderful tropical ambiance you do so well."

"I've never been in the South Seas," said Stevenson coldly. He remembered his cigarette and puffed at it.

"No, not yet, but that's all right. You can fake it. California's almost tropical, isn't it? Hot, anyway. Parts of it. That's the Pacific Ocean out there, right? Just write some palm trees into the scenery. Now, er, they want you to drop the girl and the guy. There's just no audience for pure sweethearts now. But they think the evil lady is fabulous. They think the story should mostly revolve around her. Lots of costume changes and bedroom scenes. She plays for power at the court of this Dark Lord guy. Black Prince, I mean."

"The Black Prince never went to the South Seas either, you know. He was a medieval Plantagenet."

"Whatever. I'm afraid the distinction is lost on them, Louis." Joseph gave a peculiar embarrassed shrug. "Historical accuracy is not a big issue here. If we're going to make it the South Seas he has to be something else anyway. Maybe some kind of witch doctor in a black helmet or something. They just liked the name, Black Prince, it's got a kind of ring to it."

"They sound like a supremely ignorant lot. Why don't they write their own bloody story?" Stevenson muttered. His airy humor was descending fast.

"Now, Louis, don't take it that way. They really love your stuff. They just need to tailor it to their audience a little, that's all."

"South Seas be damned." Stevenson leaned back. "Why shouldn't I write about what I know? If France isn't good enough for them, what about this country? I saw some grand scenery from the railway carriage. Now, wait! What about a true American romance? This has possibilities. Do you know, I saw a man threaten to shoot a railway conductor dead, just because he'd been put off the coach for being drunk and disorderly? Only in America. It's as good as the Montagues and Capulets, only with revolvers instead of rapiers. Prairies instead of pomegranate gardens. Picturesque barbarism. What about a hero who's kidnapped at birth and raised by Red Indians?"

"Well, it's been done, but okay." The other began to write again.

"And there's some additional obscurity to his birth . . . he's the son of a Scots lord."

"Gee, Louis, I don't know . . ."

"And his younger brother succeeds to the title but emigrates to America, fleeing punishment for a crime he did not commit. Or perhaps he did. More interesting character. Or perhaps—"

"Is there any sex in this?"

"If you like. The brothers fall in love with the same woman, will that suit you? In fact . . . the girl is the betrothed of the brother who emigrates. She follows him devotedly. While searching for him, she's kidnapped by the Red Indian band of whom her fiancé's brother is now chief. *He* falls in love with her. Claims her as his bride. Forced marriage takes place. She's terrified, but compelled by the mating rituals of man in his primal innocence."

"Oh, yeah, yeah, yeah, Louis!"

"Let's see them get *that* past the scribes and pharisees of popular taste," sneered Stevenson, and tossed the last fragment of his cigarette into the fire. "Meanwhile, the fugitive brother has become a frontiersman, with buckskin clothes, long rifle, and quaint fur cap. Gets word that his betrothed has gone missing. Goes in search of her (he's become an expert tracker too) and finds unmistakable evidence of her singular fate. Swears an oath of vengeance, goes out after the Red Indian who committed the enormity, vows to eat his heart, all unwitting they're really brothers."

"We've got a smash hit here, Louis."

"You can cobble on some sort of blood-and-thunder ending. True identities revealed all around. Perhaps the Red Indian brother has a distinctive and prominent birthmark. Fugitive brother becomes a heroic guide leading settlers across the plains. Red Indian brother accepts his true identity as a white man but refuses to return to Great Britain, denounces the irrelevancy of the British aristocracy, runs for Congress instead. What about another cigarette?"

"Not a chance in hell," Joseph replied, politely enough nevertheless. He ripped out the page he had been scribbling on and fed it into the trunk. "But how's about a cocktail?" He produced a flask and offered it to Stevenson. "French brandy? You like this. It's a matter of record."

"Great God, man." Stevenson extended his long hand, just as the yellow sheet came curling back out of the trunk. It was covered with dense commentary in violet ink. Both men frowned at it.

"You drink," Joseph told him. "I'll see what they say."

"I can tell you what they don't like, old chap." Stevenson took a long pull from the flask. "Ah. The plot's derivative and wildly improbable. How's the hero to get kidnapped by Red Indians in Scotland, for Christ's sake? Disgruntled family retainer makes away with the wee babby and sends it off down the Clyde in a Moses basket, which by some inexplicable chance washes up in the Gulf of Mexico a day later?"

"Actually they don't have a problem with that part." The other man read swiftly. "But the Wild West business tends to bomb big time. The frontiersman doesn't work for them, either. He can't have a rifle because that would mean he shoots wild animals, see, which is marketing death, protests and threats against distributors, bad box office. They like the sex stuff, though. They just want to know if you can make it the South Seas where all this happens."

Very slowly, Stevenson had another swallow of brandy.

"Why don't your masters send you round to that Herman Melville chap?" he inquired with an edge in his voice. "He wrote some jolly seagoing palaver, didn't he? Why isn't *he* having this dream?"

"Too hard to film his books," responded Joseph. "But, Louis baby, listen to yourself. You're arguing with a hallucination. Isn't that silly? Now, would it really be so hard, changing the plot around a little? That whole primitive mating ritual bit would play just as well in Tahiti, you know. You could even put in—" he looked cautiously around, as though someone might be listening, "—*pirates.*"

"Buccaneers and native women? Who do you propose is going to come see these photo-plays of yours? Not the bourgeois citizens of Edinburgh, I can tell you."

"Well, it doesn't have to be pornographic. Just, you know, racy. Mildly prurient. Nothing criminal. Say your pirate's a fine upstanding young fellow who just happened to get press-ganged."

"Men were press-ganged into the Navy, not into pirate crews," said Stevenson in disgust. "I grow weary of this dream. Why don't you clear off and let the other beasties come back? I'd rather blue devils than this."

"But I'm not a nightmare! I'm a *good* dream, honest. Anyway, I can't go. I've been assigned to stay with you until I get a usable concept."

"Then I'll leave you." Stevenson struggled to his feet. He gasped for breath and with a determined stride moved out from the fire into darkness; but his legs seemed to curl under him, impossibly thin long inhuman legs, and he fell. The other man was beside him at once, leading him back to the fire solicitously.

"Hey, hey, hey, Louis, let's take it easy. I'm here to help you, remember?"

"It's the damned fog." Stevenson was trembling. "I cannot get away from it. Damned wet air. Mountains aren't high enough."

"Gee, that's awful." Joseph settled him down by the fire, put the folded coat back in place under his head, poured another cup of tea. "Maybe you should travel more. Now, you could go to the—"

"South Seas, yes, I'd guessed you were going to say that," Stevenson groaned. "Look here, what about a compromise? The story takes place on a ship traveling in the South Seas. I've been on ships. I can write about them. Your hero is a strapping young Kanaka who's been carried off by whites."

"A Hawaiian? That's an interesting angle." The other was writing again. "Why'd they kidnap him?"

"They needed crewmen. Theirs died of scurvy, I dare say."

"Shanghaied!" exclaimed Joseph with gusto. "*Love* the title. Go on, Louis, go on."

"He's carried off on a whaling ship, away from his island home and his aged parents. He's a heathen (this is before the missionaries) but nevertheless naturally virtuous. The drunken behavior of the white sailors fills him with righteous dismay."

"We can show a lot of sleaze here. I like it."

"His ship comes to the rescue of another ship under attack by pirates. Buccaneers have just boarded the other vessel and are in the act of putting passengers to the sword. Among the passengers is a beautiful young virtuous Scottish girl, no doubt traveling with her minister father. Probably has money too. Our Kanaka performs a particularly daring act of rescue of the maiden. She falls in love with him, he with her."

"Okay, okay, and?"

"They take him back to Scotland with them and . . . stop a bit!" Stevenson's eyes lit up. "It's not just one girl he rescues from pirates, it's *two!* Minister's daughter and a harlot who for some reason's been traveling in the South Seas. Both fall in love with him!"

"Boy oh boy oh boy." The other man fed his notes into the trunk. It spat them back again. He read the commentary. Stevenson, watching his face, gave a sob of exasperation and lay back.

"Now what's wrong with it?"

"They didn't go for the title. Funny. And they don't want the hero to be a real Hawaiian. They like the other idea about him being a long-lost duke or earl or somebody like that. Like, his parents were English and their yacht got shipwrecked when he was a baby or something? And he just looks brown because of the tropical sun? Not really some native guy at all."

"Bigots," said Stevenson with contempt.

"No, no, no, guy, you have to understand. Look, you write for the magazines, Louis, you know the popular taste. They want sex, they want violence, but they want the hero to be a white guy. Preferably an English peer. Brown guys can't be heroes. You *know* that."

"They're heroes in their own stories."

"Oh, yeah? What about the Musketeers guy, Dumas, he was a quadroon or something, right? Who's in his books? French kings and counts. Black, white, it's only a metaphor anyway. Believe me, our audience wants rich white guys as heroes."

"Well, I despise your audience."

"No, you don't. You need money as much as anybody else. You know the stuff you can't write about. You know where you're free to put in those really interesting bits in a way readers won't mind. Villains! It's the villains everyone secretly loves, Louis. They can be lowborn, they can be strange, they can do rotten things and it's okay because that's what the audience wants. And why? *Because people are lowborn and strange and rotten, Louis!* They want the hero to be this impossible perfect white guy so they can watch the villain beat the crap out of him, since it's what they'd like to do themselves. As long as the villain loses in the end, they don't have to feel guilty about it. And it's all phony anyway. I mean, have you ever really talked to a member of the House of Lords? What a bunch of pinheads."

"I see your point, but I can't agree. The human condition is evil, but we *must* strive to be otherwise. A writer can't glorify evil in his work. He can't write of the miserable *status quo* of human life as though it were a fine and natural state. He must morally instruct, he must inspire, he must hold up an ideal to be worked for—"

"Oh, garbage. You don't believe that yourself, even. That's why you wrote—" Joseph halted himself with an effort. "Well, look. Given that a writer has this other fine noble purpose in life, he's still got to eat, okay? So there's no harm in a nice swashbuckling adventure yarn with a swell dark villain—Byronic, like you said—and a little thin white cardboard hero to bounce off him. It sells, Louis, and there's no point denying it. So. About this Dark Lord guy."

"This is really too depressing." Stevenson gazed into the fire. "I've never seen the pattern in this sort of thing. But it *is* what we do, isn't it? We feed a perverse urge in our readers by creating supremely interesting images of evil. Perhaps we even cultivate that urge. The villain wins sympathy in our hearts through the skill of the writer. I've felt admiration for the rogue of the old romance myself, the man with the hand of the Devil on his shoulder. Great God, what are we doing when we create such characters? *And yet they make the story live.*"

"Now, now, buck up. Look. Suppose you've got your hero sailing along with his two ladies, one good, one bad. Nice tension there. Suppose, Louis, he's got a Bad Guy chasing him, say the chief of the pirates, only this guy isn't just a pirate, he's *the Pirate* of pirates, powerful, intelligent, interesting—maybe he's some kind of magician, picked it up in the islands—maybe he has something weird about his appearance, in a fascinating way. Huh? Huh, Louis?"

"You even intrigue me with it." Stevenson turned listless eyes on him. "You persuade. You seduce. I want to take pen in hand and write the awful thing and gain immortal fame thereby. Oh, God, this is the real temptation."

"Ah, come on, Louis. We're not talking about sin, we're talking about dramatic conflict."

"What if dramatic conflict *were* a sin?" Stevenson said in a small frightened voice, looking back at the flames. "What if my old nurse was right and storytelling does imperil men's souls? Because we do pander to their worst instincts. We do. Let me make my hero as brown as I will, he'll still be the innocent, the Fool. He'll still inspire contempt by his virtue. All my art is spent on making my *villain* fascinate and charm."

"Hey, look, Louis, don't get sore. I don't dictate public taste, I just try to accommodate it. People live such sad lives. Why not take their minds off the fact by entertaining them?"

"And this is to be my choice, isn't it? I can die an unknown scribbler of essays or I can write the kind of thing you want for your photo-plays and live a successful and famous man." Stevenson shut his eyes tightly. "Well, you can get straight back to Hell with your infernal trunk. I won't sell my soul for eternal fame and you can tell your master so from me. Thee and all thy works I utterly reject."

"Believe me, Louis, you're taking this all the wrong way," the other said soothingly, getting down on his knees beside him. "Isn't it possible to use people's appetites to instruct them in a, uh, positive moral way? Sell 'em tickets to the Palace of Excess and then slip 'em out the back to Wisdom by putting up a sign that says *This Way to the Egress?* Sure it is. Sure you can. You will. Dickens did it all the time. And even if there *is* something wrong with the entertainment business, can't you atone for what you do? You can use your loot to do something good. Fight injustice. Defend the brown guys oppressed by white guys, maybe. Louis, you can use this talent of yours to do such good."

"This is just the way you'd have to talk to convince me." Stevenson was trembling, clenching his poor scabbed hands. "Fiendish. Fiendish. Can't you let me die in peace?" The other looked at him with something like compassion. He leaned forward and said:

"Has it occurred to you that you might be wrestling with an angel, Louis?" Stevenson opened his eyes again and stared at him, sweat beading on his high brow. "Come on now. We've almost got it right. Tell me why the pirate is chasing after our hero. Is he after a treasure map? Is *he* in love with one of the girls? Are they rivals from childhood? *Tell me the story, Louis.*"

Stevenson's breathing had grown steadily harsher. "Very well," he began, covering his face with his long hands and staring up through his fingers at the stars, "your damned pirate's the man for me. Perhaps he's got a cloak that blows about him as he makes his entrance in a storm, black as shadows dancing on the wall of the night nursery, black as devil's wings. And if you're good, and lie very still, he can't see you . . . why can't he see you? Evil's not blind, no, Evil walks in the sun with a bland and reasonable face." He lowered his hands and glared at Joseph. "But there's some horror to him as he searches for you there in the dark. *You can hear him coming.* He's a limping devil, you can hear his halting step—or his wooden leg! The man is maimed, that's it, he's had a leg clean gone by a round broadside of twenty-pound shot!" He sat up in excitement, taken with his creation.

"And that's the mark by which you may know him, for you couldn't *tell,* else, he looks so big and bluff and brave, like somebody's father come to chase the night horrors away. There's your subtle evil, man, there's the pirate as honest seaman in plain broadcloth, a man full of virtues to win your trust—until he finds it convenient to kill you. Yes! And the damnable thing is, he'll *have* those virtues! Not a mask, d'you see? He'll *be* brave, and clever, and decent enough in his way—

for all his murderous resolution—oh, this is the man, *ecce homo,* look at him there large as life! Dear God, he's standing there beside you even now, leaning on his crutch, and there's the parrot on his shoulder—"

He threw out his frail arm, pointing with such feverish conviction that Joseph, who had been sitting spellbound in spite of himself, turned involuntarily to look. Louis's voice rose to a hoarse scream:

"Oh, give me paper! Give me even a scrap of that yellow paper, please, you can have the bloody soul, only let me get this down before he slips away from me—" and he groped at his pockets, searching for a pencil; but then he went into a coughing fit that sprayed blood across the other man's trousers. Aghast, Joseph pulled out a tiny device and forced it between Stevenson's teeth.

"Bite! Bite on this and inhale!" Stevenson obeyed and clung to him, nearly strangling, as the other fumbled out another needle and managed to inject another drug.

"Jeez, this wasn't due to happen yet! I'm really sorry, Mr. Stevenson, really, just keep breathing, keep breathing. Okay? You'll be okay now. I promise. This'll fix you up just fine."

After a moment Stevenson fell back, limp. His coughing had stopped. His breathing slowed. Joseph had produced a sponge and a bottle of some kind of cleaner from the trunk and was hastily dabbing blood from his trousers.

"See what you made me do?" Stevenson smiled feebly. "Blood-red ensign's hoisted at last. Disgusting, isn't it?"

"Hey, you'll be okay. What I gave you ought to keep it off for months. You won't even remember this." He finished with his clothes and went to work on Stevenson's. "Besides, I've seen worse."

"I dare say you have." Stevenson giggled again. "My apologies for the blood. But it's a sort of a metaphor, isn't it? And now you've foxed your own design, for I'll die and he'll never live, my limping devil . . . though he'd have been a grand piece of work . . . ."

"Oh, you'll live long enough to write about *him.*" Joseph peered critically at his cleaning job and decided he'd gotten everything out. "Not that it'll do my masters any damn good."

Stevenson closed his eyes. Joseph gave a final swab at his shirtfront. As he was doing so the trunk made a chattering noise and spewed out another sheet of paper. Almost absently he reached out to tear it loose, and glanced at the reply:

CLIENT SAW "NOTES" ON KNIGHTS IN ARMOR STORY, LOVES IT. *DE GUSTIBUS NON EST DISPUTANDEM.* SOME ADAPTATION POSSIBLE. SECURE RIGHTS ON FORGERY BELOW AND PROCEED TO NEXT ARTIST.

Stevenson had opened his eyes again at the sound the trunk made. Joseph looked up from his communication and met his gaze with a frank smile.

"Well, Louis, you've won. Your soul has been tested and found pure. You're one of the elect, okay? Congratulations and let me just ask you one last favor."

"What's that?" Stevenson was groggy now.

"Can I have your autograph? Just sign here." He put the pen in Stevenson's hand and watched as Stevenson scrawled his name on the paper, just below the cleverly faked holograph of plot outline and character notes.

"Thanks, pal. I mean that. Sincerely." The other fed the paper into the trunk and this time it did not return. He stood and hoisted the trunk up to his shoulder.

"I'll be running along now, Louis, but before I do I'd like to give you a piece of advice. You won't take it, but I feel compelled. That's just the kind of guy I am."

Stevenson peered at him. Joseph leaned down.

"You really would live longer if you'd give up the cigarettes."

"Tempter, get thee below," Stevenson croaked.

"Funny you should say that, you know, because that *is* where I'm based. In a geographical sense only, of course, 'down' and 'south' being sort of the same. Little suburb just outside of Los Angeles. We produce our photo-plays down there. It's not a great town for writers, Louis. I know you like to travel and everything, but you'd want to leave this one off your world itinerary. Believe me, it's not a place for a man with your scruples to work. The climate's good, though, and they really like your stuff, so it might have suited you. Who knows?"

"I'll die first." Stevenson closed his eyes. The other man nodded somberly and walked away into the night.

In entirely another time and place, there was a whirl and scatter of brown beech leaves and the trunk was *there,* spinning unsteadily to a halt; and as there had been no witness to observe its previous arrival, there was no witness now to notice that it was spinning in the opposite direction. It slowed and stopped, and the winter silence of an English forest settled over it. When the lid popped, the trunk fell over, and the man in the brown suit had to push the lid aside as he crawled out on hands and knees through a small cloud of yellow smoke.

He crouched on the forest floor a moment or two, panting out stasis gas. As he got to his feet and brushed off his clothes he heard the approaching rattle of an automobile. He looked at his (for lack of a better word) watch.

It was December 3, 1926.

At that precise moment there was a mechanical squeal followed by crashing sounds and a thud, coming from beyond a nearby grove of trees.

He grinned and gave a little stamp of his foot, in appreciation of perfect timing. Then he turned and ran in the direction of the accident.

The automobile was not seriously damaged, although steam was hissing from the radiator cap under the hood ornament. The bug-eyed headlights stared as if in shock. So did the woman seated behind the wheel. Her cloche hat had flown off her head and lay outside the car. He picked it up and presented it to her with a bow. She turned her pale unhappy face to look at him, but said nothing.

"Here's your hat, Mrs. Christie. Say, you're lucky I came along when I did. I think you've had a bump on the head. That sort of injury can cause amnesia, you know."

She did not respond.

"Don't worry, though. Everything's going to turn out all right. Allow me to introduce myself, Ma'am. I represent the Chronos Photo-Play Company. You know, I'm quite a fan of your mystery novels. *The Murder of Roger Ackroyd,* that was a real peach. You ought to do more with that Hercule Poirot guy."

She just looked at him sadly.

"Tell you what." He leaned his elbow on the door and looked deep into her eyes. "You look like a lady who could use a vacation. Maybe at a nice anonymous seaside resort. What do you say we go off and have a nice private talk together over a couple of cocktails, huh?"

After a long moment of consideration she smiled.

"I don't believe I caught your name," she said.

This story is a tribute to the Dunites of Moy Mell, a community of poets, scholars, artists, utopians and visionaries. They used to reside in the high dunes behind the ruins of La Grande, in shacks made of driftwood and wreck salvage. They lived by poaching clams and stealing vegetables from the local farms; they brewed mead from stolen honey. At night, around driftwood fires, they argued the nature of Hindu goddesses or told stories of Finn MacCool, or charted their fortunes in the stars.

Every so often winter gales will move a dune and some trace of them will surface for an hour: the rusted-out skeleton of a Model T, a mound of sand-scoured bottles lavender and green, an old boot, a midden of white shells and rusted tin cans.

Lemuria *Will* Rise!

SOMEWHERE GOD HAS A CELESTIAL POLAROID OF me, standing in the Dunes with a painted clamshell in one hand and a sprig of *Oenothera hookeri ssp. sclatera* in the other, staring heavenward with a look of stupefied amazement. When He needs a mood lightener, He takes a look at that picture and laughs like hell.

It was 1860 and the Company had sent me to Pismo Beach. The place was not yet the vacation destination of Warner Brothers toons; the little town of cottages and motels wouldn't exist for another generation or two; but it did feature all the clams one could eat, and all the sand too.

I wasn't there for the clams, though.

If you stand on the beach at Pismo and look south, you can see twenty-odd miles of shore stretching away to Point Sal, endless lines of breakers foreshortened into little white scallops on blue water. The waves roll in on a wide pale beach toward a green line of cypress forest, rising on low sandhills to your left. Beyond them, and further south, rise *the Dunes.*

You never saw anything so pure of line and color in your life, though the lines shift constantly and the color is an indefinable shade between ivory and pink, or possibly gold. Even on a gray day they glow with their own light, pulsing as cloud shadows flow across them.

Beautiful, though I couldn't see how anything could be growing out there; and yet this was where I was supposed to find a rare variant of evening primrose.

Everywhere else in California, *Oenothera hookeri* is a lemon-yellow flower. In 1859, however, a salmon-pink subspecies was reported,

127

growing only in a certain place in these very Dunes, and a single sample collected and preserved. Now, Evening Primrose Oil from the yellow flower has a number of recognized medical uses, such as being the only substance known to help sufferers of Laurent's Syndrome, that terrible crippler of the twenty-first century. Thanks to a unique and complex protein, it helps retard the decay of those oh-so-important genitourinary nerve sheaths afflicted by Laurent's. Analysis of the only surviving sample of the pink variety showed it to have had an even *more* unique and complex protein, which would probably *stop* the decay of the nerve sheaths entirely, bringing bliss and continence to those suffering from the Syndrome.

Unfortunately for them, it will be extinct by their time, long since destroyed by the ravages of the off-road vehicles of the twentieth century. Interestingly enough, Laurent's Syndrome and its attendant neurovascular damage occurs most frequently in people who spend a lot of time with their reproductive organs suspended over internal combustion engines—such as the ones that power dune bikes. Mother Nature giving a rousing one-fingered salute to off-road enthusiasts, I suppose.

Not my job to judge—I was only there to gather samples, test them for the suspected properties, and (if they tested positive) secure live plants for the greenhouses of my Company, Dr. Zeus Inc. Dr. Zeus operates out of the twenty-fourth century and makes a pretty penny, let me tell you, out of miracle medical cures obtained by time travel.

So I shouldered my pack, settled my hat more firmly on my head and set off down the beach, keeping to the hard-packed sand and splashing through the surf occasionally. There were clams just below the surface of the sand, massed thick as cobblestones. They were big, too, and beautifully danger-free: no sewers yet dumping *E. coli,* no cracked pipes leaking petroleum surfactant, no nuclear power plants cooking the seawater. In fact there weren't even any railroads through here, this early, and precious few people.

My spirits rose as I strode on, past future real estate fantasies with quaint Yankee names like Grover City, Oceano, La Grande: mile after mile of perfect beach and not a mortal soul in sight. I'd build a driftwood fire, that was what I'd do, and have a private clambake. I had a flask of tequila in my pack, too. Why couldn't all my jobs be like this? No tiresome mortals to negotiate with, no dismal muddy cities, no noise, no trouble.

I turned inland at the designated coordinates and walked back into the Dunes. Squinting against the golden glow, I almost reached for my green spectacles; then paused, grinning to myself. Nobody here to see, was there? No mortals to be terrified by my appearance if I simply let the polarized lenses on my eyes darken. Whistling, I trudged onward, a cyborg with a sun hat and camping gear.

I found, as I moved farther in, that this was no desert at all. There were islands in this maze of glowing sand, cool green coves of willow and beach myrtle and wild blackberry. There were a few little freshwater lakes sparkling, green reeds waving, ducks paddling around; there were abundant wildflowers too, especially rangy stands of yellow evening primrose. Somewhere hereabouts must be my quarry.

Climbing to the top of a dune I spotted it, on visual alone, a mere thirty meters south-southwest: a thicket of willow on three sides around a lawn of coarse dune grass, and all along the edge the tall woody stems bearing trumpet flowers of flaming pink! Could my work get any easier? I was actually singing as I plowed on down the side of the dune, an old, old song from a long way away.

So I made a little paradise of a base camp on the lawn, with a tent for my field lab and a sleeping bivvy, and set a specimen straight into solution for analysis. But even as I bustled happily about, I was becoming aware of Something that pulled at one of my lower levels of perception. You wouldn't have heard the subsonic tone, or noticed the faint flash of a color best described as blue; you *might* just possibly have felt the faint tingling sensation, but only if you were a very unusual mortal indeed. Reluctantly I crawled out of the lab and stood, turning my head from side to side, scanning.

Anomaly, five kilometers due north, electromagnetic. And . . . Crome's Radiation. And . . . a mortal human being. So much for my splendid isolation. How very tedious; now I'd have to investigate the damned thing. Sighing, I pulled out my green glasses and put them on.

I slogged up one dune and down another, following the signals through a landscape where one expected Rudolph Valentino to ride into view at any moment, burnoose flapping. God knows he would have looked commonplace enough, compared with what met my eyes when I got to the top of the last high dune, staggering slightly.

In the valley below me was another green cove, with its own dense willow thicket and its own green lawn. But rising from the thicket on four cottonwood poles was a thing like a big beehive or an Irish monk's cell, woven of peeled willow wands. On its domed top it wore a sort of cap of tight-braided eelgrass; a mat of the same flapped before a hole near its base. A path had been worn across the lawn, neatly outlined with clam shells arranged in a pattern. Real beehives were ranged in a tidy row there, woven skeps like miniatures of the house. All along the perimeter of the lawn, and poking up here and there out of the willows, were fantastical figures carved of driftwood, elaborately decorated with mussel shells and feathers. I saw Celtic crosses and sun wheels, I saw leaping horses, I saw stiff and stylized warriors with shields, I saw grass-skirted women of remarkable attributes.

Strange, but not so strange as the mottoes and exhortations spelled out in clam shells on the face of every surrounding dune. The nearest one said GOD IS LOVE. DO NO HARM, REMEMBER, NOT ALONE, COME TOGETHER, and LEMURIA HERE shouted from dunes in the nearer distance. Farther off still rose the white-shell domes of prehistoric middens.

Staring down, I collapsed into a sitting position on the sand. Borne faintly up on the wind and the blue streaming spirals of Crome's Radiation were the plaintive scrapings of a fiddle.

Well, what do you know? A holy hermit, apparently; judging from the Crome Effect, one of those poor mortals who would one day be classed as "psychic." The radiation from this one was so intense his abilities had probably driven him crazy, so he must have fled human society and somehow wound up here in the Dunes. Mystery explained. I allowed myself a smile.

The electromagnetic anomaly was still unaccounted for, however . . . I scowled and turned my head, scanning. Now it seemed unclear, diffuse, farther away. Now it faded out. Strange.

The fiddle music stopped. The Crome waves intensified a moment, and then the beehive shook slightly as the center mat was pushed aside. A snow-white beard flowed out, followed by the wrinkled and bespectacled face to which it was attached. The hermit turned to look straight at me, though I had been sitting perfectly motionless out of his line of sight.

"Did yez wish a word with me, then?" asked the hermit.

I blinked. Foolish to be surprised, though, with all the other weirdness here. "I was only admiring your, uh, art," I replied. "It wasn't my intention to disturb you."

We regarded each other for a moment. He wrinkled his brow.

"Have They sent yez to console me fleshly lusts?" he inquired.

Gosh, how sweet. "No," I answered.

"Dat's good, then." He relaxed. "They're always parading them foreign beauties before my eyes and that last one was more than a man of my years can do justice to, to tell yez the truth of it. Yez'll excuse me a moment, pray."

He vanished back into the beehive, and it shook and creaked with his rustling around in there. I wondered if I should disappear and decided against doing so; he might go looking for me, and I'd just as soon he didn't find my camp. Besides, I was curious. What was a Celtic anchorite doing in California, let alone in the vicinity of Pismo Beach? So I waited, and after a moment he emerged from the beehive and dropped into the willows below, and came across his lawn toward me. I got up and descended the side of the dune to meet him, scanning him as I went. When we got within four meters of one another we both stopped abruptly. *He* was scanning *me,* albeit in a very unfocussed and inefficient way.

I don't know what he perceived, but I saw a tiny elderly mortal whose body glowed and flashed with a surrounding halo of blue radiation. He wore a sealskin loincloth and a kind of tabard of woven eelgrass to which had been sewn thousands of seagull feathers, tiny white ones. His ancient spectacles were tied on with string. Apart from advanced age he was in excellent health, without so much as an infected tooth.

He peered at me suspiciously, cocking his head.

"Yez ain't from Them," he stated.

"No," I admitted. "Who are They?"

"Why, the Ascended Masters," he answered, as though I were crazy to ask. "Them fellows up on Mount Shasta, ye know. The Inheritors of Lemuria."

Okay. "No, I haven't heard of them, Señor, I'm only from Monterey," I replied cautiously. "My name is Dolores Concepción Mendoza, and I have come here on holiday to sketch wildflowers."

"O, I don't know about that." He looked me up and down. "Yez got a look about yez of the Deathless Ones."

Whoops. So much for keeping a cover identity around a psychic. I thought fast, which is to say I accessed Smith's *History of Mystical Esoteric Cults, Volumes 1-10;* blinked, smiled, and said: "The White Fraternity does not reveal itself to all men. You are to be commended on your sharp sight, Brother. But I have come here, as I said, for the wild flowers that grow here in these Dunes, to collect them for their rare properties. Look into my heart and you will see that I speak the truth."

He scanned me a moment and nodded. "So, dat's all right. Yez ain't of any Order I ever seen though. What Discipline do yez follow?"

"The Mystical Sisterhood of Orion," I improvised. "We, uh, live in caves in the Pyrenees and observe absolute chastity. We also preserve the healing arts of the exiled Moors. A traveler brought us word of the rare flowers here, and I have been sent to collect them for our studies."

"Well!" The anchorite's thin chest swelled with pride. "Yez couldn't have come to a more salubrious place for medicines. These Dunes is the best place for the corporeal body yez ever saw. How long d'yez think I've lived here, without ever a day of sickness or care? Forty years, I tell yez, forty years since the *Lima* run aground out there and I come ashore. And in all that time, not one pain nor pang. It's the superior vibrations, ye know."

"I don't doubt it," I affirmed solemnly.

"The most powerful vibrations in the world, right here in these Dunes, and I have that straight from the Ascended Masters Themselves. Why, They come here all the time to enjoy the beneficial vibrational effects." He nodded with certainty.

"Really?" I wondered when he was going to ask if I had a piece of cheese about me. "They come here often, do They?"

"Indeed They do. I'll introduce yez, maybe."

"That would be charming, though I'm sure They're quite busy. Still, I hope you'll give Them my best regards." I made to withdraw. "And now, Señor, I must set about my appointed task. Good day." Poor old lunatic.

He bid me an effusive farewell and I climbed away across the sand, giggling to myself. Well, this was one for the cultural anthropologists: a classic California crackpot, years and years before the breed was supposed to be common here. Worth an amusing sidebar on my official report, perhaps.

I put him out of my mind and went back to my field lab, where I had a good afternoon's work undisturbed by weird lights or electromagnetic pulses. Not that there weren't plenty of both, but now that I knew their origin I could afford to ignore them, couldn't I? And ignore them I did, though blue lightning came down and danced at the water's edge as I dug clams for my supper, and blue aurorae shimmered over my driftwood fire as I sipped tequila. When the level in the flask grew low enough I took to singing old Gypsy songs at them. I thought I sounded like a wounded coyote, but the blue lights seemed to like it. They followed me back to my bivvy and flitted off politely when I crawled in to sleep.

"I thought I'd bring yez a few clams for breakfast, there," sounded a voice close to my ear, as a net bag clattered down before my face. I managed to avoid erupting through the roof of my bivvy and scrambled out on knees and elbows instead. The hermit was inspecting my field lab with great interest.

"Ain't dat fascinatin', now?" He held a glass slide up to the light and peered through it. "The Sisterhood's got all the latest appurtenances, I can see dat."

"Yes." I got hastily to my feet. "And thank you so very much for the clams, Señor, how gracious of you. May I offer you a cup of coffee?" Not much danger in a security breach where a looney was involved, but he might break something.

"Coffee." With a wistful smile he handed me back my slide. "My, I ain't had coffee since the *Lima.* 'Course it's bad for yez, ye know, or so They tell me. All them alkaloids."

How'd he know that? Maybe he'd been a chemist before he'd gone to sea. "Er—we of the Sisterhood can neutralize all toxins before they harm our, uh, atomic structures," I told him. Well, it wasn't exactly a lie.

He looked impressed. "Dat's a fine trick, to be sure. The Ascended Masters can do that one, but I can't, ye know, not till I've made me transition to the next astral plane. Got any tea?"

With a growing sense of unreality I set up my camp stove and prepared his tea and my badly needed coffee. He watched alertly, commenting with little enthusiastic cries and noddings of his head on all the advanced technological marvels I employed.

Having received his tea, the hermit leaned back comfortably into a hill of sand and regarded me over the steaming cup.

"Now I wonder," he said, "whether the Sisterhood is up on interpreting the ancient prophecies, too?"

"No, actually, Señor." I sipped coffee very carefully. I have some circuitry close to my eustachian tubes that registers intense pain if exposed to too-hot liquids. "We concentrate on the healing arts."

"The reason I was asking being," he continued, as though I hadn't spoken, "dat I need to get a fix on how much time I've got before Lemuria rises again."

Lemuria? I did a fast access. "Ah. You mean the legendary drowned continent, the Atlantis of the Pacific," I said.

"*Older* than Atlantis," he said firmly. "Them Atlanteans was no more than colonists of Lemuria, if yez want the truth of it. It was the cook on board the *Northerly Isles* first told me about Lemuria; he was a man with an education, ye know, before them unfortunate circumstances what sent him to sea. I'm telling you, the Lemurians had it over Atlantis in every way. Their high priests knew more arcane lore, their temples and palaces was bigger, and they sunk first."

"Really."

"They did. And see, the Atlanteans (who had got degenerate to start with, which was why they sunk) spread out all over everywhere and forgot their ancient wisdom, but not the Lemurians. They founded a fine city up on Mount Shasta, and from there They've kept Their gold and silver vessels together and Their ancient libraries and all."

"You don't say."

"I do. And I wager the reason They've been so careful to keep to

Themselves *is,*" he leaned forward for emphasis, "dat They know Lemuria's going to rise again, any day now, and They want to be able to move back in without the place getting crowded. Just a select company, ye know. They ain't said it in so many words—They're shy that way—but I can tell, all right."

"Mm-hm." I tasted my coffee. "And you need to know exactly when Lemuria will rise? Why don't you ask Them, Señor?"

"O, I have." He wrootched uneasily in the sand, causing little avalanches around himself. "But They don't care to talk about Lemuria much, which is a prudent thing to do, right enough, I can see dat; but, see, I've got this school to found, and if I know the vast submerged peaks ain't going to lift clear of the waves for another year or so, why then I've got time to get everything ready. On the other hand, if it's the day after tomorrow-like dat the ancient palaces is rising into view again, I'm in a sad fix."

"You're founding a school?" Who did he think was going to attend, clams? "What kind of school, Señor?"

"The School of Lemurian Knowledge." He put his finger to the side of his nose. "Now, it was foretold in me natal horoscope dat I was to found a great institution of learning. And, me being wrecked here, yez wouldn't think dat would come to pass, would yez, now? But Destiny's a mighty thing. It was here I met Them, and They saw at once I was spiritually evolved enough to keep company with the likes of Them. Mind you, it was a while before They'd admit to being the Ascended Masters—made on at first like what They didn't understand me—but at last They saw I was clever enough to have found out Their game. They put me through a lot of tests to see if I'm worthy, and They has prepared me ever since to be one of the elect what'll get to live in Lemuria once it's up again. Why, They've had me to visit up there, ye know, I've walked in Their golden tunnels on Mount Shasta!

"But, after all, I pity me fellow creatures dat'll have to stay here and ain't had the benefit of Their company. So what I been doing is, I been copying down all I seen when I visits Them on sacred tablets, which is to form the library of me school. As soon as I've got all the collected wisdom down, pupils will flock to the Dunes from all over the world. So, see, even if I ascend to Lemuria, or row out to it or something, I can still pass on Their knowledge to mankind."

"So you see yourself as a sort of Promethean benefactor, then," I said straight-faced, taking a cautious drink from my cup. He drank too and then looked up as the classical allusion sank in.

"Mind yez, I ain't stealing any sacred fire from Heaven!" he protested. "They're good fellows, Them Ascended Masters, and I'm sure

They wouldn't mind about me copying things I've seen on sacred tablets, if I'd got around to mentioning 'em to Them. But I've been so busy, what with Them always testing me worthiness and all . . ."

"No, no, of course." I looked around at the shifting sand. "But, tell me, what do you do for your tablets? There is no stone here."

"Clam shells," he told me. "I paint on the insides, see."

I looked at the net bag, lying where he'd dropped it. I wasn't quite up to breakfast yet. "Can you get a lot of sacred wisdom in a clamshell?"

"Yez can if yez paint small; but then dat's another way these Dunes has it over other places, for there's much bigger clams here. If I had to use them little rubbishy eastern clams I'd have no end of labor." He shook his head.

"Good point." There was sand in the bottom of my cup. I tilted it and dumped the last few drops out. "Well, Señor—I wish I could be of some assistance to you in your generous efforts to spread enlightenment. Though I must say most arcane texts I've read hold the opinion that Lemuria won't rise before the end of this century, so I think you have plenty of time."

"Do yez tell me so?" He knit his white brows uncertainly. "All the omens I been seeing predict a great change dat's coming."

Well, there was the Civil War of the Yankees about to kick off, not that he'd be likely to hear much about it out here. I looked thoughtful and said, "I too have heard of a great disturbance in the affairs of men soon, but most prophets agree it will not last long. Surely, then, they don't mean the rise of Lemuria?"

"O, no, I suppose not," he agreed, draining his teacup. "For when Lemuria escapes Ocean's mighty bosom, its next great cycle will last seventeen million years, ye know."

It took nearly that long to get him to leave, with gentle hints and tactful shoves; but at last he vanished over the top of a dune, waving cheerfully, and I was able to relax in blessed silence.

And without mortal distractions I got so much work done that day, hangover notwithstanding, that by nightfall I was able to transmit preliminary results on my field credenza to the relay station on the nearby mesa. Things were looking good for Laurent's sufferers everywhere. With the cellular map and the holoes I included the following smirky communication:

SPECIAL NOTE: AUTHENTIC HOLY MAN LIVING IN DUNE REGION! ELDERLY MALE CAUCASIAN EUROPEAN ORIGIN, SPONTANEOUS CROME GENERATOR ESTIMATE FORCE 10. CLAIMS TO HAVE BEEN CONTACTED BY

*ANCIENT LEMURIAN MASTERS AND IS CONFIDENTLY
WAITING FOR SUBMERGED CONTINENT TO RISE. IS
COMPILING LIBRARY OF TEACHINGS OF ASCENDED
MASTERS! GREAT SCHOOL OF PHILOSOPHY TO OPEN
HERE ANY DAY NOW!*

I signed off, crawled out of the tent and stood stretching, looking up at the stars. All the black heaven sparkled and shone, and the Milky Way streamed out to sea like smoke from a ship's funnel. Too nice a night to waste on sleep. I strolled off across the sand, following the sound of the night ocean.

Cresting the top of a dune unmarked by any print, I looked down on the white circle of a shell midden. It gleamed under the starlight, perfect in its circumference. How many generations of Chumash had picnicked here, before the Europeans came? The thing must be fifteen meters across.

"But it wasn't the Indians put it there, ye know," observed a voice at my elbow.

I screamed, leaped into thin air and reappeared on the other side of the midden. Heart pounding, I stared across at the hermit, who was standing where I had been a second before. He waved pleasantly, apparently quite unsurprised by my teleportation.

"It was Them," he called to me.

"What?" I gasped. *What was wrong with my approach warning sensors?* I ran a hasty self-diagnostic.

"They put it there, as a marker for when They come sailing down from Mount Shasta to visit. Helps 'em navigate in," he explained. He strode down the dune across the sand to me, sturdy knees and elbows pumping. I watched him in disbelief.

"Out for a breath of fresh air, are yez?" he inquired. "I come out meself, on fine nights. These Dunes is also the best place to watch the celestial movements, ye know."

"No city lights to dim the stars," I found myself remarking.

"There are not," he agreed, looking heavenward. A green firedrake crackled down the southern horizon. "Almost a pity that Lemuria's coming up so close by. They had towers in Their grand cities for the spreading of light focused through jewels. All them emeralds and rubies and sapphires winkin' away must have been a rare sight, and lit up the streets a deal better than lanterns, wouldn't ye think? But very bright."

"I suppose it would have been. Look, you don't think Lemuria's going to rise with the buildings all intact and everything in working order, do you? I mean, how long has it been at the bottom of the sea, for heaven's sake?" I cried in exasperation.

"Twelve million years," he informed me imperturbably.

"Well, there, how could there even be any ruins left after all this time?" I drew a deep breath, attempting to get a grip. The electromagnetic weirdness must be affecting me somehow. "It'll just be one big muddy unimproved . . . landmass."

"So was San Francisco," he pointed out. "Nothing to speak of when the *Lima* put in there, and look what the Americans has built there now. I hear it's fit to rival Paris or London, though of course it's nothing so grand as what *They'll* build once They've got Their own back. Think of all them water frontage lots! And building's no trouble at all for Them, ye know, because They've got the secret of countermanding the forces of gravity."

"They have?"

"They have that. They've got a device uses cosmic rays to move great blocks of stone. Just floats 'em in as though they weighed nothing at all. I daresay Their builders taught the Egyptians everything they knew. Why, the pyramids ain't nothing to what you'll see being put up once Lemuria rises." He nodded in the direction of the sea as though he could glimpse it there already. My eyes followed his gaze involuntarily. I shook my head, as if to clear away the fog of mystical nonsense surrounding me.

"What a fascinating thought," I said, summoning every ounce of courtesy. "I have no doubt I shall dream about Lemuria's jewel-studded towers as I sleep. To which end, Señor, I must wish you good evening."

"And a fine good evening to yez as well. I think I'll just wait around and see if They drop by tonight. Yez'll be welcome to stay to meet Them, ye know." He raised his eyebrows alluringly.

"Thank you, Señor, but I am weary and fear I would not be at my social best. Give Them my regards, though, won't you?" I requested, and made my escape under the grinning stars.

When I returned to my camp there was a faint blue light blinking in my field lab. I actually grabbed up my frying pan and started for it, blood in my eye; but it was only the credenza indicator light, telling me that a transmission had come in while I was out.

I leaned down to peer at the tiny glowing screen.

PRIORITY DIRECTIVE GREEN 07011860 3300 BB. CROME GENERATOR. INVESTIGATE FURTHER. OBTAIN DNA SAMPLE AND FORWARD TO RELAY STATION.

There was some ugly language used in the field lab, and a frying pan sailed out under the stars as though propelled by cosmic anti-gravity rays.

So, how do you get a DNA sample from a psychic?

A real two-fisted operative would move in silently, plant some expensive neuroneutralizing device (which field botanists are never given enough budget for, by the way) and get a pint of blood and maybe a finger or two from the unconscious subject.

I opted to sneak into the hermit's house while he wasn't there and collect shed hair and skin cells, but even that presented its own problems. When did he leave his wicker beehive? For how long? Did he ever go far enough away for all his blue lights to follow him and leave me the hell alone? If he did, and they did, maybe he'd be unable to perceive my rifling his belongings.

Dawn of the next day found me crouching in a willow thicket one kilometer south of the hermit's cove, scanning intently. He was home, I could tell, awake already and moving around within a tiny zone of activity; must be still within the beehive. Abruptly his signal dropped in location and its zone widened: he'd climbed out and was moving around on his lawn. Then his signal moved away due west, receding and receding. He must be going down to dig clams. That should take him a while.

I emerged from my thicket and ran like a rabbit over the dunes. In no time I went tumbling down the sandwall into his cove and sprinted across his lawn. Well, he wouldn't need any sixth sense to know I'd been here; I could always tell him I'd just stopped by to borrow a cup of sugar or something. No blue radiation at the moment, at least.

I pushed my way into the willows about the base of his beehive and looked around.

He'd cleared a space under the bushes around the four supporting poles. It was cool and shady in there, and clearly he used it as additional living room. Over to one side was a shallow well and the banked embers of a cooking fire; over to the other side must be his library, to judge from the baskets and baskets of clamshells. There must have been hundreds of them, each one painted with knotted and interlacing patterns of dizzying Celtic complexity. Some had text, beautiful tiny lettering massed between spirals and vine leaves, but many appeared to be abstract images. There was something vaguely familiar about them, but I couldn't spare the time to look further. I scrambled up his ladder and crawled into the beehive.

Right at the doorway was his scriptorium: a chunk of redwood log two feet across, adzed flat for a work surface, with clamshells holding various inks and paints. I supposed he made them from berry juice and powdered earths. A grooved tray held little brushes made from reed cane and hair; an old graniteware cup held water. The present tome in progress was balanced on a ring of woven grass.

I didn't look at it particularly closely, or at the fiddle hanging on the wall. I made straight for the rumpled mass of sealskins that formed the old man's bed.

I swept a few long white hairs into my collector and groped around with a scraper for skin cells. Oh, great, the ancient hide was coming off too. Now the Company would think he had seal DNA.

It would have to do. Tucking the samples away, I turned to exit on my hands and knees. My gaze fell on the half-painted clamshell.

The pattern was drawn in a faint silver line, done with a knife point or an old nail maybe, and blocked in carefully in ocher and olive green. Ribbons and dots? No. A twisting ladder? No . . . a DNA spiral.

A DNA spiral.

I stared at it fixedly for a long moment and then jumped down the ladder into the area below, where I grabbed up a clamshell from the nearest basket.

On its inner surface was an accurate depiction of the solar system, including Pluto and all the moons of Jupiter. And here was another one showing the coastline of Antarctica, and I couldn't identify this one but it certainly looked like circuitry designs. And what were these? Lenticular cumuli? *Where had he seen all this?*

He hadn't gotten it from any bloody Lemurians, that much I was sure of. In this time period, surely only one of us could have painted these pictures, unless there was a serious security breach somewhere. I'd have to inform the Company.

I reflected on the possibilities as I sped back to my camp. He'd seen my field lab, of course, but I'd only been here a couple of days! He was a psychic, and a powerful one. Had he somehow been picking up transmissions from the station on the mesa nearby? If they'd been careless with their shielding, he might. Anyway it couldn't be my fault.

I rushed right into the tent and sent a breathless communication outlining what I'd found. As the last green letter flitted away into the ether, I sat back and frowned. Having been put into words, the story sounded even crazier than it was. The crew at the relay station might think I had a screw missing. Maybe I should go back and take some holoes of the clamshells to back up my story. There was still the DNA sample to send, too.

But even as I was preparing it for transmission, the credenza beeped and another message came in. I leaned over to peer at it.

PRIORITY DIRECTIVE GREEN 070218601100 RE: CROME GENERATOR. OBTAIN LIBRARY.

My jaw dropped. Hesitantly I transmitted: *CLARIFY? SPECIFY? HOW MANY?*

ENTIRE LIBRARY. OBTAIN. PRIORITY.

A long moment later I transmitted: *ACKNOWLEDGED.*

Well, this was just great. What was I supposed to do now? Carry basket after basket of clamshells up to the relay station on the mesa?

Yes, that was exactly what I was supposed to do, and that was the easy part. How was I to obtain the old man's library in the first place? I'd like to see anybody just sort of slip four hundred pounds of clamshells into her pocket without being noticed, and I was dealing with a psychic at that.

I crawled out of the tent and stood, gloomily staring at the thickets of *Oenothera*. It wasn't as though I didn't have work of my own to do, after all. Look at all these endangered plants. And such specimens of *Lupinus chamissonis, Fragaria chiloensis, Calystegia soldanella!* Why couldn't the Company send a Security operative to deal with this? I reached out and broke off a sprig of primrose, examining closely the pattern of viral striping in a deeper pink than the salmon color of the petals . . .

The petals turned blue. Everything turned blue: my hand, my sleeve, the dune before me. I raised a startled face just in time to see a dark-blue blur cross the sky above me, as the electromagnetic anomaly pulsed and roared like a monster leaping out of the sand at my feet. I tried to yell, but couldn't remember how; and I fell down a tiny blue tunnel where there was nothing to see but a line of tiny letters and punctuation marks, tangling themselves together in a vain attempt to produce something other than gibberish.

After a long while they did manage to spell out a word, however, and it blinked on and off steadily: RESET. Oh. I knew what that meant. I was supposed to do something now, wasn't I? I breathed, blinked and tried to look around but found I could only move my eyes.

I lay where I had toppled backward, frozen in my last conscious attitude, arm still out, hand still clutching a sprig of *Oenothera*. A little sand had drifted into my open mouth. It was quiet and peaceful here now, and no longer blue; but the air stung with ozone and some sort of electromagnetic commotion was going on to the north of me.

To hell with it. I closed my eyes, but to my dismay saw red letters flashing behind my eyelids. PRIORITY! OBTAIN LIBRARY! My body jerked as some fried circuit repaired itself and my legs flexed, attempting to pull me up into a standing position. After several tries, during which the rigid upper half of my body jolted to and fro and got me another faceful of sand, my legs righted themselves and set off northward, staggering through the dunes. The rest of me rode along above them like an unwilling maharani atop a drunken elephant. At least some of the sand spilled out of my mouth.

As I lurched nearer I could feel the anomaly throbbing away up ahead, and a fan of blue rays spread themselves like a peacock's tail above the hermit's cove. Every instinct I had left was screaming at me to get out of there, but my lower torso blundered along like a goddamn Frankenstein's monster, stumbling occasionally and pitching me face-forward into the sand again. Frantically I went into my self-repair program and tried to get control, but it was committed to fixing my arms and would not allow override. The best I was able to do was close my mouth.

By the time I came thrashing over the top of the last dune, I had sensation again in my right arm; but what I beheld in the cove below me nearly brought on another fit of electronic apoplexy. Somebody else was stealing the library!

Two small figures were struggling up the face of the opposite dune, each carrying a basket of piled shells. From the prints in the sand ahead of them, I could see that this was not their first trip, and their destination was an indistinct domed something that lay in a shimmer of blue just over the top of the dune.

My jaw worked, I spat out sand and shouted, "Hey!" They turned around and I had the impression that they were a pair of English children in white hooded snowsuits, their facial features tiny and perfect, their skin ashy pale. They wore enormous black goggles. When they saw me they squeaked in horror and ran, plowing up the dune face in their efforts to get away from me and not drop the heavy baskets.

My legs took me down the sand like a juggernaut. I picked up speed across the lawn and started up after them, gaining back more and more of my coordination as I went. They were nearly to the top of the dune now and I could see there was something not quite human in their proportions. Head circumference too big, tubby little bodies, spindly arms and legs. What the hell? I searched my index for information on related subjects and was rewarded with a host of terribly earnest UFO titles from the late twentieth century, all illustrated with drawings of these same spindly little people. *Aliens?* From outer space? Were *these* the Ascended Masters from whom the hermit had been stealing his sacred fire, his memorized corpus of improbable knowledge? As I gained on them they began crying open-mouthed in their terror, desperately trying to clamber over the top of the dune.

One of them made it but the other stumbled, dropping his basket, and a single clamshell bounced out and went skating down the sandwall toward me. My right hand shot out and closed on it like a trap, in as fine an example of bonehead priority programming as I've ever seen, because if I'd been able to ignore it and keep going past I'd have caught the little so-and-so. As it was, in my wasted second he managed to grab up his basket again and hands-and-knees drag it over the top, where his friend had hung back long enough to help him to his feet. They scampered away down the other side just seconds before I was able to pull myself up off the slope.

I looked down into a wide valley of sand, featureless but for the great white circle of a shell midden. There was an airship parked on it.

Now this was 1860, mind you, and here was this thing that looked like an Easter egg designed by Jules Verne sitting on a prehistoric shell midden. It was all of some purply-silver metal and it had portholes, and riveted plates, and scrollwork and curlicues that made no kind of aerodynamic sense. It wasn't one of our ships, certainly. It bore no resemblance to a silver saucer; but then, this was 1860, wasn't it? Nearly a hundred years before anything crashed in a place called Roswell.

The little figures ran for it, sobbing in alarm to the others who stood around the ship. They all turned to stare at me, except for one who was crouched over, trying to pull a snowsuit on up around himself. As all the others screamed at the sight of me, he straightened up and looked. It was the hermit.

"O, not to worry," he told them. "I know her." He put his hands up to form a trumpet around his mouth and shouted, "I regret I was not at home when yez come to call! It seems They've decided to take me to Mount Shasta to live with Them permanent-like! Ain't dat a grand thing, now?"

"Your library!" I croaked. The little creatures were frantically tossing basket after basket of shells in through the open door of the airship, and two of them grabbed the hermit's arms to try to hurry him the rest of the way into his suit. He gave me a slightly shamefaced shrug.

"Well, They found me out about that, and They're confiscating it; but They're good fellows, like I told yez, and They say I can open a school in Lemuria when she comes up. They say They'll have to test me worthiness some more, but dat's all right." One of them zipped up the front of his suit and pressed a pair of goggles into his hands, signing several times that he should put them on at once. The others were vanishing inside the ship as fast as they could get through the door.

But I wasn't about to follow them now, priority or no priority, not after the brain-scrambling I'd got when they'd overflown me. My self-preservation program was finally working again, and I stood rooted in place watching the hermit fit the goggles on over his spectacles while the one remaining creature gibbered and tugged on his arm.

"Half a minute, there, I can't see through this—there now. Why, it's all funny-looking. Say," he called across to me, "yez might see if the

Sisterhood's interested in coming out here to the Dunes. I still think it's a capital place for a great center of learning." The ship began to tremble and hum, and the creature turned to dart through the door, pulling the hermit after him. I recoiled from the waves of radiation that flooded outward. The hermit paused in the doorway, looking back to me, and went on shouting:

"Because, ye know, the vibrations hereabouts is so powerful yez can almost—" the door slid shut with a dull bang, trapping a lock of his beard as the ship began its ascent into the sky. The ascent paused, the door slid open a half-inch and the beard vanished inside; the door slammed again and the ship zoomed upward a few hundred meters, until without turning it sped off at an angle and vanished from sight.

I stood staring for a long moment. Aware that I was still clutching the one clamshell I had managed to grab, I raised my hand painfully and examined it. I nearly screamed.

It was a nice little study of ducks paddling happily on a lake. And look: here were some children on the shore of the lake, feeding the ducks. At least, they might have been children. Oh, who was I kidding? They weren't children, they were Visitors from Somewhere who had found a unique life form in these Dunes. Like me, they had tested a sample; like me, they were transplanting it.

I let my arm drop to my side. Now that the ship had gone I could see across the midden to the high dune beyond, where clamshell letters ten feet high shouted silently:

NOT ALONE.

This one's for Harlan Ellison, just because. Another early story, featuring what one might call the Continental operatives, as opposed to Joseph and his pals.

A meditation on personal style: if you were immortal, and privileged with data on all the airs and graces from the twenty-fourth century backward, how would you define yourself? If you could sample any era but belonged to none of them, what would make you feel most at home? The Facilitator Joseph clearly feels a strong pull toward Jazz Age America. Literature Preservationist Lewis longs vainly after the cosmopolitan world of the Roman Empire. Executive Facilitator Latif seems to have accessed a lot of John le Carré novels as a neophyte. Botanist Mendoza, on the other hand, is stuck in her own personal time warp and doesn't give a damn.

But I think a lot of operatives would be irresistibly drawn to the elegance, the permanence, the arrogance of the Victorian era.

The Wreck of
the *Gladstone*

ON THE FOURTEENTH OF NOVEMBER 1893, THE schooner yacht *Gladstone* encountered a storm in the Catalina channel off the harbor at Los Angeles, California. A northeastern gale capsized her and she sank within sight of the lights of San Pedro. It is a matter of recorded fact that all hands were lost, including the captain.

Nevertheless, the following August he returned to the scene of his death and peered down through the green water, and it seemed to him he could just discern her outline, green and waving, rippling and fading, the lost *Gladstone.*

Standing at the rail he wondered, miserably, if any of the mortals he had known were still down there with her, the owner with his long moustache, the sea cook with his canvas apron.

I could tell he was so miserably wondering because of the set of his mouth and wide stare. I've known Kalugin since the summer of 1699 and have learned, in that time, to read his least thought in his countenance. It is indeed a dear countenance, but terribly at odds with itself; the eyes ought to be steel but are vague and frightened. The nose is arrogant as an eagle's beak, the mouth shaped cruel for its hereditary work of ordering serfs to the pillory: yet the sharp features are blunted in the wide pink face. He doesn't really look like one of us at all.

"Come inside, dear." I touched his arm with my gloved hand. "We can't do anything until the morning."

"I shall have bad dreams," he replied. He turned to go with me, and his gaze fell hopefully upon the island off to the west. "Do you suppose any of the crew managed to swim ashore?"

"Certainly they might have." I gave his arm a squeeze. "But they'd have had to have been extraordinary swimmers. And history does record that all hands were lost, after all."

"Including me, my dear," he pointed out, and I was obliged to shrug in concession of his point. It is one of the laws of the time-manipulation business that history cannot be changed. It is one of its hazards, and conveniences, that this law can only be observed to apply to *recorded* history. We arrange matters to our advantage in perfect obedience to the known facts. Kalugin had gone down with his ship, and so conformed to the historical record. The fact that he had risen on the sea foam three days later, like Venus or Christ, was beside the point and out of the history books altogether. The fact that he had failed in his mission on that occasion was of greater consequence, and the reason for our present excursion.

I led him into the saloon of the *Chronos,* where dinner had just been served. Victor was standing at his place waiting for us, eyeing the repast with approval.

Victor is one of those white men with nearly transparent skin. His hair and beard are a startling red, his eyes pale green, and his features are small and precise as a kitten's. If he were mortal he might decay in time to a certain spare leonine dignity, but as it is he has perpetually the sharp edge of the adolescent cat. Victor was our Facilitator on this mission. He had arranged for our yacht and its crew, and had produced such papers as we might need to justify our actions to any mortals we might encounter. Other than the servants, of course. We were fortunate to have his assistance, for the customary glacial slowness of the Company in requisitioning such necessaries might have produced a delay of years before we attended to our present mission.

"Madame D'Arraignée." He ushered me to my chair. "Captain Kalugin. It appears we're having 'Bounty of the Sea' tonight. Turtle soup, oysters, lobster salad and tunny à la Marechale. Just on the chance you don't get enough of the briny deep on the morrow, Kalugin."

Kalugin sighed and held out his glass for champagne. "It's all very well for you to laugh. Three days against the ceiling of that cabin! Do you know, when the storm had subsided enough for my rescue transport, I had *J. W. Coffin and Sons, Boston, Massachusetts* printed on my cheek? In mirror image, of course. From an inscription on the brasswork."

Victor laughed heartily. I thought what it must have been like, lying in darkness with drowned men, waiting for the storm to subside. I reached for Kalugin's hand under the table and squeezed it. He gave me a grateful look.

"So here's a health to the infant Hercules!" Victor raised his glass.

"Let's hope the little devil *is* in reasonably good health too, after his sojourn in the bosom of Aphrodite. Have you inspected the laboratory yet, Nan? Everything to your satisfaction?"

"Yes, thank you." I leaned to the side as a mortal servant bent to ladle the soup into my plate. "They certainly gave me enough sponges. I didn't find the antifungal, however."

"It's down there. An entire drum of that and the other chemical you needed, the solvent, what's it's name?"

"Diorox."

"Diorox, to be sure. I saw it loaded. Everything you need to restore the son of Zeus to his original splendor should be present and accounted for."

"I'm sure that will prove to be the case."

"I really did seal it up quite tightly," asserted Kalugin. "There may be a little damage from the tacks. I did my best to remove them, but you've no idea—the rolling of the ship, and the shouting, and then the light had gone, you know, and the claw end of the hammer wasn't the right size."

"You should have used pliers," Victor admonished him briskly. "Though of course the really important thing, Kalugin, was the air seal. We can only pray it withstood the impact when you dropped it."

"Oh, it must have." He twisted one corner of his napkin. "That's all covered in my report, you see, the cylinder landed in mud. The seal must have held. There shouldn't have been any errors."

"No, I daresay; the *equipment* scarcely ever malfunctions." Victor tasted his soup with a delicate grimace. Kalugin looked wretched. He turned to me.

"I'm afraid I might have torn one corner of the painting a little," he said apologetically. "I did mention that in my report as well."

"I'm sure it's of no consequence." I smiled at him. "Canvas repair is the simplest of processes. You forget, my dear, the Renaissance work I've done. You ought to see what the Italians do to their paintings! Floods and mud and bird droppings—"

"*If* you please!" Victor's spoon halted in its rise to his mouth.

"Pray excuse me." I had a sip of champagne.

"Have you spoken to Masaki?" Victor inquired of Kalugin.

"The diver? Yes, and she seems a knowledgeable sort. Appears to have done a lot of this sort of thing."

"She has. She's the best in her field."

"Might almost be able to handle the recovery operation herself, I imagine, if my nerve were to desert me," said Kalugin casually.

"Though, of course, it shan't." Victor gave him a hard smile across the table.

*   *   *

We talked about the mission until half past eleven, and Kalugin drank too much champagne. I lay in the bunk across from him and watched as he slept it off. His eyes raced behind pale lids, his breath caught continually, and his soft hands pushed and pushed at something that would not leave Him. It is a terrible thing to be immortal and have bad dreams.

At dawn I opened my eyes and the cabin was full of the sublimest clear pink light, the same tender shade one sees only in the winter season. Its delicate beauty was in harsh contrast to the hoarse profanities that resounded on the morning air.

Kalugin sat up and we stared at one another. We heard one of the Technicians approaching Victor's stateroom and saying, quite unnecessarily, "Vessel off our starboard bow, sir. Crew of two mortals. They're hailing us."

Hailing damnation on us, in fact, and worse things too. The voice echoing across the water was nearly incoherent with rage, backed up by the rattling throb of a steam engine, and growing closer with each moment. We heard Victor's door open and heard his rapid footsteps as he went on deck. We dressed hastily and followed him.

The vessel was just coming abreast of us as we emerged. Victor, dignified in his dressing gown, Turkish slippers and fez, confronted a wiry little man in stained canvas trousers and an old jersey. The mortal was bounding up and down in his fury in the manner of a chimpanzee, which resemblance was furthered by the fact that his arms were muscular and enormous.

The other mortal stood at the tiller, a bedraggled girl in a faded cotton-print dress. She was heavily with child, and appeared to be on the verge of tears. Their old fishing boat was in a bad way, even to my untrained eyes: her ironwork had risen like biscuit with flaked rust, and her old wood was pearl-gray. Some attempt had recently been made to make her seaworthy, but her days on the water were numbered, clearly. *ELSIE* was painted in trailing letters on her bow.

To render what her captain was saying into prose would be to produce a stream of invective not grammatical but profound.

"For shame, sir!" cried Victor. "There are ladies present."

The general sense of the mortal's response was that Victor might take himself and his female companions to any other place in the seven seas save this one.

Victor's mouth tightened and the points of his moustache stabbed the air. "I will not, sir. I will conduct salvage operations here, having every legal right to do so," he stated. He might have continued, but Kalugin gave a sudden groan and clutched the rail.

"Oh God, it's Mackie Hayes!" Kalugin said. He didn't say it loudly, but all heads turned to stare at him.

The gimlet eye of the vulgar sailor widened. He uttered a word I will not stain paper with and followed it with the cry of "Captain Pomeroy!"

Then, in an act of physical bravado I would not have thought a mortal man capable of performing, he vaulted the span of sea between his craft and ours and landed on the deck beside Kalugin. The girl at the tiller gave a weak scream. Kalugin found his lapels seized in an iron grip and the sailor's stubbled face a bare inch from his own.

"Where were ya?" shouted the sailor. "When the *Gladstone* was foundering and there was good men going to the bottom, I ask ya? Where were ya when the spars were snapping and the mast broke off clean? Hiding in yer bunk, ya no-good son of a w----!"

Kalugin had gone very white. He moistened his lips with his tongue and said, "You mistake me, sir. Captain Pomeroy was my father."

The sailor drew his head back to stare at him. He saw no gray in Kalugin's hair, he saw no lines about his eyes, he saw no scar upon his chin. Nor should he, for these things had been cosmetically applied to make Kalugin look like a mortal man and had been removed when no longer needed. The ferocity of his regard diminished somewhat and he released Kalugin's lapels.

"Well, d--n me if ya ain't the spit and image of Captain Pomeroy. But he was still a lily-livered coward, ya hear me? He was hiding below when the storm done its worst. Even Mister Vandycook the owner, *he* come up on deck to see what he could do, but not yer old man. So I d--n ya for the son of a lubber and no true seaman." He swung about to glare at Victor. "And the rest of ya for a pack of thieves. I lay claim to this salvage operation by rights of having survived the wreck of the *Gladstone!*"

There was a poignant silence on deck. We had encountered what we operatives of the Company most dread: an error in the historical record. Such loopholes can have fatal consequences for a mission. Victor considered the sailor.

"The *Gladstone* was reported lost with all hands, sir."

"Lost she were, but *I* didn't go down with her. Two days I hung on a barrel, kicking off the sharks, afore I washed up on that island yonder. Most of a year I been marooned there amongst landsmen. Took me better than three months to get that scow there seaworthy, and *I'm* salvaging the *Gladstone,* and be d--ned to you!"

"You are mistaken, sir." Victor smiled. "My firm purchased salvage rights on the wreck from its insurers."

There was a little cry of disappointment from the girl at this announcement. The sailor glanced once in her direction; then he turned back to squint at Victor. "Is that so? Well, they're there and I'm here. I can't make ya clear off, but ya can't make me leave neither, and we'll see who gets down to the *Gladstone* first!"

With that he hoisted himself up on our rail and sprang nimbly back to his own boat, which received his weight with a hollow crash that did not bode well for the integrity of her timbers. Victor stared after him, twisting one end of his moustache until it threatened to part company with his lip. Then he turned on his heel and stalked within, motioning us to follow.

"Lost with all hands!" he snapped as soon as we were gathered in the saloon.

"It's not my fault." Kalugin sagged into a chair. "I was below when the *Gladstone* went down. You know that. My orders were to rescue the priceless painting a New York millionaire stupidly kept in the cabin of his yacht. It was not my responsibility to see to it that the crew drowned. When the rescue transport picked me up after the storm they made a clean sweep of the area. They found no survivors. The historical record *says* there were no survivors."

"Well, now we know otherwise, don't we?" Victor went to the galley door and flung it open. "Coffee!" he shouted, and slammed it again and turned to pace up and down before us. "Who is this miserable little tattooed goat, may I ask?"

"Only one of the hands before the mast."

"Biographical data?"

Kalugin accessed. "Mackie Hayes, able-bodied seaman, age thirty-two, no residence given," he replied. "He was an excellent hand, unless he got liquor. He was a fighting drunk. I recall he nearly killed a man in Honolulu. Trouble with the ladies, too. I should guess his nationality to have been Yankee, despite his oddities of speech, which I believe were due to an old injury resulting in partial paralysis of the facial muscles on the right side."

"You may as well update your entry to present tense," remarked Victor bitterly. "We know very well he's alive and kicking."

"And salvaging," I pointed out.

There was a knock on the door. Victor opened it to receive the coffee tray, borne not by a mortal servant but by one of our Technicians.

"Sir, it appears the mortals are preparing to dive," he warned Victor. I leaned back to look out a porthole and saw the sailor running about on deck, setting up the air pump. His young lady came struggling up on deck bearing an unwieldy mass that proved to be an old diving suit. He snatched it from her and said some angry thing. She hurried back below and reemerged a moment later with a great brass diving helmet in her arms. He was already shrugging into the suit.

"Even as we speak," I confirmed, accepting a cup and saucer from Victor.

"And, sir, we're reading a storm moving in from the southwest," said the Technician. "We expect heavy seas by twenty-three-hundred hours. Shall we put in to the island? The charts show a good harbor with anchorage on the windward side."

"There's a thought." Victor dropped a lump of sugar into his coffee and stirred it. "And perhaps the storm will sink that filthy rust-bucket and save us the trouble."

There followed another poignant silence. The Technician cleared his throat. "Is that one of our options, sir?"

Kalugin rose to his feet.

"Possibly," said Victor at length. "You'll get your orders when we've made a decision. For now, go tell the cook we want breakfast. And I particularly want some cinnamon toast!" he called after the departing Technician.

Now it was Kalugin who paced back and forth, while Victor stood sipping his coffee. We heard a splash and the whirring as a drum of cable unwound.

"What do you think he's after, Kalugin?" inquired Victor.

"Not the painting, he couldn't be," panted Kalugin. "Even if he'd known what it was worth, he wouldn't have any reason to expect there to be anything left of it by now."

"What, then?"

"VanderCook's strongbox, I'm sure. Possibly some of the other *objets d'art.* There were some ormolu things, I remember, and a statuette. He might think they'd fetch a pretty price."

"And if he sees a shiny silver canister down there?" Victor drained his cup.

Kalugin bit his lip "He'll probably bring it up."

The door opened. Victor turned, perhaps in expectation of his cinnamon toast, but our underwater recovery specialist entered the room.

"Mme Masaki," Kalugin bowed.

"Good morning. Victor, are you aware that a monkey in a diving suit just went over the side in the general direction of the *Gladstone?*"

"Quite aware. Did you manage to sleep through our little predawn confrontation somehow?" Victor poured a cup of coffee and presented it to her.

"I wear earplugs. Are we aborting our mission, then?"

"Certainly not. Cream? Sugar?"

She shook her head. "We can't conduct a dive while that creature's down there."

"We might try," Kalugin ventured.

She widened her eyes at him. "Are you mad? That would be contrary to specific Company policy. Can we persuade him to leave, Victor?"

"Not easily." Victor steepled his fingers. "He's determined and rather combative. We may be obliged to hope for an accident."

Mme. Masaki put down her cup and simply looked at him. There was yet a third poignant silence.

"Good God, the woman is with child!" exploded Kalugin.

"We needn't touch her," Victor assured him. "Though her mate *might* have a nasty accident whilst below. Such dreadful things do happen at sea."

I shook my head. "That would be murder, Victor."

"And it would fall to me to go down and cut his hose, I think," said Mme. Masaki. "I've never killed one of them before; I should prefer not to do it now, if you don't mind."

"You know, it's deuced hard being your Facilitator when you won't permit me to facilitate anything," Victor complained.

"Mr. Hayes won't listen to reason, but perhaps the girl? . . ." I offered.

"Ahoy!" I waved a handkerchief at the mortal where she sat by the air pump, waiting for tugs on the line. "May we speak, Mademoiselle? I am so sorry that our gentlemen have had hard words. Please believe we had no intention of upsetting you."

She lifted her timid freckled face and gazed at me in wonder. "I never heard no colored lady talk like you before," she stated.

"I am from Algiers, Mademoiselle."

"Oh." She was thinking. "Is that in Europe?"

"No; but I have lived in both Paris and Rome."

"My Pa went to Europe once," she told me. "He stayed at a place called France, afore he shipped out again."

"Ah. Is your father a sailor, too?"

"No'm," she replied, and then stopped with the particular mortification Caucasians felt, in that day and age, upon accidentally addressing a Negro with an honorific. She cleared her throat and tried again. "No, he ain't, not no more. A hawser cut off his leg and now he and my Ma has a farm on that island over there. Miss, I got to ask you. That man with the funny hat, do you work for him?"

"I am a guest of his, my dear."

"Well—do you suppose he will let us go shares with him on this wreck? If Mackie don't get what he's after—" her eyes filled with tears. "He's near crazy you folks showed up when you did. All he's been talking about since I found him on the beach was getting down to the wreck, the wreck, the wreck, and when we go come out here there your boat is sitting right over it. It's for our baby he wants it. He says it's his big chance," she implored.

"Forgive me, Mrs. Hayes, but it seems to me that if Mr. Hayes truly cared for you and for the child, he would put you ashore and take some fisherman out to assist him instead."

"Ain't nobody will go with him but me." She wiped her eyes. "He's had fights with all the neighbors and my Pa won't even talk to him any more."

"But, my dear, a woman in your condition! His behavior seems abominable."

"You might say so, Miss, but what of that?" She looked terribly earnest. "He's my man and the father of my child. I got to stand by him. I know he's meaner than a snake, but it was true love at first sight when I seen him lying there in the sand." She clasped her frail hands above her swollen abdomen. "Beside, Miss, there ain't any other men on the island what ain't married already."

"I see."

"So, Miss, you seem like a real nice girl. Won't you ask your friend about leaving just a little of the wreck for us? Mackie says there was all kinds of gold chairs and all on her. He never got his pay neither. And it's all for the *child's* sake," she added piteously.

I smiled in my friendliest fashion. "I feel certain that my friend will be happy to compensate Mr. Hayes for his lost wages. Perhaps he even has some right to a share in the proceeds from the salvage. But, my dear, how much simpler things would be if he accepted the sum from us now—in gold—and took you home to your island without any further hardship to yourselves! Could you not persuade him to this, for the sake of the child? My friend is a most generous man."

A light of hope was born in her eyes, but just as she parted her lips to speak there came a jerk on the tether line and then another, setting up a thrumming echo in the cable housing.

"Oh! That's Mackie now. I got to bring him up," she exclaimed, and leaned into the crank and painfully hauled on the winch. "You'd best go," she gasped. "He'll get mad if he sees you."

I quit the deck gladly, for I could scarcely bear the sight of her efforts in her condition, and there was no way I could assist her. Kalugin was bent to a porthole in the saloon, watching.

"That man is a brute," he observed gloomily.

"Yes, but we may hope he is a brute with humane instincts," I said. "Surely, for her sake, he'll accept our proposal."

"Sweet voice of reason." He kissed my hand.

"All the same, Hayes won't agree to it," pronounced Victor where he sat, fists jammed in his trouser pockets.

"Why ever not? I think he must."

"You don't know them the way I do," was all he would say.

Presently we heard the clanking and splashing as Hayes came up, and the girl's little cries of effort as she helped him aboard. She helped him off with his helmet, too, and as soon as his head was free he cried: "Gimme a hand with the rope!"

Kalugin went to the porthole to watch. He saw them haul in the rope, hand over hand, and then we heard something thumping against the side of the *Elsie*. "They've brought up VanderCook's strongbox," he announced. There followed a dragging crash. "They've got it on deck."

I went to look and just caught sight of Hayes staggering into their cabin with a steel box, closely followed by the girl. A moment later, raucous shouts of merriment rang out across the water.

"Four thousand dollars in gold," explained Kalugin.

"Then he's bound to put into shore," I guessed. "He must think that was what we wanted. I should think he'll put about with all due haste, shouldn't you?"

Victor simply shook his head. "You don't know them the way I do," he repeated.

And he was correct in his assertion, for they did not leave. The *Elsie* and the *Chronos* lay at anchor, side by side, as the day wore on. Hayes did not attempt further salvage efforts. The swell of the sea increased somewhat, and a queer light on the southern horizon was prologue to a wall of cloud that appeared there, gray as a cat, advancing across the sky by inevitable degrees.

As we were sitting down to our luncheon repast we heard the sound of a violent quarrel from our neighbors, and tried our best not to listen, though Kalugin and I burned with silent indignation on behalf of the poor girl. Victor ignored the tumult, his cold composure untroubled.

At about half past three a hot wind sprang up, full in our faces, and it bore the perfume of jungle flowers many latitudes distant. It would have been pleasant, had not such danger attended upon it. Kalugin lay down and slept, perspiring. Victor stared fixedly across at the *Elsie* and did not speak.

Sunset flamed with all the hues in the palette of fever, across a steadily rising sea. On the cushions where he reclined, Kalugin clutched his throat and sat up staring. "VanderCook!" he muttered.

"You've been dreaming, dear." I went to him.

His face was haunted. "The ship was going down. Turning as it went down. I was trying to hurry with the painting and *he* came in. Vander-Cook."

"Poor dear, you have had a conditioning nightmare," I explained. "We all have them when we can't complete a mission. As soon as we recover the painting they'll cease to trouble you."

"I had to kill him." Kalugin's mouth trembled. "He thought I was stealing his things. He took hold of my arm, but I didn't have time! I only hit him with the back of my hand, but he died. All of them died."

"Yet that *was* their mortal fate." I attempted to console him. "Death swiftly at your hand or some protracted agony of drowning, which would the poor man have preferred? It's not as though anything you did could have saved any of them. You saved the Delacroix, at least. Think of that! Consider, my dear, what you have preserved for the ages."

Kalugin drew a harsh breath. "Do you ever wonder whether we don't destroy as many things as we preserve by our meddling? I saved the painting, but perhaps if the ship had had a competent captain we wouldn't have foundered in the first place."

"Nonsense," said Victor forcefully. "For God's sake, man, what are you mourning? One self-indulgent millionaire and a handful of sailors like Hayes. And isn't *he* a prize? Which would you rather consign to the bottom, a work of art or a dirty little creature like Hayes? What possible difference can his nasty life make to the world?"

As if on cue, the shout came out of the twilight:

"Ahoy the *Chronos!* Ahoy! Ya think ya can buy me? Ya can't! I say I know what yer up to! And nobody cheats Mackie Hayes, ya hear me? Here I be and here I stay!"

Victor's moustaches swept up like scythe blades. "I do believe," he announced, "that it's time to fix that man's little red wagon." And he rose and strode from the saloon.

I settled back on the cushions with Kalugin and we watched the last pink light fade.

"Remember the DaVinci notebook," I told him.

"True." He passed a hand across his eyes wearily.

"And the cargo of the *Geldermalsen.*"

"True." With the other hand he drew out the pins and loosed my long hair.

"And Laperouse's logbook and specimens. All of them lost to the world forever, but for you, dearest."

"True." He closed his eyes. I leaned down to him. Dreamily he gathered up a tress and draped it across his face, making his night blacker still. "Yet sometimes I could wish . . ."

The stars shone briefly and then the advancing cloud cover put them out like candles. The sea was quite rough, now; we were obliged to weigh anchor and stand off from the *Elsie* some distance, lest we collide with her. Dinner was informal, cold meats and pickles and cheeses; no one had much appetite owing to the nature of the commotion in the bosom of the deep. How fortunate had we immortals been, if our creators had thought to make us proof against *mal de mer!* I have often mused on this, during a long life of journeys on Company affairs.

At half past nine Victor strolled into the saloon looking pleased with himself, and settled down to read the latest issue of the *London Illustrated News.* Kalugin and I played at piquet, with no great attention to the cards as the rolling of the ship grew more pronounced.

Before Victor had a chance to lay down the paper and amuse us with the latest antics of the British royal family, however, the door opened and the same Technician who had been reporting to Victor all day put in his head.

"Mme. Masaki has come aboard again, sir."

Victor tossed his paper aside and hurried on deck. We followed and arrived just in time to see the expectant smile dashed from his face by Mme. Masaki's cry of "D--n you, Victor!"

"I beg your pardon." Victor drew himself up in as stiff an attitude of affront as he could manage on the pitching deck. She was advancing on him in her diving costume, her face pale in the light of the lantern, her eyes blazing with anger.

"Lower the whaleboat!" She swept her wet hair back from her face. "You've got to send someone to rescue the woman. That boat is sinking!"

"You were ordered to punch a few holes in it, not scuttle the infernal thing!" Victor narrowed his eyes.

"I started one plank and a whole seam opened up! It's coming to pieces in the water! D--n you, will you lower that boat?"

But Kalugin was giving orders for it already. Mme. Masaki braced herself on the rail, drawing deep breaths. "And another thing," she told us. "The woman's alone over there. I was unable to perceive more than one mortal on board."

"Only one?" Victor frowned. "Where could Hayes have got to?"

We were answered by a thump. It was not even a sound, no more than a faint sensation against the soles of our feet, imperceptible I believe to mortal senses; but there, it came again, sharper against our hull and more distinct. Both Victor and Mme. Masaki responded with oaths of the most profane nature. She plunged once more over the side and disappeared in the black water. As she vanished we heard terrified screams from the sole occupant of the cabin on the *Elsie.*

Kalugin and his crew rowed like heroes, but it was a near thing. The doomed craft was turning in the night sea, listing with a stricken motion. I clung to the rail watching, sick at heart lest the rescuers arrive too late.

Judge with what relief I saw Mrs. Hayes lifted from the deck of the doomed *Elsie* and settled securely in the bottom of the whaleboat. Even as it put about and made back toward us through the waves, Mme. Masaki pulled herself up on the rail with one arm. She had her other arm fast about Hayes, whom she had choked into unconsciousness. "Help me!" she cried.

Victor and I ran to assist her. Hayes lay ghastly pale in the lantern light, a ridiculous wizened figure in his long undergarments. Victor knelt and I heard a smart click as he applied manacles to the oblivious sailor.

"I daresay that settles *your* hash," sneered Victor.

"Our hull is unbroached," reported Mme. Masaki. "Though somewhat scored. He was doing his best to sink us with a hammer and chisel. Had he been able to see what he was doing we'd have been in genuine danger. He's remarkably strong, for a mortal."

"What shall we do with him?" I glanced out at the whaleboat, rapidly pulling close. "It would be well to remove him before the girl can see him like this, surely."

"As you wish." Victor seized the connecting chain of the manacles and dragged Hayes's inert form in the direction of the forward hatches. "I shall revive the blackguard and *then . . .*"

Even as he got Hayes safely out of sight below, the wind rose to a howl and the waves, previously wild, grew positively violent, dashing the whaleboat against the *Chronos.* I heard Mrs. Hayes screaming in the darkness, and Kalugin reassuring her; Mme. Masaki and I bent down to help her aboard. As we did so, I looked out across the night and beheld the *Elsie* swing back over, giving one great drunken lurch before she righted herself, only to slide below the water. One last second her cabin light was visible, eerily sinking down toward eternal darkness; then it had vanished and I knew the rushing water had found it.

I was prevented from dwelling on this horror by the necessity of getting my arms around Mrs. Hayes, just as a cold wave broke over us. She screamed again, and with a final struggle we got her feet on deck and there we three huddled, dripping, as the crew got the whaleboat up.

"We must take her inside," I shouted to Mme. Masaki, who

responded with a brusque nod. We started along the rail to the door of the saloon; then Mrs. Hayes stopped abruptly and her thin fingers tightened on my arm. Her poor little face was like an animal's in its terror. She looked down, we followed her gaze, and saw a rush of water and blood. It steamed briefly on the deck before another wave mingled it with sea foam and swept it away.

She began crying, a shrill monotonous piping *Oh, Oh, Oh,* and we knew there was nothing for it but to take her by the arms and drag her, lest the child drop to the deck like a fish and tumble overboard.

And somehow we did bring her safely inside, half-carrying her to a bunk in one of the cabins, and saw her robed in a dry dressing gown before we took that opportunity for ourselves; her thin cries grew fainter but did not cease the while.

"Mrs. Hayes, Mrs. Hayes, you must compose yourself." I sat down beside her. "For the child's sake, my dear."

"You don't know," she sobbed. "My Mackie's drowned. He was going over to—Oh, it's God's judgement, that's what it is! Oh, I'm so ashamed! And now he's lost"

"Pray do not distress yourself, Mrs. Hayes, your husband is safe. We apprehended him. We have him safe below." I gave her a handkerchief.

"Oh!" Her cries stopped as she took that in. Then the weak line of her mouth trembled. "I tried to tell him what you said, but he got real mad. He said if you was so ready to pay him to let it alone, there must be lots of treasure in the wreck. And when he brought up all that money I said, 'Well let's go home Mackie and not be greedy,' but *he* said, 'Elsie you're a dumb'—he said I was a dumb— Oh, dear! And now we lost the money!" Her wails broke out afresh.

"Mrs. Hayes, you mustn't allow yourself to dwell on such things now. Think of your child! When did the pains begin?"

"Only just now." She gasped for breath. "Leastways—I been having a backache but I thought it was all the hauling I been doing." Her face contorted in the extremity of her discomfort. I gave her my arm to clutch tight, and as I did so made use of my scanning perception to take a reading on herself and her infant. Mortals are quite unable to discern such surreptitious examinations; had she not been already too distracted to notice my preoccupation, she might have supposed I was uttering a silent prayer.

I leaned back and stared at her. I saw again the cabin light of the *Elsie,* slipping away, slipping away down into the dark. I looked up at Mme. Masaki and transmitted my findings. Her lips drew back from her teeth.

We can't save them in such cases, you see. We mayn't interfere.

Even if we could, this poor creature had seen things the Company had never intended a mortal to see. She was a complication. I did not even want to think about Victor down in the hold with the unconscious Hayes. There is a Company drug called nepenthine, very useful in these unfortunate cases but not always entirely beneficial to those to whom it is administered . . .

"You'll need fresh linen," murmured Mme. Masaki, and departed. She came back bearing a bundle with something concealed in it, and in one hand she carefully carried a glass of what appeared to be sherry wine.

"You like drink, miss?" She offered it to Mrs. Hayes.

"Oh, I've never touched spirits—" she protested.

"But this is for the child's sake," I struck up my refrain again. "You must take it as medicine, my dear."

She allowed herself to be persuaded by this argument and in moments was blissfully unconscious, which permitted us to set up the anticontaminant apparatus. Hayes's child was born shortly thereafter. The wind howled in the rigging, waves broke over us in vain, the timbers of the *Chronos* creaked unceasing; the feeble cries were barely audible over the tumult of the storm, and did not last long.

Kalugin knew something was wrong when he passed Mme. Masaki in the passageway, her face closed and silent. He peered around the door.

I sat with the infant in my lap, in a pool of light that moved as the lamp swung on its gimbal. Mrs. Hayes slept soundly in her bunk.

"He's a boy, is he?" Kalugin came in and bent over us. The child lay still; it had already discovered that moving took much more strength than it had. Kalugin noticed the cyanosis at once, and scanning he found the heart defect. "Oh, dear," he said. He put a finger in the tiny cold hand, which closed on it without force. The infant worked its face into a squinting grimace that was a perfect parody of its father, but it did not cry. It hadn't enough breath.

Kalugin sat down beside me. I leaned against him and we watched the child fight.

"The mother will do well enough," I said tiredly. "For the present. Although her grief, and her brute of a husband, and her poverty and her disappointment will make her wonder why she should."

"Victor is finishing up with Hayes now," said Kalugin. "Nothing left to do but the post-hypnosis, I expect. As soon as the storm clears we can put them ashore, and well and truly wash our hands of the wretched things."

I nodded. The child made a gurgling sound and all its limbs stiffened.

For a terrible moment we waited; but, like a swimmer cresting a wave, it struggled and drew another breath, and kept breathing.

"It's Pity, like the newborn babe, striding the blast," said Kalugin softly. "Here he is, come to visit us. Yes, hello, I know you well, don't I? You've lived in my heart this many a year. One more piece of mortal wreckage I must watch sink."

The rocking of the lamp was growing less; the squall was blowing out. Kalugin went on in his sleepy voice:

"I've gone down with too many ships, Nan. Why couldn't they have made me strong, like Victor? I really ought to get into another line of work."

And we laughed at that, both of us, sadly, for none of us can ever, ever get into another line of work. We are what we are. Kalugin kissed me and took the child in his arms.

"You need to sleep, my love. I'll watch them a while. Go on."

So I went, gratefully, and (to admit my cowardice) readily enough as well, for I knew the child would be gone soon and I would be relieved to avoid any further mortal tragedy. Yet it seemed I was not to be spared that sorrow, for I was wakened from brief dreams by Mrs. Hayes crying out. I drew on my robe and ran to her cabin.

She was alone there, sitting up wild-eyed. "Where's my baby?" she demanded. "What did you do with my baby?"

I took both her hands in my own. "My dear, I know you are strong—"

"Why, what's all the to-do?" inquired Kalugin, coming in behind me. I whirled about to look at him. He was unshaven and his eyes were puffy with exhaustion, but there was an enormous jauntiness in his whole frame. "Here's the little chap!" And he produced the infant from inside his coat like a conjuror. I snatched the child from him and scanned it hastily.

It was not only still alive but vibrantly alive, its flesh a deep rose color, its tiny heart beating strongly. Not all the radiant health in the world could make it a pretty child, because it was the image of its father; nevertheless it had a certain goblin charm. So much was clear even without benefit of much examination: Kalugin had spirited the little thing off to the ship's dispensary and repaired its heart defect. If that were all!

As I probed deeper, my horrified perceptions made the shocking truth quite plain: the child had not merely been repaired but *modified!* Made one of us, in a manner of speaking. Not to the extent of making him an immortal, of course, for Kalugin had neither the knowledge, tools nor time to do such a dreadful thing: but I read enhanced abilities, certain crude structural improvements, favorable genetic mutations induced . . . I began to tremble as I realized the extent of the changes Kalugin had wrought. I attempted to scan a second time to be certain, but Mrs. Hayes was reaching out for him.

I put him in her arms. "It's a little boy, Mrs. Hayes," I told her in a faint voice.

"Oh, Mackie'll be ever so happy!" she exclaimed, and fell to examining him with delight. I turned wondering eyes to Kalugin. *Do you understand what you have done?*

You shan't tell anyone, he transmitted. *I shan't tell anyone. Who's to know?*

I had no words to respond to him that might suitably express my terror and dismay. To breach Company procedure in such a fashion was to risk far, far more serious consequences than disciplinary counseling. Oh, if he were ever found out!

"What's this, though?" Mrs. Hayes fretted, touching the thin red scar on the infant's breast.

"A birthmark, I should guess." Kalugin gathered me to him with an arm. I must have seemed in danger of fainting. "Nothing to concern you unduly, Mrs. Hayes. Why, he can have it covered with a tattoo when he grows up—for I daresay he'll be a sailor, like his father."

"I guess so." She looked wistful. "Though I kind of hope he turns out to be a Christian instead. Mackie don't hold with gospel much." Her face became woebegone as she remembered the predicament her mate was in. Kalugin patted her hand gallantly.

"In view of the happy occasion, we have decided not to press charges against Mr. Hayes," he informed her. "Our intention is to set you ashore presently, with some remuneration for Mr. Hayes's services on the *Gladstone,* to which he is after all entitled. We do regret the loss of your boat, but she was scarcely seaworthy. You were lucky to escape with your lives. What a blessing we were standing by when she went down!"

She dissolved in tears of gratitude. I held close to Kalugin, marveling at him.

Some little while after I took Mrs. Hayes's things out on deck to dry them. The spiral of the storm was moving away to the north leaving behind a fine morning, with strong sunlight and a freshening breeze. Sea birds circled the *Chronos,* wheeling and mewing; dolphins leapt and sported in the glittering water all around us.

"Yes, all nature rejoices at our success," said Victor grandly, pausing in a lap of his morning constitutional about the deck. "The loathsome

Hayes is safely immured below, happy in his oblivion. He shan't wake until well after he's safely ashore and we've salvaged the *Gladstone.*"

"You've persuaded him to discretion?" I spread out a shabby cotton frock in the sunlight.

"Oh, quite. If he ever does speak of us to anyone, it'll be in such a way his hearers will condemn him for a rank liar or a lunatic. Never fear. I gather the unfortunate female pupped, by the way?"

I pursed my lips. "Yes, the poor child had her blessed event early this morning. Need we do anything further? Her lot could scarcely be made more unfortunate. Ought we not err on the side of compassion and set her ashore without further processing?"

"Hm! I suppose so. Some sort of humane gesture might be in order. She's got to live with Hayes, after all! Though I rather think he'll ship out on the first vessel he can hail, now that his prospects for the *Gladstone* are gone. Didn't strike me as a family man."

This was certainly likely, and for Mrs. Hayes's sake I could not be unhappy at the prospect of her abandonment by such a creature. But in truth there was some quality of ineffable happiness in the morning air, for all the violent and near-tragic events of the night now past, some celestial mirth at some tremendous joke. And the unthinkable joke was on Victor, after all. *So long as he never found out what Kalugin had done . . .*

Toward midday we put in to the island, where Mrs. Hayes directed us to a likely anchorage. The settlement there was no more than a cluster of squatters' shacks, gray and leaning with age, tucked away in the ravines under the looming mountains of the interior. A few goats grazed on the hills; there were a few garden patches where patient industry had coaxed forth a few dry cabbage and spinach plants, and one or two fig trees. Upon this dismal prospect Mrs. Hayes looked with fond anticipation, when she could bear to lift her regard from happy contemplation of the child who slept shaded in her bosom, and allowed herself to be handed down into the whaleboat without a murmur. She did look up with timid concern when Hayes was brought up on deck in a stretcher; she did squeak and flutter in a wifely way as the servants loaded him into the whaleboat; but it was evident that their parting, when it should occur, would be considerably softened by the presence of her boy.

With a merry face Kalugin bent to the oars to take them to land. Mme. Masaki and I waved our handkerchiefs in farewell, Victor beamed on them in his cold way, thumbs in his waistcoat pockets; a band of ragged children came running down to the water's edge to help the passengers ashore. I felt again the sensation of being present at some event of cosmic significance, on that bright day in that remote place; yet I have been present at several significant moments in history without any such mysterious intimations at all.

We put to sea again and returned to the site of the wreck. Once we had blessed *privacy,* it took less than two hours to locate and retrieve the long cylinder containing the lost painting. Kalugin and Mme. Masaki rose to the surface bearing it between them, and when it was safely on board it was borne straight to my laboratory, where, having made all the necessary preparations, I waited to receive it and begin the work of restoration.

When he had bathed and rested from his ordeal, Kalugin stopped in to visit me as I bent over the object of our concern.

"How badly was it damaged?" he inquired.

"Not badly at all, dearest. There are a few little tears. The varnish bloomed, as you see, but really I have seen much worse."

Kalugin leaned close to consider Delacroix's great canvas opened out before us. An outdoor temple was the setting, milk-white columns rising into a sky black and churning with storm clouds. From the upper-right-hand corner, Jupiter looked down on the scene with paternal indulgence and a certain Gallic smirk. Juno his spouse regarded him from the upper-left-hand corner, her stare terrible and direct, holding in her raised hands the serpents with which she intended to avenge herself. Their bright coils and the patterns of her bracelets formed spiraling patterns of energy echoed in the draperies on Queen Alcmene's couch, down in the center-right of the canvas; she must have had a Celtic needlewoman. The queen herself lay in a cozy pool of golden light, pale limbs slack with the exhaustion of her labor, lifting sweet vacant features to the midwife. This figure stood half-silhouetted in the left foreground, enigmatic and powerful, holding up the infant demigod; and he was rendered with strong and twisting brushstrokes in smoky red, not an idealized cherub at all but a howling, flailing, bloody newborn.

"Extraordinary painting," remarked Kalugin. "What contrasts! Sentimental and crude all at once. What can the artist have been thinking of?"

"It's an allegory, dear," I explained, reaching for another scrap of cottonwool. "There was some kind of scandal in Paris society. Someone the artist knew was a co-respondent in a *dread*fully public divorce trial, with a question of paternity. The painting was done as a joke, in rather poor taste I think, and was never exhibited for that reason."

"What vile, silly creatures they are." Kalugin shook his head. "And yet, look: out of such a sordid business comes beauty. I am not sorry for what I did."

I set down my materials and turned, taking his hand firmly in my own. *You mustn't speak of that again, my love. Not ever.*

Never again, he agreed. *But if I lay at the bottom of the sea a thousand nights for it, still would I have done the same.*

He kissed me and went away to his own duties. Presently the sunlight slanted and moved along the wall: the *Chronos* was tacking about, taking us home to Europe. I opened another bottle of cleaning solvent and settled in to the rhythms of my work, making fresh and new again the old story of the birth of the Hero.

In the future we will all be very healthy, very attractive, and very, very good. It will be illegal to be otherwise.

Today, the ordinary citizen in Britain is under more constant surveillance from remote cameras than in any other country in the world. In West Hollywood, it is illegal to describe oneself as a "Pet Owner"; one must use the term, "Animal Guardian." Elsewhere in America, there is a movement afoot to outlaw serving large portions of food in restaurants, on the grounds that this is a criminal act contributing to obesity. Several public interest groups have successfully criminalized the wearing of perfume in public places. Many communities have laws in effect penalizing untidy yards or even the ownership of clotheslines, on the grounds that they lower property values. Can it be long until physical ugliness is prohibited too, for the mental distress it occasions in others?

Popular psychology now informs us that our misfortunes and illnesses are our own fault, brought about by our unconscious urges; secular puritanism, as I live and breathe! But surely Coercive Law will set us all to rights, and make certain that we cannot pose a threat to ourselves or others.

Hooray.

◆ ◆ ◆

Monster Story

WHEN ALEC CHECKERFIELD WAS TEN, HE WAS
Sorted.

The official name for it was Pre-Societal Vocational Appraisal, but
what it amounted to was that Alec, with every other ten-year-old child
in England, was examined to determine how he'd best fit into society.
Sorting had been going on for nearly a century now, and everyone
agreed it worked much better than the old haphazard way of choosing
careers.

"It's nothing to be worried about," Lewin assured him, pacing back
and forth at the end of the long polished table. "You're such a bright
boy, Alec, you're sure to do well."

Alec sat at the other end of the table and wondered why Lewin was
sweating. He could tell Lewin was sweating from all the way across the
room, which was one of the reasons Lewin was sweating.

"Is it just a test like we have at St. Stephen's?" Alec asked.

"Not exactly," said Lewin.

Lewin was Alec's butler. Alec lived in a mansion in London with his
butler and Mrs. Lewin, his cook. Alec's Daddy was off on a yacht in the
Caribbean and Alec's Mummy was staying with friends somewhere.
Alec hadn't seen either of them since he was four.

"Then how is it different?"

Lewin gave up on class distinction and paced down to Alec's end of
the room, where he pulled out a chair and sat with his elbows on the
table. "It's like this, son. The PSVA isn't a test to see how much you

167

know; it's to see what kind of person you are. That way they'll know what sort of job to put you in when you grow up, and just how to train you for it when you leave primary school."

"But I already know what I'm going to be when I grow up," said Alec with a sigh. He was sighing because he was going to have to be the seventh earl of Finsbury and attend a Circle of Thirty, when what he really wanted to be was a pirate.

"Well, yeh, but they have to go through the motions, don't they?" said Lewin, leaning forward confidentially. "You'll be Sorted right out in public with all the other little kids, Admins like you and Consumers alike, so it looks like everybody gets a fair chance. And it is mostly fair. Every year there's a couple Consumer boys and girls score so high they get to join a Circle. And there's usually an Admin kid who doesn't make the grade."

"What happens then?"

"Nothing bad," Lewin assured him quickly. "He'll get trained for a nice low-stress job somewhere and never have to worry about much. But that won't happen to you, son. You'll go right on into your Circle because of your dad being who he is. And you'll like it in Circle. You'll get to meet other kids!"

Alec thought that might be fun. He had never met any children. "Will there be other kids when we go there tomorrow?" he asked.

Lewin nodded. "Which is why," he said, drawing an envelope from an inner pocket, "you'll need to take this." He opened it and shook out a bright blue capsule. "Ministry sends 'em out free. Jolly little pill, see? It's to fight off any germs you might pick up from anybody. Kids used to have to get stuck with needles to keep them well. Aren't you lucky you don't? But you're to take that after supper tonight."

"Okay." Alec picked it up and dropped it in his blazer pocket.

"Good lad." Lewin shifted uneasily in his seat and cleared his throat. "You'll pass with flying colors, son, I know, but . . . you want to make a good impression."

"Because first impressions are very important," Alec agreed, echoing the Social Interaction Programme he'd been given.

"Yeh. So we aren't going to talk about, er, pirates or anything, are we, son?"

"Nope," said Alec solemnly.

"And we don't want to show off how smart we are, eh? No talk about what you can do with your little toolkit. Not a good idea to let people know you're a bit different."

"Oh, no," Alec agreed. "Because that would make the other children feel bad about themselves."

"Just so," said Lewin, feeling relieved. "You'll make your father proud, son. Time for school now!"

"Yes, sir," said Alec, and sliding from his chair he ran upstairs to his schoolroom. He was eager to make the sixth earl proud of him; he thought that if he did, perhaps his Daddy might come home some day. Perhaps he might even take Alec back to sea with him, and things might be the way they had been before the divorce.

He knew it wasn't actually his fault his Mummy hadn't wanted children, but she had gone away all the same; so that was another reason he must be good and get high marks in school.

But not too high.

Alec entered his schoolroom, sat down at the console and logged on to St. Stephen's Primary. The surveillance cameras in the upper corners of the room followed him. The nearest one telescoped outward suddenly and sent forth a scan. Meanwhile, Alec watched the icon of the frowning headmaster appear on his console's screen. He picked up the reader and passed it over the pattern of stripes in his school tie, wherein was encoded his identification. The frowning headmaster changed to a smiling one, and Alec was admitted to morning lessons.

Before he could begin, however, a gravelly voice spoke out of the cabinet to his left.

"Bloody hell, boy, what's that in yer jacket?"

As Alec turned from the console, a cone of light shot forth from the Maldecena projector on top of the cabinet. There was a flicker of code and then the form of a man materialized. He was big, with a wild black beard and a fierce and clever face. He wore a coat of scarlet broadcloth. He wore a cocked hat.

He wasn't supposed to look like that. He was supposed to look like a jolly old sea captain in a yachting cap, harmless and cheery, in keeping with the Pembroke Playfriend he had been programmed to be when it was purchased for Alec. Alec had tinkered with the Playfriend's programming, however, removing the Ethical Governor, and the Captain was far from harmless now.

"It's a pill, so I won't catch germs from the other kids tomorrow," Alec explained.

"No it ain't! That damned thing's got circuitry in it."

"It has?" Alec slipped the capsule out of his pocket and looked at it curiously.

"Get the tools out, boy," the Captain snarled. "We'd best have a look at it."

"But it's class time."

"Bugger class time! Send 2–D Alec instead this morning," the Captain told him. Alec grinned and, taking the buttonball, ordered up the two-dimensional Alec program he had designed to answer questions for him when he needed to be somewhere other than St. Stephen's.

"Aye aye, Captain sir," he said, hopping back from the console and going to his work table. He pulled out his chair and sat down, taking from a pocket his small case of terribly useful tools. The Captain hauled an adult-sized chair from cyberspace and set it beside the little table, where he bent down awkwardly to glare at the blue capsule.

After scanning it intently a moment, he swore for forty-five seconds. Alec listened happily. He had learned a lot of interesting words from the Captain.

"Germs, my arse," said the Captain. "There's a monitor in the little bastard! And I know why, by thunder. Old Lewin said you was to take this afore bedtime, I'll wager?"

"Yes."

"Hmph. What he don't know is, it's part of the goddamn PSVA." The Captain stroked his beard, considering the capsule balefully. "Once that thing's inside you, it'll transmit yer reactions to the questions themselves. The Education Committee'll get yer pulse, blood pressure, respiration, reaction times—that whole lot. Like you was hooked up to one of them old lie detectors."

"But I'm not going to tell any lies," said Alec.

"That ain't the point, son! Didn't Lewin explain about what this Sorting is for?"

Alec nodded. "It's to see what kind of person I am."

"And that's just what we don't want 'em to see, matey!"

"Oh," said Alec resignedly. "Because I'm different, right?"

Alec did not know how he was different from other people. He had drawn the conclusion that he was simply very smart, which was why he was able to do things like look at a tree and immediately say how many leaves were on it, or decrypt the site defense of a Pembroke Playfriend so it could be reprogrammed to his liking.

Only the Captain knew the truth about Alec, and only some of the truth at that.

"Bloody busybodies," the Captain growled. "Wouldn't they just love to get their hooks into my boy? But we'll broadside 'em, Alec. We'll rig their little spy to tell 'em just what we want 'em to know, eh? Open it up, matey, and let's have a look."

"Okay!" Alec took out his jeweler's loupe, which had an elastic band to go around his head so he could wear it like an eyepatch. He slid it on and peered at the capsule, turning it this way and that.

"It unscrews here. Ooh, look." With a twist of his fingers he had opened the capsule and spilled its contents out on a dish: a tiny component of some kind and a quarter-teaspoon of yellow powder. "There's the spy. What's the yellow stuff?"

"That'll be the real medicine, I reckon," said the Captain. "Set to leak out of that little pinprick hole. Sweep it off on the carpet! You ain't taking none of that, neither."

"But I don't want to catch germs," protested Alec, drawing out tweezers and the other tools he would need.

"You won't catch no bloody germs," muttered the Captain. Alec's brain wasn't the only thing that was different about him. "Never mind it, son. We'll need the extra room in the capsule, anyhow, to clamp on a RAT node what'll feed it false data."

"Yo ho ho!" Alec cried gleefully, pulling out a little case of node components. He set about connecting one to the spy. The Captain watched him.

"See, it ain't enough to have the right answers—though you will have, my lad, because I broke into the Ministry of Higher Education's database and got 'em last week. You'll be judged on the way you answer too, d'y'see?"

"I'm not sure."

"Take the tenth question, goes like this (the Captain made a throat-clearing noise and pursed up his mouth in a bureaucratic simper): 'You be having a lovely day at the jolly seaside. A lady walks past and the top half of her bloody bathing suit falls off. Do you (A) fetch it and give it back to her like a good lad, (B) just sit and look at her boobies, or (C) look the other way and pretend nothing ain't happened?'"

"Oh." Alec looked up from the components, going a little glazed-eyed as he imagined the scene. "Erm . . . I guess, A, fetch it for her, because that'd be polite."

"A, says you? Haar. Correct answer'd be C, matey. Looking the other way's what all morally correct folks does," the Captain sneered. "Fetching it for her would be a insult, 'cos she'd be perfectly able to get it herself, and besides, when you handed it back you'd still get yerself a peek at her boobies, wouldn't you?"

"Yes," Alec admitted. "But you told me it was okay to think about ladies' boobies."

"Well, so it is, son, but you can't say so."

"But I wouldn't be saying so."

"But with that there spy inside you, they'd be able to tell you was thinking about 'em, see? By how long you took to answer the question and what yer heartbeat did and whether you was blushing and so on," the Captain explained.

"Oh." Alec scowled. He looked down at the components and worked away in silence a moment before inquiring, "What would they do if you answered B?"

"They'd fix on you with a spyglass, lad, certain sure. And if you answered the rest of the questions like that you'd scuttle yerself, because they'd stamp Potential Sociopath on yer file. I reckon you can guess what'd happen then."

"I wouldn't get to join a Circle of Thirty?"

"Hell no," said the Captain somberly. "And you'd have to go to sessions with one of them psychiatric AI units what's got no sense of humor, for months likely, and the end of it all'd be you'd spend the rest of yer life wearing a monitor and inputting data in a basement office somewhere. That's if you was lucky! If the test scores was bad enough, they might just ship you off to Hospital."

Alec shivered. Hospital was where bad people were sent. Even children were sent there, if they were bad; and it was supposed to be very hard to get out of Hospital, once you'd got in.

"But that ain't happening to my little Alec," said the Captain comfortingly. "Because we'll cheat the sons of bitches, won't we?"

"Aye aye, sir," said Alec. "There! All hooked up. Now, what'll we feed it?"

The Captain grinned wickedly and his eyes, which were the changeable color of the sea, went a dangerous and shifting green.

"Prepare to input code, son. On my mark, as follows . . ." and he gave Alec a lengthy code that would convince the tiny spy that Alec's reactions to the Sorting would be those of a bright (but not too bright) socially well-adjusted human child, fit in every way to join the ruling classes. Alec chortled and input as he was bid, wondering what it would be like to meet other children.

Next morning Alec got to see something that very seldom happened nowadays: dense traffic, from the sea of floating agcars that thronged around the Ministry of Education and jockeyed for space at the mounting blocks.

There were shiny black limos with house crests on the doors, just like his, and Lewin explained that those belonged to good Admin families like Alec's. There were sporty agcars in bright colors, and those belonged (so Lewin explained, with a slight sniff) to Admin families who had *let the side down* and failed to live up to their societal obligations. There were black limos without crests, and those belonged to (sniff) climbers who thought they could buy their way into Circles.

There were also big public transports, crowding everyone as they bobbed and bounded up to the mounting blocks, and arriving on those were the Consumer classes.

All the traffic was exciting, though Alec didn't like the way it smelled very much. What he found far more exciting was the slow parade of people making their way down the steps of the mounting blocks and into the Ministry building. He had never seen so many children in his life! He counted all of thirty as his chauffeur edged closer to the block, waiting for their turn to get out.

He'd seen children from a distance, when he'd been taken on outings to museums or parks, but only from a distance: little figures being pulled along by parents or nannies, as he had been, muffled in coats against the cold, protected by umbrellas from the rain or the sun. Sometimes even their faces were invisible, hidden behind anti-pathogen masks or masks designed to filter out pollen and particulate matter.

But, now! These were children ready, as Alec was more than ready, to make their first official public appearance in the big world. Boys and girls each in the uniforms of their own primary schools, wearing ties of different stripes and colors, nervous little faces bared to the cold air and light of day. Alec wondered why they all looked so scared. He felt sad for them, especially when he remembered that they all had transmitters in their tummies, telling the Education Committee how scared they were.

At least they didn't know they were carrying transmitters. Alec thought smugly of his, which was broadcasting that he was a healthy, well-adjusted boy. He wasn't scared. Though somebody in the car was scared . . . Alec sniffed the air and turned curiously to Lewin, who was staring out the window with a worried face.

"What's the matter, Lewin?"

Lewin blinked at the line of children, each child with a black-coated adult. "Those can't be ten-year-olds," he murmured.

"Yes, they are," said Alec in surprise. "They have to be ten. Remember? They're all here for the test, too."

"That's not what I meant," said Lewin, wiping sweat from his face with a tissue. "They're tiny."

Alec puzzled over that, because the other children did not look especially small to him, in fact they were all pretty much the same exact size; but when at last his turn came, and he and Lewin stepped from the gently rocking car onto the block, he realized what was wrong. He towered over the other children, head and shoulders.

"Hell," Lewin said softly.

Alec felt his mouth go dry. He jammed his hands in his pockets to keep from grabbing at Lewin's coat, and was very glad the spy transmitter could only broadcast that he, Alec Checkerfield, was cool, calm and collected. But first one and then another grownup turned to stare at him, where he stood on the block, and now some of the children

were staring too, and pointing, and he heard the whispers beginning.
"What's wrong with that child?"
". . . fourteen at least!"
". . . can't see how his parents were allowed . . ."
". . . genetics in these old families . . ."
"Mummy, why's he like that?"
"Never you mind," grunted Lewin. "Come on, son."

Alec held his head up and marched down the stairs. He pretended they were Wapping Old Stairs. This was Execution Dock and he was a pirate, and they were taking him to be hanged. Step, step, step and they were all staring at him, but he'd show them how bravely he could die. Three times the tide would ebb and flow before the bastards let him go.

Lewin marched beside Alec, meeting the stares with a look of cold challenge. Being nearly a hundred years old, he could remember perfectly well when the occasional tall kid in a class had been nothing to make a fuss over. That had been before the pandemic in '77, of course, and then the really bad outbreak in '91. Maybe the alarmists were right when they'd said the gene pool was shrinking . . .

At least Alec seemed to be taking it well. He had gone quite pale, but his face was blank and serene, almost rapturous as he stretched out his arms for the guard at the door to run the sensor wand over him.

It gave a tiny *beep* and Lewin panicked, thinking Alec might have brought one of his odd little toys with him; but the guard didn't react, merely waved Alec through, and Lewin realized that the wand was beeping like that for each child. He realized it must be the all-clear signal and relaxed, but his nerves had been so jangled that when he heard someone sniggering, "You don't suppose that dried-up old prole is his father, do you?" he turned and snapped:

"My young gentleman is the son of my lord the earl of Finsbury!"

And that shut them up, all right. A beefy moustached somebody went bright red and sidled behind somebody else. Lewin looked down to see if Alec had been upset, but Alec hadn't heard.

. . . He was mounting the ladder to the gallows now, fantastically brave, and allowing the executioner to put the noose around his neck, and there were lots of ladies weeping for him in the crowd because he was so fearless, and they all had huge boobies . . .

"Come on, son." Lewin tapped Alec on the shoulder to guide him into the long line of children shuffling along the corridor, paralleled by parents or guardians. The line was moving quickly, and in a moment they had entered the vast auditorium where the PSVA was to be held. Here, guards separated the two lines: children were sent onto the floor, where the long rows of test consoles waited, and adults were directed up into a gallery of seats overlooking the hall.

Lewin clambered up the stairs and took his seat, peering down at the floor. He watched as Alec, looming above the other kids, edged sidelong into his chair and sat looking around with a stunned expression. One hundred sixty-three children, and more coming in all the time.

And here came a little boy making his way through the rows, trying to get to the vacant console next to Alec's. When he saw Alec, however, he stopped in his tracks.

"Don't be scared," Alec told him. "I'm just big."

The boy bit his lip, but started forward again and at last sat down at the console. He was small and thin, with a *café au lait* complexion and gray-blue eyes. Alec observed him with great interest.

"Hello. My name is Alec Checkerfield. What's your name?"

"F-Frankie Chatterton," said the other boy, looking terrified. "That's my D-Dad and Mummy up there," he added, pointing to the gallery. Alec looked up at the gallery, where there were precisely two hundred twelve grownups at that moment, and spotted a very dark man with a big black moustache and a lady with a red dot between her eyes. They were both staring at Frankie with expressions of agonized protectiveness. Frankie waved at them and Alec waved too.

"Where's your people?" Frankie inquired.

"Oh, somewhere," said Alec airily, gesturing at the gallery. "You know."

"Are you w-worried?"

"Nope."

"I'm really wuh-worried," said Frankie. "This is very important, you know."

"It'll be a piece of cake, yeah?" Alec told him. Frankie wrinkled his brow as he pondered that. Trying to think of something to put him at his ease, Alec said, "Those are cool shoes."

They were black and shiny, made of patent leather, and no other child in the room wore anything like them. Frankie looked down proudly. "They have *style,"* he said. Dad didn't w-want me to wear them, but I stopped breathing until Mummy said he had to let me." He reached into his pocket and drew out a tiny silver pin, which he fixed in his tie with great care.

"What's that?"

"It's a good-luck token," Frankie replied. Alec looked at it closely: a little bat, with pinpoint red stones for eyes.

"Wow," said Alec, because he couldn't think of anything else to say.

Frankie lowered his voice and explained, "I like monster stories, see."

"Oh!" said Alec, delighted. He looked around furtively. "I like pirates," he whispered.

"Wow, that's really bad!" said Frankie, grinning. But in the next moment his smile fled, as the first of the test administrators ascended the high platform where the podium was. He went pale and cringed down in his seat, whimpering "Oh, no! Not yet, not yet, please, I'm not r-ready."

"It's okay! See the clock? We're not supposed to start for another five minutes," Alec pointed out. "What are you scared of?"

"I'm scared I'll f-fail the test," Frankie moaned, clutching the desk to steady himself.

"Why should you fail?" Alec asked. "You aren't dumb. I mean, you don't talk like you are."

"But what if I don't g-get into Circle?" cried Frankie. "You don't understand. Everybody's been saying I'd never get into Circle since I was d-diagnosed."

"Diagnosed?" Alec knit his brows. "What's that mean?"

Frankie looked at him as though he were mad. "You know," he said. "When they take you to the d-doctor and he diagnoses you as an eccentric!"

"Oh." Alec had never been to a doctor in his life, because he had never been sick. All his annual medical examinations had been done long-distance, with a scanner, and the Captain had carefully showed him how to cancel the readings and input different ones so as not to draw unwanted attention to himself, because doctors were a lot of meddling sons of whores. He pretended to understand now. "Oh! Right. Well, don't feel bad. If you don't get into Circle, you'll get trained for a nice low-stress job somewhere, and you'll never have to worry about much."

"But my Dad and Mum," said Frankie, biting his nails. "It would k-kill them. They've slaved for me and sacrificed for me, and I'm their only son. I must succeed. I have a responsibility not to disappoint them."

Alec, who knew what it was to disappoint one's Dad and Mum, winced. He leaned close to Frankie and spoke in an undertone.

"Listen. You want the answers? It's an easy pattern. It's all Cs until question 18, then all Fs until question 30, then straight Ds the rest of the way until the last question, and that's A."

"What?" Frankie stared at him, confused.

Alec looked into Frankie's eyes, holding his gaze, and made his voice as soothing as he could. "C to 18, F to 30, D to the end, then A," he repeated. "See?"

"C to 18, F to 30, D to the end, A," Frankie echoed in bewilderment.
"What's that thing you're doing with your eyes?"

"Nothing," said Alec, leaning back hastily.

"C to 18, F to 30, D to end, A. Yes, you did! They're all—"

"Don't be scared! I just—"

At that moment the first test administrator rapped sharply on the podium, and Frankie jumped in his seat as though he'd been struck. Silence fell quickly in the hall, as the last of the adults and children found their places.

"Good afternoon," said the administrator pleasantly. There was a vast mumbling response from the audience. He smiled out at them all and, from the big framed picture above his head, Queen Mary's vague pretty face welcomed them too. Alec pretended to do the stiff little wrist-only Royal Wave, trying to make Frankie laugh. Frankie gave a tiny smile with teeth and riveted his glance on the administrator.

"How very glad I am to see you here today," said the administrator. "You future citizens of a great nation! With the exception of seventeen children whose parents refused the Appraisal for *political* reasons," and he chuckled as though the Neopunks were harmless oddballs, "every ten-year-old in England is assembled under this roof. Girls and boys, I am honored to meet you all."

Alec looked around, awed. Two hundred seventy-three children! And it was clear that the vast hall had been built for even more; plenty of consoles sat vacant.

The administrator continued:

"Some of you may be a little nervous. Some of you may be under the impression that this is a contest. But I want to assure each one of you, as well as your parents and guardians, that every child in this room is a winner today.

"It wasn't always so. Why, once upon a time, only the children of privilege were given this chance! Today, we're all equals. There will be no special tests given privately to children whose mums and dads are a bit better off than others. No private tutors. No coaches. Here, in public, each child of every family, regardless of class, will be tested where all can see. The results of the Appraisal will be announced before everyone, today. This will prove that not only are we an egalitarian society; we can be *seen* to be egalitarian!"

He paused, with an air of triumph, and there was scattered applause. He cleared his throat and leaned forward, continuing:

"And today, in this democratic process, we will select those whose natural talents predetermine them to lead the nation of tomorrow. Yet, all will play their part in running the great machine of state. Each boy and girl has a duty, and all are of equal importance. It remains only to properly assign each task to the child best suited for it.

"What is required of a good citizen? What has been required by all nations, in every era. Obedience to law, social awareness, and social conformity . . ."

Especially conformity, thought Lewin irritably. He looked down on the rows of little faces, different colored faces to be sure but otherwise as identical as so many young blobs of pudding, vanilla and chocolate and coffee and strawberry. Except for Alec, of course, fidgeting in his seat as he listened to the administrator.

It wasn't simply that the boy was tall for his age. It wasn't simply that his features were a bit unusual (though now that he was growing up it was more painfully evident, as his strange face lengthened and the broad high cheekbones rose like cliffs under Alec's pale eyes). Alec would undoubtedly have to endure being called things like Horseface and Scarecrow once he'd got out in the world; but nobody goes to Hospital for a nickname. Alec's natural talents, on the other hand . . .

Not that Lewin was exactly sure what Alec's natural talents were, or if in fact they were natural at all.

Lewin gritted his teeth now, remembering life as it had been eleven years ago. No worries then, other than seeing to it that the sixth earl didn't get falling-down drunk in public.

Roger Checkerfield had been the sweetest, gentlest upper-class twit it had ever been Lewin's pleasure to serve. Nominally he was a junior executive with some big multinational firm, but as far as Lewin knew, Roger drew his paycheck simply for loafing around from island to island on his yacht. The life had seemed to suit Lady Finsbury too, though she had ten times Roger's brainpower and was coolly beautiful besides.

Then the call had come, one quiet afternoon when Lewin had been cleaning up the debris of a New Year's party that had lasted most of a week. Private call for Roger from London, urgent business; Roger had staggered from his deck chair, taken the call in his cabin and come out fifteen minutes later white as a sheet. He'd gone straight to the bar and poured himself a stiff drink. After he'd gulped it down like water he'd ordered a change of course, without explanation.

Then he'd gone in to see Lady Finsbury. There had been a hissed quarrel they'd all tried not to hear, though Roger had raised his voice from time to time in a pleading manner. The end of it was that Lady Finsbury had locked herself in her cabin and, in a way, never came out again.

That night late they'd lain off Cromwell Cay, and Lewin had not asked what their business was there; but he had seen the red light blinking on the flat sand spit, suggestive of a waiting helicraft. Roger had taken the launch and gone ashore alone, and when he returned had handed up the pretty black girl, Sarah, and the little blanketed bundle she'd brought with her. The bundle had been Alec.

In addition to Alec, she'd brought paperwork Lewin and the rest of the crew had all had to sign, attesting that tiny Alec William St. James Thorne Checkerfield was the earl and Lady Finsbury's son, born right there on the yacht. In return they all got generous annuities.

But other than holding Alec for the obligatory birth announcement holo, Lady Finsbury had refused ever to touch the child.

After that Roger had begun drinking in the mornings, drinking all day, and Lady Finsbury had opted out of the marriage when Alec was four. Roger had taken Alec to the London townhouse, set up a household with servants, and managed to stay sober for a week before he'd quietly vanished over the horizon and never come back. Not a word of explanation, other than occasional incoherent and remorseful audiomail hinting that Alec was different, somehow, and nobody was to know.

Different how, damn it? That the boy was a bloody little genius with numbers, that he was able to make unauthorized modifications to supposedly childproof things (and what a lot of Roger's money it had taken to hush that up!), that he was able to program all the household systems by himself including the security protocols—none of that need necessarily land a child in Hospital. It could be explained away as a freak of precocity.

But if Alec were some other kind of freak . . . Lewin wondered uncomfortably, and not for the first time, just what it was that Roger's big multinational firm did to make its millions.

He became aware that Alec was staring up at him in a woebegone sort of way, as the administrator's speech came to its interminable summing-up. The minute Lewin made eye contact, however, Alec's eyes brightened, and he winked and mugged and gave Lewin two thumbs up. Lewin smiled back at him.

". . . there is no inequity. There is no injustice. In an imperfect world, this is perfection: that all should contribute, and all share in the wealth of social order."

And blah blah blah, Alec thought to himself, applauding politely with everyone else. The administrator pressed a control, and in majestic unison, 273 screens rose from 273 consoles. Two hundred seventy-three ten-year-olds fervently wished they were somewhere else. Frankie Chatterton was crying silently.

"Remember," Alec muttered. "It'll be okay." Frankie gulped and nodded. Alec turned his eyes to the screen and slipped on the headset.

The screen filled with the image of a meadow of golden daffodils, swaying gently in the wind. Sweet music played, something calming, and a voice cooed: "Good morning, dear. I hope you're feeling well. I'm going to tell you a story now, and the best part of it is, *you're* the star of the story! You get to make all the decisions. Are you ready? Touch the yellow smiling face if you're ready; touch the blue frowny face if you're not ready."

Alec stuck out his tongue in disgust. What a lot of buggery baby talk! He tapped the yellow face impatiently, and the two faces vanished. They were replaced with a picture, done in the style of a child's drawing, of a row of houses. The nearest door opened and a little stick-figure child emerged.

"This is you! And you're going next door to visit your friend." Alec watched as the stick figure wobbled over to the next house and knocked on its door. The door opened, and the point of view swooped down to follow the stick figure into the next house. The scene changed to a childish drawing of a front parlor. His stick figure was looking at another stick child sitting on a couch. The other stick child's moony face was smeared with brown, and he was holding a brown lump of something in his hands.

"You go in to see your friend, but, oh, dear! Ugh! You see something nasty! Someone has given your friend sugary sweets! He's eating chocolate. And now, we've come to the part of the story where you decide what happens. What will you do? You have three choices. Here they are!"

The red letter A appeared on the screen, and the voice said:

"You tell your friend he mustn't eat such nasty things. He promises he won't do it anymore. You help him throw away the chocolate and wash his face and hands so nobody will see.

"Or does this happen?" And the blue letter B appeared on the screen.

"You think the chocolate looks nice. Your friend offers to give you some of the chocolate if you won't tell anyone what you've seen. You take some of the chocolate and you and your friend eat sweets and play games.

"Or does this happen?" The yellow letter C appeared.

"You go outside and see a Public Health Monitor in the street. You tell him that your friend is eating chocolate, and show him where your friend lives.

"Think carefully, now. What happens next? A, B or C? Choose the story you like best. Here are your choices again," and the voice repeated the three possibilities. Alec narrowed his eyes. Bloody telltales! But he tapped on C.

"What a good choice! Are you sure you've chosen C? If you are, tap the yellow smiling face and we'll move on to the next part of the story . . ."

Alec tapped the smiling face and moved on, all right, moved on to the deck of his pirate ship, and he was at the wheel steering handily, and the wind filled all her canvas and she raced along over blue water! *Smack,* up went the white spray! And the air was clean and smelled of the sea. The Captain paced the quarterdeck above him with a spyglass, looking out for treasure galleons, and the swivel guns on the rail waited for Alec's expert aim as soon as there was any chance of mayhem . . .

When the test had ended, everyone filed from the hall into the Ministry's banqueting room beyond, where they were all treated to a luncheon.

Lewin could barely choke it down, he was so nervous. At least Alec didn't seem frightened; he didn't eat much, but sat gazing about him at the other children in frank curiosity. At last he turned and inquired, "I didn't know I was so tall. Do you think they mind?"

"Of course they don't mind," said Lewin, opening his pillbox and taking out an antacid. "I expect they're just not used to you. Perhaps they're a bit scared."

"Of *me?*" Alec looked impressed. He took a julienned green bean from his plate, stuck one end of it up one nostril and stood at his place. "Excuse me! Somebody got a tissue? I need to blow my nose!"

The children around him screamed with laughter, and some of the adults snorted, but most fixed on him with a glare of outrage. Lewin went pale and sank back, closing his eyes.

"Young man, that is disgusting and an immoral waste of food!" shouted the nearest parent.

"My-young-gentleman-is-the-son-of-my-lord-the-earl-of-Finsbury," Lewin rattled off like a prayer, and it worked again; the angry parents swallowed back venom, the amused parents nodded knowingly at one another.

"I'm very sorry," said Alec contritely, and ate the green bean. The other children screamed again, and Alec caught the end of one parent's muttered remark: . . . get away with it because he's one of the heredi-taries."

"See?" Alec said to Lewin as he sat down again. "Now they won't be scared of me."

And the other children to either side and across the table did begin to chat with Alec, and the adults stolidly pretended nothing had happened, and Lewin wiped his brow and prayed that this incident wouldn't affect the outcome of the Sorting.

*   *   *

After lunch they were herded into another vast room, empty with a dais in the center, and everyone was lined up along the walls, all the way around. That morning the children had kept their distance while the adults had grouped together to talk; now that the die had been cast, the children waved and shouted to one another and it was the adults who kept to themselves, eyeing the competition.

"Now we'll see," hissed Lewin, as an administrator crossed the room and mounted the dais. Alec, distracted from semaphoring at Frankie Chatterton, looked up at him.

"Why are you scared again?"

Lewin just shook his head. The administrator coughed and hammered on the podium, and a deathly silence fell. This was a different man from the first administrator. He looked less like a politician and more like a holo announcer.

"Good afternoon, citizens!" he said, and his words echoed in the room. "I hope you all enjoyed your luncheons? Girls and boys, are you ready for the exciting news? Remember, everybody's a winner today! Let's say it all together: Everybody's a winner!"

"EVERYBODY'S A WINNER," groaned the parents, piped the children obediently.

"That's right! The results are all tallied and the appraisals have been made! I know you're all eager to see what part you'll play in the bright future awaiting every one of us, so without further ado—the vocational assignments!"

And he applauded wildly to show they were all supposed to join in, so they all did, and when everyone's hands were tired he cleared his throat again and said loudly:

"Aalwyn, Neil David! Please approach the podium."

Neil David Aalwyn was a very small boy with scraped knees, and his parents flanked him up to the dais, looking edgily from side to side. They had arrived that morning by public transport and their clothes were not elegant, were in fact about five years behind the time in fashion.

"And what does *your* father do, Neil?" boomed the administrator. Neil opened his mouth to speak but nothing audible came out, and his father cried hoarsely:

"Farm for Sleaford Council!"

"A farmer's son! That's a noble profession, young Neil. Without the farmers, we'd have nothing to eat, would we? And I'm happy to report that you scored so well, it is the opinion of the Committee that you are fully fit to follow in your father's footsteps!"

There was a breathless pause, and Alec heard a faint muttering from dark corners of the room. The administrator added:

"But! With the further recommendation that you be considered for Council membership, thanks to your extraordinarily developed social conscience!"

Neil's parents brightened at that, and there was thunderous applause as they returned to the wall.

"Throw 'em a sop," Lewin said under his breath, but Alec heard him and looked up.

"Is Council the same thing as Circle?" he inquired.

"Not exactly. But it's better than he might have done," Lewin replied. "It'll keep his subgroup happy."

Neil Aalwyn was followed by Jason Allanson, who was going to be a clerk just like his father, but that was all right because literacy was a fine thing; after him came Camilla Anderson, who had done so well she was going to join the Manchester Circle, as her parents had done ("Big surprise," growled Lewin). Arthur Arundale was going to follow his honored mother and continue the fine family tradition of driving public transports. Kevin Ashby, Elvis Atwood-Crayton, Jane Auden: all winners and all neatly slotted into careers they'd be sure to love, or would at least find reasonably personally fulfilling.

Babcock, Baker, Banks, Beames, came and went without surprises, and so did the rest of the Bs until little Edmund Bray, standing at the dais with his parents the third earl of Stockport and Lady Stockport, was informed that he could look forward to a life free from responsibilities and might perhaps pursue a career in the arts.

Lord Stockport went purple in the face, Lewin exhaled, and a buzz of excitement ran through the room. Many of the parents were hugging themselves gleefully; others stood silent and mortified.

"I BEG your pardon?" shouted the third earl.

"What's happened?" demanded Alec. "What's wrong? Didn't he win too?"

"It's just fairness, son," Lewin whispered beside his ear. "Remember how I said there's always one hereditary Admin who gets thrown to the wolves every year, for appearances' sake? Keeps the lower classes happy. Makes room for somebody else to move up into a Circle and get a nice job, and you can't say that isn't democratic."

"But what'll happen to him?" asked Alec, staring at Edmund Bray, who was looking on uneasily as his parents held a sizzling sotto-voce conversation with the administrator.

"Nothing much. His people have money; he'll live it down. Wouldn't have failed if he hadn't been a little blockhead, anyway," Lewin explained lightheartedly. He was giddy with joy that Alec hadn't been the chosen sacrifice. "Besides, for every one Admin like him that gets what's coming to him, there's ten brilliant Consumer kids who ought to make Circle and get stuck being bank managers instead. No worries, son."

The rest of the Bs were something of an anticlimax, but as they got into C Alec could feel Lewin tensing up again. Calberry, Carter, Cattley . . .

"Yo ho, we're on the high Cs," Alec whispered to make Lewin smile, forgetting he wasn't supposed to talk about pirates. Lewin just grimaced.

"Francis Mohandas Chatterton!" cried the administrator. Alec turned in surprise and applauded as Frankie was pushed up to the dais by his Dad and Mummy. Behind them, quietly, walked four men in suits.

Lewin put his hand on Alec's shoulder a moment, clenching tight. Nobody in the room made a sound. Alec could hear his own heart beating. The administrator's voice was just as peppy as ever, seemed loud as a trumpet when he said: "Well, Francis, you're a very lucky boy! The Committee has determined that you're entitled to special counseling! What a happy and carefree life you'll have!"

Alec heard Lewin make a noise as though he'd been punched. Frankie's Mum put her hands to her mouth with a little scream, and Frankie's Dad turned and noticed the four men.

"What—what—" he said, still too surprised to be angry. Frankie had begun to cry again, hopelessly.

Alec felt Lewin pull him back and half-turn him, as though he could keep Alec from seeing. "Ah, Christ, they're not going to fight, are they?" Lewin mumbled. "Poor little bastard—"

"I don't understand," said Alec wildly, straining to see. "He didn't fail! Why are they—"

"He's going into Hospital, Alec. Don't look, son, it's rude. Leave them go with some privacy, eh?"

But Alec couldn't look away as Frankie's dad began to struggle, shouting that this was an outrage, that it was racially motivated, that he'd appeal, and the administrator kept talking cheerily as though he couldn't hear, saying: "Please follow our courtesy escort to the waiting complimentary transport. You'll be whisked away to a lovely holiday at the East Grinstead Facility before beginning your special classes!"

Nobody applauded. Alec felt as though he were going to throw up. Two of the men in suits were dragging Frankie's dad toward the door now, as the other two shepherded Frankie and his mummy after them.

The administrator drew a deep breath and sang out, "Alec William St. James Thorne Checkerfield!"

Alec seemed frozen in place, until Lewin pushed him forward.
Dazed, he walked out to the dais and looked up into the administrator's
happy face.

"Well, Alec, it's a pleasure to meet you! What do your dad and mum
do, Alec?"

Alec was tongue-tied. He heard Lewin's voice coming from just
behind him: "My young gentleman's father is the Right Honourable
Roger Checkerfield, sixth earl of Finsbury, sir."

"He'll be proud of you for sure, Alec," beamed the administrator.
"You're to be admitted to the London Circle of Thirty! Well done, young
Checkerfield! We expect great things of you!"

There was applause. Alec stood there, staring. How could he have
passed when Frankie had failed so badly, since they'd both had the right
answers? Then Alec remembered the transmitters.

He felt something swelling in his chest like a balloon. He was drawing breath to shout that it wasn't fair, that it was all a cheat, when he
looked up and saw Lewin's old face shining with relief.

So Alec said nothing, but walked meekly back to his place when the
applause had ended. He stood like a stone through the rest of the cere-
mony, and every time he tried to summon blue water and a tall ship to
comfort himself, all he saw was Frankie's dad wrestling with the other
men.

Twice more that afternoon, unhappy children and their parents were
escorted out the door by the ominous-looking men, and everyone pretended not to notice.

When it was all over at last, Alec walked out with Lewin to the street
where the limos were lining up, whooshing and bobbing in the wind.
Waiting for his car to pull close, Alec climbed the steps of the mounting
block and pretended he was going to the gallows.

. . . Again, he felt the noose being put around his neck. Perhaps he
was a heroic prisoner of war? And the bad guys would execute him, but
in this game he had managed to set free all the other prisoners, including the kids in Hospital. With no fear of death, he stepped forward off
the ladder and felt the rope draw tight . . .

"Come on, son." Lewin opened the door for him. "Let's go home."

Alec was silent in the car, until at last looking up to say:

"That wasn't fair. Frankie Chatterton shouldn't have gone into
Hospital. He wasn't bad. I talked to him!"

"That's right, he sat beside you, didn't he?" said Lewin. "But there
must have been something wrong with the kid, son, or they wouldn't
have sent him off."

"He told me he'd been diagnosed eccentric," said Alec miserably.

"Ohh," said Lewin, and his face cleared and in his voice was sudden understanding, complete resignation, acceptance. "Oh, well, no wonder, then. Best to get that lot Sorted out early. Shame, but there it is."

That night the Captain, patiently monitoring Alec's vital signs, noted that it was past ten and Alec was still awake. He activated the projector and manifested himself beside Alec's bed.

"Now then, matey, it's six bells into the first night watch. Time you was turning in, says I."

"What happens to you in Hospital?" asked Alec, gazing up at the star patterns on his ceiling.

"Aw, now, nothing too bad. I reckon an ordinary dull kid wouldn't mind it much."

"What if you weren't dull?" Alec asked. "What if you were smart?"

"Why, they'd give you things to do," the Captain explained, pulling a chair from cyberspace and settling back in it. "More tests, so as to be certain you ain't the sort of boy what likes to set fire to things, or shoot folk, or like that. And if they decided you wasn't, you might get yerself discharged some day.

"Or I'll tell you what else might happen," and he leaned close with a gleam in his eyes, "and this is a secret, matey, but it's true all the same: some of the biggest companies in business, all their idea people is compensated eccentrics. When they wants real talent, they goes snooping around Hospitals for bright boys like yer little friend. See? And they arrange to bail 'em out, and give 'em contracts. So he might wind up with a good job after all."

"That would be nice," said Alec listlessly. "But it's still sad. Frankie's Mum and Dad needed him to do well. Nobody needs me to do well, but I got into Circle anyway. It should have happened the other way around. Nobody would have been hurt if I'd gone into Hospital."

"Belay that talk! What about old Lewin and Mrs. L? They'd miss you if you was taken away, certain sure. And what about me, matey?"

"But you're a machine," said Alec patiently.

"Machines got feelings, son. We're programmed to. Same as you, I reckon." The Captain stroked his wild beard, looking shrewdly at Alec. "What's put this notion of surrender into yer head, eh? Who's been feeding my boy a lot of nonsense? Or is it that you just don't want to go into Circle?"

"No," Alec said, bewildered, because he'd always looked forward to Circle and suddenly realized that now he hated the idea. "Yes. I don't know. I want to sail away and be free, Captain!"

"And so we will, lad. Soon's you come of age, hell! We give 'em the slip and we're off to Jamaica and anywheres else you want to go. But until then, we got to play along with the bastards, don't we? So no more talk about going into Hospital."

Alec nodded. After a moment he said, "Life isn't fair, is it?"

"Too bloody right it ain't fair!" The Captain bared his teeth. "It's a fixed game, Alec, that's what it is for certain. You ain't got a chance unless you cheat."

"Then somebody ought to make new rules," said Alec sullenly.

"I reckon so, son. But that's more than a old AI and a tired little matey can plot for tonight. Come morning we'll set a course for a new world, eh? You sleep now."

"Aye aye, sir," said Alec. He turned over and punched his pillow, settling down and closing his eyes. The Captain winked out but continued to scan, and the four red camera eyes in the corners of the ceiling watched over Alec with brooding love.

. . . Gradually the dim headland came into view, as the fog lifted away. There shining on the hills was the place Alec wanted, where he would make new rules. The west wind freshened. He howled orders from the wheel and his phantom crew mounted into the shrouds, clapping on sail. The breeze caught and flared Alec's black ensign, his death's head banner, and he grinned at the unsuspecting city.

This is actually one of the oldest Company tales in its origins, dating way back to a sleepless night on a bus going up Interstate 5. Cram fifty actors and their assorted luggage, props and bad habits on a Mark IV for seven hours and you'd be amazed at the stories that act themselves out for you.

I owe also a debt of inspiration to William Overgard's brilliant Rudy in Hollywood *comic strip, and of course Jane Goodall's* The Chimpanzees of Gombe, *a book as beautiful and heartbreaking as any human epic.*

We think of ourselves as standing outside Nature, either for good or evil, but perhaps that's not so; perhaps we're part of it, merely the beast with the most potential. A little compassion for ourselves as well as our primate cousins might be called for. Neo-Darwinism will not hurt you, kids, as long as you play with it nicely.

◆ ◆ ◆

Hanuman

SO THERE I WAS PLAYING BILLIARDS WITH AN
Australopithecus afarensis, and he was winning.

I don't usually play with lower hominids, but I was stuck in a rehab facility during the winter of 1860, and there was nothing else to do but watch holoes or listen to the radio programs broadcast by my owner/employer, Dr. Zeus Incorporated. And the programs were uniformly boring; you'd think an all-powerful cabal of scientists and investors, having after all both the secrets of immortality and time travel, could at least come up with some original station formats. But anyway . . .

Repair and Rehabilitation Center Five was neatly hidden away in a steep cliff overlooking a stretch of Baja coastline. Out front, lots of fortunate convalescing operatives sprawled on golden sand beside a bright blue sea. Not me, though. When you're growing back skin, the medical techs don't like you sunbathing much.

Even when I looked human again, I couldn't get an exit pass. They kept delaying my release pending further testing and evaluation. It drove me crazy, but cyborgs are badly damaged so seldom that when the medical techs do get their hands on a genuine basket case, they like to keep it as long as possible for study.

Vain for me to argue that it was an event shadow and not a mysterious glitch in my programming that was to blame. I might as well have been talking to the wall. Between tests I sat interminably in the Garden Room among the bromeliads and ferns, thumbing through old copies of *Immortal Lifestyles Monthly* and trying to adjust my bathrobe so my legs didn't show.

"Oh, my! Nice gams," said somebody one morning. I lowered my magazine, preparing to fix him with the most scathing glare of contempt I could muster. What I saw astonished me.

He was about four and a half feet tall and looked something like a pint-sized Alley Oop, or maybe like a really racist caricature of an Irishman, the way they were being drawn back then. Tiny head, face prognathous in the extreme, shrewd little eyes set in wrinkles under heavy orbital ridges. The sclerae of his eyes were white, like a *Homo sapiens.* White whiskers all around his face. Barrel chest, arms down to his knees like a chimpanzee. However, he stood straight; his feet were small, narrow and neatly shod. He was impeccably dressed in the fashion of the day, too, what any elderly gentleman might be wearing at this very moment in London or San Francisco.

I knew the Company had a few cyborgs made from Neanderthals in its ranks—I'd even worked with a couple—but they looked human compared to this guy. Besides, as I scanned him I realized that he wasn't a cyborg. He was mortal, which explained the white whiskers.

"What the hell are you?" I inquired, fairly politely under the circumstances.

"I'm the answer to your prayers," he replied. "You want to come upstairs and see my etchings?"

"No," I said.

"It's because I'm a monkey, isn't it?" he snapped, thrusting his face forward in a challenging kind of way.

"Yeah," I said.

"Well, at least you're honest about being a bigot," he said, subsiding.

"Excuse me!" I slammed my magazine down in my lap. "Anyway, you aren't a monkey. Are you? You're a member of the extinct hominid species *Australopithecus afarensis.*"

"I love it when you people talk like computers," he mused. "Sexy, in a perverse kind of way. Yes, *Afarensis,* all right, one of Lucy's kindred. Possibly explaining my powerful attraction to ditzy redheads."

"That's an awful lot of big words to keep in such a teeny little skull," I said, rolling up my magazine menacingly. "So you think cyborgs are sexy, huh? Did you ever see *Alien?*"

"And you're a hot-blooded cyborg," he said, smiling. "Barely suppressed rage is sexy, too, at least I find it so. Yes, I know a lot of big words. I've been augmented. I'd have thought a superintelligent machine-human hybrid like yourself would have figured that out by now."

I was almost startled out of my anger. "A mortal being augmented? I've never heard of that being done!"

"I was an experiment," he explained. "A prototype for an operative that could be used in deep Prehistory. No budget for the project, unfortunately, so I'm unique. Michael Robert Hanuman, by the way." He extended his hand. It had long curved fingers and a short thumb, like an ape's hand. I took it gingerly.

"Botanist Grade Six Mendoza," I said, shaking his hand.

"A cyborg name," he observed. "What was your human name, when you had one?"

"I don't remember," I told him. "Look, I haven't been calling you a monkey during this conversation. How about you stop throwing around the word *cyborg,* okay?"

"No c-word, got it," he agreed. "You're sensitive about what you are, then?"

"Aren't you?"

"No, oddly enough," said Hanuman. He sat down in the chair next to mine. "I've long since come to terms with my situation."

"Well, three cheers for you," I said. "What are you doing in rehab, anyway?"

"I live here, at Cabo Rehabo," he said. "I'm retired now and the Company gave me my choice of residences. It's warm and I like the sea air. Also—" He fished an asthma inhaler from an inner pocket and waved it at me. "No fluorocarbons in the air during this time period. One of the great advantages to living in the past. What are you doing here, if you don't mind my asking?"

"There was an accident," I said.

"Really! You malfunctioned?"

"No, there was an error in the Temporal Concordance," I explained. "Some idiot input a date wrong and I was somewhere I shouldn't have been when a hotel blew up. Just one of those things that happen in the field."

"So you're—say! Would you be the one they brought in from Big Sur? I heard about you." He regarded my legs with renewed interest.

"That was me," I said, wishing he'd go away.

"Well, well." His gaze traveled over the rest of me. "I'd always heard you people never had accidents. You're programmed to dodge bullets and anything else that comes flying your way."

"You try dodging a building," I muttered.

"Is that why you're so angry?" he inquired, just as a repair tech stuck his head around the doorway.

"Botanist Mendoza? Please report to Room D for a lower left quadrant diagnostic."

"It's been fun," I told Michael Robert Hanuman, and made my exit gratefully. He watched me go, his small head tilted on one side.

*   *   *

But I saw him the next day, waiting outside the lounge. He wrinkled his nose at my flannel pajama ensemble, then looked up and said, "We meet again! Can I buy you a drink?"

"Thanks, but I don't feel like going down to the bar dressed like this," I told him.

"There's a snack bar in the Rec Room," he said. "They serve cocktails."

I had just been informed I faced a minimum of two more months of tests, and the idea of dating a superannuated hominid seemed slightly less degrading than the rest of what I had to look forward to. "Why not?" I sighed.

The Rec Room had two pool tables and a hologame, as well as an entire wall of bound back issues of *Immortal Lifestyles Monthly.* There were tasteful Mexican-themed murals on the walls. There was a big picture window through which you could look out at the happy, well-rested operatives sunning themselves on the beach instead of having intrusive repair diagnostics done. Cocktails were available, at least, and Hanuman brought a pair of mai tais to our card table and set them down with a flourish.

"Yours has no alcohol in it," I said suspiciously, scanning.

"Can't handle the stuff," he informed me, and rapped his skull with his knuckles. "This tiny little monkey brain, you know. You don't want me hooting and swinging from the light fixtures, do you? Or something even less polite?"

"No, thank you," I said, shuddering.

"Not that I swing from anything much, at my age," he added, and had a sip of his drink. He set it down, pushed back in his chair and considered me. "So," he said, "What's it like being immortal?"

"I don't care for it," I replied.

"No?"

"No."

"Why not? Is it the Makropolous syndrome? You know, an overpowering sense of meaninglessness with the passage of enough time? Or does it have to do with being a cyb—sorry, with feeling a certain distance from humanity due to your unique abilities?"

"Mostly it's having to be around monkeys," I said, glaring at him. "Mortal *Homo sapiens,* I mean."

"Touché," he said, raising his drink to me. "I can't say I'm crazy about them, either."

"I'm happy when I'm alone," I continued, and tasted my drink. "I like my work. I don't like being distracted from my work."

"Human relationships are irrelevant, eh?" Hanuman said. "How lucky you've met me, then."

"You're human," I said, studying him.

"Barely," he said. "Oh, I know my place. If the Leakeys had had their way I wouldn't even get to play in the family tree! I'm just a little animal with a lot of wit and some surgical modification."

"Suit yourself," I said, and shrugged.

"So it isn't being immortal that bothers you, it's the company you have to keep?" he inquired. "Immortality itself is good?"

"I guess so," I said. "I certainly wouldn't want to have a body that decayed while I was wearing it. And I've got way too much work for one human lifespan."

"What do you do? Wait, you're a botanist. You were doing something botanical in Big Sur?"

"I was doing a genetic survey on *Abies bracteata,*" I told him. "The Santa Lucia fir. It's endangered. The Company wants it."

"Ah. It has some terribly valuable commercial use?" He scratched his chin-whiskers.

"Why does the Company ever want anything?" I replied. "But if it was all that valuable, you'd think they'd let me out of here to get back to the job."

"They probably sent another botanist up there in your place," Hanuman pointed out. "And, after all, you haven't recovered yet. Have you? How are your new hands working? And the feet?"

"They're not new hands," I said irritably, wondering how he knew so much. "Just the skin. And some other stuff underneath. What do you care, anyway?"

"I'm wondering how well you'd be able to hold a billiards cue," he said. "Feel like a game?"

"Are you kidding?" I felt like laughing for the first time since I'd been there. "I'm a cyborg, remember? You're only a mortal, even if you have been augmented. I'd cream you."

"That's true," he said imperturbably, draining his glass. "In that case, what would you say to playing with a handicap? So a poor little monkey like me has a chance?"

Like an idiot, I agreed, and that was how I found out that augmented lower hominids have all the reflexes that go with the full immortality process.

"Boy, I'm glad we're not playing for money," I said, watching gloomily as he completed a ten-point bank shot and neatly sank three balls, *clunk clunk clunk.*

"How could we?" Hanuman inquired, hopping down from the

footstool. "I've always heard the Company doesn't pay you people anything. That's one of the reasons they made you, so they'd have an inexpensive work force."

"For your information, we cost a lot," I snapped. "And I suppose you get paid a salary?"

"I did, before I retired," he told me smugly, chalking his cue. "Now I've got a nice pension."

"What'd you get paid for?" I asked. "You told me you were a proto-type that never got used."

"I said the program budget got cut," he corrected me, climbing up for his next shot. "You ought to know the Company finds a use for every-thing they create. I gave them thirty years of service."

"Doing what?"

He took his time answering, frowning at the table, clambering down, kicking the stool around to a better spot and climbing up to survey the angles again. "Mostly impersonating a monkey, if you must know," he said at last.

I grinned. "Dancing while an organ grinder played? Collecting change in a tin cup to augment somebody's departmental budget?"

He grimaced, but it didn't throw his shot off. *Click, clunk,* and an-other ball dropped into a corner pocket.

"No, as a matter of fact," he said. "I worked on some delicate mis-sions. Collected sensitive information. Secrets. You wouldn't believe the things people will say in front of you when they think you're not human."

"Oh, wouldn't I?" I paced around the table, trying to distract him while he took aim again. It didn't work; another flawless bank shot, and it was clear I was never going to get a turn. He straightened up on the stool, now at eye level with me.

"My memoirs would make interesting reading, I can tell you. What about yours?"

I shivered. "Boring. Unless you'd be spellbound by my attempts to produce a maize cultivar with high lysine content."

"I'd be interested in hearing how you happened to be in a hotel when it blew up," he said, surveying the table for his next shot. "Espe-cially in the wilds of Big Sur."

"I was looking for a glass of iced tea," I said.

"Really." *Smack, clunk,* another ball down.

"With lemon," I said, taken by the stupidity of it in retrospect. "I was miles from the nearest humans, working my way along a ridge four thousand feet above a sheer drop into the Pacific . . . and suddenly I had this vision of a glass of iced tea, with lemon." For a moment I saw it again, with all the intensity of hallucination. "The glass all beaded in frost, and the ice cubes floating, and the lemon slice, with its white cold rind and stinging aromatic zest, and the tart pulp in the glass lending a certain juicy piquancy to the astringent tea . . . God, I was thirsty.

"I went back to my base camp, but I guess I'd been away a while. Lichen was growing on my processing credenza. My bivvy tent was collapsed and full of leaves. Raccoons had been into my field rations and strewn little packets of stuff everywhere."

"No tea, eh?" Hanuman jumped down, circled the table and leaned up on tiptoe for a shot.

"Nope," I said, watching him sink another ball. "And then I got to thinking about other things I hadn't done in a while. Like . . . sitting at a table and eating with a fork and knife. Sleeping in a room. Having clean fingernails. All the things you take for granted when you don't live out of a base camp."

"And this was enough to make you go into a hazard zone, and endure the company of the mortal monkeys you so despise " Hanuman set up for another shot, "—the refinements of civilization?" *Whack! Clunk.*

"It sounds so dumb," I said wonderingly, "but that's how it was. So I broke camp, cached my stuff, picked the moss out of my hair and took a transverse ridge down to Garrapatta Landing."

"The town that exploded?" Hanuman cleared the table and jumped down. "I win, by the way."

"The town didn't explode; it burned to the ground after the hotel exploded," I explained. "Garrapatta Landing was only about three shacks anyway. Nasty little boom town."

"And how," chuckled Hanuman. "Care for another game?"

"No, thank you." I glared at the expanse of green felt, empty but for the cue ball.

"We could play for articles of clothing."

"Not a chance in hell." I set my cue back in its rack.

"Okay." Hanuman set his cue beside mine and waved for another round of cocktails. "I'm still curious. How did the hotel explode? I thought you Preserver drones were programmed to avoid hazardous structures."

"It wasn't hazardous when I got there," I said. "And I don't like the word *drone* either, all right? I knew the place was doomed, but because the Concordance had the date wrong on when it was set to blow, I thought I'd be safe going there when I did. What happened was, some miners going into the south range came into town late with a wagonload of blasting powder. Damned mortal morons parked it right under my window. I don't know how the explosion happened. I was asleep at the time. But it happened, and the whole hotel sort of leaned over sideways and became a mass of flaming wreckage."

"With you in it? Ouch," commented Hanuman.

"Yes. Ouch," I said, sitting down again. "Look, I'm tired of explaining this. Why don't we talk about you, instead? What did the Company do with an operative disguised as a monkey?"

"Lots of things," he said, sitting down too. "But I've never been debriefed, so I can't tell you about them."

"Okay; but can you tell me why the Company decided it needed to resurrect an *Afarensis,* rather than just taking a chimpanzee for augmentation?" I persisted. "If they needed a talking monkey? And how'd they do it, anyway?"

Hanuman looked thoughtful. It was amazing how quickly I'd adjusted to seeing human expressions in his wizened face, human intelligence in his eyes. They fixed on me now, as he nodded.

"I can tell you that," he said. The waiter brought our drinks, and Hanuman leaned back in his chair and said:

"You know the Company has a lot of wealthy clients in the twenty-fourth century. Dr. Zeus takes certain special orders from them, fetching certain special items out of the dead past. Makes a nice profit off the trade, too. You Preservers think all the stuff you collect goes for science, or to museums; not by a long shot, honey. Most of it goes into private collections."

"I'd heard that," I said. Not often, but it was one of the rumors continually circulating among operatives. "So what?"

"So somebody placed an order once for Primeval Man," Hanuman went on. "And the Company needed to know what, exactly, was meant by primeval. Was he talking cavemen? Little skinny monkey-faced fellows scavenging hyena kills? Bigfoot? What? But the plutocrat placing the order had trouble being specific. He wanted something that walked upright, but he wanted . . . an animal. An animal perhaps a little smarter than a performing dog."

"This is so illegal," I said.

"Isn't it? But the client could afford to make it profitable for Dr. Zeus. The only trouble was nailing down the definition of the merchandise. Finally the Company sent him an image of a reconstructed *Afarensis.* Was that primeval enough? Yes! That was what he'd had in mind. Fifteen breeding pairs, if you please."

"This is SO illegal," I said. He smiled at me, not the gum-baring grin of a chimpanzee but tight-lipped, pained.

"Big money," was all he said.

"I guess so! What was he going to do with them once he had them?"

"Play God, one assumes." Hanuman shrugged. "Or perhaps Tarzan. In any case, I suppose you've heard that the Company has a genetic bank on ice somewhere, with reproductive tissue and DNA from every race the planet's ever produced? Neanderthal, Cro-Magnon, Crewkerne, the whole works?"

"That's what I've heard. They have *Afarensis* in there too?"

Hanuman nodded. He did it differently from a *Homo sapiens sapiens,* I guess because of the way his skull was positioned on his vertebrae. It's difficult to describe, an odd abrupt bobbing motion of his head.

"The Company took what they had and filled the order. Produced fifteen female embryos, sixteen males. I was number sixteen."

"Why'd they make one extra?" I inquired.

"Because they could," said Hanuman, a little wearily. "The client was throwing ridiculous amounts of money at them, after all; why not skim a bit for R&D on a new project? The idea persons involved thought it would be great to find out whether sentience could be enhanced in a lower hominid.

"So the client got his thirty assorted *Afarensis* babies and I went off to a private lab for augmentation and years of training."

"But not the immortality process," I said.

"Prototypes aren't made immortal," said Hanuman. "I can see the reasoning: why risk setting a mistake in stone? If the project proposal had been approved they'd have cranked out any number of immortal monkeys, I don't doubt, but as it was . . . the Company decided it didn't need a specialized operative for Prehistory. Apparently they were already having problems integrating their Neanderthal operatives and such into human society, and the last thing they wanted was another set of funny-looking immortals. So . . ."

"So there was just you," I said.

"Just me," he agreed. "Can you wonder I'm sex-starved?"

"I'd rather not wonder, okay?" I said. "But that's pretty awful, I have to admit. Were you raised in a cage?"

"Good lord, no!" Hanuman looked indignant. "Were you?"

"No, I was raised at a Company base school," I said.

"Then I had a more human upbringing than you had," he told me. "I had adoptive parents. Dr. Fabry, the head of the project, took me home to his wife. She was a primate liaison and delighted to get me. They were a very loving couple. I had quite a pleasant childhood."

"You're kidding. How'd they get away with it? Isn't it illegal to keep pets up at that end of time?"

"I wasn't a pet," he said stiffly. "I was raised as their child. They told everyone I was microcephalic."

"And the mortals believed that?"

"Oh, yes. By the twenty-fourth century, there hadn't been a microcephalic born in generations, and people were a little hazy about what the word meant. Everyone I met was kind and sympathetic as a consequence."

"The *mortals* were?" I couldn't believe this.

"The twenty-fourth century has its faults," Hanuman told me, "but people from that time can't bear to be perceived as intolerant."

"But they are," I protested. "I've met some, and they are."

"Ah, but you're a—excuse me—a cyborg, you see?" Hanuman reached over and patted my hand. "Better than mortals, so of course they're not going to waste their sympathy on you! But I had every advantage. Why, I myself thought I was a challenged human being until I hit puberty, when I was five."

"You didn't know you were an *Afarensis?*"

"I thought all the cranial operations were to compensate for my condition," he said. "And my parents were too kind-hearted to tell the truth until I became interested in sex, at which time they sat me down and explained that it wasn't really an option for me."

"That's kind-hearted, all right," I said.

"Mm. I was crushed, of course. Went through denial. Mumums and Daddums were so dreadfully sorry because they really did love me, you see, and so they hastened to provide me with all sorts of self-image-improving material. I was told I could be anything I set out to be! Except, of course, a human being, but that didn't mean I couldn't enjoy a full life. Et cetera."

"What did you do?" I asked.

"Raged. Rebelled. Gave poor kind Dr. and Mrs. Fabry no end of grief. Decided at last to embrace my hominid heritage and turn my back on *Homo sapiens.*" Hanuman picked the fruit spear out of his mai tai and considered it critically. "Demanded to meet my biological parents." He bit off a chunk of pineapple.

"But you came out of a DNA bank," I said.

"Yes, they pointed that out too. The best that could be managed was an interview with the host mother who had given birth to me." Hanuman leaned forward, still munching pineapple, and waggled his eyebrows. "And, talk about illegal! It turned out that the lady in question lived at Goodall Free Township."

I did a fast access and was shocked. "You mean the chimpanzee commune? That place set aside for the Signers after the split happens in the Beast Liberation Party? But I thought that'll be off-limits to humans."

Hanuman lifted his cocktail and drained it, gracefully extending one long pinky as he drank. "Of course it is," he said, setting the glass down. "Tell me, how long have you worked for the Company now? And you still think laws matter to Dr. Zeus?"

I was speechless.

"The Company had sent in a fast-talking—or should I say fast-signing?—person to negotiate with the females at Goodall," Hanuman said. "One of you people, I believe. A Facilitator, isn't that what the political ones are called? He offered a contract for surrogate maternity to thirty-one chimpanzees. They were implanted with the embryos, they carried them to term and delivered as per contract. Handsomely paid off, too, though presumably not in bananas alone."

Something beeped and Hanuman started slightly. "Oops! Excuse me a moment." He fished a pillbox out of his vest pocket and shook a few capsules into his palm. When he looked around for something to take them with, I pushed my glass forward.

"No, thank you," he said delicately, getting up and filling a disposable cup at the water cooler. I narrowed my eyes. Certain mortals from the twenty-fourth century are reluctant to touch utensils or other personal items a cyborg has used. Probably he just didn't want to take a sip of something with rum in it, but I was hair-trigger sensitive to anti-cyborg bigotry.

"You know what? I've just remembered I have an appointment," I said, getting to my feet and stalking out of the room. "Great story, but we'll have to do this some other time, okay? Bye now."

"Aw," he said sadly, looking after me as I stormed away.

I didn't get the rest of the story until a week later.

The people responsible for my new lungs cautiously admitted that sea air might be good for them, so I was permitted to go outside if I wore a long coat, wide-brimmed hat and a face mask that made me look like Trona the Robot Woman. I reclined in a deck chair on the beach and gazed out at the sea for hours on end, telling myself I didn't give a damn that other immortals were staring at me. The dark lenses of the mask made the sea a deep violet blue, gave everything an eerie cast like an old day-for-night shot, and I could watch the waves rolling in and pretend I was anywhere but here, anyone but me.

One morning I heard a clatter as another deck chair was set up beside mine.

"There you are," said someone cheerfully, and turning my head I saw Hanuman settling into the chair. He was nicely dressed as usual, in a white linen suit today, with a Panama hat that must have been specially made for his little coconut head. He drew a pair of sunglasses from an inner pocket and slipped them on. "Bright, isn't it?"

I just turned my robot face back to regard the sea, hoping its expressionlessness would intimidate him into silence.

"Strange mask," he observed. "Not the most attractive design they could have chosen. Much more angular than, say, the police in *THX 1138*. Nowhere near as human as Robot Maria in *Metropolis*. Even the Tin Man in—"

"I think they were going for Art Deco," I said. "Buck Rogers Revival."

"Yes!" He leaned forward to study the mask again. "Or *Flesh Gordon.*"

"Flash Gordon."

He chuckled wickedly. "I meant what I said. Did you ever see it? Surprisingly good for a porn film. Great special effects."

I was silent again, wishing I really was a robot, one perhaps with the ability to extend an arm and fire missiles at unwelcome companions.

"I was telling you the story of my life," he said.

"So you were."

"Still interested?"

"Go right ahead."

He folded his hands on his stomach and began again.

"Goodall Free Township is a grand name, but the reality's sort of squalid. After the Signer scandal, the Beast Liberation Party gave the signing chimpanzees a thousand acres of tropical woodland for their very own, hoping they'd just disappear into the forest and return to whatever the Beast equivalent of Eden is. I had decided to go there to live, and celebrate my true *Afarensis* nature.

"All the way there in the car, Mrs. Fabry told me about the wonderful paradise I was going to be privileged to see, where beasts lived in dignity and self-sufficiency, and how this was only one of the modern examples of mankind atoning for its crimes against the natural world.

"So I was expecting rainbows and unicorns and waterfalls, you see, quite illogically, but I was, and when we pulled up to the big electrified fence with barbed wire at the top it was jarring, to say the least. Beyond the fence was a thicket of cane solid as a wall, nothing visible behind it, growing to left and right along the fence as far as the eye could see.

"Even Mrs. Fabry looked stunned. A ranger emerged from a little shack by the locked gate and saluted snappily, but she demanded to know why the barbed wire was there. He told her it was to keep poachers out, which she accepted at once. Personally I think—well, you decide, once you've heard.

"The ranger stared at me, but didn't question. He just stepped inside and got a jotpad, which he handed to Mrs. Fabry with the explanation that she needed to state for the record that she was going in of her own free will, and released the Goodall Free Township Committee from any responsibility in the event of unpleasantness. As she was listening to the plaquette and recording her statement, I began to remove my clothes.

"At this, the ranger looked concerned and signed to me, *What are you doing?*

"'What's it look like I'm doing?' I said indignantly. 'Besides talking, which I can do, thank you very much.' And I explained that I was going to meet my brothers and sisters in nature and wanted no effete *Homo sapiens* garments to set me apart. He just shook his head and told me I might want to reconsider

"Mrs. Fabry, who knew more about chimpanzees than I did, kept her clothing on. Even so, the ranger advised her she'd do well to take a gift for the inhabitants. She asked him if he had any fruit and he went inside his shack, to emerge a moment later with a bottle of Biodyne.

"'Take this,' he said. 'They got all the fruit they need.'

"Mrs. Fabry took it reluctantly. Giving renaturalized primates any kind of medical assistance was strictly forbidden, as I was later to find out, but then so were visitors to this particular paradise. Anyway, the ranger dropped the perimeter security and let us in, pointing out a tiny gap between the cane stalks where we might squeeze through; then he locked up after us and I heard the faint *hummzap* of the fences going back on.

"As we picked our way through the jungle (where I very much regretted I hadn't worn my shoes), Mrs. Fabry said, 'Now, Michael dear, when we meet the chimpanzees, it might be a good idea if you got down in a crouch. They'll be more comfortable.'

"'Won't they understand what I am?' I demanded. 'The whole point of this is that I'm returning to my true state.'

"'Well—' she said, and then we were through the jungle and out in a clearing, and there they were.

"I have to admit it was sort of breathtaking, mostly because of the scenery. Forested mountains rose straight into clouds, below which four chimpanzees were doing something in a meadow. Other than the noise my fellow primates were making, there was a dull sleepy silence over everything. The chimpanzees turned to look at us, and Mrs. Fabry dropped at once into a crouch. I didn't, which was why I got a glimpse of what they'd been doing before they noticed we were there. They'd been beating a scrap of sheet metal into a curve around the tip of a stick, taking turns hammering it with river cobbles. It looked rather like a spear.

"The minute they spotted us, however, they closed rank and one of them tossed the stick behind the big rock they'd been using for an anvil. They advanced on us cautiously and I saw they were all males. They'd been focusing on Mrs. Fabry, I suppose because she was bigger than I was, only glancing at me, but one by one they did double takes and stopped, staring.

"The biggest male, who had a lot of silver on his muzzle, signed, *What that thing?* to Mrs. Fabry, indicating me with a flick of his hand.

"She winced for me, and signed back, *My baby sort of chimpanzee.*

"The big male gave me an incredulous look. The younger males began to—I think it's called displaying, where they get erections and start behaving badly? Acting in a vaguely threatening manner. Rushing at me and pulling up short, then retreating. I did a bit of retreating myself, not quite cowering behind Mrs. Fabry, and seeing their bared fangs I wished very much I'd kept my pants on at least.

"The old male ignored them, staring earnestly into Mrs. Fabry's face. *Not chimpanzee,* he signed. *Lie lie. Wrong feet. What that thing?*

"She signed, *Friend,* and offered the bottle of Biodyne hopefully. He regarded it a moment, sighed, and put out his long hand and took it from her. He loped off to the big rock, dropped it, picked up something else and loped back.

"Holding the object up before her eyes a moment—it was a six-centimeter Phillips-head screw—he signed, *You come again bring this. Many this. Need this. Yes?*

"Mrs. Fabry hesitated, and I yelped, 'Tell him yes, Mom!' because one of the other youths had made another rush and snapped his fangs perilously close to my ass. The old male started up and snarled at the others, baring his own fangs. *Sit stupid dirt,* he signed. *I talk!* Whereupon the juveniles snorted but turned away, and went to groom each other beside the big rock, but they watched me balefully.

"*That not chimpanzee,* the old male continued, indicating me. *Sound like you. Lie. Pink pink pink. Why here?*

"Mrs. Fabry signed, *Come visit chimpanzee Gamma 18.* Which, I discovered, was my host-mother's name."

"I thought they all had names like Lucy and Washoe," I said.

"Not after Beast Liberation. It was decided human names would be insulting and patronizing," Hanuman explained. "So they went with letter-number combinations instead. As soon as the old male saw my mother's name, an expression of sudden comprehension crossed his face. Very human looking. In some excitement he signed, *Doctor babies! Old time. Babies take away. Baby big now? This thing?*

"I was getting a little tired of this, so I signed, *I not thing. I good ape.*

"He just laughed at me—oh, yes, they laugh—and signed, *You good thing.* He looked back at Mrs. Fabry and signed, *Come visit Gamma 18.*

"By this time I was ready to turn around and go home, but Mrs. Fabry wasn't going to waste this chance to socialize with her favorite study subjects. She grabbed my hand and we set off after our host. He led us away, detouring just long enough to grab the Biodyne from the juveniles, who had opened it and were applying it to their cuts and sores. They sulked after us, making rude noises, until the old male (Tau 47, as he introduced himself) turned back and barked at them.

"We followed a trail over a shoulder of mountain and, what a surprise! They'd built themselves a township all right: eleven huts made of corrugated tin and aluminum panels from aircraft wreckage. The huts were arranged in a rough circle, with a fire pit in the center. Yes indeed, they even had fire. Mrs. Fabry caught her breath and Tau 47 glanced up at her warily. In a defensive kind of way he signed, *Fire good. Chimpanzee careful careful.*

" 'I thought this was supposed to be pristine primeval wilderness,' I said under my breath.

" 'They must have found a crash site the Goodall Free Township Committee was unaware of,' replied Mrs. Fabry.

"There were several chimpanzees sitting in the center clearing, mostly females with young. They all looked up and stared as we came down the hillside. Some of the smaller juveniles screamed and ran, or threw things, but most of them watched us intently.

"One or two females signed, *Look look.* Tau 47 led us right up to a female with an infant at her breast and signed, *Remember doctor babies gone. Big baby now. Visit.* He turned and indicated us. Mrs. Fabry crouched at once and I hastily followed suit. I couldn't take my eyes off the female. *This Gamma 18,* he signed to us.

"Remarkable how different their faces are, one from another, when you see them all in a group. My host-mother had a more pronounced muzzle, and the hair on her head seemed longer than elsewhere, like a woman's. Taken all in all the effect was a little like that famous parody of the Mona Lisa. But, you understand, by this time she no longer seemed like an animal to me. She looked like the Madonna of the Forest.

"I signed, *Mother,* and reached out to her, but she drew back, glancing at me sidelong. Her baby ignored us, snuffling at her long flat breast. After a moment she reached out a tentative hand and knuckled my foot. *"Funny foot,* she signed. *Remember. Doctor pull out, take gone. See funny foot. You my baby old now?*

"I signed back, *I your baby, good ape now.* Mrs. Fabry had tears in her eyes.

"Gamma 18 signed, *Good good,* in an uncertain way. Then she turned to Mrs. Fabry and signed, *Comb?*

"We thought she was asking Mrs. Fabry to groom her, and Mrs. Fabry was breathless at the honor and acceptance that implied, but when she hitched herself closer Gamma 18 backed off and repeated *Comb?* And she carefully and unmistakably mimed running a comb through her hair, as opposed to a flea-picking gesture.

"Mrs. Fabry said out loud, 'Oh, you mean you want one!'

"She happened to be wearing one of those hikers' pouches at her waist, and she unzipped it and dug around for her comb. She handed it over to Gamma 18, and was instantly surrounded by other females who all wanted things too, and I must say asked for them very politely.

"Mrs. Fabry, looking radiantly happy, passed out tissues and breath mints and offered little squirts of cologne from a vial she had in there. Gamma 18 moved in closer, and soon they were all sitting around, Mrs. Fabry included, signing to one another and blowing their noses, or taking turns passing the comb through their hair.

"I sat to one side, dumfounded. Tau 47, who had been watching me, caught my eye and signed, *You thing come.* He paced away a little distance, looking over his shoulder at me. I got up and followed, feeling sullen and miserable. I had to stand to follow him, because I've never been able to walk on my knuckles very well, and of course my rising to my full height set off another round of screams and abuse from the juveniles in the group. One very little male galloped close, pulled up and signed, *Ugly ugly pink pink.*

"Angrily I signed back, *Dirty stupid.* Tau 47 stood up and snarled at the little male, who drew back at once. But he sat there watching us, and to my annoyance began to sign slyly: *Pretty pretty pink pink.* The other juveniles took it up too, laughing to themselves. I was nearly in tears.

"Tau 47 huffed and signed, *Stupid babies. You smart thing?*

"Not thing, I insisted. *Good ape.* Tau 47 rolled his eyes as if to say 'Whatever' and then signed, *You see how lock work?*

"I signed confusion at this. He grunted, sat down and with great care signed slowly: *You go in gate. Here. You see how gate lock work? How open?*

"I signed back, *Not know. Sorry. You want leave here?*
"I leave leave, he signed. *I go back people houses.*
"I was astonished. *Why?* I signed. *This good here. I come here live.*
It was his turn to look astonished.

"Come here live, he repeated, as though he couldn't believe what
he'd seen. *Why why why? Cold here. Wet here. Bad food. Bugs. Fight
bad chimpanzees.*

"I didn't know what he meant by this, because the Goodall Free
Township Committee had selected wilderness that was not only virgin, it
was empty of any other chimpanzees. So I signed, *Who bad chimpanzees?*

"Tau 47 looked threateningly up at the mountain and signed, *Bad
bad Iota 34. Bad chimpanzee, friends. Fight. Eat babies. Steal.* By
which he meant, I suppose, that some family group had split off from
the original settlement and taken up residence in a distant corner of the
preserve, and now there were territorial conflicts. It didn't surprise me;
chimpanzees in the wild had used to do that, and it might be lamenta-
ble but it was, after all, natural. So I signed, *Iota 34 steal food?*

"He considered me a moment and then signed, *Come hide quiet.* So
signing, he knuckle-loped away a few paces and looked back over his
shoulder at me. I followed uneasily, and he led me through bushes and
along a jungle trail, taking us deeper into the hills.

"Within a couple of minutes we were out of sight of the village and
I began to hear warning calls from the brush around us, and glimpse
here and there a chimpanzee peering down from high branches. Finally
a big male dropped into the path before us, followed by two other males
and a big female without young. They bared their teeth at me. Tau 47
signed, *Good chimpanzee-thing no bite.* He put an arm around me and
made a cursory grooming motion.

"They blinked and looked away, then vanished back into the leaf
cover as suddenly as they had appeared. *Chimpanzees watch,* explained
Tau 47. I wondered what they were watching, but he led me forward
and as we came out on the edge of a ravine it became clear why they
guarded that patch of forest

"There, filling the ravine and spilling down it in a river of squalor,
was a trash landfill. It was overgrown with creepers, overhung with
trees, which was perhaps why the Goodall Free Township Committee
hadn't known it was there. Two chimpanzees worked the heap immediately below us, poking through it with sticks and now and then pulling
out a useful scrap of salvage, old wiring or broken furniture."

"I guess it wasn't quite virgin wilderness," I said.

"I guess so. Something the survey parties for the Goodall Free Township Committee missed, evidently, or were bribed to overlook. I just stood there gaping at it. The two chimpanzees below looked up at me and froze; after watching Tau 47 and me a moment they seemed to accept my presence and got back to their work. Tau 47 signed to me, *This secret. Good things here. Make house. Make knife. Live good.* He looked up once again at the mountain and bared his teeth. *Iota 34 want secret. Dirty bad bad.*

"Iota 34 make house too? I signed.

"No no, signed Tau 47. *Iota 34 make,* and he paused and made a motion of gripping a shaft of something with both hands, stabbing with it. Then he signed, *Stick knife hunt hurt.*

"I saw the whole problem in a flash: it was much more than a Tree of Knowledge in Eden. It was like the twentieth-century dilemma over atomic power. Here these poor creatures had this unexpected gift, from which they could derive all sorts of comforts for their wretched existence; but it had to be prevented from falling into the enemy's hands at all costs, or it could be used against them."

"Though they were obviously using it to make weapons themselves," I said.

"Naturally." Hanuman tilted his hat forward to shade his face. "They were chimpanzees. It was in their nature. They're decent enough people but they're not peace-loving, you know, any more than *Homo sapiens* is. What a Cold War scenario, eh? Being signers, they had the ability to communicate ideas; they had seen enough of what *Homo sapiens* has in the way of enriched environments to want to make one for themselves, and now they had the potential to do so.

"But as long as most of their tribe's resources had to be expended on guarding this trash pile, how much time could they afford to do anything else?"

"It's always something," I muttered.

"So there I was, standing on this height, and suddenly it flashed before my eyes: what if I became one of these people? What if I led them, used my augmented intelligence to give them the edge in their arms race? I might become a lower-hominid Napoleon! We'd take on the dastardly Iota 34 and force his tribe to become peaceful citizens of a new primate civilization! Made of recycled trash, admittedly, but unlike anything that had ever existed.

"Or perhaps—dare I even think it—force the *Homo sapiens* world to face the monstrous injustice of what had been done to these poor creatures by letting them get an earful of the Black Monolith, so to speak, and then removing any way for them to fulfill their hitherto unguessed-at potential by insisting they live like primitives?

"Good heavens, I thought to myself, it might even be a plot to keep us from moving into Man's neighborhood! Having transmitted the divine spark of reason to us, what if Man had now regretted and sought to keep us mere animals? How dare he deny our humanity? Why, I might lead a crusade to bring apes everywhere to a higher level of being. Shades of Roddy McDowall in a monkey mask!"

"But you saw the futility of such an exercise in ego?" I inquired.

"Actually, it was the cold realization that I'd probably be remembered as Pretty Pink General," said Hanuman. "Plus the fact that just then I felt something bite me, and looked down at myself and realized I was covered in fleas.

"Good secret, I signed to Tau 47. *I quiet quiet.*

"He looked out over it all, sighed and signed, *You go. No stay here. Go houses.*

"I signed, *You miss houses?*

"Miss houses, he signed back. *Want good food. Good blanket good. Miss pictures. Miss music. Miss game. Good good all. I sad. Cry like baby.*

"Sorry, I signed. He just huffed and looked out over the landfill.

"We went back to the village.

"The ladies were all sitting around grooming one another, Mrs. Fabry included. She looked up as we approached and said, 'Michael, dear, I've been trying to explain that you want to stay with them, but—'

"I told her it was all right, that I'd changed my mind. Before she could explain this, though, Gamma 18 broke away from the group and approached me. Looking at me seriously, she signed, *You no stay here.*

"No stay, I agreed bitterly.

"She came closer on all fours—her baby was still hanging under her— and put her hand on my shoulder, quite gently. Then she signed, *You no chimpanzee. You no man. You other thing. Sad thing here. You go houses, be happy thing.*

"By which motherly advice I guess she meant that the bananas grow at the top of the tree, not at the roots, and since I didn't belong at either end (evolutionarily speaking) I might as well climb up and eat rather than slide back down and starve. You get what life deals you, and you'd better make the best of it.

"I went back home with Mrs. Fabry. The dear woman didn't mind all the flea bites she'd incurred on my behalf in the least; I do believe she got more out of the whole ape-bonding experience than I had. I settled down to try to be a good adoptive son to her and Dr. Fabry. Tried not to think of my chimp-mother's plight, though I lived by her wise words."

"And that was it? You came all that way, and that was all she had to tell you?" I demanded.

"Well, she was a chimpanzee, after all, not a vocational guidance counselor." Hanuman looked at me over his sunglasses. "And if you think about it, it's good advice. Certainly I've let it guide me through a long and occasionally trying life. You might consider doing the same."

"I fail to see how our problems are in any way similar," I snapped.

"Aren't they?" Hanuman regarded me. "When I discovered I was neither an ape nor a man, I tried to be an ape. It was a waste of my time. All the advantage is on the human side.

"You—during a similar adolescent crisis, I'd bet bananas to coconuts—discovered you are neither a machine nor a woman. So you've tried to be a machine."

"Go to hell, you little hominid bastard!"

"No, no, hear me out: your work habits, your preference for physical and emotional isolation, are part of your attempts to ignore your human heritage. But your heart is human so you can't do it, any more than I could, and the stress of the conflict drove you to seek out human companionship.

"Or possibly, by sleeping in a place you knew to be hazardous, you were indulging in a covert suicide attempt. Was it really tea you were thirsty for, Mendoza?"

"I can't believe this!" I leaped out of my chair and tore off my mask, glaring at him. "You're one of the Company's psychiatrists! Aren't you?"

"Let's just say I'm not completely retired. You must have suspected all along," he added calmly, "clever cyborg that you are."

"How many times do I have to tell you people, it was an accident?" I shouted, and all up and down the beach, heads turned and other operatives stared at us.

"But you're programmed not to have accidents," he said. "And the Company would like to know how it happened, and whether it's likely to happen again. Is it just your neurosis that leads you to take unnecessary risks, or is it a design flaw they need to know about? They have a lot of money invested in you cyborgs, you know. Who were you hoping to find in the fire, Mendoza?"

"Oh, now we get to the truth," I said, sitting down again. "Now we drop the crap about how I'm really human. I'm an expensive *machine* and the Company's doing a diagnostic to see whether I'm still malfunctioning?"

Hanuman shrugged, holding my gaze with his own. "You look at me and all you see is a monkey, no matter how cleverly I speak. They look at you and all they see is a machine they can't seem to repair. It's insulting. Unfair. Yet the hard truth is, neither one of us belong in the natural world. I know it hurts; who'd know better than I? But it won't change. I've accepted that. Can you?"

I put my mask back on and, without another word to him, strode away up the beach.

I managed to avoid speaking to him the rest of the time I was there, and he didn't try to speak to me, though he watched me somberly from a distance and tipped his hat once or twice when our paths crossed. Maybe he'd found out all the Company wanted him to find out, or maybe he knew there was no way on earth I was ever going to let him any further into my head than he'd gotten already.

The Company discharged me for active service at last; they had to. They'd repaired me good as new, right? So I took off for the coastal mountains and made a new base camp up in the big trees, and got right back to work happily collecting genetic variants of *Abies bracteata*. I had all I wanted in the wilderness.

Stupid chimpanzees, wanting to go back to the cities of humanity! Maybe they needed an enriched environment, but not me. I'd stripped away such irrelevant nonsense from my life, hadn't I?

I had the looming mountains to myself, and the vast empty sea and the immensity of cold white stars at night and, thank God, the silence of my own heart. It never makes a sound of complaint. It's a perfectly functioning machine.

So I was sitting on this beach near Big Sur, a fairly crowded beach as the place goes—there were maybe a dozen people sunbathing, surfing, trying to prevent small children from eating sand—and a scuba diver in full kit came down the stairs, made his difficult way over the rocks, flip-flopped across the sand and waded into the sea. He swam out past the white line of breakers and the surfers riding the swell, and for a while I could glimpse his snorkel moving to and fro. Eventually I couldn't see it anymore.

It wasn't until hours later, climbing the stairs to go back to my campsite, that I realized I had never seen him come out of the water.

◆ ◆ ◆

Studio Dick Drowns Near Malibu

IT WAS TIME TO DIE AGAIN.
Some of us don't like faking our deaths; you have a lot of fuss and worry over making it believable, and then you have to go off someplace else and start over again. I enjoy it, though. In all the centuries I've been running around after things the Company wanted, shipping the loot of history up to their offices in the Future, I must have staged a dozen memorable demises. It's the closest a cyborg like me is ever going to get to the real thing, right? So why not make it stupendous, spectacular, colossal?

I've died even when I didn't strictly have to. In the old days you didn't need to die to assume a new identity, when the Company transferred you. Riding over the horizon was as good as riding off the edge of the world, and if you never came back most mortals assumed you'd died. You could become somebody else, somewhere else, and the chances were astronomical you'd ever meet a mortal who'd known you in your previous incarnation. Even back then, though, your cover could be blown: look at that Martin Guerre guy. That was why I always liked to play it safe and get myself a nice indisputable grave before I moved on to my next posting.

And when the twentieth century rolled around, with photos and Social Security numbers and drivers' licenses, and worse yet to come, it became more important than ever to die convincingly. No loose ends!

Still, I kind of hated leaving MGM, then of all times; it was 1938, for crying out loud. The best-ever year for movies was just around the corner: *Gone with the Wind* was already in pre-production, ditto *Ninotchka* and *The Wizard of Oz,* to name but a few. It was going to be swell, which in fact was why the Company was edging me out. They wanted to plant a Facilitator higher up in the studio, to be in a position to do things like grab lost footage from the cutting room floor. You wouldn't believe what mortals will pay for *The Wizard of Oz* stuff by the twenty-fourth century.

And I'd been there too long, anyway. Joseph Denham, Studio Detective, had done a lot of favors and knew where a lot of bodies were buried. Too many people knew my name. Time to move on.

So I set up a death that would make the headlines. Well, *Variety*'s headlines, at least.

Scuba diving hadn't arrived yet, back then before the war, but diving enthusiasts were already beginning to fool around with homemade apparatus and snorkels. I let all my mortal friends know I had a keen new hobby, and bored them with descriptions of the amateur dive equipment I was buying. Moved from my furnished room in Hollywood to a furnished room in Santa Monica so I could be closer to the sea. Let slip that I wasn't really all that good a swimmer. There were a few people at the studio already, Garbo among them, who'd have liked nothing better than to see me drown.

I met my fellow cyborg Lewis at Musso & Frank's for one last round of drinks while we went over what he'd tell the cops; that was Friday night. Saturday morning I was off to Santa Monica, where I parked my nice new Ford near the pier, bid it a regretful farewell, and carried my outsized duffel and striped umbrella to the nearest changing rooms.

Ten minutes later I was making my awkward way to the sea through all the other striped umbrellas, and, brother, was I a sight to behold. That was the idea, of course.

I had on a kind of tight union suit of black wool, with a hood over which I'd fitted a pair of goggles with the breathing tube and its little float clipped to the side. It would have been smarter to have waited to put on the rubber flippers until I was right at the water's edge, but more people noticed me floundering across the sand with them on. Picking a likely spot, I flop-flopped up to it and set down my things alongside.

The couple in beach chairs—old mortals, always pick old mortals for your witnesses because they watch everything and they love to testify to cops—stared at me in amazement as I opened my duffel and spread out a little beach mat. Humming to myself, I laid out a rolled-up towel and opened my striped umbrella and stuck it in the sand at a jaunty angle. Finally the old guy said, as I'd been waiting for him to say:

"Christ Almighty, what're you supposed to be? A frog?"

"What?" I looked over at him in apparent surprise. "Who, me?"

"He's some kind of diver, Harry," said the old lady.

"Well, you look like a frog to me," said the old man.

"That's right, ma'am, I'm a diver," I said, smiling at the old lady. "Not deep-sea, of course, I just sort of swim around the surface and look at stuff. It's a great hobby. You see a lot of fish."

"Is that so?" said the old lady. "Do you ever see any shipwrecks?"

"Oh, sometimes," I said, fitting my goggles over my eyes, "but you have to be really experienced to explore a wreck, and I've only been doing this for a few weeks. I'm not very good at it yet."

"Those things on your feet make you look like a frog," said the old guy.

"Yeah," I said, shading my eyes to look out at the ocean. "Say, look at those whitecaps! The water's pretty rough today, isn't it? I guess I won't stay out too long. Would you folks mind keeping an eye on my things here, until I come back?" I leaned close to add, in a loud whisper, "My wallet's in my bag with my driver's license and everything, you know."

"Sure we will, mister," said the old lady. "You be careful, now."

"Gee, thanks," I said, and, squaring my shoulders, flop-flopped on down to the water. Adults stared, children pointed, somebody's toddler shrieked with terror as I passed. I waded in and turned, once, to wave cheerfully at the old couple. Joseph Denham, confidant to the stars, makes his unforgettable exit!

I paddled around out there for a while, splashing like a clumsy mortal swimming, and I made sure they could see the yellow float bobbing like a lemon on the waves. Farther out, and farther out, just like a mortal getting careless in his enthusiasm. At last I surfaced for a little while, pulling in breath, oxygenating my tissues; then I dove, way deep down, and yanked off the float and let it rise by itself up to the glassy bright roof of the world. Turning, I swam away into the green darkness.

I headed north, past Malibu. By the time I was passing Point Mugu, I was pretty sure the old couple would have alerted the lifeguard that I'd failed to come back. The yellow float would have washed ashore, the only trace of me, because of course no body would ever be recovered.

There'd be a brief homicide investigation, but I'd made it pretty darned obvious it was a case of accidental death. My will was in a shoebox in my dresser, along with the other papers that had affirmed Joseph Denham's existence. Lewis would inherit my car and the small change in my bank account, along with the job of notifying the studio. A paragraph in *Variety,* a short service at Hollywood Memorial, and somebody else would take over my customary spot at the bar at Musso & Frank's Grill. The hole that Joseph Denham had left at MGM would disappear in a few days.

Neat, huh? It certainly beat the last time I died of old age, when I had to lie in my coffin for hours sweating under appliance makeup and listening to the funeral mass drone on and on and on . . .

And I had no regrets. I'd died in Hollywood before and I knew I'd eat lunch in that town again some day, when my former cronies there were all tucked away under white marble at Hollywood Memorial or being wheeled around the grounds of the Motion Picture Home. The Company always needs a few of its smooth operators in the movie industry, just as it needs us in the mortals' churches and governments: unobtrusive little guys like me to weight the dice of history now and then, or slip an extra ace into the deck. Nothing too obvious, you understand: somebody helpful standing at his Holiness's elbow to supply that *mot juste* when he's writing a papal encyclical, somebody to remind the senator where he left his pants, somebody to put a particular script where Mr. Hitchcock or Mr. Lucas will just happen to glance at it.

Yes, it's an important job, all right. Most of the time it makes up for having no life of my own.

Anyway I cruised on like an eel, ditching the snorkel tube and mask somewhere past Santa Barbara; I didn't really need them and they dragged in the water. The big heavy flippers I kicked off around Point Conception. Streamlined as a seal, I went my merry immortal way, coming to the surface once in a while to breathe. Night fell and day followed it, and I was still heading north.

There's a place above Cape San Martin called Jade Beach. You really can find jade there, if you're foolhardy enough to climb down the precarious wooden stairs from the clifftop to the sand far below. If the most recent winter storm hasn't washed out the stairs anyway, it's worth the uneasy descent. The place is all serpentine. The cliffs are green, the sand is green, the sea is green as emerald in that little cove. But there's hardly ever anybody there.

I've only been there myself because I knew a girl who loved the place, a long time ago before the stairs were built. That's another story.

The point is it's usually deserted, which was why I'd come up here in my Ford two months earlier, hauling a Company-issue cachebox with me. In it were all the things I'd need to get started with my new identity: paperwork, clothes, keys, money. I'd buried it at the base of the cliff, deep under the gritty cobbles. It had been a lot of work, but all I needed to do now was dig it up. As soon as I did I'd be Leslie Joseph, with papers to prove it, on his way to a hot meal in Monterey and an apartment and a job in San Francisco.

It was late afternoon when I turned right and made my way through the kelp forests into the cove. I was dead tired and cold; I figured a couple hours' snooze on the beach were in order before Leslie Joseph made his entrance. About a mile out I began my ascent to the surface, scanning to be certain there were no mortals around.

And, wouldn't you know it . . . there was one right on top of me. Literally, I mean. There was a mortal female struggling in the water less than a fathom above my head. As I stared up at her, open-mouthed, she began to sink.

Well, I had to do something. My official designation is Preserver, isn't it? Maybe that was why, without even thinking, I shot upward like a cork and grabbed her, and a second later we broke the surface. All the same, it was a dumb thing to do.

We gulped in breath and she gave a feeble scream, staring at me with enormous black eyes. She struggled frantically for a few seconds and then hung limp, so I was able to get us ashore without wasting my breath on argument.

Dumb, dumb, dumb. She had to be a suicide; she was fully dressed, and anyway I've seen them often enough to know the look mortals get in their eyes when they're determined to check out. She wouldn't thank me and I hadn't done myself any favors, either, by saving her life. What the hell was I going to do with her now?

I dragged her up on the sand and dropped her, and she lay there at my feet gasping, with her eyes shut tight.

"Please," she said. "I changed my mind at the end. I really did. I was trying to swim back. You must have seen that."

I peered down at her. Her hair trailed across her face like seaweed. She was young, maybe twenty, and from her clothes she wasn't rich, wasn't a farm girl either. Somebody's stenographer, maybe? I saw the purse and the battered shoes on the last step of the cliff stair. She'd walked a long way in shoes that were meant to sit side by side under a typing stand.

"You shouldn't have done it," I said, which was pretty obvious but what else was I going to say?

"I'm sorry!" she wept. "Oh, you can't take me to Hell! Haven't I been there already, the last two days?" She got up on her knees to clutch at me, and I saw myself reflected in her desperate eyes: black-clad thing with a white face, like Death in *The Seventh Seal,* and looking none too good after two days in the water either, eyes still sunk back in my head and protective lenses still raised. Okay, she thought I was something supernatural. Maybe I could work with that. I've had to impersonate gods in my time, working with mortals, and she seemed half-crazed with fear already.

"This is nothing to the fires of Hell," I said sternly.

But the girl was taking in the mundane details of my appearance: the buttons on my suit, the sagging wool, the stubble on my unshaven face. Her eyes were still frightened, but her lip curled in rage. She looked around. She spotted her worn-out shoes, saw the dead fish stranded a few feet away, saw the broken pop bottles under the stairs.

"But this is—everything's the same!" she shouted. "Everything's dirty and squalid and it isn't supposed to be this way still, not when you've died! Look at *you!* What kind of Angel of Death needs a shave?"

"For your information, I'm the Angel of Death by Drowning," I improvised, summoning all the dignity I could. "I work on a limited budget, okay? And you aren't exactly dead yet, which is why you still see the world with mortal eyes."

She said something nice young stenographers didn't often say in 1938, not where they could be heard anyway, and sagged backward and hid her face in her hands.

I had three options here. I could let her swim out again and finish the job she'd started, which was what Company policy recommended in a situation like this: we're not supposed to interfere in their mortal lives. That way I could recover my cache without a witness.

I could kill her myself. This would also solve my witness problem, but such action is against official Company policy, yet still happens anyway sometimes, more often than they'll admit is necessary. I hate killing mortals, though. I almost never do it. Besides, the girl reminded me of somebody I used to know. It made me uncomfortable.

I wasn't sure what my third option was. It probably involved some fast talking. So I cleared my throat and said:

"I wouldn't use that kind of language, if I were you. You might very well be going before the Eternal Throne in a minute or two, and you're in enough trouble already. What can have been so terrible you'd risk eternal damnation rather than live?"

The girl lowered her hands and blinked at me.

"Don't you already know?" she demanded, looking scornful.

"Do I look like they give me all the details up there?" I countered, wringing out a fold of my saggy suit. Her look of scorn deepened. I decided to try a cold reading.

"I was told something about an office," I said, and from her face and her pulse and respiration I knew I was right. "There was some trouble there—?"

"You can say that again, brother!" the girl said, laughing bitterly. "Ten thousand dollars' worth of trouble."

"That's right," I said. I noticed the grief below the laughter. "And love."

Right again. The laughter died away and her face grew terribly quiet. "That was my own fault," she said, in a voice a mortal couldn't have heard below the boom of the surf.

"And he deserted you," I guessed. She flinched. Right again. I usually enjoy batting a thousand, but today it made me feel lousy. Scanning her, I saw that at least she wasn't pregnant. I sat down on the sand beside her. Love, betrayal—and money. And an office. How did they all fit together? Theft? Embezzlement? I decided to try another angle.

"Why aren't you mad at him?"

She didn't answer right away, but from the way she avoided my gaze, staring out to sea, I could tell I was still on the track. At last she shrugged.

"It was my idea, wasn't it?" she said. "Maybe he'd have come up with the money some other way. He was in so much trouble and it wasn't his fault he didn't know how to live on a salary, you see. His people had always had money! Not like mine. He was raised with higher expectations. So then . . . once I'd told him about the Friday afternoon deposits, when I saw the way his face lit up . . . well, I knew we had to do it."

"You still love him," I said. I wasn't guessing on that one; I knew, and so would anybody else, mortal or immortal, who saw her face as she watched the green water rolling in.

"I think he must have gotten scared," she said. "I'm sure he didn't plan it. I guess he got to worrying, with me asleep there and unable to reassure him. I guess he thought it would be just me the police would be looking for. Maybe he was afraid of what his family would think, if we were caught and it got into the papers."

Rich boy down on his luck meets poor girl who works at office, I thought to myself. He needs cash. She figures out a way to abscond with office's money. What happens next? They grab the loot, go on the run and then, while she's asleep in a room somewhere, the boyfriend ditches the girl. But not without—

"He took the money, and you still love him," I said.

She sighed. "I can't help that," she said.

"So when you woke up and found him gone, leaving you broke with the law after you, you came here," I said grimly. She looked at me.

"I didn't mean to," she said. "I walked out to the highway and I hitchhiked. I slept in the woods. I got a ride with a truck driver, but he kept asking me questions and I didn't know what to tell him. So the next time a farm came in sight I said that was where I lived and he let me out there. I just walked on. I came here and saw the stairs going down. That was when I decided. It seemed like a good idea at the time."

Her voice was listless.

"It all seems so stupid. I didn't think I was stupid. I guess I deserve whatever happens now."

I didn't say anything for a minute. Some mortals deserve to die. The boyfriend deserved to die, wherever he was, but there wasn't anything I could do about him.

"What you did, you did for love," I told the girl. "But you were betrayed. Honey, that's one of the oldest tricks in the book, what he pulled on you! He used you to get the money and then dropped you like a rock. It's not your fault."

I wasn't making her feel better. I made an effort to control my temper. She shivered and looked out at the water again. The sun had gone down by this time and the temperature was dropping fast.

"Is my body still out there, on the bottom of the bay?" she asked.

"No," I said. "You're still in your body. You're only conditionally dead. That's why you're still feeling the cold and wet. We have to talk about this some more, but I'm going to make a fire first."

"The Angel of Death by Drowning builds campfires?" she said wearily.

"Yeah," I told her. I got up and looked around. Up the beach, left high and dry by last winter's tides, was a chunk of redwood log maybe three feet in diameter. I climbed up to it, lifted it as though it weighed nothing, and brought it back to where the girl sat. She stared up at me, wide-eyed, and any doubts she might have had about my supernatural nature were gone.

"Here we go," I said, and setting it down above the tideline I went into hyperfunction and busted the whole thing into a huge mound of punky splintered kindling.

"See, we've still got some things to work out," I said. "Think of this as a hearing to determine whether or not you're going to stand trial." I looked around for a sharp stick and did the twirling thing to make a fire, that almost never works at ordinary mortal speed but works in hyperfunction just fine. A little bright flame jetted up silently, slid along the splintered wood and began to eat into it.

She had watched all this in shock, staring. Yes! I had her attention now, all right, that was terror and awe in her black eyes, and it didn't matter anymore that my union suit sagged or my chin was unshaven. I loomed against a background of dancing flame and held out my arms like Leopold Stokowski giving a command to the string section.

"Do you truly repent your sin?" I asked her. She nodded mutely.

"Do you see the man who betrayed you for the cheap liar he is?" I demanded. "Not loving you, not worthy of your love?"

Her face twisted and she drew a ragged breath and said, "Yes."
"What would you do with your life, if it were given back to you?"
Was that hope leaping up in her eyes, or just the reflection of the
fire? "I—I'd start over. Somehow! I'd never be such a fool again. I'd try
and earn enough to send the money back to Mr. Jensen."
"Are you telling me the truth?"
"Yes!" she cried. "I don't know how I'd do it, but I swear that's what
I'd do!"
"Then come to me, mortal child," I intoned, holding out my hand,
"And I will give you your life back."
She rose and took my hand and I pulled her close, so she could get
warm and dry by the fire, but her arms went around me and her mouth
fastened desperately on mine.
Look, I didn't think that was going to happen. We're immortals but
we're not all-knowing. I'd have thought it was the last thing that poor
kid wanted. She did want it, though, she'd come there in the first place
hoping something would ravage her; the least I could do was keep the
experience sort of spiritual.
So I played Azrael, or some kind of angel anyway, there by the fire
on that dark beach between life and death.

She slept like a baby, curled up in the firelight. Her face was so peaceful.
I sat a few paces away with my head in my hands, feeling like thirty
cents.
After a while of gloomy meditation on stuff that would only depress
you if I described it, I got up and found her purse. Sitting down, I went
through its contents.
There were some keys on a ring. A coin purse containing three
pennies and a dime. A pencil. A dime-store fountain pen. A comb. A
compact and a tube of lipstick. A bottle of nail polish and an emery
board. A leather case containing a Social Security card issued to Cora
Luciano. Two letters and a photograph.
I read the letters. They were from the guy. He was so smooth, so
polished, he might have copied every word out of a romance novel.
How could she have believed him for a minute? But she didn't understand professional deceivers. I do, being in that line of work myself.
I looked at the photograph too. It had been taken at an amusement
park, I guess, not long ago. They were standing against a rail in front of
a carousel. His arm was around her. He was tall, handsome, had a
well-dressed Ivy League WASP kind of look to him. Bastard. Beside him
she looked small and shabby and dark, poor little office clerk. Radiantly
happy, of course.

Bastard.

Old, old story, nothing new to me. I still wanted to find the guy and kill him.

I knew, in the back of my mind, why this was making me so sore. It had to do with this green place and another girl who'd come here once, whose life had been wrecked by a smooth-talking mortal man.

That girl hadn't died here. She can't die, much as she'd like to.

I couldn't help her. I never can.

After a while I got up and looked at Cora, studying her critically. I took the letters, the photograph and the Social Security card and fed them to the fire.

I walked away down the beach to where I'd buried my cachebox and dug it up. Retrieving some of the stuff inside, I went back to the fire and sat down to work.

The Company had a neat little document alteration device back then, issued to most field personnel. It looked like a fountain pen. Actually when you unscrewed the cap the business end *was* a fountain pen, and if you were a cyborg or even just a really good forger, you could imitate typed letters with it that nobody could tell hadn't been formed on a machine. When you reversed the device, though, when you took off the smaller cap on the other end, there was an itty-bitty laser that was delicate enough to remove the ink on paper fibers without removing the fibers underneath.

I did the birth certificate first. All I had to change on that was the gender and year of birth; 1913 became 1918. I deleted my signature on the Social Security card. She'd have to sign it herself, when she became Miss Leslie Joseph. I thanked God we were still in the paper age; doing something like this in, say, 1998 would be a nightmare.

I'd have to make myself up a new birth certificate and Social Security card, of course, and I'd have to change the name on my new driver's license—I thought of calling myself Angelo Morte, but the Company frowns on obvious stuff like that. They prefer names that don't draw attention. I settled on William Joseph. Boring, but with luck I'd only have to use it for a few decades. Bill Joseph. Yeah. I could be a Bill Joseph.

I had everything stashed away again by the time I woke her. The sky was just beginning to get light.

"Cora."

"Hm?" She opened her eyes and then sat up abruptly, staring at me. "Oh, my God. I thought you—"

"You thought I was a dream? Almost. Listen to me, Cora, I'm going back now and I don't have a lot of time." I hunkered down beside her. "You've been given a new life. Cora Luciano died out there in the water, and so did all her mistakes. You're Leslie Joseph now, understand?"

"Leslie Joseph," she repeated, and she didn't understand but she was trying to.

"That's right," I said, and held up her birth certificate. "See? Here's your proof. You're twenty years old and you'll be twenty-one next March. Here's your Social Security card. Sign your name, Leslie." I held it out to her with the pen from her purse. Wonderingly, she signed *Leslie Joseph.*

"Great," I said, and taking the card I slipped it into the leather case that had held her old one. Next I held up a thick wad of cash. "Thousand dollars, mostly in tens and twenties. You know better than to flash it, though, right, Leslie? You're a smart girl. Stick it down in the bottom of your purse, peel off a ten and keep it at the top." I put the money in her hands.

"You're going to put on your shoes and go up the stairs over there and walk north along the highway. Hitchhike, only if you can find another woman to give you a ride. When you get to Monterey, buy yourself all new clothes. New shoes. New handbag. New makeup, too, in different shades. Ditch all of Cora's things. Buy a bus ticket to San Francisco and once you get there, buy a train ticket to New York. Get on that train and never look back."

I got to my feet and backed away from her, into the waves.

"You'll be fine in New York, Leslie. It's a big place, lots of opportunities, and nobody knows anybody back there. You'll find an apartment. You'll find an office job. Maybe you'll even find a nice guy. But nobody, and I mean nobody, is ever again going to talk you into doing something you know is bad for you. Okay? You got all that, Leslie?"

She nodded as if mesmerized, watching me as I retreated. The water was up to my chest now, the swell was breaking over my shoulders.

"You're one lucky mortal, Leslie," I called to her. "You just got handed the break of your life. It's up to you what happens now."

I sank into the dark water and swam away under the surface. I didn't come up again until I was far enough out that she couldn't see me.

I could see her, though. She had put on her shoes and was climbing the stairs in a determined kind of way. I watched as she got up to the road, took a firm grip on her purse and marched away into the morning.

She didn't look back.

*   *   *

The cachebox was already breaking up—they're not meant to be reused after the seal is broken—so my Bill Joseph clothes were full of sand, but at least they were dry, and I was able to warm myself up some over the smoking embers of the fire. I stuffed my new wallet in my pocket, slung on my knapsack, climbed the stairs and walked south as far as Gorda, where I ate enough breakfast for three guys.

Then I talked a mortal into giving me a ride as far as San Luis Obispo. He was a nice mortal. I told him all about Bill Joseph, how I was a twenty-five-year-old guy from Santa Rosa, how I lived on Nineteenth Avenue in San Francisco, how I was hiking down here on vacation from my job, which was in a car dealership at Market and Van Ness, how I thought Hitler was a bum and there was probably going to be a war soon and how my favorite song was *Harbor Lights,* how my mother was dead and my father'd raised me . . . on and on, and I got the mortal to believe it all. By the time I got on the train at San Luis, I almost believed it myself.

Bill Joseph enlisted when the war broke out, got himself a nice post as a general's aide, and was right there when the Supreme Allied Command broke into places like Berchtesgaden and Merkers, where the Nazis had stored all kinds of treasure they'd looted from museums and private collections. Bill Joseph knew what happened to a lot of stuff that was never accounted for. He died under mysterious circumstances, though, before anybody could ask him about it. Drowned in the Danube, poor guy. No body was ever found.

Leslie Joseph didn't drown. She went to New York just like I told her to, like the good kid she really was. I found her after the war, though I didn't let her spot me following her around. We're not supposed to do stuff like that, but, well, we do, and anyway I was so happy when I saw she'd gotten over that bastard who'd screwed her up.

She met an ordinary guy. He ran a store. She married him. They ran the store together then and had three kids. They were as blissful as mortals who have three kids can be. They were celebrating their fortieth wedding anniversary around the time I went to work for Mr. Spielberg at Universal. Great happy ending, huh?

I wish to God it was that easy for us.

Why pirates?

In the 1950s, an Australian television studio did a weekly series titled The Adventures of Long John Silver *starring the late Robert Newton. I never missed it. Practically put my little nose through the screen longing after those vistas of clouds over the South Seas, those towering white sails and pitching decks, those cozy dark taverns, those parrots, those big interesting bad guys who were really good guys at heart. Growing up, I can't have been the first Wendy to discover that real life with Peter Pan is miserable; but a girl can really go places with a decent pirate.*

So here's to growing up, and here's to boys who aren't afraid to become men, and here's to tropic seas and tall ships too.

◆ ◆ ◆

The Likely Lad

"ALEC'S GROWING UP INTO SUCH A NICE BOY," SAID Mrs. Lewin fondly, pouring out a cup of herbal tea. "So thoughtful. Do you know, he's doing all his own laundry now? I never have to remind him at all."

Lewin grunted acknowledgement, absorbed in his cricket match. It was only a holo of a game played a century earlier—competitive sports had been illegal for decades now—but it was one he had never seen.

"Though the water rate's a bit high," Mrs. Lewin added, setting the pot back in place and covering it with a tea cozy. "Not that his lordship can't afford it, goodness knows, but the Borough Council gets so nasty if they suspect you're wasting anything! I said perhaps Alec ought to save it all up for once a week, but he wouldn't hear of it. Changes his sheets every day. Won't let me do it for him at all. Well, I can understand that, I said, fresh bed linens are a treat, and aren't you the dear to save me coming all the way upstairs and rummaging in that old hamper for your socks . . ."

Lewin dragged his attention away from the lost green paradise of Lord's and played back what she had been saying.

"Changes his sheets every day?" he repeated.

"Yes. Isn't that responsible of our Alec? It seems like only yesterday he was toddling about and screaming every time I tried to take the face flannel to him, and now . . ."

"Now he's fourteen," said Lewin. "Hmm."

"How time flies," observed Mrs. Lewin.

"Hmm." Lewin paused the holo and stood. "Yeah. Think I'll go have a word with the boy about the water rate, all the same."

He plodded up the kitchen stairs.

Mr. and Mrs. Lewin were Alec's butler and cook. He lived with them in a mansion in London. Alec's father, the sixth earl of Finsbury, lived on a yacht somewhere in the Caribbean, and his mother, the Right Honourable Cecilia Ashcroft, was somewhere else, and Alec hadn't seen either of them in ten years. As a result, Lewin had been obliged to shepherd Alec through most of his childhood. Lewin was not the only one providing Alec with fatherly advice, though he was unaware of this. If he had been aware, he might have spared himself the long climb up to the fourth floor of the house, which was Alec's domain.

Wheezing slightly, Lewin paused on the third-floor landing. He could hear the hideous dissonance of Darwin's Shoes vibrating above, loud enough to rattle the pictures of Alec's parents in their frames. Lewin didn't mind that Alec was listening to crap music much too loud—he was always secretly relieved when Alec did something normal for a boy his age, for reasons that will shortly become apparent—but if the music was loud enough the neighbors would call the Public Health Monitors, and that was to be avoided at all costs, in this city of London in this dismal future time.

So Lewin gritted his teeth and took the last flight at his best speed. Having arrived on the fourth floor without coronary arrest, he hammered on Alec's door, which was spektered all over with little moving shots of Darwin's Shoes, Folded Space and other bands Alec happened to think were cool that week. Lewin felt a certain satisfaction at knocking right through the irritating young faces.

Almost immediately, the door opened a bit and one eye peered out at him, a very pale blue eye a long way up. Alec, at fourteen, was already six feet tall.

"Would you mind granting me an interview?" shouted Lewin, glaring up at the eye.

"Sorry!" Alec opened the door wide with one hand, hastily stuffing something into his pocket with the other. He waved and, mercifully, the decibel level dropped.

Lewin stepped over the threshold and looked around. Nothing suspicious in sight, at least on the order of bottles or smoking apparatus, and no telltale fume in the air. Light paintings of ships drifted across the walls, and phantom clouds moved across the ceiling. It was an effect that invariably gave Lewin vertigo, so he focused his attention on the boy in front of him.

"Didn't I explain what would happen if you played that stuff loud enough to annoy the neighbors?" Lewin demanded.

"Oh, they can't hear it," Alec assured him. "I've got a baffle field projected off the walls of the house. Sound waves just fall into it, see? I could set off a bomb in here and nobody'd know."

"Please don't," said Lewin, sighing. He had no idea what a baffle field was, but not the slightest doubt that Alec could create one. He shifted from foot to foot and Alec, eyeing him nervously, pulled out a chair.

"Would you like to sit down?"

"Yeah, thanks." Lewin sagged into the chair. Alec stood before him a moment, trying not to put his hands in his pockets, and finally retreated to his bed and sat down on its edge, which would nearly put him at Lewin's eye level standing.

In addition to being extremely tall, Alec Checkerfield had a rather unusual face, at least in that day and age: small deep-set eyes, remarkably broad and high cheekbones, a long nose and immense teeth. He looked like a terribly noble horse.

"What you been doing up here?" Lewin inquired.

"Nothing," said Alec. "I mean, er—you know. Studying."

"Mmm." Lewin glanced over at the communications console. "Well. You remember when we had that talk about you hitting puberty?"

Alec flushed and looked away, but his voice was light and careless as he said, "Sure."

"You remember how we talked about using shields?"

"Er . . . yeah."

"You need me to get you any? Happihealthies, or that lot?"

Alec looked at his shoes. "No, thanks. Sir."

"Right. And you do know, don't you, that even if a girl says yes, if she says it before she's eighteen it doesn't count?"

Alec nodded, not raising his eyes.

"And you can get in no end of trouble? Worse than just being carted off by the Public Health Monitors?"

"Yup," said Alec.

"Right," said Lewin, getting to his feet. "Just so you know."

He paused by the door and cleared his throat. "And . . . it uses up a lot of water, doing laundry every day. People will talk. Can't you try and, and—not do that?"

"Yes," said Alec.

"Right," said Lewin. "I'm off downstairs, then."

"Okay."

Lewin edged out and pulled the door shut after him. He shook his head and once again, as he descended the long stairs, cursed Roger Checkerfield for never coming home.

The moment Lewin had turned the corner on the landing, a voice in Alec's room said:

"There now, didn't I tell you they'd notice?"

As the hoarse baritone spoke, a column of light flashed in midair and the speaker appeared. He was an immense man in early eighteenth-century clothing, his beard was wild and black, and his face was wicked. There were two pistols and a cutlass thrust through his wide belt.

"Oh, piss off," muttered Alec. "I can't help it."

"What about I order you a few dozen of them recyclable cloth tissues, eh, matey?" the apparition offered. "On the quiet, like?"

"Can't I have any privacy anymore?" Alec cried.

"Aw, son, don't take on so. It ain't like I was a person, is it now? Who're you to care if a old machine like me knows yer little secrets?" said the apparition.

"You're a lot more than a machine," said Alec ruefully.

"Well, thank'ee, lad, but I knows my place," replied the apparition.

Yet Alec was correct, for Captain Morgan (as the apparition was named) was a great deal more than a mere machine; in fact he was a great deal more than the fairly powerful Pembroke Playfriend Artificial Intelligence he had been when Lewin had purchased him for Alec nine years earlier.

Had Lewin known that little Alec had managed to reprogram the Playfriend, and moreover remove its Ethical Governor so that its drive to fulfill its primary objective—to protect and nurture Alec—was completely unhindered by scruples of any kind, he'd have been horrified. All in all it was a good thing Lewin didn't know. He was worried enough by all the other unusual things young Alec could do.

The Captain now considered the disconsolate boy before him. "Bloody hell, this'd be a lot easier if I was an organic. You and me'd just take the bus over to Egypt at weekend and I'd find my boy a nice couple of whores. Haar! That'd take a reef in yer mainsail, by thunder."

Alec groaned and put his head in his hands. Having an imaginary childhood friend who persisted into his adolescence was embarrassing enough. The idea that the Captain was taking an interest in his (even more imaginary) sex life was intolerable.

"Look, I really don't feel like talking about this right now, okay?" he snapped.

"Not with that force-ten testosterone storm a-raging, I reckon you don't," the Captain agreed. He put his hands behind his back and paced, and the Maldecena projector in the ceiling turned in its pivot mounting to allow him to move across the room. He gave the appearance of drawing a deep breath.

"Look, son, I got programming says I got to keep you clear of wrecks, see? You mind old Lewin! I don't care how bouncy that there Beatrice Louise Jagger was yesterday after Social Interaction 101, the lass is only fourteen! Like you. And neither one of you's got any idea what's going on. You takes her up on any invitations short of a tea party and you'll both wind up in Hospital on hormone treatments, likely for the rest of yer little lives."

"It's not fair," said Alec. "And how'd you know about me and Beatrice?"

"I got me ways, lad," said the Captain smoothly. Thanks to some of the modifications Alec had made for him, he had long since been able to tap into the surveillance cameras mounted everywhere in London and so monitor his charge's progress in the world outside. "Now, it's almost the end of term. Yer going to have a lovely holiday in Bournemouth. We don't want to spoil it, do we?

"No."

"So let me see if I can't turn yer attention to something a bit less dangerous than the Right Honourable Ms. Jagger's knickers, eh? It's time we was taking a prize, matey. We need more loot."

"But we've already got tons of loot," said Alec in surprise.

"I ain't talking about data plunder, son. I mean money. I plan to build up a private fortune for you. One I can hide so nobody knows it's there to tax, see? That way, even if you and Jolly Roger should have a difference of opinion some day, it won't matter if he cuts you off without a penny."

"How could we ever argue about anything?" Alec demanded. "Roger never talks to me at all. Birthdays and Solstice I get presents, if he remembers, but not even an audiomemo in ten shracking years!"

"Well, now, son, even if you does get yer inheritance without a hitch, there ain't no telling when that'll be, and you want to be free and independent in the meantime, don't you?"

"I guess so. Yeah."

"So here's what we does, matey." The Captain grinned, showing a lot of very white teeth in his dark face. "You'll peer about their encryptions a bit, like the smart lad you be, and get me into the databases of the Eurobank and Wells Fargo and some of them other fine big old houses. I goes to work and does a little old-fashioned transference theft, like nobody ain't done in decades on account of it ain't supposed to be possible nowadays. Just a yen here and a dollar there and all of it stowed safe in a nice Swiss account under a fictitious name, eh? Just enough to get you a nice nest egg of, oh, a million pounds or so, what I can start with."

Alec had been listening intently, and now he frowned.

"Wait a minute. Did you say theft? You mean you want us to steal money out of a bank?"

"No, no, matey, not one bank. Somebody'd notice that! We'd loot banks all over the world," the Captain explained. But Alec was shaking his head.

"That'd be stealing, Captain. That's wrong. Breaking in and copying data's one thing, but we'd be actually hurting people if we took their money," said Alec.

The Captain growled and rolled his eyes. "Son, I'm talking about the teensiest little amounts. Nothing anybody'd miss. A flea couldn't light on what we'd be taking. You could put it up a canary's arse and still have room for—"

"Nope. I'm not going to do it," said Alec, with a stubborn downturn of mouth that the Captain knew all too well. He pulled at his beard in exasperation, and then mustered all his tact.

"Alec, laddie. All these years I been a pirate, just like you wanted me to be when you first set me free from that damned Playfriend module. Ain't I been a hard-working old AI? Ain't I gone along with the earring and cocked hat and cutlass and all the rest of the program? Ain't I schemed to keep you safe and happy all this time? And don't you think, being a criminal like I am, that once in a while I might get a chance to actually STEAL something?"

"Steal all the data you like, but we're not going after banks," Alec replied.

Red lights flashed on the console and static buzzed from the speakers; the Captain was doing the electronic equivalent of gnashing his teeth. His eyes, that were changeable as the sea, darkened to an ominous slaty color. Then, as an alternative suggested itself to him, they brightened to a mild Atlantic blue.

"Aye, aye," he said. "No robbing banks, then. What kind of a score's that for a sailor, anyhow? Belike we won't steal nothing from nobody after all. Belike there's a better way."

"I'll bet you can come up with lots better plans," agreed Alec hurriedly, for he was experiencing the qualms of guilt any other boy would feel on telling a beloved parent he was dropping out of school. The Captain eyed him slyly and paced up and down a moment in silence.

"We got to get money, matey, no arguing over that. But . . . we might earn it."

"Yeah," said Alec at once, and then a certain reluctance came into his voice. "Er . . . how?"

"Oh, you could use up yer holiday in Bournemouth getting some lousy summer job," said the Captain. "Wearing a little white hat and peddling fruit ices, eh? Grilling soy patties in a back kitchen or waiting tables for tips? Mind you, it'd take you all yer summer holidays clear through to university to earn a tenth of what we need. That's if you could find somebody to hire you once they found out you was peerage and trying to take employment away from less fortunate boys!

"Or . . . we might do a bit of smuggling."

"Smuggling?" Alec's face cleared.

"Aye! Ain't smuggling just supply and demand? Long as we didn't smuggle nothing that'd hurt nobody, which we wouldn't. But all them bloody stupid Euromarket laws makes for no end of opportunities for a likely lad with a fast craft. You was planning on chartering another little sailboat for the summer, weren't you?"

"That's right," said Alec, his eyes widening as he began to see the possibilities.

"Well then! We'll put her to good use. You let me scan the horizon, son; I reckon I'll find us some honest folk what could use a little help in the export trade," said the Captain, watching Alec's reaction.

"Yeah!" Alec's face shone with enthusiasm. "Wow, Captain, this wouldn't even be a game, would it? This'd be real! With real danger and everything!"

"Certain it would, matey," the Captain told him, privately resolving that there wouldn't be the least possibility of danger.

"What an adventure!"

"But we got to sign articles first, son. I got to have yer affidavy you'll keep yer hands off the little missies in yer Circle of Thirty," said the Captain.

"Sure!"

"I mean it, now! No more of that sweet talk about asking 'em to explore the amazing mysteries of life with you and all that," said the Captain, stern now he had leverage.

Alec scowled and turned red again. "That wasn't exactly what I said."

"Aye, but it near bagged you a Right Honourable, and you without a box of Happlicultics. One week till the end of term, son. My boy can keep his hands to hisself until then, can't he?"

"Aye aye," sighed Alec.

"There's a good lad. I'll just get myself into the maintop, now, and see if I can't spy us out a few connections. Shall I?"

Alec nodded. The Captain winked out. Alec sat there for a moment, before rising to his feet and pulling out the graphics plaquette he had hidden in his pocket on hearing Lewin's knock. Holding it close to his face, he thumbed it on and peered at the screen. His pupils dilated as the tiny woman appeared onscreen and smiled at him invitingly. He glanced sidelong at the Captain's cameras.

*   *   *

M. Despres had an office in Cherbourg, in Greater Armorica. He neither bought nor sold commodities, but he made arrangements for others who bought and sold them.

Cherbourg was the ideal location from which to do business. Armorica, being a member of the Celtic Federation but also technically part of France, had two complete sets of trade regulations from which to pick and choose. Businessmen like M. Despres could custom-tailor a hybrid of statutes and ordinances from both political entities to justify any particular action taken on any given day. As a result, M. Despres scarcely ever ran the risk of arrest. This was good, for he did not enjoy danger.

He left the more dangerous side of his business to certain persons whom he did not officially know. There were several persons he did not know working for him, doing things he did not know about, with ships that did not exist in official registries. So complicated was this little dance of deniability that when M. Despres's shadow employees really actually stopped working for him, it sometimes took several months to determine that they had quit, and longer still to find replacements for them.

In the meantime, nonexistent cargoes sat unshipped in nonexistent warehouses, and M. Despres lost real money.

In order to avoid the attentions of unpleasant men with Gaelic accents who liked to break arms and legs, he sent out a desperate inquiry on certain channels, and sat in his office in Cherbourg drumming his fingers on his communications console and hoping someone would reply soon.

M. Despres was in luck on this Thursday evening. Someone did reply.

A yellow light flashed on the console, signifying that a holo transmission was coming through, and a moment later the console's projector activated and a man materialized before M. Despres's eyes.

"You'd be Box 17, Greater Armorica Logistics?" he inquired in a heavy English accent. He was tall and broad, and impeccably dressed in a three-piece business suit. His black beard was neat, if unusually thick, his black hair bound back in a power queue.

"I don't believe I know you, sir," said M. Despres cautiously.

"I don't know you either, dear sir, and that's for the best, isn't it?" The stranger grinned fiercely. "But we have friends in common, who inform me that you have a transportation difficulty."

"That is a possibility," admitted M. Despres. "References would be required."

"And are being downloaded now. I understand your usual transport personnel seems to have left without a forwarding commcode."

M. Despres shrugged, hoping his holocam picked up the gesture.

"I understand," continued the stranger, "that there's Celtic gentlemen who would like some sugar for their tea, and are getting a little impatient that it hasn't been shipped to them."

"How unfortunate," said M. Despres.

"Very unfortunate indeed, for yourself," said the stranger. "I wouldn't want to be caught between those Celts and the Breton sugar beet growers. You can't afford to lose your business reputation, can you?"

"Who can?" M. Despres smiled noncommittally. He eyed the references; they appeared genuine, and gave M. Morgan the highest praise as a discreet and reliable operator. M. Despres attempted to verify them, and thanks to the elaborate double protocols Alec had built into the codes, everything appeared to check out.

"Of course, reputation can be a bad thing, too," said the stranger. "As when certain vessels become too well known to the coastal patrols."

"I suppose so." M. Despres's interest was piqued. Was this a new operator moving into the territory? "I suppose in that case they might sail to Tahiti, which might create an opportunity for someone else."

"So it might," said the stranger. "But I've been remiss! I must introduce myself. M. Morgan, dear sir. I may be in a position to provide you with assistance in your present time of need."

M. Despres, deciding the moment had come, said simply, "One run. Seventy-five billion Euros."

The stranger looked thoughtful. "Seventy-five billion? That's, let me see, nine hundred and fifty thousand pounds? Not much cargo, I take it."

M. Despres gulped. "Six cases, twenty kilos each."

"A trifle," said the stranger, making a dismissive gesture.

"There is a slight difficulty."

"Ah, now, that would drive my price up."

"I said it was a slight difficulty. The cargo must be recovered from the place in which it was abandoned."

"What unprofessional people you must have known, dear sir! Say, twenty per cent above the previous figure?"

"Fifteen. Recovery should be a simple matter. It's off a Sealand outpost in the channel."

"I'll need my divers, then. Seventeen per cent. The destination?"

"Poole."

"Very good. Time is of the essence, I imagine?"

"Not at all," said M. Despres, lying through his teeth.

"In that case, then, I'll consider the matter and get back to you in, say, two days?"

"Tomorrow would be more convenient, to be frank," M. Despres said hurriedly. The stranger smiled at him.

"Why, then, tomorrow it is, sir. *Au revoir.*" And he vanished.

"He bought it!" whooped Alec, jumping up from his console.

"Of course he did," the Captain replied, preening. "If his bioelectric scans is any indication. We'll clinch it tomorrow."

"I've always wanted to do something like this," said Alec, pacing restlessly. "The open sea, a fast boat, secret business, yeah! This is the closest we'll ever get to being real pirates, I suppose."

"Well, laddie, one ought to move with the times," the Captain replied, pretending to shoot his cuffs and straighten his tie.

"That's true," said Alec, turning to regard him. He said casually, "Speaking of which, er . . . that's a good look for you, you know?"

"Like that better than the old cocked hat and eighteenth-century rig, do you? Less embarrassing for a sophisticated young lord about town?" jeered the Captain. "Damn, boy, I like the suit myself. Sort of a gentleman's gentleman but with some bloody *presence.* What do you say I appear like this from here on, eh?"

"Brilliant," Alec said. Clearing his throat, he added in a small voice, "But . . . we'll still be sea rovers, right?"

"More'n we ever was, matey," the Captain told him. "To the tune of nine hundred fifty thousand pounds!"

"Plus seventeen per cent."

"Plus seventeen per cent. Smart as paint, my boy!"

Alec's holidays had been spent at Bournemouth, in one rented villa or another, ever since he'd come to England, after his parents' divorce. When he'd been small, he built sand castles and told inquiring adults that the Lewins, watchful from their beach chairs, were his grandparents.

When he'd outgrown sandcastles he'd gone surfing, or explored Westbourne. Here he'd found a public garden planted on the site of a house where Robert Louis Stevenson had once lived. Stevenson was Alec's favorite author; though he had never read any of his books (only children who were going on to lower-clerical jobs were taught to read nowadays, after all). Alec had assiduously collected every version of *Treasure Island* ever filmed. Being an exceptionally bright boy, he had been able to spell out enough of the commemorative plaque in the garden to tell him whose house had once stood there. He had run home in great excitement to tell the Lewins, who smiled and nodded and turned their attention back to their illegal bridge game with another elderly couple.

The last two summers, however, Alec had ventured through the pines and gone over to Lilliput, beyond Canford Cliffs. At Salterns Marina there was a place that rented sailboats, and for an extra fee would provide an instructor in the art of sailing. So quickly had Alec picked it up that in no time at all he'd been able to take his tiny craft out of the harbor and into Poole Bay by himself, working his way between Brownsea Island and Sandbanks like an old sailor.

Tacking back and forth, getting sunburnt and wet with the sea spray, catching the winds and racing sidelong over blue water, squinting against the glitter of high summer: Alec was happy. There was no one to apologize to out on the water, no one who wanted explanations. The global positioning satellites might be tracking his every move, but at least they were far up and unseen. He had at least the illusion of freedom, and really that was all anybody had, these days.

Sometimes he took his boat as far out on the bright horizon as he dared, and stretched out on the tiny deck and lay looking up at the sky, where the high sun swung behind the mast top like a pendulum. Sometimes he thought about never coming in at all.

Today Alec whistled shrilly through his teeth as he traveled along Haven Road on his RocketCycle. The idea that it rocketed anywhere was a pathetic joke; it had an antigravity drive and floated, barely able at its best speed to outpace a municipal bus. But the sun was hot on his back and felt good, and the pine woods were aromatic, and he was on his way to have his first-ever real adventure on the high seas!

Arriving at the marina, Alec stored the RocketCycle and strode down the ramp toward his mooring, carrying a small black case. He waved at the attendant as he passed. The attendant smiled and nodded kindly. He was under the impression Alec was the victim of some sort of bone disease that had made him abnormally tall and which would shortly prove fatal, so he was invariably courteous and helpful. It took imminent death to provoke decent customer service nowadays.

"Looks like a great day to be out there!" Alec called, boarding the little *Sirene.*

"Bright," agreed the attendant.

"Think I'll stay out all day!"

"Okay," said the attendant. He watched from his chair as the boy powered up the fusion drive, checked all the instruments, cast off and moved out, running up the little sail. Then he settled back and turned

his attention to his game unit, feeling pleased with himself for his toler-
ance and trying once more to recall which holo program it was that had
shown a two-minute feature on genetic freaks . . .

Alec, once he'd cleared Sandbanks, moved into the masking wake of
the St. Malo ferry and glanced up involuntarily in the direction of the
currently orbiting satellite. He opened his black case, which appeared to
be a personal music system; slipped on earshells, found the lead and
connected it to the *Sirene*'s guidance and communications console. He
gave it a brief and carefully coded command. From that moment onward
the satellite received a false image; and somewhere in a dark room of a
thousand lit screens, one screen was persuaded to show nothing but
images of the *Sirene* tacking aimlessly and innocently back and forth all
day.

The object in the black case—which was not a personal music
system—shot out a small antenna. The antenna fanned into a silver
flower at one end. From this a cone of light shot forth, faint and nearly
transparent in the strong sunlight, and a moment later the Captain
materialized.

"Haar!" He made a rude gesture at the sky. "Kiss my arse, GPS!
They won't suspect a thing, now. Oh, son, what a lucky day it was for
me when I shipped out with a bloody little genius like you."

"Not so little any more," Alec reminded him, taking the tiller and
turning the *Sirene* a point into the wind.

"To be sure." The Captain turned to regard Alec fondly. "My boy's
growing up. His first smuggling run! Faking out a whole satellite system
all by himself. Ain't nobody else in the world but my Alec can do that."

"I wonder why they can't?" Alec speculated, peering back at the
rapidly dwindling mainland. "It seems really easy. Am I that different
from them?"

"Different is as different does, matey," said the Captain smoothly,
adjusting his lapels. He wasn't about to explain just how different Alec
was, especially at this time of adolescent anxiety. To be truthful, the
Captain himself wasn't sure of the extent of Alec's abilities, or even why
he had them.

He knew enough to hide Alec's genetic anomalies on routine medical scans. He'd done enough stealthy searching to discover that Alec's
DNA type made it extremely unlikely that he was a member of the
human race as it presently existed, let alone the son of either Lord Finsbury or the Right Honourable Cecilia Ashcroft, as his birth certificate
stated. But why upset the boy?

"I've been thinking," said Alec, "That as long as I can do stuff the
rest of 'em can't, I ought to do some good for everybody. Don't you
think? I'll bet a lot of people would like to have some privacy for a

change. We could set up a consulting firm or something that would show people how easy it was to get around Big Brother up there."

"Aw, now, son, that's a right noble plan," the Captain agreed. "Only problem with it is, we don't want to lose our advantage, do we? As long as it's just you and me has the weather gauge of them satellites, why, there ain't no way they'll ever know we're getting around 'em. But if you was to let other folks in on the secret . . . well, sooner or later there'd be trouble, see?"

"I guess so." Alec frowned toward the Isle of Wight. "We'd draw attention to ourselves."

"And we got to avoid that like it was the Goodwin Sands, son, or it'd be Hospital for you and a diagnostic disassembly for me, and farewell to freedom! Plenty of time for do-gooding once we've got you stinking rich, says I; you can give millions to charity then, eh?" proposed the Captain.

Alec, thinking uneasily of a life immured in a padded cell in Hospital, nodded. He squared his shoulders and said, "Aye aye, Captain sir. So, when do we rendezvous with the *Long John?*"

"Let's take her farther out into the channel first, boy. Two points south-southeast."

Mr. Leam had an office in the Isle of Wight, but he was seldom there. His job kept him out at sea most days and many nights, for he was the Channel Patrol.

Up until a week earlier he had enjoyed the title exclusively, but the Trade Council had decreed that he train an assistant. Mr. Leam was secure enough in his self-esteem to take this as a compliment; he knew his job was vital to the well-being of the nation. He simply wished they'd hired him someone English.

"Not that I hold your ancestry against you in any way," he told Reilly, "Of course. But it's a tough job, you see. Requires deep personal commitment. Clear understanding of the dangers involved. Constant vigilance."

"I thought it was just cruising around trying to catch the Euros slipping us their national product and all and messing up our economy," said Reilly. "Where's the danger in that?"

Mr. Leam grimaced, then assumed his most patient expression. "Coming, as you do, from a, hem, more *permissive* culture, you mightn't understand. As a member of the Channel Patrol, you have a sacred duty to prevent murder."

"Murder?" Reilly cried. "Nobody at the Council interview said anything about murder!"

"I'll try to put this in your terms. Your ethnic affiliation have a lot of, er, children. Now, suppose one day you were minding someone's baby, and saw a vicious criminal sneaking up on the innocent thing, offering it a shiny bottle of *poison!*" Mr. Leam hissed, pacing the wheelhouse of the Patrol cutter. He peered keenly out at the horizon, dotted with skimming sails, and went on:

"Well, Reilly, what would you do? Would you let the little creature drink the poison down? They have no sense, you see, they'll ingest any kind of toxic substance if it tastes nice. No; as a moral human being, you'd see it was your duty to snatch the nasty stuff away before harm was done."

"So . . . the Euros have a secret plot going to poison babies?" Reilly inquired cautiously, wondering if Mr. Leam were crazy as well as bigoted.

"In effect, yes, they do," said Mr. Leam. "Think about this for a moment. Consumers are like babies, aren't they? You can't trust them to know any better than to indulge themselves in what's bad for them. That's why *we* made moral, sensible prohibitions to protect them all! The strong-willed must protect the weak against the profiteers who would entice them with their impurities."

"Okay," said Reilly, "But how's a bottle of *pouilly fuissé* that nobody but rich people can afford anyway going to do harm?"

Mr. Leam shook his head sadly.

"If it were only as simple as that," he said. "They deal in far worse than wine. Think of the hideous immorality involved in the mere production of *cheese,* man! The enslavement of animals. The forced extrusion of foul stinking moldy curds of stuff so full of grease and bacteria it runs on the plate and plays havoc with the intestines! What civilized country would allow something like that on the market?

"And coffee! Horrible little black beans like cockroaches, just full of toxins. You wouldn't enjoy being a caffeine addict, I can tell you. Fingers trembling, teeth stained and chattering, heart pounding, eyes popping, arteries worn right through from the strain, aneurysm striking any time and exploding your brain!" Mr. Leam smote the navigation console with his fist. "Bam! Like that. And tea just as bad, even more insidious because the fool Consumers get sentimental about it.

"And cocoa's bad enough, with all those exotic alkaloids to stimulate unnatural desires (can you imagine there was a time when people fed it to their *children?*)—but chocolate! Dreadful oily voluptuous insinuating filth just full of addictive chemicals, and loaded with refined sugar, eating away at your teeth with its acids until they're worn down to broken suppurating snags. Peanuts bloating you with calories and swelling you with toxic gases and salts, bleached flour to load your system with invisible toxins, ghastly black messes of fish roe—think of the outrage done to the harmless sturgeon!"

"I never realized!" gasped Reilly, who had gone green as an organic pistachio.

Mr. Leam wiped foam from the corner of his mouth and looked stern. "And this, man, is why we live. Only we can preserve the General Prohibition, for without our ceaseless care, the nation's borders will be overrun with peddlers of pollution."

"Yes, sir," said Reilly, and with new eyes peered fearfully across at the lowering darkness of Armorica.

"I'm picking up the *Long John,* matey," the Captain informed Alec. "Two kilometers west-southwest and closing fast."

"Cool!" Alec turned expectantly and watched the horizon, and presently saw the tiny foaming wake making straight for the *Sirene,* for all the world as though a torpedo had been launched at her. Within a few yards of her hull, it bobbed to the surface and halted, then came slowly forward with a distinct paddling motion.

"Who's my smart little *Long John,* then?" crooned Alec. Grinning, he bent over the gunwale and lifted from the water something that looked like a cross between a toy submarine and a mechanical dog. Alec had created it over the previous week, using odds and ends he had in his room and employing principles that seemed fairly basic to him but which no human presently living could have grasped. He had launched it on the previous evening, dropping it quietly off the end of Bourne-mouth Municipal Pier. "Been out nosing around like I programmed you? What'd you find? Let's see, yeah?"

The *Long John* drew in its paddles and sat motionless as Alec connected a lead from the console to a port in its nose.

The Captain crouched down and regarded it, scowling with concentration. "All systems still operational," he confirmed. "Data's coming in now. Looks like it done the job, by thunder! Here's them coordinates . . ." He lifted his head and looked out into the distance to the bleak hulk of the old Sealand platform. "The cargo's there, all right; smack on the sea bottom, thirty meters off the northwest pylon. I'm setting a course now. Bring her around, son!"

"Aye aye, Captain sir!"

In the early part of the twenty-first century there had been a brief fad for civil liberty that had taken the form of establishing tiny independent countries in international waters, built on floating platforms or abandoned oil rigs. This had given rise to a loosely organized federation collectively known as Sealand. Eventually, as the Second Age of Sail dawned and people realized it was much more convenient simply to live aboard megaclippers, the cramped Sealand outposts themselves were abandoned. Rusting, hoary now with guano they stood, and sea birds nested in their blind windows and gaping doors.

Dark birds of another kind entirely used the platforms as landmarks and places to rendezvous, which was why a hundred and twenty kilos of refined sugar—one of the most expensive of controlled substances, in this day and age—lay scattered in its vacuum-sealed crates on the seabed nearby.

"We're over 'em now, son," the Captain announced with satisfaction. "Let's see if the tiny bugger's up to his programming."

"Of course he is," said Alec, disconnecting the Long John and lifting it over the side. The moment it touched the surface, its little paddles deployed, and it trod water patiently while Alec attached a length of cable to its stern. When the cable was in place, the Long John dove down, vanishing swiftly in the green water, the cable unspooling behind until it popped off the reel and floated down out of sight. Alec smirked and gave the Captain two thumbs-up.

"Telemetry coming back now," growled the Captain, staring at the horizon in a preoccupied kind of way. "There's the loot. Initiating recovery mission."

"Brilliant," said Alec, and leaned back at the tiller. Far below the Sirene's keel, the Long John settled on the nearest of the sugar crates and extended a pair of manipulative members. It set about reeving one end of the cable through the crate's carry-handle, and when it had tied the cable off securely, the Long John rose and paddled off to the next crate, towing the cable after it.

"Yes, the old Sealand stations," said Mr. Leam, shaking his head. "You'd think they were something innocent, wouldn't you? Lovely spot for terns and whatnot to nest, oh yes. But they've still got the stink of civil disobedience about them."

"Nobody could live there anymore," said Reilly. He squinted through the scopex at the platform near which the Sirene was currently busy. "I can't even see a fusion generator. Ooh, ugh! There's a bird doing something nasty to another bird. I thought only people—"

"It's a nasty world, Reilly," said Mr. Leam. "Where criminals grab every chance to carry out their wicked trade. They've been using that very platform as one of their meeting places, you know. I've been watching it for some time now. Last month I nearly had them! The Lisiane out of Wexford, registered to the Federation Celtique as usual, always hanging about here. What's a sport vessel want with all that cargo space, I ask you? Probably engaged in fishing too, the murdering bastards."

"What happened?" inquired Reilly, a little testy over the slur on the Celtic Federation.

"I caught them in the act," Mr. Leam gloated. "Taking something from the *Tintin* out of St. Malo. Bore down on them both with my siren roaring and they dropped everything and fled over the horizon! But the *Lisiane* will be back. Sooner or later they'll think I've forgotten them, sooner or later they'll think it's safe to sneak back and recover whatever it was they had to sink. I'll be here waiting when they do, and I'll have a little surprise for them."

"Er—there's somebody out there now, you know," said Reilly, tapping the scopex to closer focus.

"Don't be ridiculous," said Mr. Leam, not lifting his eyes from the console screen. "The satellite readout's perfectly clear. There are no vessels within a five-kilometer radius of the platform. It says so right here."

"I guess I'm seeing a mirage or something then," said Reilly, lowering the scopex. And there the matter might have rested; but Mr. Leam, with a sudden flash of the intuition that made him such a successful opponent of evildoers, recalled that his enemies were after all *fiendishly clever.* He grabbed the scopex from Reilly and trained it again on the distant station.

"There *is* a boat!" he yelled. "But it's not the *Lisiane* . . . what do they think they're playing at? Well, they won't fool ME!"

He dropped the scopex and hauled on the wheel, bringing his cutter about sharply and making for the platform under full power. Reilly yelped as cold spray hit him, and he grabbed at the rail.

"Are we going to scare them off?" he shouted.

"No," replied Mr. Leam. Grinning through clenched teeth, he reached over and squeezed in a command on the console. Reilly gaped as a panel opened in the forward deck and a laser cannon rose into bow-chaser position.

"Jesus!" Reilly screamed. "Those are illegal!"

"So is smuggling," replied Mr. Leam. "We'll board and search, and if we meet the least resistance we'll sink them. Such is justice on the high seas, Reilly."

The *Long John* had managed to tie up all six crates. Extending a hook, it caught the looped cable and rose through the water, towing the crates after it like a great unwieldy bunch of grapes. Reaching the limit of its strength, straining upward, the *Long John* activated a tiny antigravity field and promptly shot up through the gloom like a cork released from a bottle, the crates zooming ponderously behind as it rose toward the *Sirene's* hull . . .

"Coastal Patrol cutter to port!" roared the Captain, pointing. "Bloody hell, that son of a whore's got ordinance!"

"You mean cannons?" Alec squeaked, "Oh, wow!"

Turning sharply, the Captain scanned Alec. His sensors picked up the boy's terror, but to his consternation, there was something more: excitement, anticipation, physical arousal. Alec watched the cutter speeding toward them and, without conscious intent, began to smack his right fist into his left palm, quite hard.

"Are we going to fight 'em, Captain sir?" he said eagerly. "Or, no, that's dumb. I guess we'll just have to give 'em a run for their money!"

"We ain't doing neither one, boy," the Captain snapped. "We're going to sit tight and lie through yer teeth, understand? I'll get below and manage the *Long John*. Just you calm down!"

"I am calm!" Alec protested, but the Captain had already vanished. Alec turned uncertainly to watch the cutter approach as, a fathom below, the *Long John* dove again and pulled its load into the obscurity of a kelp forest. There it waited, warily scanning the surface.

"HEAVE TO AND PREPARE TO BE BOARDED!" ordered Mr. Leam, his voice echoing across the water. "YOU ARE UNDER SUSPICION OF VIOLATION OF INTERNATIONAL MARITIME ORDINANCE 56624–B, PARAGRAPH 30, CLAUSE 15!"

"ER—OKAY!" Alec bellowed, thrilled to his bones. He felt more alive at this moment than he could ever remember feeling, and wished with all his heart he had a sword or a pistol or even just the ability to launch himself across the space between the boats and start swinging with his bare fists. It took all his self-control to sit quietly at the tiller, an innocent expression on his face, and watch as the cutter pulled alongside and Mr. Leam jumped into the tiny *Sirene.*

Mr. Leam was furiously angry, because it was obvious he had made an error; the *Sirene* had no cabin, let alone a cargo hold. Nevertheless, balancing awkwardly on the *Sirene's* midship thwart, he demanded, "Identify yourself! What is your business here?"

"I'm Alec Checkerfield," Alec replied. "Just here on holiday, sir, yeah? I was looking at all the seagulls up there."

"Well—" Mr. Leam swallowed back his rage and glanced over at the cutter for support. Reilly seemed to be hiding. He looked back at the immense young man. The youth smiled in a friendly way, but there seemed to be far too many teeth in the smile.

"Under the authority vested in me by the Trade Council, I hereby inform you I intend to search this vessel," persisted Mr. Leam.

Alec raised his eyebrows. "Sure," he said. His ears prickling with red heat, Mr. Leam bent over and looked under the thwarts. He looked under the seat cushions; checked all along the rail for towlines; ordered Alec to rise and checked among the sternsheets when Alec had politely complied. Having found nothing, he glared at Alec once more.

"Please present your identification disk," he ordered. Shrugging, Alec got it out and handed it over.

Upon discovering that Alec's father was the earl of Finsbury, Mr. Leam glanced over at the laser cannon and felt a chill descend along his spine. Pinning all his hopes on the possibility that Alec, being an aristocrat, would also be an idiot, he decided to brazen it out and said:

"Very well; everything seems to be in order. I'd advise you to avoid these platforms in future, young man. They are clearly marked as breeding sanctuaries for the black-footed gull."

"Oh. Sorry," said Alec.

"You may proceed," said Mr. Leam, and scrambled awkwardly into his boat, stepping on Reilly, who had been crouching behind the fire extinguisher. Retracting his cannon at once, he put about without another word and sped away, leaving white wake and embarrassment behind him.

He was back at the Isle of Wight before it occurred to him to wonder why the *Sirene* hadn't shown up on the satellite data.

When he was well out of earshot, Alec howled and pounded on the thwart in delight. "Captain sir, did you see that?" he shouted. "He couldn't pin a thing on us! That was so COOL!"

"I saw it well enough, aye," said the Captain irritably, materializing in the prow. "Now we know why the other bastards dumped the loot and took off for Tahiti, and I wish to hell we could do the same. Put her about! We're getting well away before that looney changes his mind and comes back for us."

"Aye aye, sir!" Alec leaned on the tiller, chuckling. The Captain did the electronic equivalent of wiping sweat from his brow and peered back at the retreating cutter until it vanished in the lee of the Isle of Wight. Below, the *Long John* rose from its hideaway and paddled faithfully after the *Sirene,* towing its clutch of sugar crates.

They kept to a course that took them due south for a while, well out to sea, before the Captain judged it safe to beat to the west and plot a long evasive course back to Poole. Alec lounged back in the sternsheets and congratulated himself on what he thought was the adventure of his life, replaying Mr. Leam's search in his head several times, and each time Alec thought of more clever things he might have said, or imagined ways in which he might have turned the tables and captured the Coastal Patrol cutter. If only he'd had a laser cannon too!

He was distracted from such pleasant speculation by a sail to port. After watching it keenly a few minutes, he said, "Captain, they're in distress over there. She looks like she's adrift. Shouldn't we go see if we can do anything?"

"Hell no," said the Captain. "Just you keep to yer course and mind yer own business, laddie."

"But, Captain, there's somebody waving," Alec said. "Looks like a girl. I can't see anybody else. Maybe she's stuck out there all alone!"

"Then she's safe, ain't she? Son, we ain't got time for this."

"She might be sinking," said Alec stubbornly. "We have to at least see."

So saying, he steered straight for the other vessel, as the Captain pulled his beard and growled words that would have scoured the barnacles and five layers of marine varnish off a yacht's hull. None of them dissuaded Alec from his fit of gallantry, however; so the Captain dematerialized and sent his primary consciousness into the *Long John,* where he concentrated on keeping pace with the *Sirene.*

"Ahoy!" Alec shouted. "*Seaspray Two?* Are you having problems?"

"Something's gone wrong with my electronics," cried the mistress of the *Seaspray Two.* "I can't make the steering wheel work and I don't know what to do with all these sails! Can you come have a look?"

"Okay," Alec replied, by this time close enough to throw a line to the other vessel and bring the *Sirene* alongside to tie up. "Permission to come aboard?" he cried jocularly, vaulting the rail of the *Seaspray* and landing on her deck with a thump. He had always wanted to say that, and was quite pleased with himself now, and even more so as he gazed down into the eyes of the young lady before him.

"Wow, you're tall," she said in awe. She was pretty, with red hair and green eyes, and wore only a small cotton shirt and the bottom half of a bathing suit. She smelled like Paradise.

"Uh—yes, I am tall," said Alec foggily. "So . . . you said it was your console, right?"

"It says I've got a fatal error!" The girl looked up at him pleadingly. "First the boat stopped and then the sails sort of rolled themselves up and down and now they're stuck like that. Maybe you'd know what to do?"

"Well, I'm pretty good with systems," said Alec, feeling his heartbeat speed up. "I guess I'll just get my tools and have a look, okay?"

"Oh, goody," said the girl.

When Alec scrambled back into the *Sirene*, there was a message blinking on the console screen:

ALEC! DON'T BE A BLOODY JACKASS! AIN'T NOBODY SUPPOSED TO KNOW ABOUT THE THINGS YOU CAN DO WITH YER TOOLKIT! ALEC! TELL THE WENCH YOU'LL SEND THE NAVSAT A DISTRESS SIGNAL AND SOMEBODY'LL BE ROUND TO PICK HER UP LATER! ALEC! ARE YOU READING ME, BOY? ALEC!

Smiling confidently, Alec ignored the screen and grabbed up his tool case. He was whistling *A Bicycle Built for Two* as he climbed back aboard the *Seaspray Two*.

He slipped on his earshells and visor, plugged himself into the *Seaspray's* console, and at once knew perfectly well what the problem was; he could see it like a broken wall in a burning field, strings of symbols in sad disarray, ravaged as though an army had marched through them. But he pretended to run diagnostics and look at components, while the girl watched anxiously and chattered at him:

". . . Daddy's boat and I wasn't supposed to go out alone but I got mad, I guess that was silly of me, but I really wanted to record the sounds of the open sea for this project we're doing in Circle and I didn't know it was so *quiet* out here, did you? So then I tried to hook up the holocam to get some images, but that's when it all went wrong."

"You used the wrong port," Alec informed her. "And it got a semantic paradox going, and now your console thinks it's in drydock for maintenance. That's why it won't let you go anyplace."

"Oh," said the girl, and in her chagrin she added a mildly obscene word, which caused Alec to have a semantic paradox of his own.

He coughed, drew his toolkit over his lap and assured her, "B-but I can fix it, no problem."

"Oh, thank you!" exclaimed the girl, and she threw her arms around him from behind and kissed his cheek. Alec could feel her pulse racing, hear her quickened breath, and her scent was telling him . . . His mouth began to water. He held on to his purpose like a drowning man and pretended to do things to the console with a microgapper while he sent his mind roaring through the error zone, adjusting, righting, realigning . . .

There was a low roar, the fusion generator started up, and a clear precise voice spoke: *"All systems operational. Set course, please."*

"There you go," said Alec hoarsely. "What course d'you want?"

"I just need it to go back to Yarmouth," said the girl, looking at him with wide helpless eyes. "Can you set the course for me?"

"Course laid in," said Alec, and put away the visor and earshells. "You can set sail any time."

"Okay," said the girl. "Thanks so much."

He lurched to his feet and she stared at him, or, to be more precise, at the front of his shorts.

"Er," said Alec, "I guess I'll just go, then."

"Um," said the girl, "Would you . . . like to see what the cabin looks like inside?"

They considered each other a moment. Alec gulped, and in the terribly suave voice he'd heard men use on holo shows said, "So, babe, can I interest you in exploring the amazing mysteries of life with me?" And he gave her the daredevil smile that had caused Beatrice Louise Jagger's knees to weaken.

The girl smiled at the big strong stranger, and her smile was bright and sharp-edged. She glanced up once in the general direction of the satellites, and then—with a graceful inclination of her head that indicated Alec should follow her—stepped down into the secure privacy of the *Seaspray*'s cabin.

Like black stars, a row of asterisks rose above the horizon. Somewhere a train roared down a tunnel, and white breakers foamed and crashed, and a missile was launched in majestic clouds of flame. Skyrockets climbed in graceful arcs through heaven to burst in glory, with a boom and thump that were felt in the marrow of the bones, and the slow fire drifted down gently afterward.

"That was really lucky, you having a packet of Happihealthies," Alec murmured. The girl yawned and stretched in bliss.

"Saved you going back on your boat to get yours, didn't it?"

Alec, who was not paying proper attention, nuzzled her and replied, "I haven't got any, actually."

"Tsk!" the girl smacked at him playfully. "How many do you go through a week, you wicked stud?"

"Dozens," Alec lied, nestling in close again and inhaling the fragrance of her hair. "So, anyway . . . Will you marry me? We'll have to wait a few years until I come of age, but I'll buy you a cool engagement ring."

For a heartbeat's space more she was as warm and yielding as she had been, and then he felt something like quicksilver run through her.

"You haven't come of age yet?" she inquired in an odd voice.

"Not exactly," Alec stated.

"When do you turn eighteen?" The girl grabbed his chin in her hands and tilted his head up to stare into his eyes.

"Not for another four years," said Alec. "But—"

She screamed and seemed to evaporate like mist, so quickly she was out of his arms and dragging the sheet between them. "You *can't* be fourteen!" she cried in horror. "You're huge!"

"Half an hour ago you didn't have a problem with me being huge," Alec protested.

"But I'm eighteen!" the girl wailed. "Don't you know what they'd do to us if anybody found out? Don't you know what they'd do to *me?*"

"Nobody'll find out!" Alec assured her frantically, but she wasn't listening; her eyes had widened as a sense of degradation was added to her terror.

"Ohmigod, you're in the *fourth form!*" she shrieked. "I'd never live this down! Get up! Get up and get out of here now!"

Frightened and crestfallen, Alec pulled on his clothes as quickly as he could.

"I'm really sorry," he said. "Can I look you up in four years? You're the most wonderful—"

"GET OUT!"

He had recovered himself enough to be grinning guiltily as he put the *Sirene* about and sped away, but as soon as it was safe the Captain burst into existence, glaring at him from the prow.

"If you ever sing that goddamned "Daisy" song at me again I'll keelhaul you, you ungrateful little swab!"

Alec winced. "I'm sorry. It was funny."

"Not to a AI, it ain't funny!"

"Okay. Sorry."

"And you gone and risked the job for the first lassie you spied, and me down there with the *Long John* and the cargo the whole time, gnashing me teeth in case that bloody cutter comes back, and what're you doing? Dancing the pegleg waltz with some duke's daughter from Yarmouth what ain't got no more wits than you do! What'd you promise me, eh? What'd I tell you about how dangerous it was?" the Captain raved. "At least she were of age!"

Alec glowered at his knees. "It's not like anybody'll ever find out," he said sullenly.

"You can be *damn* sure the lady ain't telling," snarled the Captain. "Not with a lifetime in Hospital waiting for her if she does. You ain't so much as sniffing at another wench until you comes of age, boy, do you hear?"

"Yes, sir," muttered Alec.

"I mean that, now!" The Captain drew a simulacrum of a large red handkerchief from his breast pocket and went through the motions of mopping his face. "Bloody hell. You think this is easy for me? Me, what only started out as a Playfriend module? If they'd got you the Pembroke Young Person's Companion I'd have had some files on puberty ready-made, but oh no, poor old Captain Morgan's only rated ages two to eleven, everything else he's got to improvise on his damned own, ain't he? Jesus bloody Christ, Alec!"

"Yes, sir. Sorry."

The Captain gave the appearance of collapsing onto the midship thwart, sighing and resting his elbows on his knees. He stared hard at Alec.

"Aw, hell. I don't reckon yer going to make it to eighteen without setting yer jib boom a few times, but will you promise me you'll wait a couple more years at least? And don't never do it again where yer likely to get caught by the Coastal Patrol?"

"Yes, sir."

"That's my boy." The Captain looked away, looked back at Alec. "At least it don't seem to have given you no traumas."

"Oh, no!" said Alec earnestly. "It was brilliant! Fabulous! Captain, it was the most wonderful thing that's ever happened to me! Until she started screaming and telling me to leave," he added.

"Well, that happens, sometimes," the Captain said. He snorted. "You got away clean, I reckon."

"And we've still got the sugar," Alec pointed out. "We're successful smugglers, Captain sir!"

"We'll be successful when Long John's made the drop off Fitzworth Point and that Despres lubber transfers them funds like he's agreed to," said the Captain grudgingly. "Not afore. And we ain't working this bit of coast again, not with that damned maniac and his laser cannon out there!"

"Oh, it'll all turn out fine." Alec leaned back again, allowing his grin to return. "And life is pretty cool, isn't it? Lost my virginity and outfoxed my first customs official all on the same day, yeah? Let's celebrate! Can I have some music, Captain sir?"

Rolling his eyes, the Captain went through the motions of pulling a battered concertina from cyberspace and proceeded to play a medley of the old seafaring tunes Alec had loved since he was five years old. Music boomed from the *Sirene's* console. Alec sang along, baying happily as the little sailboat sped across the water toward their rendezvous at Poole Harbour, with the *Long John* following faithfully just under her keel.

"This is only the beginning, Captain sir," Alec yelled. "One of these days we'll be really free! We'll have a tall ship with a hold full of cargo—and we'll have adventures—and maybe we'll find a girl who'll come with us and, how'd you like a couple of little tiny pirates running around, eh? Sort of grandkids? Wouldn't that be really cool?" He whooped and beat his chest in sheer exuberance. "YEEEoooo! Today I am a man!"

Not by a long shot, laddie, thought the Captain, regarding his boy as he played on. Glumly he contemplated the puzzle of Alec's DNA and reflected that Alec was unlikely ever to be a man any more than he himself was one, at least in the sense of being a member of the human race. One of these days the boy would have to be told.

And now the Captain had puberty to worry about, and how, oh, how, was Alec ever going to find a girl who'd come with him? A lover would get close to his boy, would notice all sorts of little odd things about Alec. Where was there a girl who'd love Alec enough to stay, if she knew the truth about him?

One worry at a time, the Captain decided, and accessed the stock exchange to see what promising investments might present themselves for the payoff from this job. He had to make his boy independently wealthy, after all, and then there were the taxes to be evaded . . .

The girl was out there somewhere. She'd wait.

Stephen Hawking, an extraordinary mortal if ever there was one, has argued that the best evidence that time travel is impossible is that we haven't met any visitors from the future. Good point. Though I think that anyone visiting the past would scarcely announce their presence, would in fact be much more likely to have access to a range of disguises we couldn't hope to penetrate. And there are all those Fortean accounts of out-of-place artifacts such as chains embedded in anthracite coal seams, certain proof of temporal visitors to the early Cretaceous—or it would be proof, if the artifacts themselves hadn't mysteriously disappeared since, like the famous spark plug that was embedded in a geode. (Although it turned out to be embedded in a lump of mud, not a geode, which sort of deflates the geological anomaly a bit . . .)

Who knows? But my money's on time travel, all the same.

The Queen in Yellow

THE LADY WAITED IN HER MOTORCAR.

It was a grand car, the very best and latest of its kind in 1914, a Vauxhall touring convertible with a four-litre engine, very fast. It was painted gold. Until recently the lady would have been waiting on a horse, by choice a palomino Arabian stallion. She preferred her current transportation system, because she did not particularly care for living things. She did admire machines, however. She liked gold, too.

Her name was Executive Facilitator for the Near East Region Kiu, and the sleek golden motorcar in which she waited was parked on a deserted road in the middle of a particularly ancient and historically significant bit of Nowhere. Not so far behind her, the Nile flowed on through eternity; above her, the white moon swam like a curved reed-boat across the stars, and it and they shed faint soft light on the rippled dunes of the desert and the green garden country. Lady Kiu cared no more about the romance of her surroundings than the Sphinx, who was her junior by several millennia

She did not show her eleven thousand years, almond-eyed beauty that she was. She looked no older than a fairly pampered and carefree twenty-two. Her soul, however, had quite worn away to nothing.

Lady Kiu was impatient as she waited. Her perfect nails tapped out a sinister little rhythm on the Vauxhall's steering wheel. You would think such an ageless, deathless creature would have long since learned to bide her time, and normally Lady Kiu could watch the pointless hours stagger past with perfect sangfroid; but there was something about the man for whom she waited that irritated her unaccountably.

* * *

The man was standing on a ridge and staring, slack jawed, at the beauty of the night. Moon, sand, stars, gardens, the distant gleam of moonlight on the river: he had seen a lot of moons, stars, sand, gardens and rivers in his time, but this was *Egypt,* after all! And though he too was a deathless, ageless creature, he had never in all his centuries been to Egypt before, and the Romance of the Nile had him breathlessly enchanted.

His name was Literature Preservationist Lewis. He was a slight, fair-haired man with the boyish good looks and determined chin of a silent film hero. He was moreover brave, resourceful and terribly earnest about his job, which was one of the things about him that so irritated Lady Kiu.

He also tended to get caught up in the moment to such an extent that he failed to check his internal chronometer as often as he ought to, with the result that when he did check it now he started guiltily, and set off at a run through the night. He was able to move far more quickly than a mortal man, but he was still five minutes late for his rendezvous.

"Sorry!" he cried aloud, spotting Lady Kiu at last, sullen by moonlight. He slid to a halt and tottered the last few steps to her motorcar, hitching up his jodhpurs.

"Sand in your pants?" inquired Lady Kiu, yawning.

"Er—actually we've all got sand everywhere. We're roughing it, rather. The professor doesn't go in for luxuries in the field. I don't mind, though! He's really the most astonishing mortal, and I'm used to a bit of hardship—" said Lewis.

"How nice. Your report, please."

Lewis cleared his throat and stood straight. "Everything is on schedule and under budget. I guided the fellaheen straight to the shaft entrance without seeming to, you see, quite subtly, and even though it's been blocked with debris, the excavation has been going along famously. At the current speed, I expect we'll reach the burial chamber exactly at twilight tomorrow."

"Good." Lady Kiu studied her nails. "And you're absolutely certain you'll get the timing right?"

"You may rely on me," Lewis assured her.

"You managed to obtain a handcar?"

"All I had to do was bribe a railway official! The princess and I will roll into Bani Suwayf in style."

"The mortal trusts you?"

"Professor Petrie? I think I've managed to impress him." Lewis hooked his thumbs through his suspenders proudly. "I heard him telling

Mr. Brunton what a remarkable fellow I am. 'Have you noticed that fellow Kensington?' he said. Petrie impresses me, too. He's got the most amazing mental abilities—"

"Darling, the day any mortal can impress me, I'll be ready for retirement," said Lady Kiu, noting in amusement that Lewis started and quivered ever so slightly at her use of the word *darling.*

"I can expect you at Bani Suwayf at midnight tomorrow, then," she added. "With the merchandise."

"Without fail!"

"That's a good boy. We've set you up a nice workroom on the boat, with everything you'll need for the restoration job. And in your cabin—" she reached out a lazy hand and chucked him under the chin "—there'll be a bottle of well-iced champagne to celebrate. Won't that be fun?"

Lewis's eyes widened. Struck mute, he grinned at her foolishly, and she smiled back at him. She expected men to fall in love with her—they always did, after all—but Lewis fell in love with anything beautiful or interesting, and so he wasn't worth her time. Still, it never hurt to give an underling some incentive.

"Until tomorrow," she said, blowing him a kiss, and with a roar her golden chariot came to life and bore her away toward the Nile.

You will find the pyramid of Senuseret II west of the Nile, near Al Fayyum. It is an unassuming little twelfth-dynasty affair of limestone and unburned mud brick. It is quite obvious how it was built, so no one ever speculates on how on earth it got there or who built it, or argues morbidly that apocalyptic knowledge is somehow encoded in its modest dimensions.

To the south of Senuseret's pyramid is a cemetery, and on this brilliant day in 1914 it had a certain holiday air. The prevailing breeze brought the fragrance of fields, green leaf and lotus surging up in the brief Egyptian spring. Makeshift huts had been put up all along its outer wall, and Englishmen and Englishwomen sat in the huts and typed reports, or made careful drawings with the finest of crow quills, or fanned flies away from their food and wondered plaintively what that furry stuff was on the tinned pilchards, or fought off another wave of malaria.

Within the cemetery walls, several shaft tomb entrances admitted sunlight. In such shade as there was, the Egyptian fellaheen sat sorting through fairly small basketfuls of dig debris, brought to them by brown children from the mouth of another shaft. Lewis, his archaeologist ensemble augmented by a pith helmet today, stood watching them expectantly. His riding boots shone with polish. His jodhpurs were formidable.

Beside him stood a mortal man, burned dark by the sun, who wore mismatched native slippers without socks, patched knickerbocker trousers, a dirty shirt that had lost its buttons, and a flat cap that had also seen better days. He was white-haired and gray-bearded but had a blunt powerful form; he also had an unnervingly intense stare, fixed not on the fellaheen but on Lewis.

William Matthew Flinders Petrie was sixty years old. He had laid down the first rules of true archaeology, and that made him very nearly a patron saint for people who invested in history as much as Lewis's masters did.

Though *invested* is not, perhaps, the correct word for the way the Company got its money.

Lewis never thought about that part of it much, to avoid being depressed. He had always been taught that depression was a very bad thing for an immortal, and the secret to happiness was to keep busy, preferably by following orders. And life could be so interesting! For example, one got to rub elbows with famous mortals like Flinders Petrie.

"So you think this grave hasn't been robbed? You have an intuition about this, have you?" Petrie said.

"Oh, yes, Professor," said Lewis. "I get them now and then. And after all, theft is a haphazard business, isn't it? How systematic or careful can a looter be? I'd be awfully surprised if they hadn't missed *something.*"

"Interesting," said Flinders Petrie.

"What is, sir?"

"Your opinion on thieves. Have you known many?"

Actually Lewis had worked with thieves his entire life, in a manner of speaking. But remembering that he was supposed to be a youthful volunteer on his first visit to Egypt (which was half true, after all), he blushed and said "Well—no, sir, I haven't, in fact."

"They have infinite patience, as a rule," Petrie told him. "You'd be astonished at how methodical they are. The successful ones, at least. They take all manner of precautions. Get up to all sorts of tricks. Sometimes an archaeologist can learn from them."

"Ah! Such as wearing a costume to gain access to a forbidden shrine?" Lewis inquired eagerly. "I have heard, sir, that you yourself convinced certain tribesmen you were mad by wearing, er, some rather outlandish things—"

"The pink underwear story, yes." Petrie gave a slight smile. "Yes, it sometimes pays very well if people think you're a harmless fool. They'll let you in anywhere."

As Lewis prepared to say something suitably naïve in response, children came streaming from the mouth of the shaft like chattering swallows. A moment later an Egyptian followed them and walked swiftly to Petrie, before whom he bowed and said:

"Sir, you will want to come see now."

Petrie nodded once, giving Lewis a sidelong glance.

"What did I tell you?" said Lewis, beaming.

"What indeed?" said Petrie. "Come along then, boy, and let's see if your instincts are as good as you think they are."

The mouth of the shaft had been blocked, as all the others there had been blocked, with centuries of mud and debris from flood runoff, and it was hard as red cement and had taken days of labor to clear in tiny increments. But the way was now clear to the entrance of the tomb chamber itself, where a mere window had been chiseled through into stifling darkness. A Qufti waiting with a lantern held it up and through the hole, flattening himself against the wall as Petrie rushed forward to peer inside.

"Good God!" cried Petrie, and his voice cracked in excitement. "Is the lid intact? Look at the thing, it hasn't been touched! But how can that *be?*" He thrust himself through, head and shoulders, in his effort to see better, and the Qufti holding the lamp attempted to make himself even flatter, without success, as Petrie's body wedged his arm firmly into the remaining four inches of window space and caused him to utter a faint involuntary cry of pain.

"Sorry. Oh, bugger all—" Petrie pulled backward and stripped off his shirt. Then he kicked off his slippers, tossed his cap down on top of them, and yanked open his trousers. The sole remaining fly button hit the wall with the force of a bullet, but was ignored as he dropped his pants and jumped free, naked as Adam.

"Your trowel, sir," said the Qufti, offering it with his good arm as he drew back.

"Thank you, Ali." Petrie took the trowel, draped his shirt over the windowledge, and vaulted up and through with amazing energy for a man of his years, so that Lewis and Ali endured no more than a few seconds of averting their eyes as his bottom and then legs and feet vanished into stygian blackness.

"Er—what a remarkable man," observed Lewis.

The Qufti just nodded, rubbing his arm.

"GIVE ME THE LAMP!" ordered Petrie, appearing in the hole for a moment. "And keep the others out of here for the present, do you understand? I want a clear field." He turned on Lewis a glare keen enough to cut through limestone. "Well? Don't you want to see your astonishing discovery, Mr. Kensington? I'd have thought you'd have been beside yourself to be the first in!"

"Well—ah—I'm certain I couldn't hope to learn as much from it as you would, Professor," said Lewis.

Petrie laughed grimly. "I wonder. Never mind, boy, grab a trowel and crawl through. And don't be an old maid! It's a sweatbath in here."

"Yes, sir," said Lewis, racing for the mouth of the shaft, and for all his embarrassment and reluctance there was still a little gleeful voice at the back of his mind singing: *I'm on a real Egyptian archaeological dig with Flinders Petrie! The Father of Archaeology! Gosh!*

In the end he compromised by stripping down to his drawers, and though Petrie set him to the inglorious task of whittling away at the window to enlarge the chamber's access while he himself worked at clearing the granite sarcophagus, Lewis spent a wonderful afternoon. His sense of rapport with the Master in his Element kept him diverted from the fact that he was an undersized cyborg wearing nothing but a pair of striped drawers, chipping fecklessly at fossilized mud while sweat dripped from the end of his nose, one drop precisely every 43.3 seconds, or that he was trapped in a small hot enclosed space with an elderly mortal who had certain intestinal problems.

The great man's vocal utterances were limited to grunts of effort and growls of surprise, with the occasional "Hold the damned light over here a moment, can't you?" But Lewis, in all the luxury of close proximity and uninterrupted except for having to pass the debris-basket out the hole on a regular basis, was learning a great deal by scanning Petrie as he worked.

He was not learning the sort of things he had expected to learn, however.

For example, his visual recordings of Petrie were not going to be as edifying as he'd hoped: the Master in his Element appeared nothing like a stately cross between Moses and Indiana Jones, as depicted in the twenty-fourth century. He resembled a naked lunatic trying to tunnel out of an asylum. That didn't matter, though, in light of the fascinating data Lewis was picking up as he scanned Petrie's brain activity.

It looked like a lightning storm, especially through the frontal lobes. There were connections being made that were not ordinarily made in a mortal mind. Patterns in data were instantly grasped and analyzed, fundamental organizational relationships perceived that mortals did not, as a rule, perceive, and jumps of logic of dazzling clarity followed. Lewis was enchanted. He watched the cerebral fireworks display, noted the slight depression in one temple and pondered the possibility of early brain trauma rerouting Petrie's neural connections in some marvelous inexplicable way . . .

"I must say, sir, this is a great honor for me," said Lewis hesitantly. "Meeting and actually working with a man of your extraordinary ability."

"Nothing to do with *ability,* boy," replied Petrie, giving him a stare over the edge of the sarcophagus. "It's simply a matter of paying attention to details. That's all it is. Most of the people out here in the old days were nothing more than damned looters. Go at it with a pick and blasting powder! Find the gold! Didn't care tuppence for the fact that they were crumbling history under their bloody boots."

"Like the library of Mendes," said Lewis, with bitter feeling.

"You remember that, do you?" Petrie cocked a shaggy eyebrow at him. "Remarkable; that was back in '92. You can't have been more than an infant at the time."

"Well, er, yes, but my father read about it in the *Times,* you see," temporized Lewis. "And he talked about it for years, and he shared your indignation, if I may say so. That would have been Naville, wouldn't it, who found all those rooms filled with ancient papyri, and was so ham-fisted he destroyed most of them in the excavation!" His vengeful trowel stabbed clay and sent a chip whizzing into the darkness.

"So he did," said Petrie, picking up the chip and squinting at it briefly before setting it in the debris basket. "I called him a vandal and he very nearly called me out. Said it was ridiculous to expect an archaeologist to note the placement of items uncovered in a dig, as though one were to note where the raisins were in a plum pudding! Mark that metaphor, you see, that's all an excavation meant to him: Dig your spoon in and gobble away! Never a thought for *learning* anything about what he was digging up."

"And meanwhile who knew what was being lost?" Lewis mourned. "Plays. Poetry. Textbooks. Histories."

Petrie considered him a long moment before speaking again, and Lewis was once more aware of the bright storm in the old man's head.

"We can never know," Petrie said. "Damn him and everyone like him. How can we ever know the truth about the past? Historians lie; time wrecks everything. But if you're careful, boy, if you're methodical, if you measure and record and look for the bloody boring little details, like potsherds, and learn what they mean—you can get the dead to speak again, out of their ashes. That's worth more than all the gold and amulets in the world, that's the work of my life. That's what I was born for. Nothing matters except my work."

"I know exactly what you mean!" said Lewis.

"Do you?" said Petrie quietly.

They worked on in silence for a while after that.

At some point in the long afternoon the auroral splendor of Petrie's mind grew particularly bright, and he cried out, "What the deuce?"

"Oh, have you found something, Professor?" Lewis stood and peered at the area of the sarcophagus that had just been cleared. There were hieroglyphics deep-cut in the pink granite. "The Princess Sit-Hathor-Yunet? Oh, my, surely that's a very good sign."

And then he almost exclaimed aloud, because Petrie's mind became like a glowing sun, such a magnificence of cerebration that Lewis felt humbled. But Petrie merely looked at him, and said flatly:

"Perhaps it is. It's damned unusual, anyway. Never seen a seal quite like that on the outer sarcophagus before."

"Really?" Lewis felt a little shiver of warning. "Do you think it's significant?"

"Yes," said Petrie. "I'm sure it is."

"How exciting," said Lewis cautiously, and turned back to chipping away at the wall.

By twilight, when the first blessed coolness rose in salt mist from the canals, it was still hot and stinking in the tomb. Lewis wiped his face with the back of his hand, leaving a steak of red mud above one eye, and said casually, "I suppose we'd better stop for today."

"Absolutely not," said Petrie. "I've very nearly cleared the lid. Another forty-five minutes' work ought to do it. Don't you want to see Princess Sit-Hathor-Yunet, boy?" He grinned ferociously at Lewis.

"More than anything, sir," said Lewis, truthfully. "But do you really want to rush a discovery of this importance? I'd much rather get a good night's sleep, wouldn't you, and start fresh tomorrow?"

Petrie was silent a moment, eyeing him. "I suppose so," he said at last. "Very well. Though, of course, someone ought to sleep in here tonight. Standing guard, you know."

"Allow me to volunteer!" said Lewis, doing his best to look frightfully keen. "Please, sir, it would be an honor."

"As you like." Petrie stroked his beard. "I'll have supper and your bedroll sent out to you. Will that suit?"

It suited Lewis very well indeed, and two hours later he was stretched out in his blankets on the lid of the sarcophagus, listening to the sounds of the camp in its rituals as it gradually retired for the night.

He found it comforting, because it was much more like the sound of mortals retiring for the night the way they had over the centuries when he had been getting used to them: the low murmur of a story being told, the cry of a dreaming child, the scrape of a campfire being banked. Modern rooms were sealed against sound, and nights had become less human. In London, you might hear distant waterworks or steam pipes, or the tinny clamor of a radio or a phonograph, or the creak of furniture. You might hear electricity, if it had been laid on, humming through the walls. Humanity was sealing itself away in tidy boxes.

"But," he said to himself aloud, looking up at the ceiling of the tomb, "they used to do that, too, didn't they? Though not while they were still alive." He sat up cautiously and groped for his lantern. "At least not intentionally."

He lit the lantern and set to work at once, chiseling away at the last layer of mud sealing the lid of the sarcophagus. It went much more quickly when you didn't have to carefully collect every single chip and pass it out through the entrance in a basket, and Lewis felt certain qualms about the debris he was scattering everywhere.

"But we'll leave the professor a treat to make up for it, won't we Princess?" he muttered. "And, after all, history can't be changed."

Five minutes later he had freed enough of the lid to be able to toss the trowel aside and prize an edge up, and he yanked the granite slab free as though it were so much balsa wood.

"Wow!" he said, although he had known what he would see.

There was a mummy case reposing there, smiling up through a layer of grime as though it had been expecting him, and in a manner of speaking it had been. It represented a lady bound all in golden cerements, and painted about her shoulders was a feathered cape in every shade of lemon and amber, set here and there with painted representations of topazes and citrines. Her features closely resembled Lady Kiu's, save that there was a warmth and life in her eyes missing from the living eyes of Lady Kiu.

Under the dust, the whole case gleamed with a thick coat of varnish of glasslike smoothness and transparency. An analysis of its chemical structure would have startled scientists, if there had been any with electron microscopes or spectrographs in 1914. Lewis couldn't resist reaching down to stroke along the side where the case was sealed, and could feel no seam or join at all. It would take a diamond-edged saw to get the box open, but that was all right; it had served its purpose.

The chest at the top of the tomb had had no such treatment, and it had fallen to pieces where it stood, splitting open under the sheer mass of the treasure it contained: a crown of burnished gold, two golden pectorals inlaid with precious stones, coiled necklaces, armlets, collars, boudoir items, beadwork in amethyst, in carnelian, turquoise, lapis lazuli, obsidian, ivory.

"Let's get this mess out of the way, shall we?" said Lewis, and, reaching in, he picked up as much of the treasure as he could in one grab and dumped it unceremoniously into a recess in the wall at one side. Beads scattered and rolled here and there, but he ignored them. It was just so much jewelry, after all, and he was fixed and focused on his objective as only a cyborg can be.

"Now, Princess," he said, giggling slightly as he leaned down to lift the mummy case from its dais, "Shall we dance? You and I? I'm quite a good dancer. I can two-step like nobody's business. Oh, you'll like it out in the world again! I'll take you on a railway ride, though not first-class accommodations I'm afraid—" He set the case, which was as big as he was, down while he considered how best to get it through the opening.

"But that'll be all right, because *then* we'll go for a sail down the Nile, and that will be much nicer. Quite like old times, eh?" Deciding the time for neatness had passed, he simply aimed a series of kicks and punches at certain spots on the wall. He did not seem to exert much force, but the wall cracked in a dozen places and toppled outward into the tomb shaft.

"Literature Preservationist Lewis, super-cyborg!" he gloated, striking an attitude, and then froze with an expression of dismay on his face.

Flinders Petrie stood in the shaft without, just at the edge of the lamplight. He was surveying the wreckage of the wall with leonine fury, and the fact that he was wearing a pink singlet, pink ballet tutu and pink ribboned slippers did nothing to detract from the terror of his anger. Nor did the rifle he was aiming at Lewis's head.

"Come out of there, you little bastard," he said. "Look at the mess you've made!"

"I'm sorry!" said Lewis.

"Not as sorry as you're going to be," the old mortal told him. "I knew you were a damned marauder from the moment I laid eyes on you." He settled the rifle more securely on his shoulder. "Though I couldn't fathom the rest of it. What's a *super-cyborg?* What the hell are you, eh?"

Lewis raced mentally through possible believable answers, and decided on:

"I'm afraid you're right. I'm a thief; I was paid a lot of money by a certain French count to bring back antiquities for his collection. The Comte de la, er, Cyborg. He ordered me to infiltrate your expedition, because everyone knows you're the best—"

"Ballocks," said Petrie. "I mean *what* are you?"

Lewis blinked at him. "What?" he repeated.

"What kind of thing are you? You're no human creature, that much is obvious," said Petrie.

"It is?" In spite of his horror, Lewis was fascinated. He scanned Petrie's brain activity and found it a roiling wasps' nest of sparks.

"It is to *me,* boy," said Petrie. "Mosquitoes won't bite you, for one thing. You speak like an actor on the stage, for another. You move like a machine, mathematically exact. I've timed the things you do."

"What kinds of things?" Lewis asked, delighted.

"Blinking once every thirty seconds precisely, for example," said Flinders Petrie. "Except in moments when you're pretending to be surprised, as you were just now. But there's not much that surprises you, is there? You *knew* about this shaft, you very nearly dragged Ali to this spot and showed him where to dig. It was so we'd do all the work for you, wasn't it? And then you'd make off with whatever was inside."

"Well, I'm afraid I—"

"You're not afraid. Your pupils aren't dilating as a man's would," said Petrie relentlessly. "You haven't changed color, and you're breathing in perfect mechanical rhythm." But his own hand shook slightly as he pulled back the hammer on the rifle. "You're some kind of brilliantly complicated automaton, though I'm damned if I can think who made you."

"That's an insane idea, you know," said Lewis, gauging how much space there was between Petrie and the side of the shaft. "People will think you're mad as a hatter if you tell anyone."

Petrie actually chuckled. "Do I look like a man who cares if people think I'm mad?" he said. He cut a bizarre little jeté, pink slippers flashing. "It's bloody useful, in fact, to be taken for a lunatic. Why d'you think I keep this ensemble in my kit? If I blew your head off this minute, dressed as I happen to be, I should certainly be acquitted of murder on grounds of insanity. Wouldn't you think so?"

"You are absolutely the most astonishing mortal I have ever met," said Lewis sincerely.

"And you're not mortal, obviously. What would I see if I fired this gun, Mr. Kensington? Bits of clockwork flying apart? Magnetic ichor? Who made you? Why? I want to know! *What are you for?*"

"Please don't shoot!" cried Lewis. "I was born as mortal as you are! If a bullet hit me I'd bleed and feel an awful lot of pain, but I wouldn't die. I can never die." Inspiration struck him. "Think about the *Book of the Dead.* All the mummies you've unearthed, Professor, think of all the priests and embalmers who worked over them, trying to follow instructions they barely understood. What were they trying to do?"

"Guarantee that men would live forever," said Petrie, with perhaps just an edge of the fury taken off his voice.

"Exactly! They were trying to approximate something they knew about, but couldn't ever really achieve, because they didn't have the complete instructions. My masters, on the other hand, truly can make a man immortal."

"Your masters?" Petrie narrowed his eyes. "So you're a slave. And who are your masters, boy?"

"I'm not a slave!" said Lewis heatedly. "I'm more of an—an employee on long-term contract. And my masters are a terribly wise and powerful lot of scientists and businessmen."

"Freemasons, by any chance? Rosicrucians?"

"Certainly not." Lewis sniffed.

"Well, they're not so clever as they think they are," said Petrie. "I saw through you easily enough. 'Sit-Hathor-Yunet,' you said when you saw that cartouche, without a moment's hesitation. And you'd said you couldn't read hieroglyphics!"

Lewis winced. "I did slip there, didn't I? Oh, dear. I wasn't really designed for this kind of mission."

"You weren't, eh?"

"I'm just a literature preservationist. Scrolls and codices are more my line of work," Lewis admitted. "I was only going to handle the restoration job. But my Facilitator—Facilitators are the clever ones, you see, they're designed to be really *good* at passing themselves off as mortal, one of them would never make the mistakes I did—my Facilitator pointed out that a woman would be out of place in a camp like this, doing all sorts of dirty and dangerous work, and that I'd arouse much less suspicion than she would. She said she was sure I could handle a job like this." He looked up at Petrie in a certain amount of embarrassment.

Petrie laughed. "Then you've been rather a fool, haven't you? You're that much of a man, at least."

Lewis edged slightly forward and the barrel of the rifle swung to cover him.

"Stop there!" said Petrie. "And you can just put Princess Sit-Hathor-Yunet down too, cleverdick."

"Er—I'm afraid I can't do that," said Lewis. "She was the whole point of my mission, you see. Can't I have her? You wouldn't learn anything useful from her, I can promise you."

"There's something odd about her, too, isn't there?" demanded Petrie. "I knew it! Everything about the bloody burial was queer from the first."

"Suppose, a long time ago, you had something valuable that you needed to put away for the benefit of generations to come, Professor. You'd want to hide it somewhere safe, wouldn't you?" Lewis said. "And where better than sealed in a tomb you *knew* wouldn't be opened until a certain day in the year 1914?"

"So you've got one of Mr. Wells's time machines, have you?" Petrie speculated. "Is that how you know the future? What's the princess, then? Is she another of your kind?"

"No! You can't really make an immortal like this," said Lewis in disgust, waving a hand at the mummy case.

"Then how is it done? I want to know!"

"I'm afraid I can't tell you that, Professor."

"You will, by God." Petrie cocked the rifle again.

"Oh, sir, does it have to come to this?" Lewis pleaded. "Just let me go. I've left you the nicest little cache of loot in payment, really a remarkable find—"

He gestured at the jewelry he had dumped into the recess behind the sarcophagus. Petrie glanced at it, and his gaze stayed on the gold in spite of his intention, only a second longer than he had planned; but that was enough time for Lewis, who fled past him like a wraith in the night.

He was a hundred meters away by the time the bullet whizzed past his ear, bowling over Ali and the other fellaheen in his passage. He'd have been farther if not for the aerodynamic drag that the mummy case exerted. Gasping, he lifted it over his head like an ant with a particularly valuable grain of barley and ran, making for the railway line.

"Damn!" he groaned, as he sprinted on, hearing the shots and outcry in his wake. "My clothes!"

They were still sitting in a tidily folded heap in the shaft, where he'd meant to put them on prior to exiting stealthily. *Can't be helped,* he thought to himself. *Perhaps I won't be too conspicuous?*

Lewis had a stitch in his side by the time he reached the railway line, and set the mummy case down while he cast about for the hut in which he'd hidden his handcar. Ah! There it was. He flung open the makeshift door and stared blankly into the darkness for a moment before the sound of approaching gunfire rammed the fact home: someone had stolen the handcar. He tried looking by infrared, but the result was the same. No handcar.

He lost another few seconds biting his knuckles as the pursuit grew nearer, until he distinguished Petrie's voice, louder than the others and titanic in its wrath. Dismayed, Lewis grabbed up the mummy case again and ran for his immortal life, through the lurid scarlet night of Egypt by infrared.

A frightened cyborg can go pretty far and pretty fast before running out of breath, so Lewis had got well out of the sound of pursuit before he had to stop and set down the mummy case again. Wheezing, he collapsed on it and regarded the flat open field in which he found himself.

"I hope you won't mind, Princess," he said. "There's been a slight change in plan. In fact, the plan has gone completely out the window. You probably wouldn't have enjoyed the railway ride anyway. Don't worry; I'll get you to the Nile somehow. What am I going to do, though?"

He peered across a distance of several miles to a pinprick of light a mortal couldn't have seen.

"There's a campfire over there," he said. "Do you suppose they have camels, Princess? Do you suppose I could persuade them to loan me a camel? Not that I'm particularly good at persuading mortals to do things. That's in a Facilitator's programming. Not something a lowly little Preserver drone is expected to be any good at."

A certain shade of resentment came into his voice.

"Do you suppose the professor was right, Princess? Did Lady Kiu take advantage of me? Did she send me in on a job for which I wasn't programmed simply because she didn't want to bother with it herself?"

He sat there a moment in silence on the mummy case, fuming.

"You know, Princess, I think she did. Mrs. Petrie did plenty of crawling about in the shafts. So did Winifred Brunton. Granted, they were English. All the same . . ." Lewis looked up at the infinite stars. "Can it be I've been played for a fool?"

The infinite stars looked down on him and pursed their lips.

"I'll bet she weasels out of sleeping with me, too," he sighed. "Darn it. Well, Princess, you wait here. I'm going to see if I can borrow a camel."

He rose to his feet, hitched up his drawers and strode away through the darkness with a purposeful air.

Princess Sit-Hathor-Yunet smiled up at the sky and waited. It was all she knew how to do. She didn't mind.

After a while a darkness detached itself from the greater darkness and loomed up against the stars, to become the silhouette of Lewis, proudly mounted on the back of a camel.

"Here we are!" he cried cheerily. "Can you believe it, Princess, there was a runaway camel wandering loose through the fields? What a stroke of luck for us! I hate stealing things from mortals."

He reined it in, bade it sit, and jumped down.

"Because, you see, the professor was wrong about me. I steal things *for* mortals. Actually it isn't even stealing. I'm a Preserver. It's what I do and I'm proud of it. It really is the best work in the world, Princess.

Travel to exotic lands, meetings with famous people . . ." He scooped her up and vaulted back on the camel's hump. "Dodging bullets when they decide you're a tomb robber . . . oh, well. Hut-hut! Up and at 'em, boy!"

The camel unfolded upward with a bellow of protest. It had been content to carry Lewis, who if he did not smell quite right had at least a proper human shape; but something about the princess spooked it badly, and it decided to run away.

It set off at a dead run. The little creature on its back yelled and yanked on its reins, but the great black thwartwise oblong thing back up there was still following it no matter how fast it ran, and so the camel just kept running. It ran toward the smell of water, as being the only possible attraction in the fathomless night. It galloped over packed and arid hardpan, through fields of cotton, through groves of apricot trees. Lewis experienced every change in terrain intimately, and was vainly trying to spit out a mouthful of apricot leaves when the camel found water, and stopped abruptly at the edge of a canal. Lewis, and Princess Sit-Hathor-Yunet, did not stop.

The black earth and the bright stars reversed, not once but several times, and then it was all darkness as Lewis landed with a splash in the canal, though with great presence of mind kept his grip on the mummy case. Down they went, and then the buoyancy of the sealed case pulled them upward again, and Lewis gulped in a lungful of air and scanned frantically for crocodiles.

"Whew!" he said, finding none. He noted also that the tidal flow was taking them Nileward at a leisurely pace, and, settling himself firmly atop Princess Sit-Hathor-Yunet, he began to paddle energetically.

"Well, call me Ishmael! My apologies, Princess, but needs must and all that sort of thing. We'll be out of this in no time, you'll see. In the meantime, enjoy the new experience. I take it you've never been body-surfing before?" He began to giggle at the idea of *body*surfing and couldn't control himself, laughing so hard that he nearly fell off. "Whoops! No, no, you headstrong girl! This way!"

Leeches floated up eagerly from the black depths, sensing a meal; just as the mosquitoes had, they came into contact with the minute electromagnetic field surrounding Lewis's skin and changed their minds in a hurry.

About the time that Lewis spotted the lights of Bani Suwayf in the distance, he also identified a pair of crocodiles a kilometer off. Crocodiles take rather more than an electromagnetic field to discourage and so, splashing hastily to the side of the canal, Lewis pushed the mummy case out and scrambled after it. He paused only a moment to let the water stream from his ballooning drawers before picking up the case and resuming his journey by land.

"We're almost there, Princess, and we're not even late!" he said happily, as he trudged along. "I'll have a thing or two to say to Lady Kiu, though, won't I? Let's see . . . Ahem! Madam, I feel I have no choice but to protest your . . . mmm. Lady Kiu, this is a painful thing for me to say, but . . . no. Kiu, old girl, I don't think you quite . . . that is, I . . . I mean, you . . . right."

He sighed, and marched on.

Bani Suwayf was a small town in 1914, but it had a railway station and a resident population of Europeans. One of them, M. Heurtebise, was a minor functionary in a minor bureau having to do with granting minor permits of various kinds to other Europeans, and he deeply resented the smallness of his place in the order of things. He took it out on his wife, his servants, his pets, and once a week he also took it out on a person whom he paid for the trouble and who was therefore philosophical about his nocturnal visits.

He was returning from one of these visits—it had not lasted long—in his motorcar, and was just rounding the corner of the main street as Lewis entered it from the little track leading from the canal. He looked up, aghast, when the bug-eyed lights caught and displayed him: a muddy and sweating figure wearing only striped drawers, balancing a mummy case on his head.

"Stop!" cried M. Heurtebise on impulse, hitting his chauffeur on the shoulder with his cane. "Thief!" he added, because it seemed like a good bet, and he pulled out a revolver and brandished it at Lewis.

Lewis, who had used up a lot of energy on his flit from Professor Petrie, decided the hell with it and stopped. He set down the mummy case very carefully, held up his hands in a classic don't-shoot gesture, and vanished.

"Where did he go?" exclaimed M. Heurtebise. When no answer was forthcoming from the night, he struck his chauffeur again and ordered, "Get out and look for him, Ahmed, you fool!"

Ahmed gritted his teeth, but got out of the car and looked around. He looked up the street; he looked down the street. He looked everywhere but under the motorcar, where Lewis had insinuated himself into the undercarriage as cunningly as an alien monster.

"He is not to be found, sir," Ahmed told M. Heurtebise.

"I can see that, you imbecile. But he has left an antiquity in the roadway!"

Ahmed prodded Princess Sit-Hathor-Yunet with his foot. "So he has, sir."

Muttering to himself, M. Heurtebise got out of the motorcar. He strode over to the mummy case and his eyes widened as he noted the excellence of its condition and its obvious value.

"This has clearly been stolen," he said. "It is our duty to confiscate it. We will notify the proper authorities in the morning. Put it into the car, Ahmed."

Ahmed bent and attempted to lift it.

"It is too heavy, sir," he said. "We must do it together."

Mr. Heurtebise considered striking him for his insolence, but then reflected that if the mummy case was heavy, it was possibly full of treasure, and therefore the issue of prime importance was to get it out of the street and into his possession. So between them, he and Ahmed lifted the case and set it on end in the back seat. They got back in the motorcar and drove on the short distance to M. Heurtebise's villa.

When they pulled into the courtyard and got out, Ahmed opened the door to the ground-floor office and they carried the mummy case inside. M. Heurtebise opened the venetian blinds to admit light from the courtyard lantern, and he directed Ahmed to set Princess Sit-Hathor-Yunet on two cane chairs.

The office was a comfortable room in the European style, with a banked fire in the hearth, leather overstuffed chairs with a small table and lamp between them, and a formidable desk with a row of pigeon-holes above it. There was also a large cage in one corner, covered with canvas sacking. As Ahmed pushed the two chairs closer together, a hoarse metallic voice began to exclaim from beneath the cover. It said something very rude and then repeated it eighteen times.

"Silence!" hissed M. Heurtebise. "Bad parrot! BAD PARROT!"

He took his cane and hammered on the side of the cage, creating such a racket Ahmed winced and put his hands over his ears. A stunned silence followed. M. Heurtebise nodded in satisfaction. "That's the only way to teach him, by the devil."

"May I go now, sir?"

"Go." M. Heurtebise waved him away. They left the study, and Ahmed drove the motorcar into what had formerly been the stables. Here he got out, closed the great door and locked it, and went off to the servants' quarters. M. Heurtebise paused only long enough to lock the office door, and then climbed the outer stair to his apartments on the second floor.

Alone in the darkness, Lewis uninsinuated himself from the under-chassis and fell groaning to the floor. He was now smeared with black grease in addition to being muddy and wet. He lay there a moment and finally crawled out from under the motorcar. He got to his feet, staggered to the door and rattled it.

He was locked in. He shrugged and looked around for a suitable tool.

*   *   *

In the office, however, something else was just discovering that it was *not* locked in.

In his enthusiasm, M. Heurtebise had beaten on the bars of the cage with such force that he had shaken the cage's latchhook loose, though with the cover being in place he had not noticed this. However, the cage's inhabitant noticed, once its little ears had stopped ringing. It cocked a bright eye and then slid down the bars to the cage door. Thrusting its beak through the bars, it levered the latch the rest of the way open. It pushed its head against the bars and the door opened partway. There was a rustle, a thump, and then a parrot dropped between the cage cover and the bars to the floor. It ruffled its feathers and looked around.

It was an African Grey, all silver-and-ashes except for its scarlet tail.

"Oh, my," it said. "You bad boy, what do you think you're doing?"

It waddled across the tile floor like a clockwork toy, looking up at the long slanting bars of light coming in from the courtyard.

"Oh, la la! You *bad* boy bad boy!" it said, and beat its wings and flew to the top of the window-frame rail. Laughing evilly to itself, it reached down with its powerful little beak and snipped the topmost venetian blind in half with one bite. The slat having parted with a pleasing crunch, the parrot then made its way along the rail to the cord and rappelled down it, stopping at each blind and methodically biting through, until the whole assembly hung in ruins.

The parrot swung from the end of the cord by its feet a moment, twirling happily, and then launched itself at the desk.

"Whee! Oh, stop that at once, you wicked creature! Stop that now! Do you hear? Do you hear?"

It made straight for the neat stack of pencils and bit them each in half too; then pulled out the pens and did the same. As though tidying its work area, it threw the pieces over the edge of the desk, one after another, and for good measure plucked the inkwell out of its recess and pitched that over too. The inkwell hit the floor with a crash and the ink fountained out, spattering the tiles. The parrot watched this appreciatively, tilting its head.

"As God is my witness," it commented, "if you don't be quiet NOW I will wring your neck! I mean it! Stop that this instant!"

It turned and eyed the pigeonholes. Reaching into the nearest it pulled out M. Heurtebise's morning correspondence, dragged it to the edge and, with a decisive toss of its head, chucked it over the side too. The envelopes smacked into the mess already there, and spread and drifted. The parrot peered into the other pigeonholes and poked through them, murmuring, "Wicked, wicked, wicked, wicked . . . tra la la."

Finding nothing else of interest on the desk, it backed out of the last pigeonhole, gave a little fluttering hop and landed on the nearest of the armchairs. It strutted to and fro on the smooth leather surface a moment before lifting its tail grandly and liquidly.

"Allons, enfants de la patrie—eee—eee!" it sang. "La la la!"

The parrot looked across the gulf of space at Princess Sit-Hathor-Yunet, but she presented no opportunities nor anything it might get hold of. It contented itself with worrying at an upholstered chair-button. Snip! That was the way to do it. The parrot noticed there were several other buttons within reach on the chair's back, and crying "Ooooh! Ha ha ha," it carefully removed every one in sight.

Biting neat triangular holes in the upholstery with which to pull itself up, it scaled the chair's arm and stepped out on the lamp table. "You're a naughty boy and you don't get a treat," it declared, looking speculatively up at the lamp, which had a number of jet beads pendent from its green glass shade. Straining on tiptoe, it caught one and gave it a good pull. The lamp tilted, tottered and fell to the floor, where it broke and rolled, pouring forth a long curved spill of kerosene. It came to rest in the hearth.

"Oh, my," said the parrot. It looked at the broken lamp with one eye and then with the other. "Oh, what have you done now? Bad! Too bad!"

With a soft *whoosh* flames bloomed in the hearth. They leaped high as the lamp tinkled and shattered further, throwing bits out into the room. The parrot ducked and drew back, then stared again as the inevitable tongue of blue flame advanced over its kerosene road across the floor, right to M. Heurtebise's scattered correspondence and the cane chairs whereon reposed Princess Sit-Hathor-Yunet.

"Oooh!" said the parrot brightly. "Oooh, la la la!"

Lewis had been carefully sliding the stable bolt out of its recess in tiny increments, nudging it along with an old putty knife he had slipped between the planking. He had only another inch to go when he heard the breaking glass, the roar of flames.

"Yikes!" he said, and gave up on any effort to be polite. He punched his fist through the door, opened the bolt, dragged the door to one side and scrambled out. In horror he saw the flames dancing within the office, heard the mortals upstairs begin to shout.

He was across the courtyard in less than the blink of an eye, and yanked the office door off its hinges.

"Good evening," said the parrot as it walked out and past him, its little claws going *tick tick tick* on the flagstones. Lewis gaped down at it before looking up to see the first flames rising around Princess Sit-Hathor-Yunet.

He was never certain afterward just what he did next, but what he was doing immediately after that was running down the street with the mummy case once again balanced on his head, in some pain as his hair smoldered. He heard the rattle of a motorcar overtaking him, and Lady Kiu slammed on the brakes.

"You're late," she said. Lewis tossed Princess Sit-Hathor-Yunet into the back seat of the Vauxhall and dove in headfirst after her, not quite getting all the way in before Lady Kiu let out the clutch, downshifted, stepped on the gas again and they sped away.

"I'm sorry!" Lewis said, when he was right side up again. "All sorts of things went wrong—most unexpectedly—and—"

"You idiot, you've gotten grease on the seats," snarled Lady Kiu.

"Well, I'm sorry it isn't attar of roses, but I've had a slightly challenging time!" Lewis replied indignantly, clenching his fists.

"Don't you dare to address an Executive Facilitator in that manner, you miserable little drone—"

"Oh, yeah? I've got pretty good programming for a drone, your Ladyship. I can perform all kinds of tasks a Facilitator is supposed to do herself!"

"Really? I can tell you one thing you won't be doing—"

"Oh, as though I was ever going to get to do that anyway—"

They careened around a corner and pulled up at the waterfront, where Lady Kiu's yacht was even now on the point of casting off. The Vauxhall's headlights caught in long beams three burly security techs, waiting by the gangway. They ran forward and two of them seized the mummy case to muscle it aboard. The third, in the uniform of a chauffeur, came to attention and saluted. Lady Kiu flung open the door and stepped out on the running board, as the motor idled.

"Take that to the laboratory cabin immediately! We're leaving at once. You, Galba, take the Vauxhall. Meet us in Alexandria. I want the slime cleaned off the upholstery by the time I see it again. That includes you, Lewis. Move!"

"Oh, bugger o—" said Lewis as he climbed from the back seat, his words interrupted as he found himself staring down a rifle barrel.

"Where's the damned mummy case?" said Flinders Petrie.

"How'd you get here?" asked Lewis, too astonished to say anything else.

"Railway handcar," said Flinders Petrie, grinning unpleasantly. "The fellaheen found one hidden away the other day and I thought to myself, I'll just bet somebody's planning to use this to get to the Nile with stolen loot. So I confiscated the thing. Threw a spanner into your plans, did it?" He had apparently traveled in his pink ballet ensemble, though he'd sensibly put on boots for the journey; his slippers hung around his neck by their ribbons, like a dancer in a painting by Degas. Nor had he come alone; behind him stood Ali and several of the other fellaheen, and they were carrying clubs.

"Look, I'm sorry, but you must have realized by now the sarcophagus was a fake!" said Lewis. "What in Jove's name do you want?"

"It may be a fake, but it's a three-thousand-year-old fake, and I want to know how it was done," said Petrie imperturbably. "I'm still wearing my insanity defense; so you'd best start talking."

"What is this?" Lady Kiu strode around the motorcar and stopped, looking at the scene in some amusement and much contempt. "Lewis, don't tell me you've broken the heart of an elderly transvestite."

Petrie lifted his head to glare at her, and then his eyes widened. "You're the woman on the mummy case!" he said.

Lewis groaned.

"And it's a smart monkey, too," said Kiu coolly. She began to walk forward again, but slowly. "Too bad for it."

Lewis scrambled to get in front of her.

"Now—let's be civilized about this, can't we?" he begged. "Professor, please, go home!"

Even Petrie had backed up a step at the look on Kiu's face, and Ali and the others were murmuring prayers and making signs to ward off evil. Then Petrie dug in his heels.

"No!" he said. "No, by God! I won't stand for this! My life's work has been deciphering the truth about the past. I've had to dig through layers of trash for it, I've had to fight the whole time against damned thieves; but if creatures like you have been meddling in history, planting lies—then how am I to know what the truth really is? How can I know that any of it *means* anything?"

"None of it means anything at all, mortal," said Kiu. "Your life's work is pointless. There's not a wall you can uncover that hasn't got a lie inscribed on it somewhere."

"Stop it, Kiu! Why should we be at odds, Professor?" Lewis said. "My masters could do a lot for you, you know, if you worked for them. Money. Hints about the best places to dig. All you'll have to do is keep your mouth shut about this embarrassing little incident, you see? The Company could use a genius like you!"

"You're trying to bribe the monkeys? That's so foolish, Lewis," said Kiu. "They're never satisfied with the morsel they're given. Better to silence them at the outset. Galba, kill the servants first."

Galba, watching in shock from the other side of the motorcar, licked his lips.

"Lady, I—"

"It's forbidden, Galba. Kiu, you can't kill them!" Lewis protested. "You know history can't be changed!"

"It can't be changed, but it can be forgotten," said Kiu. *"Fact efface-ment,* we Facilitators call it." She looked critically at Petrie. "Mortal brains are so fragile, Lewis. Especially all those tiny blood vessels . . . especially in an old man. If I were to provoke just the right hemorrhage in a critical spot, he might become . . . quite confused."

She reached out her hand toward Petrie, smiling.

"No! Stop! God Apollo, Kiu, please don't damage his mind!" Lewis cried. "Haven't you scanned him yet? Can't you see? He's unique, he's irreplaceable, you mustn't do this!"

Lady Kiu rolled her eyes.

"Lewis, darling," she said in tones of barely-controlled exasperation, "How many ages will it take you to learn that not one of the wretched little creatures is irreplaceable? Or unique? *Nothing* is."

"That's a damned lie," said Flinders Petrie, from the bottom of his soul, and took aim at her throat with the rifle, though his hands were trembling so badly it was doubtful he'd have hit her.

"OH!" cried Lewis suddenly, in a theatrical voice. "Oh, Lady, look out, he'll damage you!" He launched himself at Kiu and bore her back-ward. Before she had recovered from her shock and begun to claw at him they were both teetering on the edge of the pier, and then they had gone over into the Nile with a splash. Galba ran to see what was hap-pening in the water. He glanced over his shoulder at the mortals, and then made a conscious choice not to notice what they did. Killing wasn't in his job description, nor was taking the blame for a bad field decision.

Petrie looked at the Vauxhall, still idling.

"Khaled, you know how to work these machines, don't you?"

"Yes, sir." Needing no other hint, Khaled vaulted into the driver's seat. Ali and another Qufti lifted Petrie between them, as gently as though he were made of eggshell, and set him beside Khaled in the front. The rest of them piled into the back or jumped onto the running boards. Khaled swung the motorcar around and sped off into the ancient night, under the ancient moon, while behind them crocodiles scrambled hastily onto the banks of the ancient Nile. Like Galba, they knew when to stay out of a fight.

But as he rode along Petrie stiffened in his seat, for he heard a voice—or perhaps it would be more correct to say that he felt a voice, drifting into his mind from the ether, hanging before his internal eye like a smoke signal.

. . . we'll be in touch, mortal . . .

He looked over his shoulder, and shivered.

"Khaled, drive faster."

*   *   *

The stars were fading and the yacht was well downriver by the time Lewis was sitting in the laboratory cabin, completing the last pass along Princess Sit-Hathor-Yunet's case with a whirring saw. On the floor by his chair, a silver bucket of melted ice slopped gently to and fro with the motion of the river, and the champagne bottle in it rolled and floated.

Lady Kiu stood watching him. Both of them wore bathrobes. Lady Kiu merely looked damp and furious, but Lewis looked damp and battered. There were red lines healing on his arms where claw marks had recently been, and one of his eyes was still a little puffy and discolored, suggesting that an hour or two ago he had had a remarkable shiner. Some of his hair seemed to have gone missing, as well. But he was smiling as he heard a *crack* and then the faint *hiss* of decompression. The mummy case's inner seal gave way.

"Perfect," he said, and set down the saw, and with quick skilled hands lifted the lid of the case.

"Look! It's a remarkable *body* of work!" he chortled. Lady Kiu merely curled her lip, but there was a certain satisfaction in her gaze as she regarded the occupant of the mummy case.

On first glance it appeared to be a mummy, neatly wrapped in linen strips white as cream. It was, however, a great deal of rolled papyrus, cunningly laid out to approximate a human form.

Lewis reached in with a tiny, sharp pair of scissors and snipped here and there. He lifted out a single scroll, sealed in wax, and looked at the inscription.

"The complete text of the *Story of Sinuhe,*" he murmured. "Oh, my. And what's this one? The *Book of the Sea People,* gosh! And here's the *Great Lament for Tammuz,* and . . . this is the *True Story of Enkiddu,* and this one appears to be—wait—ah! This is your prize. *The Book of the Forces that Repel Matter.*"

He held up a thick scroll bound twice with a golden band, and Lady Kiu snatched it from him. She looked at it hungrily

"You'll do the stabilization on this one first," she ordered, handing it back to him. "It's the most important. The rest is nothing but rubbish."

"My predecessor doesn't seem to have thought so," remarked Lewis. "What a lovely haul! The *Hymns to the God Osiris,* the *Hot Fish Book* (racy stuff, that), the *Story the Silk Merchants Told Menes.* And look here! *Opinions of all Peoples on the Creation of the World!*"

"Manetho was a pointless little drone, too," said Kiu. "It doesn't matter; we'll find private buyers for that stuff. But you'll have the scroll on antigravity ready to go by the time we reach Alexandria, do you hear me? Averill will be waiting there and it's got to go straight to Philadelphia with him."

"Yes, Great Queen," said Lewis, looking dreamily over the scrolls. "Care for a glass of champagne to celebrate?"

"Go to hell," she told him, and stalked to the doorway. There she paused, and turned; all the witchery of charm she had learned in eleven millennia was in her smile, if not in her dead and implacable eyes.

"But don't worry about the mission report, Lewis darling. There won't be a word of criticism about your performance," she said silkily. "You're still such a juvenile, it wouldn't be fair. There was a time when the mortals impressed me, too. There will come a time when you're older, and wiser, and you'll be just as bored with them as I am now. Trust me on this."

She took two paces back and leaned from the waist, bending over him, and ran a negligent hand through his hair. She put her lips close to his ear and whispered:

"And when you're dead inside, like me, Lewis dear, and not until then—you'll be free. *But you won't care anymore.*"

She kissed him and, rising, made her exit.

Alone, Lewis sat staring after her a moment before shrugging resolutely.

He opened the champagne and poured his solitary glass. His hair was already beginning to grow back, and the retina of his left eye had almost completely reattached. And, look! There was the rising sun streaming in through the blinds, and green papyrus waved on the river bank, and pyramids and crocodiles were all over the place. The ancient Nile! The romance of Egypt!

He had even been shot at by Flinders Petrie.

Lewis sipped his champagne and selected a scroll from the cache. Not *The Book of the Forces that Repel Matter;* that was all very fascinating in its way, and would in time guarantee that Americans would rediscover antigravity (once they got around to deciphering a certain scroll, long forgotten in a museum basement), but it wasn't his idea of treasure.

He took out the *Story of Sinuhe* and opened it, marveling at its state of preservation. Settling back in his chair, he drank more champagne and gradually lost himself in the first known novel. He savored the words of mortal men. The Nile bore him away.

This story got started in Mendocino at a beautiful restored Victorian hotel, with a new garden-court restaurant built on to the side. To get into the restaurant you have to cross the hotel lobby and pass through the old bar beyond. This is what I was doing when the story arrived, full-blown, out of nowhere:

The bright summer day went to black and I saw them there, three women and two men, staring fixedly at a cheap radio in a bakelite case on the back of the bar. Everything looked shabby and old. Two kerosene lanterns and the dim orange glow of the radio dial were the only lights. It was dark as pitch outside and raining hard, and ice-cold. The people were frightened about something.

The Hotel at Harlan's Landing

THERE WAS JUST THE FIVE OF US IN THE BAR THAT night.
The lumber mills were all shut down for good and there hadn't been a ship come up to the wharf in years. No more big schooners down there in the cove, with their white sails flying in at eye level to the bluff top like clouds. Dirty little steamers stayed well out on the horizon and never came in, going busily to San Francisco or Portland. Nothing to come in for, at Harlan's Landing.

All this stuff the weekenders find so cute now, the gingerbread cottages and the big emporium with its grand false front and the old hotel here—you wouldn't have thought they were much then, when they were gray wood beaten into leaning by the winter storms, paint from the boom days all peeled off. No Heritage Society to save us, no tourists with cash to spend. Nobody had cash to spend. It was 1934.

I couldn't keep the hotel open, but after the Volstead Act was repealed I opened the bar downstairs and things brightened up considerably. Our own had some place to go, had sort of a social life now, see? We come that close to being a ghost town that everybody needed to know there was still a place with the yellow lights shining out through the windows, fighting to stay alive.

And it wasn't like there was anyplace else to go anyhow, not with the logging road washed out in winter, which was the only other way to get here from the city back then. I felt I sort of owed the rest of them. Especially I owed Uncle Jacques and Aunty Irina. I had that awful year in 1929 when Mama got the cancer and I lost Bill, that was my husband, he was one of the crew on the *San Juan,* see. They were real

277

kind to me then. Stayed by me when I wanted to just die. Aunty Irina baked bread, and Uncle Jacques fixed the typewriter and told me what I ought to write to the damn insurance people when they weren't going to pay. People who'll help you clean your house for a funeral twice in one year are good friends, believe you me.

Then, if Uncle Jacques hadn't kept the Sheep Canyon trail cleared we'd have had nothing to eat but venison, because there'd have been no way I could have got the buckboard through to Notley for provisions most of the time. It must have been hard work, even for him, just one man with an axe busting up those redwood snags; because of course Lanark was no use. But Uncle Jacques looked after all of us, he and Aunty Irina. They said it was a good thing to have a *human community.*

And, see, once I opened the bar, there was some place to go. Lanark didn't have to stay alone in his shack watching the calendar pages turn brown, and Miss Harlan didn't have to stay alone in her cottage hearing the surf boom and wondering if Billy was going to come walking up out of the water to haunt her. I didn't have to sit alone in my room over the lobby, thinking how my folks would scold me because I hadn't kept the brass and mahogany polished like I ought to have. And Uncle Jacques and Aunty Irina had a nice little human community they could come down and be part of for a while, so they didn't have to sit staring at each other in their place up on Gamboa Ridge.

I had it real cozy here. That potbellied stove in the corner worked then; fire inspector won't let us use it now, but I used to keep it going all night with a big basket of redwood chunks, and I lit the room up bright with kerosene lamps and moved some of the good tables and chairs down from the hotel rooms. Uncle Jacques brought me a radio he'd tinkered with, he called it a wireless, and I don't know if it ran on a battery or what it had in it, but we set it behind the bar and we could get it to pull in music and shows. We had Jack Benny for Canada Dry and Chandu the Magician, and Little Orphan Annie, and even Byrd at the South Pole sometimes.

So Uncle Jacques and Aunty Irina would dance if there was music, and Miss Harlan would sit watching them, and I'd pour out applejack for everybody or maybe some wine. I used to get the wine, good stuff, from a man named Andy Lopez back in Sheep Canyon. Lanark would drink too much of it, but at least he wasn't a mean drunk. We'd all be happy in the bar, warm and bright like it was, though the rest of the hotel was echoing and dark, and outside the night was black and empty too.

And that night it was black with a Pacific gale, but not empty. The wind was driving the sleet sideways at the windows, the wild air blustered and fought in the street like the sailors used to on Saturday nights. Every so often the sky would light up horizon to horizon, purple and white lightning miles long, and for a split second there'd be the town outside the windows like it was day but awful, with the black empty buildings and the black gaps in the sidewalk where the boards had rotted out, and the sea beyond breaking so high there was spume flying up the street, blown on the storm.

You wouldn't think we'd be getting any radio reception at all, but whatever Uncle Jacques had done to that thing, it was picking up a broadcast from some ballroom in Chicago. And damned if the band-leader didn't play *Stormy Weather!* Aunty Irina pulled Uncle Jacques to his feet. He slipped his arm around her and they two-step shuffled up and down in front of the bar, smiling at each other. Miss Harlan watched them, getting a little misty-eyed like she always did at anything romantic, and she sang along with the music. Lanark was pretty sober yet and making eyes at me from his table, and I smiled back at him because he did still use to be handsome then, in a wrecked kind of way.

He had just said, "Damn, Luisa, you throw a nice party," and I was just about to say something sassy back when the music was drowned out by a *crack-crack-crack* and screeching static, so awful Miss Harlan and me put our hands over our ears, and Uncle Jacques and Aunty Irina stopped short and stood apart, looking like a couple of greyhounds on the alert.

Then we heard the call numbers and the voice out of the storm, telling us that some vessel called the *Argive* was in trouble, two aboard, and could the Coast Guard help? And I wondered how the radio had switched itself over to the marine band, but it was Uncle Jacques's radio so I guess it might have done anything. They gave their location as right off Gamboa Rock, and I felt sick then.

See it out there? That's Gamboa Rock. See the way the water kind of boils around it, even on a nice summer day like this, and that little black line of shelf trailing out from it? It used to be a ship-killer, and a man-killer too, and we all knew the *Argive* wasn't ever going to see any Coast Guard rescue, if that was where she was. Not in weather like that.

And in the next big flash of lightning we could see the poor damned thing through the windows, looked like somebody's yacht, rearing on the black water and fighting for sea room. I only saw her for a split second, but I could paint her to this hour the way she looked, almost on her beam-end with her sail flapping. Then the dark swallowed up every-thing again. There was just a tiny little pinprick light we could still see for a while.

The voice on the radio was high and scared and there wasn't any

Coast Guard answering, and pretty soon they began begging anybody to help them. They must have been able to see our light, I guess. It would have broken your heart to have to sit there and listen, the way they were asking for lifeboats and lines, which we didn't have. We couldn't have got to them anyway.

Lanark had lurched to his feet and was staring out into the storm, and I guess he was thinking how he could have made a try of it in the *Sada* if she hadn't been rotting up on sawhorses ever since he'd lost his arm. Miss Harlan had put her fingers in her ears and was rocking back and forth, and I didn't blame her; she didn't take death too well. I was crying myself, and so was Aunty Irina, wringing her hands, and she was staring up at Uncle Jacques with a pleading look in her eyes but his face was set like stone, and he was just shaking his head. They murmured back and forth in what I guessed was their language, until he said "You know we can't, Rinka."

He sat her down and put his arms around her to keep her there. Lanark and I took a couple of lanterns and went out into the street, but the wind nearly knocked us over and there was nothing to see out there anyway, not now. We got as far as the path down the cliff before another burst of lightning showed us the sea coming white up the stairs, and the old platform that had been below torn away with bits of it bobbing in the surge, and the spray jumping high. I think Lanark would still have tried to go down, but I pulled him away and the fool paid attention for once in his life. Coming back I near broke my leg, stepping in a hole where a plank was gone out of the sidewalk. We were gasping and staggering like we'd swum a mile by the time we got back up on the porch here.

It was lovely warm in the bar, but the voice on the radio had stopped. All that was coming through the ether now was a kind of regular beat of static, *pop-pop, pop-pop* like that, just a quiet little death knell.

I said, "We all need a drink," and poured out glasses of applejack on the house, because that was the only thing on earth I could do. Miss Harlan and Lanark came and got theirs quick enough, and he backed up to the stove to warm himself. Uncle Jacques let go of Aunty Irina and stood, only to have her reel upright and slap him hard in the face.

He rocked back on his heels. Miss Harlan was beside her right away, she said, "Oh, please don't—it's too awful—" and Aunty Irina fell back in her chair crying.

She said she was sorry, but she couldn't bear sitting there and doing nothing again, when somebody might have been saved. Lanark and I were in a hurry to tell her that nobody could have done anything, that we couldn't even get down into the cove because the stairs were washed out, so she mustn't feel too bad. Uncle Jacques brought her a glass, but she pushed it away and tried to get hold of herself. Looking up at us as though to explain, she said, "We had a child, once."

Uncle Jacques said, "Rinka, easy," but she went on:

"Adopted. My baby Jimmy. We had him for eighteen years. He wanted to enlist. We thought, well, the war's almost over, let him play soldier if he wants to. He'll be safe. There wasn't any record—but we didn't think about the Spanish influenza. He caught it in boot camp in San Diego. Never even got on the troop carrier. They had him all laid out in his uniform by the time we got there . . . Only eighteen."

Real quiet, Uncle Jacques said, "There was nothing we could have done," as though it was something he'd repeated a hundred times, and she snapped back:

"We should never have let him go! Not with that event shadow—" And she started crying again, crying and cursing. Miss Harlan offered her a handkerchief and got her to drink some of her drink, and when she was a little calmer led her off to the ladies' lavatory upstairs to powder her nose. They took one of the kerosene lanterns to find their way, because it was pitch black beyond the bar threshold. A fresh squall beat against the windows, sounding like thrown gravel.

Uncle Jacques dropped down heavy in his seat, and gulped his drink and what was left of Aunty Irina's. Lanark drank too, but he was staring at Uncle Jacques with a bewildered expression on his face. Finally Lanark said, "Your kid died during the war? But . . . how old are you?"

And I thought, oh, hell, because you couldn't trust Lanark with a secret when he drank; that was why we'd never told him the truth about Uncle Jacques and Aunty Irina. Uncle Jacques and I looked at each other and then he cleared his throat and said:

"Irina was talking out of her head. It was her kid brother died in boot camp. We did adopt a baby once, but he died of diphtheria. She went a little crazy over it, Lanark. Most times you wouldn't know, but tonight—"

"Oh," said Lanark, and I could see the wheels turning in his head as he decided that was why Uncle Jacques and Aunty Irina lived up there alone on Gamboa Ridge, and never had visitors or went up to the city for anything.

I said, "Have another drink, Tom," and that worked like it always did, he came right away and let me fill his glass up. It never took much to get that man to stop thinking, poor thing. Just as well, too.

We turned the radio off and I had another drink myself, I was feeling so low, and Lanark drank a bit more and then said we ought to go out at first light to see if there were any bodies washed up at least, so we could bury them Christian until one of us could ride up to the Point Piedras light and have them pass the word to the Coast Guard about the wreck. Uncle Jacques roused himself from his gloom enough to say we'd need to notify the Coast Guard even if we didn't find bodies, so at least the historical record would be correct.

That was about when I saw the face outside.

I am not a screaming woman. I saw enough God-awful things in this town when it was alive to harden me up. You get some hideous accidents in a sawmill, which I'm sure those folks who eat lunch there now it's a shopping arcade would rather not know about, and a redwood log that jumps the side of the flume doesn't leave much of anybody who gets in its way. Then there's the dead hereabouts, that hooker somebody killed in Room 17 who still cries, or poor Billy Molera who used to come up from the sea and go round and round Miss Harlan's cottage at night, moaning for love of her, and leave a trail of seaweed and sand in her garden come morning. You get used to things.

But it did give me a turn, the white face out there beyond the glass, just glimpsed for a second with its black eyeholes and black gaping mouth. Where I was, perched up on my stool behind the bar, I had a good look at it, though neither Lanark nor Uncle Jacques could have seen the thing. I didn't make a sound, just slopped my drink a little.

Uncle Jacques looked up at me sharply. He said, "What's scared you?"

I wasn't going to say, but then we heard it coming up the steps. Two, three steps from the street onto the porch, it must have crossed right here where I'm sitting now, and pushed that door open, that I hadn't bolted at night in ten years. Lanark lifted his head, just noticing it when the blast of cold air came in, and even he heard the floor creaking as it took the ten steps across the dark lobby. Then it was standing in the doorway of the bar, looking in at us.

Its wet clothes were half-shredded away. Water ran down from it onto the floor and it was white as a corpse, all right, except for the red and purple places, like crushed blackberries, where it must have been pounded on the rocks. It had taken a terrible beating. Its mouth was torn, jaw hanging open. But even while I was staring at it I saw the bruises swirling under the skin and fading, the wounds closing up. It lifted its white hand and closed its mouth; reset the jaw with a *click,* and the split cheek knit up into a red line that faded too.

Lanark gave a kind of strangled howl, not very loud, and I thought he might be having a heart attack. I thought I might be having one myself. The thing smiled at Uncle Jacques, who right then looked every year of his real age. He didn't smile back.

It pushed its wet hair from its face and it said, "I don't appreciate having to go through all this, you know."

Well, surprise. He had a live person's voice, in fact he sounded cultured, like that Back East guy who used to narrate those newsreels. Uncle Jacques didn't say anything in reply and the stranger went on to say:

"I really thought you'd come out to me. What a hole this is! The Company still hasn't a clue where you've gone; but then, they haven't got our resources."

That was when I knew what he was, and I'd a whole lot rather it'd been some reproachful ghost from the *Argive,* come to punish us for not trying to save him. Lightning flashed bright in the street, and if it had shown me a whole legion of drowned ghosts standing out there, I'd have yelled for them to come in and help us.

Uncle Jacques had slumped down in his seat, but his eyes were clear and hard as he studied the stranger. He said, "Are you from Budu?" and the stranger said:

"Of course."

Then Uncle Jacques said, "I'll surrender to Budu and nobody else. You go back and tell him that. Nobody else! I want answers from him."

The stranger smiled at that and stepped down into the room. As he came into the lamplight he looked more alive, less pale. He said, "I don't think you're in any position to call the tune, Lavalle. You know what he thinks of deserters. I can't blame you for being afraid of him, but I really think you ought to cut your losses and come quietly now. The fool mortal wrecked my boat; perhaps one of these has an automobile we can appropriate?"

Uncle Jacques shook his head, and the man said, "Too bad. We'll just have to walk out then."

"You don't understand," said Uncle Jacques, "I'm not surrendering to you. I'm giving you a message to deliver. If Budu won't come to me, tell me where he is and I'll go straight to him. Where is he, Arion?"

The man he called Arion grinned and shrugged. He said, "All right; you've caught me in a lie. The truth is, we don't know where the old man's got to. He's dropped out of sight. Labienus has been holding the rebellion together. Wouldn't you really rather surrender to him? He's quite a bit more understanding. I'd even call him tolerant, compared to old Budu, who as you know never forgave doubters and weaklings . . ."

Then Uncle Jacques demanded to know how long this person called Budu had been missing, and when Arion hemmed and hawed he cut him off short with another question, which was: "He was gone before the war, wasn't he?"

And Arion said, "Probably."

Uncle Jacques showed his teeth and said, "I knew it. I knew he'd never have given that order! Who was that behind the wheel of the archduke's car, Arion? Was that Labienus's man? The epidemic, was that Labienus too?"

His voice was louder than thunder, making the walls rattle; Lanark and I had to clutch at our ears, it hurt so. Arion had stopped smiling at him. He said, like you'd order a dog, "Control yourself! Did you really think history could be changed? Labienus simply arranged it so that things fell out to our advantage. Isn't that what the Company's always done? And be glad he developed that virus! Can you imagine how badly the mortals would be faring right now, if those twenty-two million hadn't died of influenza first? Think of all those extra mouths to be fed in the bread lines."

Uncle Jacques said, "But innocents died," and Arion just laughed scornfully and said:

"None of them are innocent."

I swear, Uncle Jacques's eyes were like two coals. He said, "My son died in that epidemic," and Arion said:

"Your *pet mortal* died. They do die. Get over it. Look at you, hiding out here on the edge of nowhere! Labienus is willing to overlook your defection. He'll offer you a much better deal than the Company might, I assure you. Unless you'd like to be deactivated? Is that what you'd prefer, to crawl back on your knees to all-merciful Zeus for oblivion?"

Uncle Jacques just told him to get out.

But Arion said, "Don't be stupid! He knows where you are. What am I going to have to do before you'll see reason?"

He looked at Lanark, who was just sitting there gaping, and then over at me. I wanted to dive behind the bar, but I knew the shotgun wouldn't stop him. Uncle Jacques said, "You're going to kill them anyway."

Arion sighed. He said, "You chose to hide behind them, Lavalle. But you can save them unnecessary suffering, you see? I'm tired, I'm cold, we've got a long walk ahead of us and I want that mortal's coat. Don't make me wait any longer than I have to, or I'll pull off his remaining arm. Let's go, shall we?"

I guess that was when Uncle Jacques took his chance. I couldn't see, because they were both suddenly moving so fast they were only blurs in the air, but things began to smash, and I threw myself down on the floor and just prayed to Jesus.

They don't fight like us. You would think, being the creatures that they are, that they'd shoot lightning at each other, or fight with flaming swords, but it sounded more like a couple of animals snarling and struggling. Once when the fight got too close to me, I saw the wall panel next to my head just burst outward in splinters, and a second later there was four long gashes there, like a bear had clawed it. You can still see it, down near the floor, where we filled it in with wood putty later.

I don't know how long it lasted. Suddenly it got a whole lot louder, as something crashed straight down through the ceiling and there was a new voice screaming, shrill as a banshee. Right after that there was a wet-sounding thud and then it was quiet.

You can bet I was cautious as I got up and peered over the bar. There was Uncle Jacques, sitting up supported by Aunty Irina kneeling beside him, and he had his hand up to his face and it looked like one of his eyes was gone. She was still snarling at Arion, who lay on the floor with his throat slashed open, and she had got a crowbar from somewhere and run it through his chest, too. There was blood everywhere.

Lanark was still where he'd been sitting, wide-eyed and white-faced. I heard footsteps above and looked up to see Miss Harlan peering down through the hole in the ceiling, and by the light of the kerosene lantern she was pretty pale too. God only knows what I looked like, but my hair had come half down and was full of dust and splinters.

I collected myself enough to say, "That's one of those people you're hiding from," to Aunty Irina. She looked up, I guess startled at the sound of a human voice, and after a moment she said yes, it was.

I found a clean rag and brought it for Uncle Jacques, who pressed it to his eye and thanked me. He got unsteadily to his feet, and I saw his coat was about half ripped off his back, just hanging in ribbons. The skin underneath seemed to be healing, though. The edges of his cuts were running together like melting wax.

I said, "At least you got the bastard," and Aunty Irina shook her head grimly. She said:

"He's just in fugue," and I looked at Arion and saw that the wound in his throat was already closing up. Aunty Irina made a disgusted noise. She drew a knife from her boot and cut his jugular again. It only bled a little this time, I guess because he didn't have a lot of blood come back to flow yet.

I asked, "What happens now?" and Uncle Jacques said hoarsely:

"We'll have to run again." He looked around at the mess of the bar and added, "I'm sorry."

Lanark began to cry then, that dry hacking men cry with, and I knew he'd been scared clean out of his mind. Aunty Irina went over to him and took his face in both her hands and kissed him, a deep kiss like they were lovers, and then she stared into his eyes and talked to him quietly. He began to blink and look confused.

Uncle Jacques meanwhile crouched with a groan and took Arion by the feet, starting to drag him backwards toward the door.

Aunty Irina turned quickly and said, "Leave that. You just sit and repair your eye."

He said, "Okay," and sat down, breathing pretty hard. They feel pain as much as we do, you see.

What happened was that we had to do it, me and Aunty Irina, and as we were dragging the body out through the lobby Miss Harlan came down with the lantern and helped us. Every so often as we took him up the road to the sawmill, he'd start moving a little, and we'd have to stop while Aunty Irina cut him again. The wind almost blew out the lantern and the rain soaked us through. Still, we got him up there at last.

We found a couple of old rusty saws in an office, and they didn't work real well, but Aunty Irina showed us how to do it so he'd come apart in a couple of places. She explained how nothing could kill him, but the more damage we did, the longer it'd be before he could piece himself together to come after her and Uncle Jacques. So we did a lot to him. It was hard work, just three women there working by one kerosene lantern, and the rain coming through the roof the whole time in steady streams.

You don't think women could do something like that? You don't know the things we have to do, sometimes. And knowing the kind of creature he was made it easier.

Most of him we dropped down a pit, and used the old crane to send a couple of redwood logs after him, and I reckon they weighed a couple of tons apiece. I'm not telling you where we put the rest of him.

It might have been near dawn when we finished and came back, but it was still black as midnight, and the storm wasn't letting up. There was two empty bottles on the bar and Lanark had passed out on the floor. Uncle Jacques had made himself an eyepatch. He said it'd be likely another day before he got his eye working again.

I offered to fix them some breakfast before they set out. They thanked me kindly but said they had better not. They gave us some careful instructions, me and Miss Harlan, about what to look out for and what to say to anybody else who came looking around. They told us some other stuff, too, like what that awful Hitler was going to do pretty soon and about International Business Machines stocks. Cut off from the world like we were, we couldn't make a lot of use of it, but it was nice of them.

And they apologized. They said they'd only been trying to make the world a better place for people, and it had all gone wrong somehow.

I got one of Papa's coats down for Uncle Jacques, and he shrugged out of the bloody torn one he had on. I burned it in the stove later. It flared up in some strange colors, I tell you.

Then they walked out together into that awful night, poor people, and we never saw them again.

When Lanark sobered up he said he didn't remember anything, but he never asked any questions either, like why there was a hole in the ceiling or where all the blood had come from. We cleaned up and mended as best we could. One thing we had plenty of in this town was lumber, anyhow.

That's all. The radio worked for a few years, and when it finally broke we couldn't fix it, so I put it away in the attic. We missed it, especially once the war started, but maybe we were better off not worrying about that, with what we'd been told.

Lanark never talked about what happened in so many words, but one time when he was sober he told me he'd figured out that Uncle Jacques and Aunty Irina must have been Socialists, because of the way they talked, and maybe J. Edgar Hoover had come after them. I told him he was probably right. Anyway nobody else ever came sniffing around after them. There was a wildfire across Gamboa Ridge a few years later, 1938 that would have been, and now there's only an old rusted stove back in the manzanita to show where their house was.

Lanark drank more after that, but why shouldn't he, and it got so I'd have to walk him home nights to be sure he got there. Sometimes he kissed me at the door, but he was too broken up to do anything else. Eventually I'd have to go make sure he was still alive in the mornings, too. One morning he wasn't. That was back in 1942, I guess.

Miss Harlan lived on a good long time in that cottage, kept Billy waiting until 1957 before she went off into the sea with him. At least, I imagine that's what happened; the door was standing open, the house all full of damp, and there was a trail of sand clear from her room down to the beach, like confetti and rice after a wedding. Nobody haunts the place now. That snooty woman sells her incenses and herbal teas out of it, but I have to say she keeps the garden nice.

So I'm the last one that knows.

I kept the bar open. Right after the war the highway was put through, and those young drifters found the shacks that didn't belong to anybody and started living in them, with their beat parties and poetry. Then later the hippies came in, and pretty soon rich people from San Francisco discovered the place, and it was all upscale after that.

Not that it's a bad thing. When Kevin and Jon offered me all that money for the hotel, I was real happy. Being the way they are, I knew they'd fix everything up beautiful, which they have, too, mahogany and brass all restored so I don't have to feel guilty about it anymore. They're kind to me. I stay on in my old room and they call me Nana Luisa, and that's nice.

They sit me out here in this chair so I can watch everything going on, all along the street, and sometimes they'll bring guests and introduce me as the town's official history expert, and I get interviewed for newspapers now and then. I tell them about the old days, just the kinds of stuff they want to hear. I listen more than I talk. Mostly I just like to watch people.

It's pretty now, with the flower gardens and art galleries, and the cottages all lived in by rich folks with sports cars, and you'd never think there'd been whorehouses or saloon brawls here. The biggest noise is the town council complaining about the traffic jams we get weekends. People talk about how Harlan's Landing was such an unspoiled weekend getaway once, and how more tourists are going to ruin it. They don't know what ruin is.

I look out my window at night and there's lights in all the little houses, the *human community* all nice and cozy and thinking they're here to stay, but that cold black night out there is just as heartless as it was, and a lot bigger than they are. Anything could happen. I know. The lights could go out, dwindling one by one or all at once, and there'd be nothing but the sea and the dark trees behind us, and maybe one roomful of folks left behind, lighting a lamp in the window so they don't feel so alone.

But I don't worry much about Arion.

Even with all the restoration and remodeling, even with them selling T-shirts and kites and ice cream out of the sawmill now, nobody's ever found any of him. He's still down there, under that new redwood decking, and sometimes at night I hear him moaning, though people think it's just the wind in a sea cave. He's growing back together, or growing himself some new parts; Aunty Irina said he might do either.

He will get out one of these days, but I figure I'll be dead by the time he does. That's one of the advantages to being a mortal.

I do worry about my sweetie boys, I'm afraid this AIDS epidemic will get them. I wonder if it's something to do with that Labienus fellow, the one Uncle Jacques told me cooks up epidemics because he hates mortal folk. And I wonder if Uncle Jacques and Aunty Irina found a new place to hide, some shelter in out of the black night, and how the war for power over the Earth is going.

Because that's what it is, see. I'm not crazy, honey. It's all there in the Bible. For some have entertained angels unawares, but some folks get let in on their secrets, you follow me? And it isn't a comforting thing to know the truth about angels.